Chapter 1

Torrential rain had washed away earth and leaves from the shallow mounded grave so that the top of the head and a smooth forehead were exposed. Water dripped from the branches of the tree above and made its way in slow rivulets through the hair and down into the eye sockets where ochre leaves that had lodged there were being gently lifted clear. It was a young brow, suffused by the nature of death but unmarked by time and experience. The hair, darkened by the wet, was thick and strong, washed back from a pretty widow's peak. The body had been there only a few days and so far no scavenging animals or insects had intruded, the constant rain during the past week perhaps having suppressed the body's odour and kept them at bay.

Detective Chief Inspector Simon watched as handfuls of earth were thrown into the obscene hole and the vicar intoned the words from the Book of Common Prayer. 'Earth to earth, ashes to ashes. In sure and certain hope of the resurrection of the body and the life everlasting . . . .'

Personally, he'd take a chance on the resurrection of the body and go for cremation. He had a horror of the burial hole. Fire was good and clean. So long as you had your amalgam fillings removed, he told himself, reminded of the ecologically-minded Jessie, his long time partner. Though, if as he hoped, they were still together when the time came, should he go first, Jessie would probably see to it that he had a cardboard box and was planted under an oak tree in one of these new woodlands for the dead. If people found ordinary woodland spooky after dark he couldn't begin to imagine what those burial woods would be like when the trees came to maturity. He couldn't somehow picture people tripping along primrose paths and sniffing the bluebells even in daylight.

5

People were turning away as the burial men waited to finish the interment. It was a perfect day for a funeral – all rain and black umbrellas. He was not closely affected by the burial. It was the wife of a colleague from Westwich Police Headquarters and Simon had met her only a few times at official functions. She had been blonde and pretty and pleasant though not wholly memorable, looking like thousands of well-preserved middle-aged women. He couldn't recall a single thing she had said to him, though police functions were the kinds of affairs where conversation rarely moved beyond the mundane, especially with the spouses of colleagues. Ironical that she should have died after all in a car crash. He glanced across at Jack Fielding, reluctant to intrude on his grief but concerned that he should not be isolated. His face still showed the cuts and bruises caused by the accident, a piece of sticking plaster adhering to the right side of his forehead. A young woman Simon thought was his daughter was sheltering him under an umbrella, her arm around him, he with his head bowed.

God, how he hated funerals, Simon thought. If the church believed, as they preached, in a hereafter, why couldn't they make funerals less gloomy affairs and more of a celebration of the life lived here and to be lived hereafter? He looked around for Longman. The Detective Sergeant had firm and positive faith in everlasting life without seemingly adhering to any particular creed, and managing to be robustly matter of fact on the subject. But funerals always faced people with their own mortality as much as with the death of the immediately departed and it wasn't a subject that Simon wished to dwell on. He hoped Longman would be coming to the wake, his good-natured cheerfulness usually managing to rise above circumstance.

Simon didn't manage to speak to the sergeant until they were among the crowd at Fielding's place, an attractive late Georgian building in a square close by the church, not unlike the one in which Simon kept a flat he seemed to live in rarely these days.

'Funny to see you in a suit,' Longman remarked, his chunky fingers clutching a diminutive glass of sherry.

'Very funny.'

'No, just not used to seeing you look so . . . .'

'Smart?' Simon gave an uneasy smile.

'Uncomfortable,' Longman said with a quick snort of laughter.

A woman close by looked over her shoulder in disapproval at the sound of levity.

'I might say the same about you.' Simon surveyed Longman's sturdy frame straining at the seams of his jacket. 'How long have you had that suit?'

'Got married in it,' Longman admitted, turning to view the other people in the room. 'Jack seems to be coping reasonably well.'

Simon followed the direction of his glance to where Fielding, his daughter still at his side, was talking to Simon's boss, Detective Superintendent Munro. She towered over the figure of the widower, exotic even in black among the drab figures, her dark skin glowing amid the pale faces.

'I never really had much to do with them as a couple,' Simon said. 'I can't judge.'

'I worked with him when I was in uniform as a constable and he was a sergeant. Decent bloke and his wife Heather was a nice woman. Seems cruel she should have died like that after being ill and seeming to be getting better.' Longman looked at Simon over the rim of his glass. 'Perhaps there really is an appointed time for us to die and we can't escape it. Despite all the nursing and the treatments, maybe she was meant to die when she did.'

'You're a fatalist. You think we can't escape what's in store for us?'

'Maybe not the death part of it.' Longman tossed back the remains of his sherry.

'What was her illness?'

'Some sort of cancer. Leukaemia? Is there any beer here do you know?'

Simon didn't. 'Is Julie here?' he asked. There had been such a crowd at the church he hadn't spotted either Longman or his wife.

'She's here somewhere.' Longman moved his head in the direction of a slender man with a fine head of dark hair sprinkled with grey, now standing with his hand on the shoulder of Fielding's daughter. 'I see the vicar is still on duty.' The man looked younger than his greying hair suggested, smooth skinned, his muscles taut under the shoulders of his well-cut dark suit. 'Fielding and his wife were regulars at the church. His wife was a helper there until she became ill.'

Longman always seemed to know such details about colleagues, Simon reflected. It was something he envied while admitting to himself that he was too watchful of his own privacy not to accord the same to others. Such diffidence, though, could easily in the force be taken for indifference or standoffishness.

The vicar was moving on, making polite sounds accompanied by a gentle smile to one figure and another. He was now close to Simon and Longman.

'You gave a good service, Vicar,' Longman said, turning to include him.

'Very kind of you,' the man said, his smile widening marginally.

'It makes a difference when you know the person who has died, I suppose,' Longman added.

The vicar's expression tightened, as if in momentary pain. 'Easier and harder, I think.' He held out his hand. 'Adrian Swan.'

Longman introduced himself and Simon. 'Do you believe in God?' he asked Swan.

Swan gave a startled smile. 'Depends what you mean by God.'

Longman let out a breath. 'That reminds me of Prince Charles's engagement, on being asked if he was in love, when he replied, "whatever being in love means". I mean, if you don't know, you're not, are you?'

Simon looked on in faint alarm as the colour rose slowly in Swan's cheeks.

'I assure you that is not a fair analogy,' the vicar replied.

'So you do believe in God?' Longman persisted.

'Of course I do,' Swan said with obvious forbearance. 'I simply meant that I acknowledge that peoples' perceptions of God may differ.'

Longman nodded. 'True enough.'

'And please don't ask me to define just at the moment what my own conception of God is,' Swan said hurriedly. 'Though if you would like to visit me at the vicarage for a fuller discussion you would be very welcome.'

'That's very kind of you,' Longman said amiably. 'I might take you up on that. But there is something else I'd like to ask.'

Simon looked on, bemused and excluded, yet keen to know what Longman would say next. He knew Longman well enough to know he was not teasing the cleric. Longman had a fascination with all things esoteric.

'Yes?' Swan said cautiously.

'Do you believe in life after death?' Longman asked.

Swan hesitated, perhaps as much in care of his words as his meaning. Then he answered with an uncompromising 'Yes'.

Simon wondered if he had decided it was the simplest route.

'Do you mean that you believe our bodies will be raised from the grave at the last trumpet? Or that we immediately move on to another form of life at the end of this one?' Longman put his head on one side, his bright eyes fixed on those of the vicar.

'The bible teaches . . .' Swan began tentatively.

'Partly what a Roman emperor and a group of powerful people decided a few hundred years after Christ's death,' Longman finished for him. 'And, of course, the last trumpet bit. But that rather excludes those who are cremated or those whose bodies are accidentally destroyed by fire, doesn't it? And as a policeman I'm very well aware of the corruption of the physical body after death so that line doesn't really reassure me very much.'

Swan ran his tongue over his lower lip and glanced at Simon who smiled encouragingly. 'He's not baiting you, Reverend Swan. He's very serious.'

Swan cleared his throat and lifted his schooner of sherry to his lips. 'Perhaps now is not the time,' he said more firmly.

'A funeral would seem a perfect occasion,' Simon said mildly.

'I have other people to speak to—'

'It won't take long, surely?' Longman persisted. 'I'll say something of why I ask, shall I?'

'Please do,' Swan said dryly.

'It's because I've just been to a funeral service. The funeral of the wife of a friend and colleague. And although it was a very pleasant service in which kind things were said of the departed, nothing at all was said about her current destination until we got to the bit about "in sure and certain hope of the resurrection of the body" which, as I've said, I have particular problems with.' Longman raised his shaggy eyebrows enquiringly. 'So why is the Church of England so mealy-mouthed about the issue of the life everlasting?'

Swan's lips twitched in sudden humour. 'Perhaps because the Church teaches that it is God who decides what happens to us after death.'

'Up, down or limbo, you mean?' Longman suggested.

'One way of putting it,' Swan agreed, a genuine smile more evident.

'So you don't mention the destination of the dear departed because you're not sure where they are going?'

'I suppose that might be the case.'

'You maintain a tactful and democratic silence on the issue?' Simon asked.

Swan looked up at him, the smile still in place. 'You could say that.'

'But you do believe we go somewhere, that we don't just disappear like a puff of smoke?' Longman said.

'Are you perhaps worried about your own destination?' Swan asked, noting Longman's shift to the personal pronoun.

Longman considered. 'No, I'm not worried about that. You see I don't have any fears I shall cease to exist after my physical body has died. What worries me is the teachings of our church on the subject, and its apparently weak faith in the certainty of everlasting life.' His voice hardened slightly. 'And I wish that when people lose someone they love very much, the church would give them more positive faith in the indestructibility of life and celebrate both the life lived and the life to come.'

Swan lowered his head and appeared to study his shiny black shoes. 'You very probably have a good point.' He raised his head and fixed Longman with dark eyes. 'Perhaps sometimes we are overly cautious in toeing the doctrinal line and not sufficiently alert to human needs.' He nodded to both of them. 'It's been interesting to talk to you but now I really must move on.' His smile was professionally benign as he turned away.

'He took that rather well,' Simon said, watching the fine head of hair bending again to another.

'He ought to. It's his job,' Longman said stoutly 'The main body of the Church of England is far too diffident for my tastes.'

'You prefer the happy-clappy brigade?' Simon asked with a grin.

'No.' Longman pursed his lips. 'But I wish I could find some religious system that suited me sometimes.'

'It's lonely out there on the cutting edge, is it?' Simon asked, immediately regretting the implicit mockery. Longman was sincere. Just a little too earnest at times.

'I think I'll go and find that beer,' Longman said with a dismissive glance at his senior officer.

Simon stood alone, idly watching others in the room sip their drinks and take tentative mouthfuls of food, their faces appropriately solemn. Detective Superintendent Munro was now in discussion with the Reverend Swan who seemed to be finding his current conversation less bracing.

'Have you seen Geoff? I thought he would have been with you.'

Simon looked around and down to find Longman's wife Julie at his elbow. She was tiny and pretty with a small heart shaped face and dark wavy hair.

'He was.' Simon explained Longman's current errand. 'Where have you been until now?'

'Helping in the kitchen,' she said with a grimace. 'I'm not very good on these occasions at making polite small talk. Especially when we're here because of something so sad, but everyone is trying to pretend we're just having a rather sedate party. It's amazing what a taboo death is, even at a funeral.'

She was right, Simon thought. It was probably somewhat less indecent to take off one's clothes in public than to talk about death, or worse, anyone who had had the bad taste to actually die.

'It's tragic what happened, isn't it?' Julie said. 'I managed to have one genuine conversation in the kitchen.'

'I'm not really up on much detail,' Simon said.

'You know that Heather had been ill for some time, though?'

Simon nodded.

'She was supposed to be in remission. A form of cancer, it was. And as she was feeling better, Jack took her out for a meal for the first time in ages for a treat. It was on the way back that a van came out of a side road and hit the passenger side of Jack's car.' Julie gave a sad smile. 'It seems so unfair after all she had gone through. And Jack was hardly hurt at all. Just a few cuts and bruises and he didn't even have to stay in hospital.'

'Perhaps it was a good way for her to go,' Simon suggested. 'Since we all have to go sometime. I mean, she had a good evening with Jack, went out on a happy note, you might say. And if she was just in remission she may have had a lot more suffering to come. Whereas she was killed instantly, wasn't she?'

'Not so nice for Jack, though,' Julie said, her mouth tightening. 'It must have been terrible for him.' She looked across to where the widower was talking to another member of the force, an inspector in uniform branch, as Jack was.

Fielding did look very pale and strained, as if the effort of talking was getting too much for him.

'It's always worse for the ones left behind,' Simon said prosaically.

'Perhaps you get blasé about death in the job you do,' Julie said sharply. 'I sometimes wonder if Geoff does.'

'You're wrong,' Simon said defensively. 'Geoff has his own way of coping, which involves more faith than I have, but life never ceases to be precious. And sudden death, especially murder, is never anything but painful in the extreme. Don't ever believe we feel otherwise.'

'Sorry,' she said. 'I suppose you have to find ways of coping in the job you do.'

'We also have to care,' Simon said. 'It's why we do the job we do.'

She looked up at him, her eyes brighter than before. 'Of course you do.' She said quietly. 'I just don't know how you bear it. I have trouble with funerals,' she said with a small smile. 'And that's the tidy bit of death. I couldn't cope with what you and Geoff deal with.'

It wasn't just the feelings of outrage at murder, Simon thought, wondering if it might be a good thing to confide some of this to Julie. It was the misery of dealing with the bereaved, of turning peoples' lives, including those of the bereaved, upside down during the ensuing investigation, and so much more.

There was a sudden frisson of activity over by the door. DC Tremaine, whom Simon knew to be on duty, stood there, almost wedged beside Longman who was holding his beer aloft and listening intently to what Tremaine was saying. The DC's eyes were at the same time searching the room and came to rest on Detective Superintendent Munro. She seemed to become aware of him at the same moment and moved towards him. Longman eased out of the way and headed for Simon and Julie.

'A body's been found in Eltham Woods,' he said.

Chapter 2

Eltham Woods were about five miles south of the city boundaries on a fold of hills between the river and the Cotswold escarpment. They were a pleasant and popular walking place, being largely composed of beech and oak trees, but on the most southerly edges where the woods joined privately owned land the trees took on a wilder, more overgrown aspect and brambles deterred any but the most determined. It was not an area that Simon was familiar with, being on the other side of the river from where he lived most of the time with Jessie.

'Who found the body?' Simon asked Longman who was beside him in the passenger seat. They had left quickly after Superintendent Munro had directed them to, and Longman had been the only one to have gathered what sparse information they so far had.

'Some farmer out with his dogs,' Longman said, grabbing support as Simon took an unfamiliar corner too fast. 'He owns that bit of woodland apparently but it's not clearly fenced off and is easily accessible to the general public.' He gave a quick laugh. 'I expect he'll do something about that after this happenning.'

'It's female?' Simon asked.

'He thought so. The dogs had scratched a bit at the grave but he couldn't see much. And I don't suppose he wanted to hang about.'

Simon turned off the main road into a narrower one, directed by a uniformed officer. 'It's about half a mile along here to a right turning, sir,' the officer said, bending to Simon's window. 'They'll direct you from there.'

Simon nodded and drove on. The day was still dismal, foggy and drizzly rather than anything more emphatic, leaves seeping water and ditches overflowing with the recent heavy rain. The car splashed through pools of water red as blood from the iron ore deposits that were common in the area. He turned right where directed and bumped along a rutted lane for another quarter of a mile until he came to the group of marked police cars, one unmarked saloon beside them.

'This is as far as we can get, sir,' a uniformed sergeant said as Simon opened the car door, turning up the collar of his overcoat against the drips from the branches overhead. It was early autumn and already the trees were shedding their leaves, which lay soggy and churned in the mud turned over by the car tyres.

'Isn't it likely, then, that this is where the murderer stopped off with the body?' he asked the sergeant, annoyed that no care seemed to have been taken over possible evidence from tyre prints.

The sergeant – his name was Toplin, Simon remembered – shrugged. 'There are other points of access to the woods, sir.' He shook his head to one side, sending the water on his cap flying in all directions and giving an involuntary shiver. Though obviously damp and uncomfortable he held himself with a military stiffness.

'Let's hope he got in elsewhere, then,' Simon said shortly. Having to view a dead body, one that had come to its end through violence, did nothing for his good humour.

'Dr Starkey's just arrived,' Toplin said, unperturbed.

'Chris!' Evelyn Starkey, the Home Office pathologist moved into view around the broad back of the sergeant, already kitted out in her white overalls, her plump body looking dumpier in this outfit. She put up a hand as the mortuary van pulled in behind Simon's car.

Simon liked Evelyn Starkey. She was compassionate, even reverent in her dealing with the dead, and she didn't play games with the police, making every effort to give as accurate an assessment of death as she could, and never being patronizing as some pathologists Simon had met could be.

'My, you look elegant,' she said, eyeing him from his snowy-white shirt to his polished black shoes, mud now oozing over them.

'We've just come from a funeral,' Longman said glumly, looking around at the dismal damp scene.

'Ah,' she said. 'A colleague?'

'A colleague's wife,' Simon said, reaching into the car for his kit. With boots, and covered in the anonymous overalls, he felt more prepared for the scene ahead. Toplin held out a hand and the three of them followed him along a narrow muddy track through the woods.

'Where's the person who found the body?' Simon asked Toplin.

The sergeant glanced over his shoulder. 'The dogs were playing up so

Chapter 3

There was no missing person report that fitted the young woman. The autopsy had confirmed that she had been dead for about five days, that she was in her early twenties and had eaten a meal several hours before her death. There was no evidence of needle marks on the body, though if she was an inhaler evidence would be harder to trace. There was skin tissue under her nails, probably from her attacker, which would be of help when they had a firm suspect. Dr Starkey had said she would send them a full report as soon as possible.

On their return to Westwich from the woods, Simon and Longman had called at the administration offices of the further education college. There the slip of paper they had found in the young woman's pocket had been identified as a receipt for payment for an evening class, though which one was not clear.

'Classes started at the beginning of this week,' the woman informed them.

If she had been dead since Sunday she would not then have attended her first class. Perhaps a tutor could be found who had noted the absence of an expected student?

The woman shrugged. 'They keep their own records. This receipt could be for a class held in one of the outreach venues anywhere in the surrounding areas as well as the city.'

Perhaps she had a list of classes and the names and telephone numbers of tutors holding them?

It took a little while but finally, and with little grace, the list was produced. Today the team was trying telephone numbers and attempting to track down a tutor who had a female student who had missed her first class. As the gloomy administrator had informed them, any number of people might not have turned up for a first session. For the moment it was all they had to go on though.

we sent him home. He doesn't live far away – you can speak to him at the farm if you need to.'

Simon hoped it wouldn't be necessary. There would be enough to do without traipsing around farmyards. 'What was he doing out here? It's not exactly prime walking terrain, is it?'

'He said there'd been druggies out here using the woods. He'd found needles and foil around.'

'You mean he found them where the body was?'

'No, sir. He was just following the path on and was going to do a circular walk back to the farm. He said he hadn't found anything new as far as drugs went. Seems they were using his part of the woods because they are a bit more impenetrable and they were less likely to be discovered.' Toplin paused as he spoke and they all came to a halt behind him.

Simon urged him on. 'Funny place to come to get their fixes.' Perhaps the dead body, then, was linked to drug taking.

'Happens all over. Especially when they're dealing and if they think they're being watched. It's not so far from the city and there are a few small towns near here.'

It could of course be merely coincidence and the body dumped by someone unconnected to drugs. 'Were the police aware locally that this place was used?' he asked Toplin.

'Apparently not. The farmer, a Mr Mackleton, was intending to pass it on to us but thought he'd just check again before he did so.'

'Did he fancy a confrontation or something?'

Toplin gave a short laugh. 'Wouldn't surpirse me. He's a bit of a bruiser.'

The undergrowth was thick with brambles, the trees now consisting mainly of birch and sycamore. After about a hundred yards or so where the trees grew more sparsely they could see the white tent and screen that had been erected in a small clearing.

Dr Starkey entered first, treading carefully. Efforts had obviously been made to keep the area as pristine as possible and only paw prints and one set of footprints showed beside the raised pile of earth.

'The killer obviously scratched over his tracks after burying the body,' the photographer commented, standing back ready with his camera.

Nevertheless, Simon moved forward carefully to see what little had been exposed of the corpse. There was a muddy streak across the forehead, probably the result of one of the dogs pawing fretfully after finding the body. They had scratched little away from the shallow burial mound though, and only the top of the head and the face as far as the nose were exposed even now.

'She's young,' Dr Starkey said beside him, her voice low. The horrible suffusion of the face made it difficult to tell what she might have looked like, whether pretty or plain, or even, yet, whether she was overweight or slim. But the nose was a good shape, straight and finely modelled.

Dr Starkey stood back, allowing Simon and Longman to examine the site, and find nothing other than the photograher had remarked. Then began the task of carefully uncovering the body, the photograher marking each stage.

'Strangled,' Dr Starkey said, revealing the purple contusion around the neck. 'Manually. You can clearly see the thumb marks.' She pointed to the dark rounded marks either side of the oesophagus.

'How long dead?' Simon asked. 'Approximately.'

She gave him a bleak smile. 'Approximately,' she said with emphasis, 'four or five days. I may be able to be more accurate later, but we've no insect infestation to go with. The earth and then the torrential rain we've had seems to have protected her. Though it's possible the body was moved some time after death.'

Today was Friday, so that meant she was likely to have died on Monday or Sunday.

As the head came clear of the soil they could see the hair properly. It was straight, cut level to the shoulders and appeared to be a fine light brown. 'Any needle marks?' Simon asked as the top half of the body became exposed.

She held out a slender arm on the left side of the body and smoothed away the earth on to a collecting sheet. 'Nothing evident as far as I can tell at the moment.' Discolouration could hide them in these conditions. It might need a magnifying glass at the lab. She examined the other arm. 'She appears to be a healthy well-nourished young woman,' she continued. 'But it would be wise not to place too much faith in anything until I can do a proper examination.'

The body was dressed in a blue shirt and red fleece, the lower part of her body in blue denims, showing no obvious signs of a sexual attack. On her feet were brown laced boots.

'Anything in the pockets?' Simon knelt beside Dr Starkey. They investigated a side of the body each, feeling carefully in jacket and jeans.

'Just this.' Dr Starkey held up a thin fold of paper between tweezers.

'It was pushed down tight in her jeans pocket.'

Simon dropped the paper into an evidence bag and used the tweezers to gently unfold the damp narrow strip of paper. It was a form of some sort, a signature blurred and illegible at the bottom. Longman pointed to the top of the sheet.

'That's the logo for Westwich College, the further education college in town. Looks like she signed up for a course.'

It was now late September, so the form may well relate to a course beginning in the new autumn term.

'Have any checks been made yet on missing persons?' Simon asked Toplin, who watched on from the entry to the tent. He himself had initiated nothing yet, preferring to start from the beginning and without prejudice. But there was nothing with the body to identify it and it was unlikely that a seemingly well-cared-for young woman would have disappeared without someone having reported the fact.

'As far as I know they got on to it right away, sir, but we haven't had anything back. Course, she might not be from around here and a wider search will take longer.'

Simon waved the evidence bag at him. 'This suggests she's local,' he pointed out.

They found nothing else on the body that might help to identify the young woman. Her clothes were of good quality, but not distinctive enough to be likely to offer any leads. Finally Dr Starkey signalled for the body bag and the unknown young woman was carefully lifted and carried away.

Meanwhile a graphic image had been produced from a photograph of the dead girl. Regional television had promised to show this on the evening news together with a description of the clothing she was wearing. There had been some useful liaison with the media recently and everyone was trying hard to be nice. Local and regional radio were also broadcasting a description. And the newspapers would carry the report tomorrow. The city paper had said they would try to get the photograph in their evening edition.

'It's odd,' Simon said to Longman, his feet resting on his desk at the end of a long day. 'She's not some poor malnourished girl from the streets. She's obviously looked after herself, dresses unimaginatively but in good quality clothing. She must have family and friends, and judging by the quality of her clothes, she probably has a job. So why has no one missed her?'

'Sign of the times,' Longman said, hooking his hands behind his head. 'Lack of community life. People want independence and that's what they've got. The "I am not my brother's keeper" society, where people keep to themselves and don't interfere in their neighbour's business. They hate to be seen to be nosy, or concerned. It's not cool.'

'Especially among the younger generation,' Simon agreed. 'But if the girl's got family, they would have noticed her disappearance.'

'Which means she probably hasn't. Perhaps she moved to the city for her job and it's too few days for any relations to have missed her. Or,' Longman put his own feet on the desk, 'no one's missed her because she was going away somewhere.'

'But she'd booked an evening class,' Simon objected.

'Perhaps it interfered with earlier plans. That woman at the college said it wasn't that uncommon for people to miss first sessions.'

'And if she had a job, they might not have missed her if she had leave.' Simon pulled his feet to the floor and went over to the window. He had a smaller office than Detective Superintendent Munro, but by far the better view, her office overlooking the car park at the back of the building. He looked over to where the floodlights were warming the stones of the cathedral. The rush of traffic was over and this part of the city was relatively quiet by evening, so that the lit-up spires appeared to soar serenely over the crowded roofs of the West Gate. Simon looked at his watch. 'Let's get a bite in the canteen before all those calls start coming in.'

'With stories of little green men abducting nubile girls, the head cases

19

confessing to murder, and just maybe one or two sane and concerned friends or relations of the deceased,' Longman said, joining Simon at the door.

There were in fact quite a lot of calls, all of them sifted by those members of the team who weren't speaking to evening class tutors. Most of the calls were not causing the lights to go on in the eyes of the officers dealing with the phones Simon noted, as he watched on from a corner of the room.

'Sir?' A police constable looked in through the door. Simon went over to her. 'There's a young woman in reception who thinks she knows who the dead girl is.'

'Bring her up to my office,' Simon said, beckoning to Detective Sergeant Longman.

She was in her early twenties, plump and homely, but with fine blue eyes, which lowered nervously as she was shown into the room. She clutched her shoulder bag into her lap as she sat down on the chair Simon indicated, then looked around the room, her eyes lingering on the lit-up cathedral.

'It's a good view from here, isn't it?' Simon said quietly.

'Oh yes,' she agreed quickly. 'I've never seen it from high up.'

Her name was Vanessa Peel and she had known Kate Milliner for several years, she said. They went to the same church. 'That was where I saw her last, at morning service last Sunday.'

Simon produced the digitally enhanced picture and pushed it over the desk to her. 'And you believe this is Kate?'

She nodded, her plump cheeks quivering slightly, her eyes wide. 'I mean, I hope it's not.' She sank back in her seat. 'She's prettier than that but I suppose you . . . .' She swallowed and her eyes slid away again. 'But it looks like her,' she said hurriedly, 'and I haven't been able to get her on the phone. We were supposed to be going to the pictures this week and I was trying to get in touch to arrange where we'd meet.'

'Has Kate no relations who might have missed her?'

'Her mother lives in Westwich. That was where Kate was going after church. They always had Sunday lunch together if her mother wasn't at work. She was expecting her mother to be at church but she didn't turn up.' She flicked her heavy brown hair back, leaving her hand touching her cheek. 'I don't know why Mrs Gaston hasn't been in touch with you. Except,' she paused, 'I suppose if she was working all week she might not have expected to hear from Kate.'

Simon noted the different surnames of mother and daughter. 'Had her mother remarried, or had Kate married?'

'Oh no, it was Mrs Gaston who married again after she divorced Kate's father. He is a doctor and lives up north somewhere. I don't think Kate had anything much to do with him. Mrs Gaston's second husband died about two years ago.' Vanessa pulled the collar of her raincoat closer around her neck. The coat was an unexceptional beige colour and rain had made dark patches on the shoulders. Her large shoulder bag was the only overstated thing she had about her, her appearance being a clear indication of indifference to fashion or vanity.

'What was Kate wearing when you saw her on Sunday?' Longman asked.

'She had a new navy blue overcoat on and some navy blue shoes with low heels and a pretty pale blue scarf,' Vanessa said promptly.

'Was she likely to have changed her clothes before going to her mother's?'

Vanessa hesitated. 'She did say she was going to help her mother do some clearing up in the back garden, so I expect she did get changed.'

'Any idea what she might have worn?' Simon asked. The girl obviously took an interest in her friend's clothes.

Her forehead puckered. 'Perhaps if you described the clothes the girl was wearing – ?'

Simon did so, seeing unhappy recognition dawning in her eyes.

'She did have all of those,' Vanessa agreed. 'And she probably would have worn her old brown boots if she was planning to work in the garden.'

'Did she have a car?'

'No, she didn't. She liked to walk as much as possible.'

'So would she have walked from the church to her own home and then to her mother's house?'

She nodded.

'Which church do you both attend?'

'St Biddulph's in the North Gate.'

It was the church where the funeral they had attended had been held. So the Reverend Swan would know both of these girls.

It was looking increasingly likely that the girl they had found was indeed Kate Milliner, but they needed a clear identification of the body and the mother was the obvious person. Besides which she would have to be notified of the possible death of her daughter and it couldn't be done by phone. Simon hesitated, unwilling to put anyone through such an ordeal without some further confirmation than the word of the young woman sitting in front of him. He had no reason to doubt her, but would be easier in his mind if something had come through in the phone calls to back up her belief that it was Kate Milliner lying on a mortuary slab.

He asked the young constable standing by the door if she would fetch some tea for Vanessa and returned to the incident room, leaving Longman to take care of her.

After he had signalled for quiet and half a dozen hands had placed callers on hold he asked if anyone had called suggesting the name Kate Milliner. Three hands went up. He nodded first to DC Rhiannon Jones.

'Someone from where she works, sir. In fact there were two calls from there but one of them wasn't so certain. It seems a Kate Milliner didn't turn up for work on Monday and they tried her number but got no reply.' She looked down at the list she had made. 'She's a teacher at Linden Road Primary School.'

'No one went round to check on her?'

'No, sir. They just telephoned and got no reply.'

DC Tremaine said, 'I got a similar call from her head teacher.'

'I got a call from a man giving the name,' Sanders said.

'Was he from work too?' Simon asked.

Sanders shook his head. 'He didn't say and didn't give his name. Rang off rather quickly.'

Simon told them about the arrival of Vanessa Peel. 'Carry on, but I'm going to follow this up. Apparently Kate Milliner has a mother in the city.'

Vanessa knew which road Kate's mother lived in but couldn't remember the number of the house. Telbury Avenue was on the north side of the city, inside the inner ring road.

'Try the telephone directory,' Simon said to Longman.

'She went ex-directory,' Vanessa said. 'A while ago.'

'Would you remember where the house is if we took you to the road?'

Anxiety puckered her features. 'I think so. The houses all look alike but she's got a bird bath in the front garden and she had the garage door painted recently,' Kate said.

'Ah, but what colour?' Longman asked with a reassuring smile.

'It was bright yellow. I remember because Kate said that the neighbours thought it was too bright and flashy.' She flushed slightly. 'They're big houses. People are quite well-off around there.'

'Did Kate have a boyfriend?' Simon asked.

'No.' She gave a quick frown. 'Well not seriously, I don't think.'

'But there was someone?'

She gave a curious grimace. 'Well, she might have gone out with Rupert Colville a couple of times. He's another teacher at her school. He was keen on her but I don't think she was that bothered,' she said with a minute toss of the head.

Was there perhaps an element of jealousy here? Simon wondered. Was the dismissiveness part of the fear of someone coming between Vanessa and her friend Kate?

'Is there any chance that Kate might have been involved in drug taking?' Simon asked, perching on the desk near to her.

She lifted her face with a horrified expression. 'Never! No, not Kate. She'd never have done that in a million years. So if the girl you've found has been taking drugs, it's not my Kate.' She made as if to get up from her chair, clumsily half-rising to her feet, still clutching her bag.

Simon held up his hand. 'We haven't found evidence of drug taking. It's routine to ask,' he said, avoiding going into details.

Her heavy body sank back and her shoulders lowered. 'I really hoped just for a moment that it couldn't be Kate,' she said, her voice indistinct. She looked up, her blue eyes blurred with tears. 'I still can't believe it. I still hope it's not true.'

'Of course you do,' Simon said gently, unfolding his long frame. 'So let's try and confirm it or otherwise. Would you mind guiding us to Mrs Gaston's house, Vanessa?'

'No, not at all.' She rose heavily to her feet and stood waiting, a dignified and rather lonely figure, her features tight with tension. She asked hesitantly, 'How did the girl, the one you found, how did she die?'

'She was strangled, Vanessa,' Simon said.

She swallowed then hesitated, as if to ask more, then gave a brief shrug and went over to the door where Longman was waiting.

It was now fully dark and a fine rain was still falling as they drove out of the station car park. 'First,' Simon said, 'we'd better double-check that Kate is not at her own home.' The address Vanessa had given Longman earlier was for a flat in one of the large Edwardian houses fronting the municipal park in the centre of town, little over half a mile from police headquarters. As he slowed down the car Vanessa pointed uncertainly to one of the houses near the centre of the row. 'I can't make it out clearly in this rain,' she said.

Simon stopped the car on a single yellow line and she led them to a house with a high privet hedge at the front. There was a list of three names by the front door, MILLINER the middle one, clearly inscribed in black capitals under the yellowing plastic cover. Simon pressed the bell.

Vanessa leaned back from the porch entrance. 'There's still no light showing,' she said peering up at the bay front window she had indicated.

Simon tried again to no response, then pushed the button for the ground floor flat. Light was showing in the window and they could hear the sound of heavy rap music.

A thin girl with long pale hair opened the door to an increased blast of sound and leaned against the jamb. 'Yeah?' she asked, without interest.

Simon explained that they were looking for Kate Milliner.

With a glance full of pity for their ineptness she pointed at the bell for *Milliner* and pushed herself sufficiently upright to turn away.

'Police,' Simon said, producing his identification.

She turned quickly at that and began unobtrusively to pull the door to behind her. 'What's the matter?' she asked, her voice sharp and irritated.

'When did you last see Kate?'

The girl shrugged, pushing her hands into the belt of her tight jeans, her narrow shoulders in a sleeveless sweater gleaming in the dim light. 'Can't remember.'

'Perhaps you could try,' Simon said shortly, pushing past her.

He let Vanessa go ahead, her heavy footsteps falling loudly on the vinyl-covered staircase. She stopped at the door at the front end of the landing and knocked. It was a fruitless exercise, as Simon had expected it to be. They trailed back down the staircase, the beat of the loud music making the very boards shudder. Simon wondered how Kate and the other residents coped with it.

'Kate was trying to find somewhere else,' Vanessa said to him with a knowing look, rolling her eyes.

A young man in a vest and jeans had appeared in the doorway of the ground floor flat, the pale girl beside him. He was heavily built, unpleasantly hirsute and looked as if he worked out. Probably the reason why others living there dared not complain and could only suffer or compete.

The three of them passed by, Longman swinging the big front door to with an expressive bang. They headed out to the inner ring road and took only a few minutes to reach Mrs Gaston's house.

No lights were on, though a blue Vauxhall car was parked on the short drive. The curtains were open Simon noted as he rang the bell. After several minutes there was still no response and Longman went to check at the back of the house. He returned to say that there was no sign of anyone.

'She might be at work, I suppose,' Vanessa said, wiping the sheen of rain from her face.

'Where does she work?' Simon asked.

'She's a nurse.' Vanessa blinked at him through the rain which had suddenly begun to fall more heavily and insistently.

Simon led them back to their car. 'Where?' he finally asked, as the obviously required information was not forthcoming. 'The city hospital?'

'No.' Vanessa huddled forward in the back seat. 'She's a sort of private nurse. Looks after people at home. That sort of thing.' Her eyes widened as a figure approached the car.

'Can I help you?' The high voice of a woman sheltering under a large umbrella was aimed at Simon in the driving seat.

He turned and let down the window. 'We're looking for Mrs Gaston,' he said, producing identification from his inside pocket and holding it up in the ineffectual light.

'Police!' she exclaimed, her voice higher still. 'Why? What's happened? Has something happened to her son?'

'I'm not able to tell you any details,' Simon began, realizing that the woman could not have seen the evening news or had failed to make any connection.

'Oh no! It *was* Kate!' she said excitedly, her sharp nose tightening. 'My husband said it looked like her but I didn't really think so and you don't believe in things like that happening to people you know. And anyway, we never saw much of her. Nor her mother either,' she added more grudgingly.

'Do you know where we might find Mrs Gaston?' Simon interrupted the flow, shoving his identity folder back into his pocket.

She cocked her head and looked sideways as if in search of inspiration, the rain catching on her blonde curls and shining white in the light of the street lamp.

'Do you know, I don't think I've seen her since Saturday. She was coming in with some shopping and we briefly said hello. She's never one to stand gossiping. Not that I am, and we had all that trouble over her garage door.' She paused briefly to indicate the offending article with a leftward toss of her head. 'No, I haven't seen her since but I expect she's at work. I understand she looks after people at home. Nursing them, you know, after they come out of hospital. Or people who don't want to go into homes. That sort of thing. If they can afford it,' she said with a lift to her thin arched eyebrows.

'Did she not usually take her car?' Simon asked.

A puzzled look appeared on the woman's face and she peered through the rain at the glistening blue car. 'Oh!' she said, her voice a fraction lower. 'I see what you mean. We did wonder about that.'

It was absurd trying to carry out any sensible conversation with the woman in the circumstances and it was obvious that she and Mrs Gaston had not been in any way intimate friends, but he tried another question.

'Have you seen her daughter here recently?'

'Well not that recently.' The woman crouched a little closer to the car window. 'Come to think of it she was here last Sunday around lunchtime. My husband and I were just coming back from the garden centre where we'd been buying bulbs for autumn planting and she was ringing her mother's doorbell. I called out to her, but I don't think she can have heard me because she just put the key in the lock and pushed open the door.'

'Was her mother's car here at the time?'

Her face creased in concentration. 'Yes, yes it was. I remember because she'd parked it a bit close to our drive and Kenneth had trouble getting our car in straight.'

Perhaps Mrs Gaston had simply run away from obnoxious neighbours, Simon thought. He could see no infringement on to their section of the communal parking area that they shared.

'Did you happen to notice what Kate was wearing?'

She pursed her lips. 'She had a jacket and jeans on but I can't remember what colour. The jacket was a fleece one I think. They're so common now aren't they?'

'You didn't see either Kate or her mother after the times you've mentioned?' Simon asked, buckling his seat belt.

'No,' she conceded after thought. 'We had our Sunday dinner shortly after we got back and I didn't see Kate leave.' Her eyes glinted briefly. 'It is Kate, is it? The missing girl on television?'

Simon ignored the question, asking for her name.

'Mrs Susan Wright,' she said, peering in as he wrote in his notebook and staring at Vanessa in the back of the car. 'Number 54. And you'll want my telephone number.'

Simon duly made a note of it. 'You've been very helpful, Mrs Wright. We'll be in touch.' He started the engine and pressed the window button to firmly shut out Mrs Wright's inquisitive nose, forcing her to back away swiftly.

'Nice sort of neighbourhood if the only concern they've got over a neighbour who's not been seen for a week is that their car might be taking up an inch of their drive space,' Longman sighed. 'I tell you, it's a sign of the times. There's just no community spirit left anywhere any more.'

'I suppose Mrs Gaston is alright?' an anxious voice said from the back seat as they drove off.

In the circumstances it was a bit worrying that the mother had either disappeared or was behaving in any way out of her normal routine. 'It's within the realms of possibility that a relative of one of her clients picked her up from her home I suppose,' he said over his shoulder. 'But we will look into it.'

He was meanwhile faced with the possibility of the body remaining unidentified and he needed that sorted as soon as possible. 'Mrs Wright mentioned a son, or brother, Vanessa. Where does he live?'

'He's backpacking somewhere,' she said sorrowfully. 'In Nepal unless he's moved on. Mrs Gaston was worried about him, Kate said, because she hadn't heard from him for some time.'

And the girl's father lived 'up north somewhere' and seemed to have little or no contact with his daughter or wife. So he was unlikely to be of use for identification purposes because they might not be able to track him down as soon as they'd like. And if they did it might be so many years since he had seen his daughter in the most formative years of her life that his identification might be uncertain at best.

He pulled the car over to the side of the road.

'Vanessa, do you think you could carry out the identification of the body? We need to know for certain whether it is Kate or not. I'm really sorry to have to ask you, but in the circumstances . . . .'

There was silence from the back, a faint rustle of clothing before she answered. 'I think I have to, don't I? It's my duty.' Her voice sounded small and his sympathy with her made Simon ignore the use of the cold word 'duty'.

27

Chapter 4

Simon and Longman picked up Vanessa and took her to the mortuary next morning. She had said she would like to get it over with before she attended morning service, if they would take her there afterwards.

She was visibly trembling when they got out of the car, pale with a faint sheen of sweat above her upper lip.

'Are you sure you're feeling up to this?' Simon asked, concerned.

She nodded mutely and gestured to follow them into the building where they waited for an attendant to wheel in the body.

Simon said awkwardly, 'She won't look quite as you remember her, because of the way she died. But take your time.'

Again she nodded, then closed her eyes as the trolley was brought in.

The attendant glanced at Simon and Longman and peeled back the sheet.

'When you're ready, Vanessa,' Simon said gently.

She half-opened her eyes before she lowered them to the shrouded figure. Only the head was revealed, the mottled skin purple against the whiteness of the sheet. Her eyes widened and immediately filled with tears. She nodded quickly and turned away, fumbling for a hankerchief in her coat pocket.

'Do you identify this as the body of Kate Milliner?' Simon asked formally.

'Yes,' she said, almost angrily, her voice muffled. 'It's Kate.'

Simon gestured to the attendant, who as silently as he had come, wheeled away the trolley through the heavy plastic sheeted screen.

'Would you like to sit down for a moment, Vanessa?' Simon asked, a hand on her shoulder.

'I'd like to get out of here,' she said, blundering towards the door through which they had entered.

In the fine rain outside she took a deep breath, her face flushed, her eyes pink rimmed.

'I'm sorry we had to put you through that,' Simon said. 'It was brave of you. Thank you.'

She blew her nose. 'Nothing can prepare you for it,' she said. 'I've never seen a dead body before.'

'But you have no doubts that it's Kate?'

'Unfortunately, no,' she said, her voice still shaky. 'That was awful.'

'Can we get you a cup of tea or something?' he asked. For himself it would be 'or something stronger', but he doubted if Vanessa would choose to enter church breathing alcohol fumes.

'No, thanks.' She looked up at him, brushing her fringe away with the palm of her hand. 'She wasn't, you know, assaulted or anything, was she?'

'If you mean sexually assaulted, no, she wasn't.'

Vanessa let out a breath. 'I'm glad about that, anyway.'

Longman opened the car door for her but she turned back to Simon. 'I can't understand it. Kate wasn't stupid. She didn't do things that put her in any danger like some girls do. Why did it have to be Kate?' she said fiercely, glaring at him.

'It's what we have to find out,' Simon said flatly. 'And we're going to need to talk to you again, to get as much information as we can about Kate's life.'

She bent under Longman's arm and took her seat. 'I've given you my address and phone number but I shall be at work tomorrow and they probably won't take kindly to me being interrupted.'

Simon started the car and Longman got in beside him.

Vanessa leaned forward. 'I can't understand what's happened to Kate's mum.'

'You say she was a nurse in private homes. Did she work for an agency?' Longman asked.

'Yes I think so,' she said. 'Maybe one of the agencies might know where she is.'

'We'll try them,' Simon assured her.

They drove on through the weeping rain to the North Gate and St Biddulph's. Vanessa awkwardly ducked her head at them as she left the car, and hurriedly moved to join the other members of the congregation filing up the path to the church.

They watched her go, fading inconspicuously into the line of other worshippers, her plump rounded shoulders giving her the appearance from the rear of a woman much older.

'Kate wasn't so wise and wary as all that,' Longman commented. 'Not if she got about the city on foot rather than by car.'

'Sad but true,' Simon agreed. Even his fervently ecologically minded Jessie saw no alternative to the car as an instrument in women's independence.

'Well at least we've got a firm identification and we can get started,' Longman said. 'So what now?'

'There's not much we can do with agencies and people at Kate's school today, it being Sunday. Let's check her mother's house again. After that we'll search Kate's flat.'

The blue Vauxhall had not been moved, the drive surface still dry beneath the car, and there was no answer to their knock at Mrs Gaston's house. Simon noticed the curtain twitch next door at number fifty-four and led them hastily back to the car.

At the house that Kate had lived in the same thin blonde girl answered the door, looking as if she had just risen from her bed. Mercifully there was no loud music playing.

'We'd like to ask you a few questions,' Simon said without preamble.

'I don't think I'd like it,' she said idly.

Longman ostentatiously sniffed the air. The stuffy emanations from the hallway could discernibly hold the sweet scent of cannabis. 'It might of course be some strange incense sticks I can smell,' he suggested. 'Or perhaps someone is burning rubbish around here.'

She appeared unmoved. 'I thought you lot had given up on a bit of innocent grass smoking.'

'Sometimes not,' Longman said.

She unpeeled herself slowly from the door jamb and mockingly held out a welcoming arm. The door to her flat was open and she led the way in.

'Who is it?' a male voice called from an adjoining room.

'Nobody,' she said, barely raising her voice.

They heard what sounded like a satisfied snort and a rustle of bedclothes as he apparently settled himself to rest once more. The girl glided over to the door and closed it firmly then turned to face Simon and Longman, her arms folded across her small breasts.

They looked around for a place to sit but most surfaces were littered with clothes, CD covers and tabloid newspapers. The smell of the place years. They keep to themselves a lot. Except when they complain about the music.'

They thanked her for her time and left, taking the stairs to the first floor. Longman produced a useful bunch of keys and tried them in the lock. The third gained them entry.

The contrast with the flat below could not have been greater. Here all was order and fragrance, the only jarring note a vase of dead chrysanthemums on the table near the window. Certainly there was no sign that any struggle might have taken place here, that this might have been where Kate had died before being transported to her muddy grave. The room was inexpensively and simply furnished, some of the furniture probably junk shop finds that Kate had restored to some new glory. The curtains, an ethnic check design of orange and maroon, were open and there were no signs of recent occupancy, a thin film of dust lying on the polished table and on the mantlepiece. It seemed preternaturally quiet, seeming to Simon haunted with the presence of the young woman who had left it a week before never to return. A veil of depression overcame him, as it often did on such occasions – it was the familiar fear that he would fail to get justice for the dead.

He and Longman put on gloves, Longman first going to the telephone on a painted box next to the sofa. 'No answerphone,' he said, lifting the receiver, 'and no answer service.' He pressed some numbers and scribbled in his notebook. 'Last call to Kate was last Wednesday,' he said pressing 1471. He punched in the number of the most recent caller. 'No answer.' He replaced the phone. 'Probably Vanessa. Or Kate's mother.'

'Or the boyfriend, perhaps?' Simon was looking at an enlarged photograph hanging in the alcove to the right of the fireplace. 'This is Kate. With her mother maybe?' The picture showed a glowingly healthy young woman, her glossy hair blowing in a breeze, her arm around the shoulders of an older woman who stared into the camera lens with a tolerant half-smile. Kate's hair was light brown; her mother's, if that was who she was, nearer to blonde and stylishly waved. She was an attractive woman, her colouring more emphatic than her daughter's, her features more defined, her mouth wider, her eyes dark and sparkling with humour.

Longman stood beside him. 'I wonder where the hell she is. If she doesn't turn up soon after all the publicity I think we're going to have reason to worry. It's a bit of a coincidence after all, her going missing. She wasn't there when Kate turned up last Sunday and she hasn't been

was in keeping with its sordid appearance, the smell of unwashed socks almost overwhelming even the scent of illegal substances. The girl herself looked clean enough, her hair shining even if at present uncombed. She moved to push several piles of muddles into one large pile and gestured for them to sit on the stained sofa. The detritus from last night's takeaway she shoved into a capacious woven basket. She remained standing, lifting a bored eyebrow. 'Well?'

'You may have heard that a young woman was found strangled in woods to the south of the city,' Simon began. 'She has been identified as Kate Milliner who lived in the flat above yours.'

This, at least, occasioned a reaction in the form of a blink and widened eyes. The shutters quickly came down. 'Well, I don't know anything about it,' she said.

'We're not suggesting that you knew of her murder,' Simon said. 'But we do need to find out something of her activities before she died.'

She let herself down on to the arm of an overstuffed armchair. 'Why didn't you say anything about her being dead when you came yesterday? I didn't know what you wanted her for, did I?'

'She was formally identified this morning,' Simon explained. He looked around the dismal room. 'This is your flat, is it?'

'Yeah. Well, I rent it. All of us rent.'

'Perhaps we could have your name?'

She folded her arms tighter about her thin body. 'Sandy Stoddart.'

'Is that a shortened name, Sandy?' Longman asked, pen poised.

'For Alexandra, after my grandmother.' She pulled a face.

'How long have you lived here?'

'About a year.'

'And Kate?'

She shrugged. 'She was here when I moved in.'

'Did you get to know her at all?' Simon asked.

'Not really. Just to say hello going in and out. Sometimes to borrow some milk, that sort of thing.'

'Have you had any thoughts about when you last saw Kate?'

She tightened her small mouth. 'I did think about it after you'd gone. I think it was last Sunday, round about this time, maybe a bit later.'

'Where did you see her?'

'I was just going out to get the Sunday papers and she was coming in. She was smartly dressed. I think she'd just been to church. She went to church, she told me once. Perhaps that was what put me off her.'

'The fact that she went to church?'

Sandy wriggled her torso uncomfortably. 'I s'pose it sounds a bit bad put like that, but I always think people who go to church are a bit holier than thou.' She shrugged again. 'I didn't think we could have anything in common.'

'You didn't like her then?'

'Oh no. It wasn't that. She was nice enough. Always friendly and everything. Just made me feel uncomfortable, that's all.'

Perhaps it was the judgement Sandy placed on herself in contrast with the comparatively clean-living Kate that was at the root of her discomfort, Simon thought. A not unusual reaction in a young woman like Sandy whose bored air probably disguised some inner uncertainties.

'Did you happen to notice when Kate went out again?'

'She was going back out when I got back with the papers. She'd done a quick change into something a bit more casual. Said she was off to her mother's and she had to hurry because it was a bit of a walk.' Sandy tossed her hair back. 'The buses in this city are a waste of space. Especially on Sundays.'

'And you don't remember seeing, or hearing her again.'

'No. I went to my sister's in the afternoon. I suppose Kate could have come back when I was out. But I don't think she did because I left a note out for her and it's still there. The landlord rang. He'd tried to speak to Kate as well but couldn't get hold of her, so he asked me to leave a note telling her that he'd need access to the flats and could she ring him and give him a date.' She looked down, scuffing the edge of the chair with her bare foot. 'When did she die?'

'We think it was probably the same day you last saw her. Last Sunday.'

'Oh.' She looked down, her curtain of hair swinging to hide her face. 'I'm sorry. She was alright really.'

'Was anyone else in your flat when you were out? Or does your boyfriend live here with you?' Simon asked.

'No he doesn't live here and no he wasn't here when I went out that day. I chucked him out earlier.' She tilted her pointed chin at them.

'Did Kate ever have any friends to visit that you noticed, Sandy?'

She looked up. 'That girl who was with you yesterday came round the most I suppose.'

'Anyone else? Any boyfriends?'

She chewed on her lip. 'There was one bloke who came now and again. Big bloke with dark curly hair. Looked like a rugby player.

Thick neck like they have.'

'Can you remember when he was last here?'

'No.' She shook her head. 'Couple of weeks ago? Can't ren

'Did you see them together? Did they seem like an item?'

'I s'pose I assumed they were, but I never saw them with th all round each other if that's what you mean. I just saw her the front door to him once or twice and he followed her u flat.'

'Did he stay the night?'

She flushed slightly, the colour in her cheeks making her look and more animated. 'I don't think he did, no,' she said, lookin 'Lenny and me laughed about her being Miss Innocent so wh bloke started calling we listened out to see if she was as good pretended to be.'

'Sleeping with a steady boyfriend would hardly make her a woman,' Longman suggested. Simon cast him a glance and he su into the sofa. 'She just didn't seem the type, even so,' Sandy shru;

'And you always heard him leave?' Simon asked.

'I couldn't swear to always, but whenever we knew he'd arrive always heard him leave and not later than ten.' She thought moment. ''Course, if she'd come back with someone some nig| wouldn't know about that. I'm not a curtain-twitcher.'

With all the self-righteousness of youth she had failed to equa with 'listening out'.

They heard a low groan from the next room. 'Sandy?' a croaky v called. 'Any chance of a cup of tea?'

'No!' she yelled back in decibels Simon would have thought her sl frame incapable of.

More movements and more groans. Sandy got up as if to forestall entry into the room.

Simon asked, 'Sandy, can you remember what Kate was wearing wh she left here last Sunday, after she had changed her clothes?'

With her back to the bedroom door she folded her arms again, as barring entry, or exit. She frowned in concentration. 'She was wearing red fleece and jeans,' she said after a moment's pause.

So she had not changed again before she had been killed.

'Just one last question. Did Kate have anything much to do with th people in the flat above her?'

'Not that I ever noticed. It's an oldish couple who've been here fo

seen at home since. I hope it is just a coincidence and nothing more.'

Simon turned away. 'I'll take the bedroom.'

They searched for over an hour, looking through what paperwork they could find and searching for anything that might throw some light on Kate's personal life. The bedroom was as orderly as the living room and looked over the gardens at the back of the house. When Kate had changed her clothes, though apparently in a hurry, she had carefully and neatly hung them in the fitted wardrobe. The new blue overcoat hung there on a padded hanger.

School work stood in an orderly pile on the table in the sitting room. Her personal paperwork was as orderly as someone's might be if they anticipated their own death and wished that things should be as comprehensible as possible to the executors. Her bank statements showed that she paid all bills by direct debit and amongst receipts they found one for a health and sports club that had opened within the last year off the South Gate and not far from Kate's flat. They found no trace of a handbag, barring an empty one hanging in the wardrobe. Presumably she had had it with her and the murderer had disposed of it. The only tangible sign of outside interests was the squash racket lodged in the wardrobe.

Simon moved on to the bathroom and Longman looked around the small kitchen. Both were wedged tightly into the space over the downstairs hall and next to the living room.

'She was on the pill,' Simon called out, lifting a small narrow box from the shelf of the bathroom cabinet.

'Was she indeed?' Longman said, coming to lean in the doorway. 'Not quite such a dull life as young Sandy seemed to suppose then.'

'It isn't necessary to have a man stay all night to accomplish a sexual relationship,' Simon commented. 'Perhaps Kate just liked her privacy and independence.'

'I was wondering about that,' Longman said. 'I mean, why she didn't stay with her mother rather than go to the expense of paying for her own accommodation.'

'As I said, privacy.'

'Yes, but with her mother working away a lot she'd have had that anyway, wouldn't she?'

Simon looked over his shoulder. 'True. Perhaps it was more that she needed symbolic independence.'

Longman shrugged and turned away. Simon, finding no evidence of any chronic illnesses and diseases among the usual painkillers in the cabinet, followed Longman.

'She liked history,' Longman said. 'Belongs to a History Book Club.' She apparently also had a taste for the classics, Penguin editions of Elliot, Dickens, Hardy and Lawrence being prominent. Several poets were also represented, most of them Romantic poets. Simon took down a beautifully bound edition of Shakespeare's Love Sonnets and flicked through it, feeling his usual glow of pleasure at the seductive lines. As he closed it he noticed an inscription at the front: 'To darling Kate on your 23rd birthday, everlasting love, R.'

He showed it to Longman. 'What was the name Vanessa mentioned? Rupert?'

'Yes, poor lad,' Longman said. 'Do you think everyone calls him Rupert Bear? He must be the one Sandy saw coming here.'

They found nothing else of interest. Any address and phone numbers they had to assume would have been in Kate's handbag.

Simon wandered over to the window and stared out at the trees lining the park. The leaves had thinned enough in the high winds to give glimpses of the stretches of grass and tattered municipal flower beds. It was a better outlook than was usually to be had in city dwellings, another reason for Kate to favour it over the road in which her mother lived. The thought of Mrs Gaston roused Simon's unease anew. Tracing her had to be the first priority.

'Ready?' he asked Longman. 'I think we can knock off for today.'

'I suppose so,' Longman said, obviously reluctant. 'Julie's parents are there.' Simon gave a sympathetic grin. 'Sorry I can't offer you a way out.'

'It's easy for you to laugh. You haven't got some old bore waiting for you at home with all his holiday photos and the life history of every single person they met while staying on some Greek island or other. I think he's collecting them.'

'People or islands?'

'Both probably,' Longman said glumly.

'Well there's no one waiting at home for me. I think I'll go to my flat for a change. It probably needs a bit of an airing.'

'Jessie still away? I'd have thought she was due back for the beginning of term.'

Simon's partner Jessie, Professor of Psychology at the University of Westwich, had been at a conference in Chicago, but had decided to delay her return until the last minute in order to do some sightseeing.

'She's gone to New England in the hope that the Fall is under way. She'll be back this week,' Simon said.

'I bet you've missed her.'

He had. A lot. He had stayed at Jessie 's cottage for much of the time she'd been away, under the illusion that being there would make them feel closer. It hadn't, only lonelier and emptier. He should have returned to his flat sooner, he realized. It was faintly ridiculous of him to have remained moping about in Oxton.

The sun blinked briefly through racing clouds as they got into the car and Longman heaved a heavy sigh. 'Sure you can't think of anything else I can do today?'

Simon put the car in gear and moved off. This Rupert fellow would need questioning but Vanessa had no information on his address or telephone number. The only thing they could do today was get hold of Mrs Gaston's telephone number so that he could continue to check if she had arrived home and he intended going back to his office to do that himself. He was in no hurry to go home either.

'There's the church,' he said, thinking aloud. 'The one Kate attended.' He glanced amused at Longman who sat glumly staring ahead. 'But that's maybe not a good idea, it being the Reverend Swan you'd be speaking to.'

Longman brightened. 'He asked me round to talk to him if you remember.'

'Sorry. It may be the one day that they're open for sure for business but I think he's likely to be a bit occupied centre stage. Anyway, it's hardly a priority. We'll speak to him some time but I doubt if the Reverend Swan knows much about Kate's private life.'

'I suppose not. It's not Catholic or High Church.' Longman folded his arms and sighed again.

'And even if it were he'd be bound by the confessional.'

'Mrs Gaston was a church member as well. He might know her better, being more of an age.'

'We'll speak to him. Soon,' Simon said firmly.

'We should have a word with the people in the top flat, too,' Longman suggested.

'Give up Geoff. It's likely to be routine. Others on the team can do that soon enough.' Simon turned off the major road on to the new estate where Longman lived. He always had difficulty in finding his way in this homogenous-seeming cluster of housing, despite the efforts of architects and planners to promote the illusion that the house designs were not all identical.

'Left here,' Longman said quickly as Simon prepared to pass his turning. 'I know, it all looks the same to me as well. I don't know why Julie had to insist we moved here. It's like a goldfish bowl with everybody looking at you from all angles.'

It was true. In an attempt to keep the roads of the estate free from any resemblance to a grid system, they had simply turned houses in on one another in a series of gratuitous curves. Resulting, as Longman had said, in no privacy, or space either, for anyone. Simon, relieved to be able to identify Julie's curtains, if nothing else, pulled the car to a halt.

'Sure you can't think up any emergency?' Longman pleaded as he got out.

Simon smiled and shook his head. 'But make sure you're in early tomorrow.'

'That shouldn't be a problem. They're staying the night.' Longman pulled a face as Simon reversed, lingering to wave as the car disappeared.

Simon, having got hold of Kate's mother's telephone number tried it several times. An answerphone replied each time, the recorded voice, sensibly for a woman living alone, that of an anonymous male.

Finally he climbed the stairs to his first-floor flat in St Mark's Square. Its downtrodden comparison with its famous namesake had amused and attracted him when he had first moved here a few years ago. He was still fond of it and the pleasant outlook on to the small grassed park at the centre with its fine old birch, beech and horse chestnut trees. He opened the floor-length windows giving on to the small balcony, letting in some fresh air. It was cool but not uncomfortably so and the rain seemed to be holding off for the moment. He put on some Charlie Parker, poured himself a malt and sat in the low armless chair by the open window. It was quiet and peaceful and no one was about at this time of a late Sunday afternoon, apart from the old man opposite who was letting himself out with his small dog.

The square had been moving up in the world since Simon had moved in. At first there had been a motley collection of house owners and flat-dwellers none of whom had seemed flush enough to do the necessary repairs to the crumbling stucco frontage of the late Georgian houses. Money had taken over in the meantime, and though Simon had to be glad that the houses should not crumble too far, he had been sad to see the departure of some of the more colourful residents. Respectability had cast its pall over St Mark's, along with shrewd investment.

He shifted himself moodily to silence Charlie Parker and put on a Mozart symphony instead. He had read that Mozart was stimulating to the thinking and creative processes. Then he decided that he didn't want to be either encouraged to be maudlin, nor to think or be creative, but he was feeling too inert to get up again.

His thoughts, as they so readily did, returned to Jessie. It troubled him how lost he had felt with her away. This was the longest break that they had had from each other and it had left his feelings of insecurity in the relationship more intense and troubled than before. It was the old problem: he wanted them to put their relationship on a permanent committed basis, i.e. marriage. He also wanted to have children with Jessie; not children in abstract, Jessie's children. But, if he asked her to marry him, to interrupt her career to any degree by having a child, or children, would she decide that they should part company so that he could find a partner who *would* give him children? And he didn't want anyone else's.

And interrupting her career, her new post as Professor of Psychology, was not an idea he thought she would warm to. She had a passionate interest in her work. His own relationship to his job was more equivocal. It was one of the reasons why he was feeling so bereft without her.

He sank back the remainder of his whisky. Alcohol, as he knew it would, had served only to intensify his feeling of desolation. He stood up a little too quickly and clutched at the chair, castigating himself for his continued procrastination. It couldn't go on, this situation. He had to ask Jessie to marry him and put an end to all this insecurity one way or the other. He would do it. And what if she refused? He would deal with that when and if the situation arose. He looked at his watch. She would probably be ringing him soon: it was a civilized hour in the States.

Chapter 5

The headteacher of Linden Road Primary School was grim-faced as she showed Simon and Longman into her room. Corina Hanson was a small woman who carried herself as if she were tall. Blonde spiky hair, well-applied make-up, a retroussé nose and rounded cheeks made her look younger than her probable years. She was dressed professionally, a city type in her smart blue pants suit and discreet earrings and was aeons away from Simon's own memories of headteachers.

She indicated the two comfortable chairs in front of her desk and took the one behind, linking her hands in front of her and gazing solemnly at them. After a pause she said 'It must be a cliché but I can't believe this has happened to Kate.'

'Is that why you didn't contact us when Kate failed to turn up to work for a week?' Simon asked mildly.

Her eyes sparked at the veiled criticism. 'We did try to contact her by phone. And someone went round to her flat. But you can't get beyond the front door if no one answers.'

'But surely it worried you?' Simon said. 'Or was this not unusual behaviour in Kate?'

She tightened her hands and looked at him levelly. 'No, it wasn't. Kate was highly reliable and an excellent teacher. In hindsight I can see that I was wrong not to have raised the alarm. But I assumed that she might have gone to stay with her mother. We did try to contact her there but the number had changed from the one Kate gave us for next of kin.'

She got up and walked over to the window which faced the now deserted play yard. All around them was the faint hum of young voices chanting tables, singing and generally setting about their studies. 'It's no excuse, but experience perhaps shapes one's responses. We've had so many staff absences for one reason or another – mostly stress and over-work – that when even a reliable teacher goes absent you tend to put it down to the same cause. And this is only Kate's second year in teaching. I suppose I assumed she had been having a harder time dealing with things than I had thought.'

'You have no idea then of any problems that Kate may have had in her personal life?' Longman asked. 'I mean, you assumed it was work difficulties.'

She returned to her seat, placing her well-manicured hands flat on the surface of the desk. 'No,' she said. 'I have no knowledge that Kate was having any personal problems. Do you have some reason to think, then, that Kate was killed by someone she knew, rather than attacked by a stranger?'

'Most murders are carried out by someone known to the victim,' Simon murmured.

She sighed. 'Yes. I know that, of course.'

'What do you know of Kate's personal life, Mrs Hanson?' Simon asked. 'I assume as her senior teacher you had some interest in her general welfare?'

She lifted her hands and splayed them. 'As far as I know, Kate led a blameless existence. I know of nothing in Kate's life that might have led to this terrible thing happening to her.' She wrinkled her brow, examining her hands. 'And I'm more sorry than I can say. I was fond of Kate, as was everyone here, not least the children. She will be very hard to replace.'

'Did she have any special friend on the staff here?' Simon asked.

'Not any particularly intimate friend I don't think. The other female members of staff are married and are too busy to have much of a social life, what with their children and husbands. As for the male staff, Bob Goodenough is married also and Rupert is our only other single member of staff. Rupert Colville,' she amended, seeing the light of interest in their eyes. 'Kate used to play squash with Rupert and they were good friends I think, but nothing more.'

There was a tap at the door and a man's head appeared briefly. 'Oh! Sorry,' he said, withdrawing.

'Come in Bob,' Mrs Hanson called.

He came, carrying a sheaf of papers under his arm and standing near the door, looking at them all enquiringly.

'This is our deputy head, Bob Goodenough, whom I mentioned,' she said, grammatically immaculate. 'Bob, this is Detectice Chief Inspector Simon and Detective Sergeant Longman who are investigating the death of poor Kate.'

He ducked his head. 'Terrible,' he muttered. He looked at Simon. 'The trouble is you find that everything is a cliché when someone dies. We never seem to find the original words to convey how truly devastated we feel.'

He had echoed the words of Mrs Hanson, Simon noticed. No doubt they would have already discussed Kate's death at length. To be fair, the man did look troubled, though that might be his usual manner. He was lean bodied and lean faced, his hair wavy brown, overlong with a studied casualness, his eyes dark and watchful. Simon was reminded of the lean and hungry Cassius: 'Such men are dangerous'. But he reminded himself that this was a primary school teacher, not a plotter in ancient Rome.

'We were just discussing whether there might be anything in Kate's personal life that may throw some light on what happened to her,' Simon said.

Goodenough looked at Mrs Hanson. 'I said I couldn't think of anything,' she said firmly and Simon wondered fleetingly if there was some note of warning in her voice.

He gave a small cough. 'I used to tell Kate she should get a car,' he said. 'It's not safe walking about the city like she did. But she used to laugh and say we'd all get fat never walking anywhere.' He looked down at his feet, clutching his bundle of papers more tightly. 'She was keen on keeping fit was Kate.'

'She used to play squash with Rupert Colville, Mrs Hanson says,' Simon said. 'Perhaps we could speak with him before we go.'

'Of course,' Mrs Hanson agreed. She looked at the clock on the wall. 'It will be lunch break soon.'

'I've a few more questions though,' Simon said.

She subsided into her chair and looked across at Goodenough. 'Was it anything urgent you wanted, Bob?'

'It can wait,' he said, backing towards the door. He nodded to Simon and Longman, before disappearing.

Mrs Hanson leaned forward again, clasping her hands once more. 'I really can't think of anything I know of that can help you, Chief Inspector. I only wish there were.'

'I understand,' Simon said. 'But at this stage we're just looking for a fuller picture of the person Kate was. So anything you tell us may help. Any conversations you had with her that involved her personal life.'

She gave a short laugh. 'I'm afraid we're far to busy with the work in hand to spend much time thinking about leisure, Chief Inspector,' she said patronizingly. 'You must be aware that the education system has as many problems as the police force these days and we struggle to keep our heads above the piles of paperwork.'

'So you're saying you have no knowledge of your staff members' personal lives?' Simon said, lifting an eyebrow. 'Don't they come to you if they have any problems?'

Her rounded cheeks grew a little pinker. 'Do your officers confide in you, Chief Inspector?'

'It's been known,' Simon answered. Beside him, Longman gravely nodded in agreement.

She gave a small toss of the head. 'Well, my staff do, also. *If* they have problems, including those of a personal nature.' She spread her hands. 'But Kate didn't have any problems. Certainly none that she needed to confide.'

'But you must have learned something about Kate's private life?' Simon persisted.

'She came here just over a year ago. She was a fully active member of staff, despite last year being her probationary year. She was a church member, she liked to keep fit, she had a mother living here in the city.'

'What did she do in the holidays, for instance?' Simon asked in the face of such dry facts.

Mrs Hanson paused and thought. 'She went on some activity holiday for children, arranged through the church during this last summer holiday. She said how much she enjoyed it.'

'And she never mentioned having a man in her life to you or any other staff member?'

'I'm not aware of one,' she said, drawing her mouth in a firm line.

'You say you weren't able to contact Kate's mother by phone. Did no one call at the mother's house?'

'I'm afraid not, Chief Inspector.'

A buzzer sounded loudly outside the room and was repeated throughout the building. She stood up. 'I'll get my secretary to find Rupert for you. You can speak to him here if you like, while I go for my lunch.'

Simon and Longman stood up as she left the room.

There was a roar as of crashing waves as the children rushed out into corridors. Raised voices of teachers could be heard chivvying and cajoling their charges into order.

'She was a bit buttoned up,' Longman said.

'Defensive,' Simon commented. 'She's probably embarassed and feels guilty that she didn't do more about Kate's failure to turn up or contact her.'

'It does look bad,' Longman agreed. 'People seem to hate to interfere in other people's lives these days.'

A few moments later another face appeared cautiously around the edge of the door. Simon wondered if such caution were habitual on entering this room or whether it was the presence of the police that was inhibiting.

'Rupert Colville,' the young man said, revealing himself more completely.

Simon could see why Sandy had thought him a likely rugby player. He had the stature of a prop forward and the thick neck she had described. His expression though was genial in a broad open face topped by fair close-cropped hair.

'Take a seat, Mr Colville,' Longman said. He introduced himself and Simon while Colville uncertainly studied the only other chair vacant, behind the headteacher's desk. After a moment's thought he dragged it from behind the desk and sat down nearer Simon, crossing his massive thighs and leaning back with his arms hanging beside his seat. He studied them, his eyes half-closed.

'You're aware of why we are here, are you?' Simon asked.

'Because of Kate,' Colville said in a flat northern accent.

'We understand that you saw more of Kate than other members of staff here and wondered if you knew of anything in her life that might have led to her death.'

'Kate and I played squash together once or twice a week. I don't think it made me privy to any intimate details of her life.' Colville continued to examine them through half-closed eyes. 'I hope what's happened to her isn't going to give rise to the usual press innuendoes about her private life.'

'I can't think of any reason why it should, can you?' Simon asked mildly.

'No, of course I can't,' Colville said almost angrily. 'Kate was a nice decent girl.'

'But you didn't think to report her missing,' Simon said.

Colville uncrossed his legs and tipped his chair back on its hind legs. 'That was up to the head.'

The chair tipped forward with a thump. It was steel framed, or Simon might have anticipated it splintering at the joints under the assault of Colville's weight and maltreatment. 'I did go round to Kate's flat on

Tuesday after school,' Colville admitted. 'But she wasn't in and I could-
n't get anyone else in the house to answer the front door. Probably a bit
early for them if they were out at work.'

'So when did you last see Kate? Mr Colville,' Simon asked.

'The week before on the Friday at school. We were supposed to have
played squash at half past four on the Sunday but she rang me in the
afternoon to put me off.'

'What reason did she give?' Simon asked, his interest quickening.

'She said she was going to be busy, that she had to see someone.'
Colville said, pursing his lips.

'And what time did she call you?'

Colville scratched his short-cropped head. 'About one or just after? I
remember thinking she hadn't given me much notice.'

'And that was all she said? No further explanation?'

'No. She just said she'd see me in school next day and rang off.'

'And when she didn't see you in school next day weren't you at all
concerned?'

'No, not really. Staff absences happen and you don't think much
about it.'

'But I understand that Kate was not prone to taking time off.' Simon
was thinking that, for a young man who had at least some kind of friendship with the dead girl, he was taking the situation so calmly as to be
almost cold. Then Colville slapped his large hands on his thighs and
raised his voice.

'Look Chief Inspector, you don't have to rub it in, all right? It's easy
to be wise in hindsight but I should have made more effort over Kate. I
feel terrible about it. Does that satisfy you?' Colville's mouth turned
down at the corners and he blinked rapidly, showing that there was some
emotion after all.

'I'm not trying to make you feel guilty,' Simon said calmly. 'I'm just
trying to understand how a young woman in Kate's situation can lie
dead for almost a week without anyone apparently missing her.'

'Didn't her mother report her missing?' Colville asked, passing a hand
over his eyes. 'No, she couldn't have done, or you wouldn't have asked
for information from the public. So where's her mother?'

That was something to which Simon would like the answer. He said,
'Apparently Kate was planning to have a midday Sunday meal with her
mother after church, but we can't be sure it took place. Kate did go to
church that morning and apparently went home to change and then she

was seen letting herself into her mother's house afterwards. As far as we know that was the last anyone saw of her.'

'So she might have called me from her mother's,' Colville said.

'It seems possible,' Simon said. In which case what had happened that Kate had suddenly to 'see someone' after letting herself into her mother's house? 'Did Kate ever mention a boyfriend to you?'

The young man's broad face coloured up. 'No. Why would she? We were just mates, Kate and me.'

Simon wondered if Colville had wished the relationship might be something more.

'And she had no problems that you are aware of. Nothing was bothering her?'

Colville shrugged, his eyes on the playground where the sharp cries of children let loose after confinement were penetrating the room. 'No.'

'How did she sound when she called you on the Sunday?'

His eyes returned to Simon. 'All right. The same as usual. But Kate wasn't the fussy sort. She was always pretty calm about everything.'

'Tough, too?' Simon said with a half smile.

'What d'you mean?' Colville frowned.

'Having you as a squash partner. You have certain advantages.'

The young man smiled for the first time, eclipsing the dour expression that had closed his face since he entered the room. 'She was a match for me though. She was agile, was Kate.'

'If you think of anything that might help us, here's my number,' Simon said, handing him a card. 'And perhaps you'd give your phone number and address to Sergeant Longman.'

That done, they left the room together, Colville heading off down a corridor with a muttered goodbye while Simon and Longman walked out into the playground. Children nearby fell silent, watching them curiously as they made their way to the car.

'She seems to have led a remarkably blameless existence,' Longman remarked.

'It happens,' Simon said.

His phone rang as they were getting into the car. It was DC Tremaine. He had tracked down the agency that used Mrs Gaston's services. 'We'll go there now,' Simon said and rang off.

'So I wonder who it was that Kate had to see on Sunday afternoon,' Longman said, buckling his seat belt as Simon took off.

'If her mother wasn't there on Sunday when Kate turned up, it maybe had something to do with that.'

'We need to find Mrs Gaston.'

Guardian Angels Nursing Agency was just off the centre of town in one of a warren of complex backstreets. Simon drove into their private parking area and they entered by the gleaming plate glass doors that opened from the street.

A glossy brunette with perfect *maquillage* surreptitiously pushed a paperback into her desk drawer and looked up with a professional smile.

Simon showed his identification and explained that they were trying to trace a nurse who was on their books.

'Ah, yes,' the girl said, her smile disappearing. 'Mrs Jones dealt with that when the police telephoned earlier. I'll tell her you're here.' She picked up the phone and spoke into it in a low voice. 'I'll show you up,' she said, rising to her feet and going to a door to the left of her desk.

If the appearance of the place were anything to go by, nursing agencies must be doing good business. They followed her up thickly carpeted stairs to the first-floor landing where the receptionist opened a door for them and stood back for them to enter. A voice called, 'Thank you Delia,' and the girl turned away.

Thelma Jones was a full-bosomed lady of mature years. She rose from her desk and came to shake their hands before asking them if they would like coffee. Simon declined and she gestured them to a pair of upholstered chairs in front of her desk.

'I understand that you are trying to find Sylvia Gaston?' she said, peering at them over half-moon glasses as they sat down.

'She is on your books, you told DC Tremaine.' Simon said. 'Can you tell us where she is working at the moment?'

'I'm afraid I can't. I did try to explain this to the policeman who telephoned but he was in too much of a hurry to listen,' she said reprovingly.

'But she is registered for work with you?' Simon said.

'Yes. Unfortunately she failed to turn up for her latest assignment and she hasn't been in touch since. The people she was supposed to go to telephoned us in some dismay to say she had not arrived and had not contacted them.'

'When was this?' Simon asked.

'She was due to start with them a week ago today. Last Monday. Of course we telephoned her house but got no reply.'

'Weren't you concerned?'

Mrs Jones gave a plaintive smile and took off her glasses. 'It happens sometimes that nurses find their own employment through personal recommendation. I assumed that Mrs Gaston had gone somewhere else.'

'Had she ever done such a thing before?' Simon asked.

She twirled her glasses in her fingers. 'No, I confess she hadn't. She has always been very reliable.'

'And you haven't heard from Mrs Gaston since?'

'I'm afraid not. May I ask why you need to contact her so urgently?'

'Her daughter has been found murdered,' Simon said.

Mrs Jones looked suitably aghast. 'The young woman found strangled in the woods? How terrible. The name was different though, wasn't it? Of course I made no connection.'

'And you have no idea where Mrs Gaston might be?'

She thought for a moment. 'I suppose I could give you the names of former clients of Mrs Gaston's. It's possible that she was contacted directly by one of them and has gone to help out in an emergency. But it seems very unlikely that she would do so without letting us know, especially as she was already booked for that week.'

'Mrs Gaston worked in private homes, did she, rather than in hospitals or nursing homes?' Simon asked.

'Yes. It was what she preferred. She sometimes lived in, depending on circumstances. She mainly worked with the chronically or intermittently ill, or with people who needed care after coming out of hospital.'

'We'd be grateful then for that list of former clients of Mrs Gaston's,' Simon said.

She looked troubled. 'I feel a little uneasy about having the police question such clients. Often they are in a very vulnerable state for obvious reasons. Surely when Sylvia sees the publicity surrounding her daughter's death she will be contacting you directly.'

'We were hoping she would already have done so. I suppose it's possible that if she is busy caring for a client and not watching television, listening to radio or reading newspapers that she may have missed out on publicity. But we can't leave things indefinitely.' Simon stood up to add weight to the urgency of his appeal.

After hesitating for a moment she went over to the computer on a table by the window and pressed a few keys. 'I hope you'll be as discreet as possible,' she said over her shoulder. 'Perhaps I should warn them of your possible impending contact with them.'

'If you want,' Simon agreed. 'But we are capable of sensitivity, Mrs Jones. We have training for it these days.'

She pressed a few more keys and the printer began to disgorge a list of names and dates, addresses and telephone numbers. 'The last dozen clients are here,' she said looking up at Simon. 'Will that be enough?'

'You tell me,' he said. 'I assume it's possible that an earlier client may have contacted her though.'

'It all depends on the nature of their illness or difficulty,' she said, starting the printer. 'Some assignments were for a week or so, others of longer duration. But in some cases the client will have died. I'd really rather check them out myself first before I pass these names to you. It would be distressing for people to have the police telephone to ask if Mrs Gaston was currently caring for a spouse who is now deceased.'

Simon had to allow that she had a point. 'Can you let me have the names tomorrow?'

She sighed. 'I suppose so. I'll have to get on with this today and I have a million other things I should be doing.'

If so, Simon thought, she had a remarkably clear desk. 'It is important, Mrs Jones,' he said. 'I am feeling some concern about Mrs Gaston herself.'

Her eyes widened and she paused in the act of extracting the printed list. 'You don't think something has happened to Sylvia as well?' she asked, her voice lowered.

Simon wasn't sure. He had an uneasy feeling about it though, and it did no harm to convey that to the woman in front of him.

'I don't know. But Sylvia Gaston has not to our knowledge been seen since yesterday week, the same day that Kate, her daughter, disappeared. It seems an unhappy coincidence.'

'It does,' she said thoughtfully, returning to her desk, the list clutched firmly in her left hand. 'I'll do my best for you, Chief Inspector,' she said, holding out her right hand and terminating the interview. Longman stirred from an apparent inertia and got to his feet, accepting her hand in silence. She looked at him a little curiously before showing them to the door.

'I'll send someone for the list in the morning,' Simon said. 'Unless we learn something in the meantime.'

She nodded pleasantly. 'I expect you can find your way out.' She gave a tolerant smile and pulled the door to behind her, its closing making a sibilant sigh on the thick carpet.

The receptionist didn't bother this time to hide her book and looked up with a distant smile before returning to it.

'I think you're right,' Longman said as they appraoched the car. 'I'm very much afraid that something nasty has happened to Sylvia Gaston.'

49

Chapter 6

On the way out of headquarters next day Simon and Longman passed Jack Fielding.

Fielding stopped. 'Chris, is that right that you're looking for Sylvia Gaston?'

'Why? Do you know her?' Simon asked.

Fielding was showing all the stress that the inner man had been going through over the last week. The fact that the bruising on the side of his face had still not completely disappeared didn't help his appearance. His uniform though was faultless and pristine. Simon was surprised to see him back at work so soon after his wife's death.

'She looked after Heather,' his voice broke for a moment. 'For a while after she came out of hospital. She was a really good nurse. What's she done? She can't be in any trouble, surely?'

'Not that we know of. She seems to have disappeared though.'

'Has someone reported her missing?' Fielding's face furrowed in concern.

'No, but she's the mother of the girl who was found strangled last week in Eltham Woods. No one seems to have seen her mother since around the same time the girl disappeared.' They pressed themselves against the stair rail as someone passed.

'I didn't realize. The girl had a different name then?'

'Her mother was married twice. The girl kept her father's name.'

Fielding frowned. 'I'm really sorry Mrs Gaston's had such a thing happen. She's a lovely person, wonderful with Heather. I wish I could help.' He made a move to continue up the stairs. 'Let me know if there's anything I can do. I wish I could think of something.' He was shaking his head as he passed them, still frowning.

'He doesn't look so good,' Longman commented as Fielding moved out of earshot.

'Probably helps to be back at work, though, taking his mind off things a bit.'

They went out through the rear of the building to the car park. A radio appeal the night before had brought no response from Sylvia Gaston or anyone who might know of her whereabouts. That fact, combined with the fact that the newspaper and television coverage of the murder of her daughter had brought no word from her, was enough to justify concern over her own safety. They had obtained a search warrant for her house – which was where they were now headed.

Telbury Avenue in bright autumn sunlight, the leaves of the trees showing brilliant colours, seemed entirely different from its remote, indifferent appearance on the rainy night that they were here before. Sylvia Gaston's car remained in the same position though. As they pulled on to the drive behind the blue Vauxhall Simon glanced at the house next door, but no face appeared, no curtains twitched.

'The decline in milk deliveries has done nothing to help us spot when people are in trouble,' Longman remarked in another of his little homilies on the decline in caring standards among the British people.

'Newspaper deliveries, too,' Simon agreed solemnly and Longman cast him a quick glance as he went ahead to try the Yale lock.

'Working away a lot I don't suppose she'd have had either anyway.'

After a few minutes Longman pushed open the door to allow Simon to enter ahead of him. They both pulled on gloves.

Simon picked up some mail that had accumulated on the mat and looked through it before placing it on the hall table. It consisted mostly of what looked like quarterly bills and a letter with the logo of the Guardian Angels Agency – perhaps stiffly enquiring where Mrs Gaston had got to.

The hall was spacious, with four doors leading off it and fitted carpet continuing up the staircase to a half-landing. There was no sign of any disturbance here or in the sitting room that they entered next. It was on the left of the hall and stretched the depth of the house to French windows opening on to a patio and long lawn, edged conventionally by herbaceous borders. The room was immaculately tidy. Books were fitted neatly on to a bookshelf that stood in an alcove, magazines were neatly placed in a rack beside an armchair at the fireplace. The room was furnished comfortably with a green three piece suite and fitted cream carpet. The only personal touch was in the form of some photograph frames on a sideboard against the right hand wall. Some showed Sylvia

Gaston with one or both of her children, others were of the son and daughter individually. The young man was darker than his mother and sister and thinner faced, but showed the same open smile and bright eyes. Simon wondered where he was now and whether he had access to British newspapers. It would be hard for him if so, far from home. He picked up a postcard-sized frame of mother and daughter and extracted the photograph. They had as yet had no photographs for publicity purposes than the enhanced picture of Kate. Sylvia, wearing a low-cut top, a silver medallion in the shape of a large star around her neck had her arm around Kate's shoulders. It looked as if the picture had been taken in the back garden.

Longman had wandered ahead into the kitchen at the back of the house. He called out as Simon crossed the hall. 'She and her daughter have a strange habit of leaving their homes as if they're never coming back. This whole place looks like a showhouse.'

Simon joined him. There were no signs that any meal had been prepared for the Sunday that Kate had called. Nothing was out of place, not even washing up left to dry on the draining board. Sylvia Gaston had probably spent very little time in her own home, being occupied as she was in other people's.

Longman flipped open a tall stainless steel bin. Inside, still in their cellophane covering, was a spray of roses, their red petals brittle and patched with brown. He lifted them out. 'No card with them.'

'Perhaps an unwelcome attention from someone,' Simon said. 'Maybe we can track down the sender.'

Longman pushed them back into the bin. 'There are quite a few florists in the city. And how many do you think deliver red roses in a week?' he said doubtfully. 'And they might have been ordered outside the city.'

'They'd still pass the order on to a local branch,' Simon said.

'Would they?' Longman said, eyebrows twitching. 'I wouldn't know.'

'I believe so,' Simon said flatly. 'She's removed any sender's card whether it came from a florists or a supermarket, and was delivered by hand. Perhaps she didn't like what it said.'

The dining room seemed to be used mainly as an office. A PC was set up in the corner on a wide table. 'She's on the internet,' Longman noted, pointing to the modem.

'We'll have to check her email,' Simon said. 'Maybe it will yield the name of some friends and relations.'

Upstairs Sylvia's bedroom was at the front of the house overlooking the avenue. It was tidy, the bed carefully made, but there were a few signs of habitation, even some powder spilt on the dressing table amid pots and potions. Her nightdress and dressing gown in midnight blue satin were draped over the bottom of the bed. Simon went through to the ensuite bathroom. Electric toothbrush and paste were on the shelf above the basin and a bag of toiletries sat on a stool, opened and showing what amounted to a complete kit of anything needed for an overnight stay or longer.

Longman was half in the wardrobe. He emerged with a handbag dangling from his wrist. 'Let's see what's here.' From inside he produced a wallet and chequebook. 'Speaks volumes I think,' he said, delving further.

Simon mentioned the overnight toiletries bag. Longman looked up. 'So it doesn't look as if she has gone away intentionally. When she left here she either was forced or she planned to come back very soon.'

'Why would she willingly go out without her wallet and chequebook?' Simon objected.

Longman thought about it, wallet in hand. 'Suppose she was taken for an evening out by someone where she wasn't expecting to need any money?'

'It's possible,' Simon agreed. 'But would a single woman take the risk of being that dependent on a date?'

'Depends how well she knew him,' Longman said, producing a handful of bank notes from the wallet.

'Are her car keys there?'

Longman found them in a side pocket. 'No house keys on the key ring and I can't find any other keys.'

'Which fits with the scenario that she was out for the evening with someone she knew well enough or was comfortable enough with not to need get-out funds,' Simon said, wandering to the window to peer into the road where steady traffic streamed past. 'We'll have to speak to other neighbours soon,' he said. 'But I think we've seen enough here for now.' He turned for the door. 'We'll get the others to go through any personal papers. I'm satisfied Sylvia Gaston's disappearance must be involuntary.'

Longman produced a large evidence bag and pushed the handbag into it.

Simon went down the stairs to check the phone. He pressed a few buttons and noted down a number. 'Last call made from here,' he said.

Longman handed him the number Rupert Colville had given him. 'It's not his.' He tapped out some more numbers. The 1571 service yielded the voice of Mrs Jones from the agency asking Sylvia to get in touch please. Another call was from a garage asking if she was bringing her car in for service as planned. The next caller could only be Kate Milliner. Simon shivered as the clear voice reached from beyond death. 'Mum, wherever are you? Thought I'd see you at church. Perhaps you've popped out for the Sunday papers. Or maybe you're having a lie-in. I'll be over for lunch as planned. Love you.'

Simon repeated to Longman the content of Kate's call.

'So she came here on Sunday, found her mother wasn't here. She rang Rupert Colville to say that she had to see someone –'

'Sometime after she arrived. And she must have called someone else as well since the last number she rang is not Colville.'

'So she must have hung around here for a bit using the phone and then going off to wherever it was she went.' Longman sank onto the seat next to the hall table.

'According to Colville she was going to see someone,' Simon said.

Longman leaned over and picked up the phone. He pressed 1571 again and waited for Kate's voice, listening intently. 'She might have known if her mother was dating someone,' Longman said. 'And if she'd known who her mother's boyfriend was she would presumably have tried to contact him. So the last call she made could have been to the man her mother was dating.'

'It's something we can check. Let's not hang about here any longer. Too many ifs and buts give me indigestion.'

'That's hunger,' Longman said. 'There's a good pub down the road.'

Heedless of injunctions to eat in the staff canteen whenever feasible, Simon made no objections.

Chapter 7

'Bob Goodenough,' Longman said, putting down the phone. 'That was who Kate rang from her mother's.'

Simon rested his long legs on his office desk. 'So your optimistic theory that it was her mother's boyfriend is out the window. Though she might have phoned him beforehand.'

'Why would she phone Goodenough?' Longman said.

'Perhaps he's *Kate's* boyfriend.' Simon abruptly pulled his feet to the floor and went over to his cathedral view.

'Sir?' Simon nodded for DC Rhiannon Jones and DC Tremaine to come in.

As always, Rhiannon's face flushed when confronting Simon. Her silent admiration of him was irritating and endearing by turn. 'Sir, we went to interview the neighbours in the flat above Kate's.'

'And?' Simon turned back to the room more fully.

'They say that they saw a man entering Kate's flat last week.'

'He had his own key?'

Rhiannon nodded. 'They said he had.'

'Any description of the man?'

'He kept his head turned away from them and slipped into the flat quickly, so all they could say was that he looked youngish with longish brown hair and slim build.'

'Bob Goodenough,' Longman said.

'One of the teachers at Kate's school?' Tremaine asked.

'That's the one. Did they see him leave, or notice how long he was there?' Simon asked.

Rhiannon shook her head and looked contrite. 'They didn't take that much notice, sir. Said they would have of course if they had realized that Kate was missing, but since they saw so little of her they didn't really think much of it. Just thought it must be a boyfriend letting himself in.'

'Did they have anything else to add on the subject of Kate?'

'No, they just said she was quiet and they hardly ever saw her as they don't get out much. They're a fairly old couple and they've lived there for over twenty years and keep themselves to themselves.'

'I think we'd better go and speak to young Bob,' Simon said to Longman.

Longman looked at his watch. 'We'll need to hurry if he's planning to leave school when the bell goes.'

'By the sound of it we'll be doing him a favour if we can question him at school rather than his home.' Simon turned to Rhiannon and Tremaine and gave them a brief account of their morning's activities. 'We need Sylvia Gaston's phone calls checked, and Kate's as well. Perhaps you two could get on with that straight away.'

'Did they have mobile phones?' Tremaine asked.

'No sign of them in either case, though they could have had them with them when they disappeared. If so their numbers may turn up on the landline records.'

'So could our little book of love sonnets from 'R' be from R for Robert rather than R for Rupert?' Longman suggested as he and Simon went down the stairs.

'It looks likely. Presumably he had a key and went round in the week to check up on Kate.'

'If they were having an affair they'd have wanted to keep it quiet I imagine,' Longman said, puffing slightly as he hurried to keep up with Simon.

'Extra-marital affairs are commonplace enough,' Simon commented over his shoulder.

'It's frowned on though. The board of governors wouldn't like it. There was a hell of a fuss at the junior school my sister's children go to when a couple of staff started an adulterous affair.'

Simon could think of many on the force who would have described the relationship in more earthy language. 'Didn't know you were an uncle,' Simon said, easing his long frame into the driver's seat.

'Yes, lovely kids,' Longman said, smiling benignly.

Longman and his wife had no children of their own, whether through choice or otherwise Simon didn't know. From the beatific expression on Longman's face, it seemed it might be the latter. Simon felt a twinge of unease and recognized it as his own unsatisfied desires in that direction. He and Longman had never discussed such issues, both preferring the discussion of work issues to intimate revelations. Unerringly male of them, Simon thought.

Linden Road was a chaos of parents' cars when they arrived. They waited for the rush to subside and when they finally pulled into the school car park it appeared that most of the staff were still at work.

Their arrival had obviously been noted: Corina Hanson, high heels clicking on the polished surface of the corridor was approaching them as they came through the door. 'Did you think of something else?' she asked, her brow furrowed, a twist of impatience on her lips. 'Or,' her eyebrows lifted, 'perhaps you have some news?'

'We need to speak to Mr Goodenough,' Simon said.

Her chin tilted and from her small height she managed to look at him along her nose. 'Would you mind explaining why?'

'I rather think I would,' Simon said with a disarming smile.

It did not, however, disarm. 'Perhaps you would both take a seat,' she said curtly, indicating some plastic chairs lining the wall. 'I'll see if I can find him. It's possible he has left.' She turned away, clicking along the opposite corridor, her shoulders held stiffly.

'I told you,' Longman said. 'She's not happy with what this implies.'

'It may be something other than mere disapproval or fear for the school's reputation. Maybe she's friendly with Mrs Goodenough.' Simon, ever restless, wandered over to examine a wall full of childrens' artistic efforts. Their inventiveness and vision cheered him. He still had a smile on his face when Mrs Hanson reappeared, Bob Goodenough at her side.

She said, 'You can use my office if you wish. I shall be in the staffroom if you need me.'

Simon thanked her and waited until she had turned away before moving into her room.

Goodenough, his hair more dishevelled even than Simon's, remained silent as he chose a chair near the door.

Simon saw no reason to prevaricate. 'Mr Goodnenough, why didn't you tell us that Kate telephoned you on the Sunday that she disappeared?'

'I must have forgotten,' he said quickly, his eyes on the bright blue carpet. He must have realized that the police would trace the call at some point and still hadn't managed to come up with a more original response.

Useless to argue the point. 'Would you tell us why Kate phoned you, what she said?'

Goodenough shrugged and leaned back in his chair. 'Something to do with a school meeting, I think. She thought she'd forgotten to prepare for it.'

Simon and Longman regarded him silently as his colour began to rise. He kept his eyes focused on the view through the window.

'Did that have anything to do with why you went to Kate's flat on the Wednesday following her disappearance?' Simon asked.

Goodenough's eyes darted back to Simon's face. 'Who says so?'

'Kate's neighbours saw you quite clearly, letting yourself in with a key to her flat.'

Goodenough's shoulders sank.

'You were obviously in a relationship with Kate, Mr Goodenough. It might be best in the circumstances, and if you have nothing to do with Kate's death, to be a little more forthcoming with us,' Longman said.

'Of course I've got nothing to do with Kate's death,' Goodenough said contemptuously.

'We know only that you are the last person known to have spoken to her before she disappeared. So why did Kate really telephone you?' Simon was beginning to feel comfortable in the head teacher's chair. He resisted his habitual temptation to lift his feet to the desk.

'She shouldn't have phoned,' Goodenough said grudgingly. 'We agreed she wouldn't phone me at home.'

Simon suppressed a rush of contempt for the man's egregious criticism of Kate. Despite the horror of what had happened to her, he seemed concerned only about himself, protecting himself from the consequences of his involvement with her. 'What did she say?' he repeated.

Goodenough's mouth twisted into a petulant line. 'She wanted me to meet her. On a Sunday afternoon, for God's sake! I mean, my wife's parents were there. How was I supposed to explain swanning off in the middle of a Sunday when they were there?'

Simon didn't dignify such self-pleading with a response. 'What did she actually say? What were her words?'

'I can't remember,' Goodenough said irritably, crossing one leg over the other and hunching forward to grab his ankle.

'Try,' Simon said, and waited.

The young man's features creased with apparent effort.

'You realize that we shall have to check your alibi that you stayed with your family after Kate called,' Longman said pseudo-sympathetically.

Goodenough jerked his head in Longman's direction. 'All she said was would I go and meet her.'

'Did you ask her why?' Longman enquired.

'Yes, yes I did,' Goodenough's head nodded agreement, his memory apparently jogged. 'She said she had to go and see someone and she wanted me to go with her.'

'And you said?' Simon asked.

'Why didn't she ask Rupert instead. She said she'd already put Rupert off because she wanted me to go with her.'

'How did she sound? Did she seem very bothered that you wouldn't?' Longman asked.

'I suppose so.' Goodenough scowled at his shoe and fiddled with a lace.

Simon said impatiently, 'But did she give you no reason why she was so anxious to have company? Or who it was she was going to see?'

'No, she didn't,' he said in an aggrieved tone. 'She was just unreasonable when I said I couldn't possibly get out that afternoon, and she rang off quite quickly making sure I knew that she was pissed off with me.'

'Tough for you,' Longman said expressionlessly.

Goodenough's deepset dark eyes darted back to Simon. 'Surely there's no need for you to check with my wife? I mean it would cause unneccessary grief if my relationship with Kate came out.'

Did he really expect sympathy? Simon wondered. Any discretion on the part of the police would be for the sake of Goodenough's wife and family rather than the errant husband. Though he wondered for a moment if the alternative might not do them a greater favour. 'Why did you go to Kate's flat on the following Wednesday?' he asked, ignoring the appeal.

'To see if she was all right of course.'

'Of course. And did you perhaps decide to remove any incriminating evidence of your relationship with Kate, as she seemed to have disappeared?'

Goodenough coloured up again. 'I know that seems pretty low to you. But it wasn't going to do Kate any good to have me dragged into any investigation,' he said defiantly.

'You did think then that something must have happened to Kate?' Simon asked mildly.

'Something must have,' Goodenough muttered. 'I'd tried her several times on the phone before then. I even tried her mother's number but there was no one there.'

'And you were so concerned about your own precious hide that, believing that something had happened to her, you made no effort to inform the police?' Longman made no effort to hide his contempt.

'I had other people to worry about,' the young man said in a low voice.

'So you did, Mr Goodenough,' Longman said, distaste on his face. 'And had you responded to Kate's request, it's possible she would still be alive today.'

Goodenough uncrossed his legs and got to his feet. 'Don't put that on me! It's not my responsibility if Kate went off on her own to meet some madman that she was obviously nervous about seeing.'

'He does have a point, Geoff,' Simon said, also standing. 'You can go now, Mr Goodenough, though we may want to speak to you again.'

Goodenough's hand was already on the door.

'Just one more thing,' Simon said.

He turned back, his face closed.

'Did Kate ever talk to you about her mother?'

'Not really. I know she lives in Westwich and Kate used to see her regularly, but we didn't really discuss family. We talked about other things.'

'Not surprising I suppose,' Longman said.

'As you say, Sergeant,' Goodenough said sarcastically. He slipped through the door and was gone.

'Unfeeling sod,' Longman commented.

'Didn't you like him?' Simon asked. 'I'd never have known.'

'I just can't believe how little he seems bothered by Kate's death. All he cares about is his own skin,' Longman said hotly.

'The Queen is dead, long live the former Queen?'

'Something like that,' Longman sighed disgustedly.

Chapter 8

'He forgot to remove the little book of love sonnets he gave Kate,' Longman said as they drove back to headquarters.

'I wonder if something similar happened with Kate's mother,' Simon said. 'What if she was out with a man on Saturday night and something happened to her with him.'

'He might have sent her love poems, you mean, or love letters?'

'She had her house keys on her. He might have let himself into the house and taken any evidence of their relationship, just as Goodenough did.'

'Or she could have had trouble with the admirer who sent her the flowers she binned,' Longman suggested.

'Not likely if she was out with him that night. So perhaps there were two different men.' Simon pulled to a stop at some traffic lights.

'We haven't spoken to the other neighbours yet. Maybe someone will have seen something. Like a man delivering a bunch of roses.'

'Maybe. It could be that rather than Mrs Gaston having gone out with a boyfriend, that someone came to her house on Saturday night, attacked her after she rejected him and cleared any evidence of any assault.' Simon pulled forward again as the lights changed.

'And in either case, her mother might have confided in Kate any problems or relationships she was having with men so that Kate took off after him when she found her mother had disappeared,' Longman said, winding down the window. The autumn sun, now that it had appeared at long last, was warm and soporific. 'That bunch of roses says something. They must have been from someone whose attentions she didn't welcome.'

'But there's no way of knowing if she threw them away because of some kind of tiff or because she wanted nothing to do with the man in the first place.'

Simon pulled into the car park at headquarters. 'There should be prints on the cellophane.'

'That's only of use if he delivered the flowers himself.' Longman's sigh turned into a groan as he released his seatbelt. 'The fact is, we don't have enough facts and we're speculating too much.' He ducked his head, peering up through the car windscreen. 'There's Munro at her window, keeping a lookout for you I wouldn't be surprised.'

Simon winced and kept his eyes averted. He hadn't put in his report last night to Detective Superintendent Munro. He was meeting Jessie at Heathrow tonight so instead he had gone out to Jessie's cottage to check that everthing was in order, and that enough food was in the house so that she could recover from any jet lag without having to think about shopping needs. The cat was alive and well, he was relieved to find, the appointed neighbour having done her duty in that direction. And now Munro would be insisting on a verbal update. He extracted his legs from the car and headed into the building.

There was indeed a message for him to see Munro and he decided it was politic to get to her office without delay.

Despite the unnerving effect this impressive woman always had on him it was always a pleasure to enter her room. Though it lacked his lovely view, it caught the westering sun that lit on the warm fabrics she had chosen for the upholstery and illuminated the colourful prints she had placed on the walls. It was far from the masculine sanctum that her predecessor Detective Superintendent Bradley had made of it – designed to relax rather than intimidate. Though, as Simon was conscious at the moment, the disarming effects of the atmosphere could catch the unwary unprepared. Detective Superintendent Munro was no slouch when it came to discipline. He stood waiting just inside the room after his call to enter, expecting a mild verbal onslaught over his omission of the previous evening.

'I didn't know you possessed a suit, Chris,' she said. 'How charming you looked at the funeral. You should wear it more often.' She looked up from one of the several easy chairs in the room. This was another departure from Bradley who, without exception, greeted one, if that was the appropriate term, from behind his large oak desk. Munro used the desk rather more selectively so he intuited that she was not overly concerned by his omission.

He made no reply to her remark. His sartorial shortcomings had become a theme in their communications, a constant tease, he thought without any real resentment.

She beckoned to a seat opposite her, across the coffee table. 'Tea? Coffee?' she asked.

'Coffee, thanks.' He lowered himself into his seat while she got up, tall and elegant, and moved with her usual grace to a side table.

'Perhaps you could bring me up to speed with the case of Kate Milliner,' she said over her shoulder, the omission the more pointed for being unspoken.

He told her what little they had so far uncovered since Sunday about Kate Milliner's life. The warm aroma of coffee filled the room as she waited by the cafetière and finally pushed home the plunger.

'So it seems that Kate's mother has disappeared in suspicious circumstances and that her disappearance and Kate's death may be linked?' she said, handing him the steaming porcelain mug. 'Cream, sugar?' she offered.

It was very civilized and very calming and she knew what she was doing. She knew just when to pull the line tight and just when to metaphorically soothe the fevered brow 'That's fine as it is,' he said after a sip of the hot liquid.

She sat opposite him and waited for his response to her former question.

'It's difficult to see it any other way. Mrs Gaston's handbag and purse were in her bedroom. So she either went out with someone voluntarily where she knew she wouldn't need them, or she was forced out by someone who removed her from the house. I can't think of any other explanation, except the unlikely one that she's disappeared out of choice.

'Kate's own disappearance was after she arrived at her mother's house where she was expecting to have lunch with her and do some work in the garden. She cancelled an appointment to play squash with a friend and rang her married boyfriend to ask him to keep her company to where she was going next, though she offered him no explanation.'

'And what about this married boyfriend? Presumably he's in the frame?' Munro crossed her long legs, the fabric of her skirt pulling tighter against her thighs.

'We'll check his alibi obviously. But if he is involved I can't see the connection between Kate's death and her mother's disappearance and I can't believe they're not connected. I suppose there's a possibility that he went to Mrs Gaston's and killed the pair of them, but it doesn't seem very likely.'

'Keep an open mind, Chris,' she reminded him. 'You don't know enough yet to come to any kind of conclusions.'

'Of course,' he agreed, nettled that she should think him unaware of his own favourite maxim. 'We'll check what we're told.' He took a mouthful of coffee.

'So what are your plans?' she asked with a slight smile touching the corner of her mouth.

'They'll change according to what evidence emerges of course,' he said a trifle sententiously, causing her smile to widen and his discomfort to increase. He cleared his throat. 'The first priority as I see it is to look into Sylvia Gaston's life, find out about any men friends.'

'What about women friends?'

'That too. We got her address book from her handbag and the team are due to do a thorough check on both womens' homes for any possible leads.'

'A friend Sylvia Gaston confided in would be a help,' Munro commented.

'Another possiblity is the vicar of their church. Apparently Kate and her mother were regular attenders at St Biddulph's.'

Munro raised an eyebrow. 'Where Mrs Fielding's funeral was. The Reverend Swan seems a pleasant type. He might be the sort either of them might have confided in if in trouble of any kind. Mrs Gaston was a widow, wasn't she? And Kate was the product of her first marriage. Has her father put in an appearance?'

Simon explained that he worked as a doctor in the north somewhere and that they were trying to trace him though the medical authorities.

She frowned. 'Surely they should have caught up with him by now?'

Simon shrugged. 'There might be some news.'

'And then there's the putative unwanted admirer who has his roses spurned.'

'Fingerprints are checking the cellophane wrapping. It looks as if the flowers may have been bought from a supermarket rather than a florists, so it's not likely anyone is going to remember who purchased them.'

The phone on Munro's desk beeped sharply and Munro rose slowly to answer it. He had never seen her hurry. She spoke briefly in response to the caller and replaced the handset. 'It seems Kate's father has turned up. Dr Milliner is waiting for you.'

Simon's first thought was that he hoped this didn't mean any delay in

his trip to Heathrow. It was already almost 6 p.m. He got to his feet quickly.

'Take your time, Chris. He'll keep,' she said with a smile. Did she know what he was thinking? Was there more she wanted to say about the case? He waited, the strain showing in his face.

She relented. 'All right. You can go. But get your reports to me daily. Now we've talked I can wait until tomorrow for a full update.'

He gave her a quick smile and made for the door. 'How's Jessie?' she asked presciently as he put his hand on the door knob. 'Is she still in the States?'

He turned to face her. She had probably somehow divined it anyway. 'I'm meeting her at Heathrow at ten tonight,' he said.

'You'd better get your skids on then.'

Milliner had been put in Simon's office. A silent Sergeant Longman seated behind Simon's desk, waited with him. Milliner had chosen no to sit, his back to the room, he was studying the view and turned slightl as Simon entered. 'The most beautiful cathedral in England, I think. Yor are fortunate to have such a view. Mine, in my place of work, is less salu brious.'

'Dr Milliner?' Simon held out a hand and the man turned fully to fac him.

'You're Detective Chief Inspector Simon, the officer in charge (Kate's case.' It was a statement, and made as if his daughter were merel on a medical treatment list rather than lying cold in the mortuary.

Simon gestured to a chair and Longman got up and moved to a se against the wall. Milliner took his time settling himself, placing his brie case on the floor beside him.

Simon's first impression was of sleekness and cleanliness, or perha sanitariness was a more apt word: he supposed grubbiness would harc have aroused confidence in a doctor. It was unlikely that they rea were cleaner than the average professional male but they someh looked it. Simon found the quality slightly repulsive, wondering if were some kind of genetic trait common to the profession. Not to own genes for sure – however fastidious he himself might be in ways t counted, he lacked the ability to *look* it.

Milliner was as tall as Simon himself and had not developed compensatory stoop that some less confident tall men displayed. hair, greying evenly, was a bit overlong but carefully groomed. The f too, was long and narrow with deepset pale eyes and a sharp nose.

looked altogether distinguished.

'We've had trouble locating you, Dr Milliner,' Simon said. 'What took you so long in contacting us?'

'I've been on duty in my public and private practices and much too busy to look at newspapers or watch television.' There was no apology in the well-modulated voice and the egotism of his remark put Simon's temper on edge.

'You are certain that the dead girl is my daughter Kate? I gather that her mother can't be found.'

'We have some concerns about Mrs Gaston's whereabouts,' Simon put him straight. 'Kate has been formally identified by a close female friend. Would you be willing to, or wish, to confirm the identification, Dr Milliner?'

He gave a deprecating little cough. 'I imagine her friend more qualified than I. Kate has not chosen to have much to do with me since her mother and I divorced.'

'You work in the north somewhere I understand?' Simon leaned back in his chair and linked his hands behind his head in an effort to ease the tension in his body.

'You are out of date. I have been working in Westwich for the past two years.'

So Kate had for some reason not mentioned the fact to her friend Vanessa. 'At the Westwich Royal?' Simon named the city's main hospital.

'And the Cossingham, as consultant there as well.'

The Costly Cossingham, as it was called locally, was a well-established private hospital. 'What is your area of medical expertise, Dr Milliner?' Simon asked, his eyes on the man's perfectly manicured white hands that had not twitched or shifted since he had arranged them over the very slight mound above his waist.

'I'm a gynaecologist.' Milliner crossed one leg over the other. 'Chief Inspector, I've come, as I ought, to speak to you today but I'm not sure what help I can be to you. Sylvia managed to poison relations between myself and my children so that there has been little or no communication between us. I really know nothing about their lives or what might have led to Kate's death.'

'When did you last see Kate, or her mother, Dr Milliner?'

The man tilted his thin nose at the ceiling and pursed his narrow lips. 'I really can't remember. I ran into Kate in town one day last year I think and we spoke briefly, but she was obviously as prejudiced as before

against me so I didn't prolong the encounter.'

'And your ex-wife?' Simon asked.

'I called to see Sylvia soon after I returned to Westwich to work, after being in the north for several years. I thought it was as well to let her know I was in the area again, especially as she works in the medical profession herself and our paths might cross. She is, of course, still living in the marital home.'

The bitterness he felt towards his wife and daughter could be detected in his voice. Though Simon could not warm to the man he had to remind himself that there were two sides usually in any marriage breakup. 'What was the cause of your divorce?' he asked.

'I don't think that's any of your business,' Milliner replied smoothly.

Longman stirred in his seat. 'You might be surprised what becomes our business in a murder case,' he said mildly.

Milliner looked at him in surprise. He turned back to Simon. 'As I said, I don't think there's anything I can help you with. My visit here is merely a formality.'

Did the man really have no feelings about the fact that his only daughter had been murdered? Simon wondered. Perhaps the man had another family by now. 'Have you remarried, Dr Milliner?' he asked.

'I married again five years ago. I have a young son.'

'And your first son, by Mrs Gaston. Do you see anything of him?'

A fleeting expression crossed Milliner's face. 'A little more than the others. Ian came to see me after he heard that I had returned to Westwich. He came again just before he set off on his backpacking tour for his gap year. He wanted some money. Which I gave him.'

Neither of Milliner's children, despite the acrimonious divorce, had chosen to adopt the name of their mother's second husband. Simon wondered just how much of the rift between father and children had been kept alive by their mother.

'Do you know where he is now?' he asked. 'We need to let him know what's happened. Though it's possible that copies of English newspapers might have reached him wherever he is.'

'I had a postcard from him about a month ago. He was in Nepal, but he's likely to have moved on by now so I'm afraid that's unlikely to be of any use to you.'

They would probably have to rely on Ian contacting them. He was unlikely to be in any centres of civilization if he was backpacking.

'Did Mrs Gaston have any relations?'

'Her parents are dead. She has one sister, though I never met her because they had nothing to do with each other. She lives in Scotland I think.'

How long ago did your marriage to Mrs Gaston end?' Simon asked, still wondering about the estranged children having hung on to Milliner's surname despite everything. Perhaps they had been relatively mature and decided it was too late for change.

His supposition was in part confirmed. 'Ten years ago,' Milliner said, closing his lips firmly after he had spoken.

'And she married again soon after?'

'Quite soon. To a GP,' Milliner said. 'He died, a couple of years ago.'

Simon nodded. 'So we understand.'

Milliner uncrossed his legs and unfolded his hands, laying them on the arms of his chair. 'I really ought to be getting back to the hospital. Unless there's anything else I can help you with?'

'We really would prefer you to do an official identification of your daughter's body, as a next of kin,' Simon said, aware of a desire to confront this apparently unfeeling man with the reality of the death of his daughter. Then he glanced at his watch, remembering Jessie in flight somewhere over the Atlantic at this moment. Longman could accompany Milliner. His in-laws were still staying with him, he wouldn't mind.

Milliner's nose twitched. 'If you insist.' He rose to his full height.

Yet he had asked for no details of Kate's manner of death or the circumstances. Simon found that extraordinary. Although some details had been revealed in the press, it was in the nature of a bereaved parent to want to know as much as possible, as if in doing so it confirmed the link, held the loved one closer until the inevitability of the reality of death had sunk in. 'So you know of nothing in Kate's life that might have led to this happening to her?' he asked.

Milliner dragged his eyes from the view through the window. 'As I said, I have nothing to do with Kate's life. I assumed she was killed in some random act of brutality as is all too common these days. Have you any reason to think otherwise?'

'We mentioned the disappearance of your ex-wife. We may have to treat it as suspicious,' Simon said.

'I got the impression from your sergeant that Sylvia had simply gone away somewhere and couldn't be located.'

Longman shook his head slightly but said nothing.

Simon explained what they had found at the house in Telbury

Avenue. 'It appears at the moment as if Kate disappeared – until she was found dead – shortly after she may have gone looking for her mother.'

'But you can't know that for sure?' Milliner's expression was patronizing and quizzical at the same time. Simon was grateful that he was not a woman and would never have to come under this man's ministrations in the course of his existence.

Simon admitted, 'No, we don't know anything for sure at the moment. But we shall be checking alibis of known contacts of both women. Perhaps, before he takes you to see your daughter, Dr Milliner, you could give Sergeant Longman an account of what you were doing during the weekend they disappeared?'

Chapter 9

Simon was late leaving Westwich but made good time until he met a traffic snarl-up approaching the airport. Concentrating on driving as
effectively and speedily as possible on the journey kept his mind off the
case for much of the way, but his thoughts kept returning to Dr Milliner
and his extraordinary sangfroid. What, he wondered, had happened in
that family to have caused such a degree of coldness and even hostility?
Between divorced partners it was not uncommon, almost inevitable
when one or other proved unfaithful, but for the estrangement to have
extended to the children it required a consistent and articulate fury on
the part of the one who considered themselves injured. And in this case
it might mean the greatest hostility arose in Sylvia Gaston, since it was
she that the children of the marriage had remained with.

Had Milliner been unfaithful? Or had his injury of his ex-wife taken
a different form? It seemed there was no one to answer the question –
unless young Ian reappeared from his remote backpacking trip and was
willing to talk. And was it relevant to the case? Was it possible that the
old bitterness between the formerly married couple had boiled over
again since Milliner had moved back to Westwich and its medical frater-
nity? Would his ex-wife's path and his own have been likely to cross,
with her working in the private home care sector of nursing? He was a
gynaecologist. Sylvia Gaston might have been providing home care for
patients after he had operated on them.

They had received a short list from Thelma Jones of Sylvia Gaston's
recent patients and had begun contacting them. Simon no longer had
much hope that she would be discovered staying with one of them,
though they might possibly offer some lead as far as her recent activities
were concerned, although for the moment he couldn't think how.

Perhaps it was infidelity he thought, returning to the spectre of Dr
Milliner, and probably on his part as she had kept the house and the chil-

dren and must have been bitter to have turned the children against their father fairly comprehensibly. Ian's contact with his father, being apparently for the sole purpose of demanding funds, was not indicative of a true rapprochement. Perhaps Milliner had started a relationship with the woman who was now his wife while still married to Sylvia. Simon tried to imagine what that would feel like. He had never suffered infidelity in a relationship himself. His relationships before Jessie had ended mutually and with no bad feeling on either side. And though he had been fond of the women concerned he had suffered no jealousy of them and could imagine no torment had they ditched him for another man. Jessie though was a different matter, his feelings here being sometimes painfully engaged. He had experienced jealousy when he had felt other men were getting too close to her. The memories even now made the heat rise in his face.

Why should it be so different with Jessie? Why should he, a formerly fairly diffident lover, have discovered a whole nest of insecurities where she was concerned? Why suddenly find that he was capable, if not of murder, then certainly of murderous thoughts? It was a question that, as a psychologist, she was eminently qualified to answer, and disqualified by him because of the nature of their relationship. He was aware that she had picked up on this weakness of his but he could never bring himself to openly admit it to her.

It was linked in some way to his hesitation in broaching the subject of marriage. He was terrified she would say no and send him on his way with a kindly pat on his head and an injunction to go forth and multiply with some biddable and fertile female of a different mettle. But he had to do it. His hands tightened on the steering wheel and the blast of a horn behind him accompanied by rudely waving fingers woke him to the fact that he had slowed to a cruise in the fast lane.

He returned the wave less amiably than was usual with him and moved over, glancing at the clock. He was going to be late. With tightened security regulations, though, it would probably take some time to come through immigration. He longed to see Jessie again but all these self-promptings over marriage had got him so screwed up that she would sense the tension in him and think that her prolonged absence was at the root of it. Better – absolutely necessary – to put it out of his mind for a while. She would need to get over jet lag and settle back into term time before he should say anything on the subject. He breathed a sigh of relief, both at the decision and at the sign for the turn-off for the airport.

He felt ridiculously nervous as he entered the Arrivals section, searching among the milling bodies for her distinctive hair, distinctive height. He imagined her standing alone, suitcase at her side, hand luggage slung over her shoulder, looking for him as he was looking for her. The line of a poem came to mind with a feeling of warm satisfaction: 'The woman who looks for me in the world'. So that it came as an unpleasant and unexpected shock to find her not looking for him but looking instead into the eyes of another man and talking animatedly, and with obvious pleasure.

Simon was beside her, the curious eyes of her companion on him, before Jessie was aware of his presence. Her delighted 'Chris!' went some way to comforting him, and the fact that she dropped her bag and hugged him. But then she turned to the other man, introducing him. 'This is Perry Parton, Chris, Cambridge University.'

Simon hoped his students called him Dolly: he was pretty enough, despite his very formal suit. He looked like a member of the new breed of business academics, those who assiduously fed industry their research rather than studied and researched for the pure purpose of learning – as academics had appeared to do in his own university days. He noticed belatedly that Perry had put out a hand to be shaken, and belatedly and briefly took hold of it.

'Were you at the same conference in Chicago?' he asked.

'That's right. Very worthwhile, too, wasn't it, Jessie?' Perry replied, smiling at her with white even teeth.

So how come he had travelled back with her if Jessie had spent several days after the conference in New England? 'So how was the Fall?' he asked Jessie exploratively.

'It hadn't really got started,' Jessie answered Simon.

'Too early for it, isn't that so?' Perry said unneccessarily, smiling at Jessie.

'I rather think that's what Jessie meant,' Simon said.

A faint expression of irritation crept across her face. 'Perry here just happened to be on my flight by coincidence,' she said abruptly. She picked up her hand luggage, leaving her suitcase for Simon. 'Shall we go?'

'Don't forget to call,' was Perry's parting remark as Jessie made a brief farewell and Simon nodded to him.

She said nothing as they made their way to the car. His ventured 'You look well,' went unanswered. As they buckled their seatbelts he asked if she were tired.

'I thought you said I looked well,' she said shortly.

'Oh Hell,' he thought as he started the car. They drove on in silence for several miles, Simon thinking back over the encounter at the airport and wondering what he had said or done that was so very bad. The trouble was, these things were so subtle. She would have read his body language, his facial expressions, which he was not so very expert at dissembling, and sharp as she was, she would have read him like the proverbial book. He knew she had no patience with his insecurities as far as she was concerned, regarded them as a kind of lack of faith. And she was right to feel that way. He pulled himself together mentally and tried to step aside from the pain that the incident had produced in him. He had wanted things to be so different.

'Are you hungry?' he asked as they approached a turn-off for a motorway stop.

'I'm OK. I ate on the plane.' Her tone was muted but not hostile.

Encouraged, he ventured, 'I missed you. Hope you had a good time.'

'I missed you too,' she said. 'It was worthwhile, the conference. Useful. And New England was lovely even without the proper Fall. But I'm glad to be back.' She put out a hand and rested it on his knee and he lowered his from the steering wheel and gave it a squeeze.

'Tell me about the conference,' he said.

She shifted, raising herself in her seat a little. 'It was a mixed bag in some ways – a lot of different experts in various fields of psychology. There was a profiler from the FBI you would have found interesting. I found the Industrial Psychology sessions a bit of a bore but that's all my reservations about some of the more manipulative aspects of psychology – and that's where the money is when it comes to investment in university departments.'

Simon bit back a question about whether that was Perry's sphere. Either that or commercial – advertising perhaps.

She talked on for a little while, becoming more animated, describing some of the contacts she had made. Her own particular sphere of interest was interpersonal – she had her own private practice – but in her professorial role, all directions the study of psychology was taking were relevant.

'Any parapsychologists?' he asked with a smile, recalling Hermione, a colleague of Jessie's, who had involved herself in a previous case of his.

'Certainly parapsychologists. It's big in America. But I attended only one of their sessions, bagging what I could for Hermione.'

'Perhaps I should consult her again. I've got a bit of a mystery on my hands at the moment,' he said, glancing at her with a sideways smile.

'I read about it on the plane. You've got some poor murdered young woman and her mother seems to have disappeared. Do you think something's happened to her as well?'

Simon had long since got over any reservations about Jessie's interest in his cases, at least in a discreet role. She had frequently been of great help with her insights into personalities involved or implicated in investigations. In this particular case, though, at the moment he could see little scope for her expertise just yet. He gave her an account of what had happened and the little they had discovered so far.

'No woman would voluntarily leave home without her money and money sources – unless as you suspect, she was out for a date with a man she trusted.' She sat up even straighter. 'Unless she was forced out, which you say you've thought of. And you say her house keys aren't there?'

'That's right.'

'So, if she was forced out he might have taken those with them. Did the neighbours see anything?'

'Not so far.' The house-to-house inquiries had yielded nothing as yet. If it had been after dark when Sylvia left her home, either to be picked up by a date or under duress, it was unlikely in that leafy road, where houses were fronted by fairly large gardens, that anyone would have seen. They were all probably watching television on that Saturday night, or were out socializing. 'Our best hope might be that someone was out walking the dog at the relevant time – perhaps someone from a neighbouring road whom we haven't got to yet.'

'But you think Kate's behaviour after she arrived at her mother's suggests she had some idea who her mother was with?' Jessie said, and continued without waiting for Simon's reply. 'If so, I wonder why she felt the need to ring her boyfriend for support? Was she expecting some kind of confrontation?'

Simon thought about it for a moment. 'Or was she expecting a confrontation with her mother? Maybe she was annoyed that her mother wasn't home as promised and had stayed over with her own boyfriend. Maybe it had happened before and she was more angry with her mother as a consequence.'

'It's a lot of "maybes",' Jessie said. 'What you need is a close friend of the mother – someone in whom she may have confided. Or even a close friend of the daughter.'

'Mmm. Well the apparently close friend of the daughter that we have interviewed didn't even know that Kate's father was back in town.'

'Could he be a suspect? Perhaps there's some ongoing problem there.'

'Husbands, ex or otherwise, are always in the frame,' Simon commented. He made a sharp exclamation as a driver came up at high speed behind him, forcing him into the middle lane.

'Take his number,' Jessie said. 'He was doing at least a hundred.'

He should, of course. The driver was a menace to others on the road as well as himself. But he could do without any more paperwork at the moment – and, besides, the car was out of sight before Jessie had finished speaking. They drove on in silence for a few more miles until Jessie spoke again.

'The flowers that were dumped in the bin might lead to something. Does it mean she had had a row with her boyfriend – the fact that she threw them away? Or were they a gift from an unwanted admirer? Her ex-husband?' Jessie said exploratively. 'Or some sort of stalker maybe.'

'Her ex didn't seem to cherish any romantic illusions about her. It might be someone with a fixation on her though,' Simon agreed.

'She is a nurse,' Jessie said thoughtfully. 'Transference maybe?'

'Tranference?' Simon repeated, vaguely aware of the meaning of the term.

'It's something you have to guard against in psychotherapy. The kind of focused attention that clients get from a therapist is more than people often get in their everday lives and is associated in their minds with loving interest, so that they can come to believe that the therapist's interest is personal rather than professional. Sylvia Gaston was a nurse, giving home care which would have involved very personal attention to her patients. It's possible one of those became attached to her and believed that Sylvia's professional interest was something more.'

It was quite possible, Simon thought, grateful for Jessie's insights not for the first time. 'We're going to be following up on her recent cases,' he said. 'I'll keep it in mind when I see any of her previous patients.' It could mean a lot of work if they had to check on all Sylvia's patients, and he didn't have much manpower.

'And study their husbands, if the patient was female,' Jessie added emphatically. 'Being around twenty four hours a day means a growth of intimacy with the household and inevitably means giving support to the spouse. And don't limit yourself to recent cases. This could have been going on for some time.'

Simon groaned inwardly. It was all very well for Jessie to try and direct the case but she had no idea of the restrictions placed on him. 'We don't even know if the person who left the flowers was anyone other than a boyfriend – who, admittedly, she must have fallen out with if she stuffed the flowers in the bin,' he protested. 'Or it could even be a current boyfriend that she kissed and made up with later. Have you any idea of the limited resources I'm working with?'

He felt her shrug beside him. 'You still can't afford to ignore the possibility. How you go about it is your own affair. As I said, you need to find out if Sylvia had any close friends. Or if her daughter did. She might have confided in her boyfriend about any problems her mother was having. Haven't you found *anyone* yet who was close to Sylvia Gaston?'

Invigorating she was, and exasperating too at times, Simon thought. It was so good to have her back, but it was nearly midnight and he was exhausted. Jessie, on the other hand, felt that it was around seven in the evening, he realized.

He explained how little he had gleaned from Vanessa Peel and Bob Goodenough and that they would be going through Sylvia Gaston's telephone book and emails. 'The vicar might possibly hold out some hope. Sylvia and her daughter were regulars at his church.' He realized he was already speaking of Mrs Gaston as if she were dead. 'She might have friends through the church I suppose. Her job is a bit isolating, living in so much of the time with different patients.'

'Depends on the vicar, I suppose,' Jessie said. 'How much he involved himself with his flock, I mean.' She shifted in her seat, examining Simon's profile. 'What did you make of her ex-husband?'

'Cold, arrogant, remarkably unconcerned about either his ex-wife or his daughter.'

'Sounds like some consultants I've come across.' Jessie's voice was amused. 'They need training in interpersonal skills, but, like alcoholics, that being the case, they are the last to realize it, or care. What did you say his name was? Milliner, the same as Kate's?'

At Simon's affirmative she said, 'I'm sure that's who Hermione had to see about some gynaecological problem last term. She was absolutely livid about him, said he had humiliated and insulted her.'

'I can't imagine Hermione taking that lying down, so to speak,' Simon said, grinning.

'It's not funny, Chris. It's no matter for amusement that women are still treated to that sort of behaviour from professionals who should know better – especially when women are at their most vulnerable.'

Suitably chastened, Simon apologized. 'Sorry. I completely agree. It was more the impossible thought of Hermione being bested by any mere man.'

'Which goes to show how little you thought of the implications. And what kind of man Milliner might be.'

'Hasn't Hermione made any protest, any official complaint?'

'She thought about it long and hard, first because she's due to follow up with some surgical procedure and she had images of a slip of the knife cutting off a fertile future in some act of medical solidarity. But she has gone ahead with a complaint to the authorities.'

'Brave of her,' Simon said soberly.

'Quite an inditement of the medical profession, isn't it, to think such thoughts? That's power, I suppose, but only if it gets into the hands of the wrong people.'

'But as we know, all power corrupts,' Simon agreed, realizing as he spoke, that he himself had power over the lives of others – that decisions he made had the power to influence or even break the lives of others. It was a power he used cautiously, though, and it was one hemmed around by the constraints of the system he worked within. Yet the police force could be as wrong-headedly protective of its own as the members of the British Medical Association.

'She's hedging her bets, though, by going private,' Jessie said neutrally.

'So she'll be able to get a different doctor? Let's hope he or she is not a pal of Milliner.'

'Let's hear more about Milliner,' Jessie demanded as they crossed over the river west of the city. 'Do you know what caused the breakup in the marriage to Sylvia?'

'No idea. She subsequently remarried and so did he. Her second husband died but Milliner has a young son by the second marriage.'

'There is so much you need to know in a murder investigation, isn't there?' Jessie observed as the neon lights came to an end.

They were left with a world defined by the headlights – arching trees, their limbs whitened by the beams of light and brittle leaves scurrying like small animals from the predatory wheels of the car.

'You just don't know what might be relevant and what might not,' she added. 'And if you don't cover every avenue and it turns out that one you didn't was relevant you look totally incompetent.'

'Thanks for that insight, anyway,' he said.

'You should find out about their marriages. What peoples' marriages are like tells you a lot about the two people involved.'

Simon's heart gave a slight lurch. What was coming next? Marriage was somehow a subject that was never raised between them, and he never was sure whether that was deliberate evasion on Jessie's side. He knew what it was on his: cowardice and fear of rejection.

'Yes?' he said cautiously

'Fascinating institution, marriage,' Jessie mused, and his heart sank somewhat at the objectivity in her voice. Did she really never think of marriage in relation to the two of them? Could she really be so indifferent? Perhaps she was just perfectly happy with things as they were. He felt depressed.

'Mmm,' he agreed, keeping his own tone indifferent.

'The way some work so well, and the reasons that others fall apart, I mean,' she went on.

'And why do some work so well?' he asked lightly.

'Well, you can't generalize too much, I suppose. Marriages can be as different as the people in them, in theory. But in practice, a marriage that seems rock solid seems to me to resemble nothing so much as a conspiracy.'

'An odd thing to say,' he said, his voice failing him for a moment. This did not sound promising.

She sounded amused. 'Not really. It's the "Us against the world thing" in part.'

'Perhaps it's just strong loyalty,' he said quickly.

'That, too, certainly,' she said slowly. He felt her face turned towards him and his own burned.

Aware that she couldn't see him clearly in the circumstances, he went on, 'Surely loyalty, support, *love*, would be a necessary part of any decent marriage.'

Jessie cleared her throat. 'Mmm,' she said after a thoughtful pause. 'And not a part of any unsuccessful marriage. Didn't someone say that all successful marriages are alike and all unsuccessful ones different, or words to that effect?'

'Something like that,' he agreed, thankful to be able to do so. 'Or it might be the other way around. Or it might have been about a different subject.'

'I still think that some so-called successful marriages are a bit of a lie.'

'Why?' he asked.

'Oh,' she said consideringly, 'perhaps because they are based on lies. Because there seems to be a sort of agreement to ignore the less acceptable aspects of one's partner, or of the relationship itself and behave as if everything is quite wonderful, when it isn't.'

'In that case they are not, by definition, successful marriages then,' Simon said.

'True. Just rather smug ones all too often.'

He wanted to ask her *now* what she felt about marriage for herself. All the mysteries he had had to solve in the course of his work had never been as baffling to him as the mystery of this woman in his life. But he didn't dare. It was not promising, all this.

'I suppose at the root of it is the nature of love itself and how that is perceived or practised within marriage,' Jessie continued relentlessly.

'Meaning?'

'Caged birds,' she said.

He glanced left but in the faint light from the dashboard could see only that she was gazing ahead expressionlessly, her eyes slightly hooded.

'You mean marriage is like a prison,' he asked heavily.

'Some marriages,' she corrected. 'The love within them is like the love that people have for their caged birds.' She stirred in her seat, her voice becoming more animated. 'I mean, *how* can anyone call it love to keep a free-flying creature shut up in a cage? Is there anything much more outrageous – and to have the unmitigated gall to say they *love* their little caged bird!'

' "A robin redbreast in a cage puts all heaven in a rage",' Simon quoted.

'Exactly,' she said hotly.

There was silence for a few minutes as they drove past some woodland, the headlights picking out the trunks of trees in an hypnotic rhythm.

Jessie cleared her throat. 'Some marriages are like that and can survive, provided both partners go along with the lie. Especially if they both agree to live in cages.'

'My parents have a good marriage,' Simon said quietly.

'They have a partnership,' she said. 'That's what a good marriage means.'

'Like us,' he said, the words slipping out before he considered the challenge that might be implicit in them.

'Yes, like us,' she agreed, and there was no hesitation in her words.

He exhaled silently and slowly, a sweet sense of relief flowing through him. It was as if he had been granted a stay of execution.

'In view of which, we're straying a little from the subject of Dr Milliner.'

Simon gestured with his head to the road in front of them 'We're almost home, and it's well past midnight.'

'Is he the kind of man who wanted his wife in a cage?' Jessie continued, ignoring Simon's plea. 'If so, there may have been unfinished business there.'

'I'll bear it in mind,' he said wearily.

She laughed, squeezing his hand. ' It's still early by my body clock. I find I'm ravenous after all.' She leaned sideways and planted a lingering kiss on his cheek.

Chapter 10

An extended list from Thelma Jones arrived next morning, delivered by hand by her languid receptionist. It consisted of only eight more names, two of them deceased, patients Sylvia had cared for over the last three to four months. It was not enough. If any former patient or spouse were involved in Sylvia's disappearance the association might date back earlier.

'See Mrs Jones and impress on her the need for a list going back at least over this year,' Simon said to DC Rhiannon Jones at the meeting that morning.

'Are we going to interview all of them, sir?' she asked, her Welsh accent exaggerating the interrogative.

'Not if some of them are dead, Rhiannon,' said DC Savage amid laughter.

'Yes, we are Rhiannon,' Simon spoke to the room in general and the noise subsided. 'That is, the partners or spouses of any patients, even if the patient is now deceased. They might have some information on Sylvia's private life.' Simon would want to speak to certain patients himself, he said, but some of the team could begin a filtering process, selecting out any possible clients who might have formed some fixation, as Jessie had suggested, on Sylvia Gaston. Or they might have formed a more normal relationship with her – perhaps someone that Mrs Gaston may have been with the day she was last seen.

'We need as much information as we can get on Sylvia and on Kate, their lives and circumstances. Kate's life appears fairly straightforward but she may have talked to other friends we don't know about. Her phone records need checking, personal effects at her flat, and so on. And the same for Sylvia Gaston – she's on the net, so check emails. Which

81

should keep you all busy enough for a while. I'm off to see the Reverend Adrian Swan to see how well he knew these particular members of his congregation.'

It was bright and sunny as Simon and Longman approached the church and vicarage. Dried-out leaves lay in gutters and under the large horse chestnut at the entrance to the vicarage garden, the tree providing a screen and division from the church next door. Simon had phoned Swan earlier and the man was waiting for them on a seat by the front path, immaculate in clerical garb, and in sharp relief to the blowsy decay of the autumn garden.

'A muddled autumn this year,' Swan greeted them. 'We need a good frost to colour the leaves.' He got up from the seat, straightening his trouser legs. 'Would you like to go inside?'

Swan ushered them through the front door into the dark hallway. The house was large and Victorian, stonebuilt and chilly. An old oak chest stood on the flagged floor, an ancient carved chair beside it; otherwise the hall was bare, apart from a dark oil painting of a stern-looking cleric frowning down on them, a look of acute distaste about his mouth.

Swan followed Simon's gaze. 'That's Joseph Biddlethorpe, the first incumbent who lived in this house. It's become a tradition with all his successors to leave him where he is. I believe his immediate successor was formerly Joseph's curate and was probably afraid the old man would haunt him if he were removed. That vicar was here well into the twentieth century and I think that after that old Joseph was allowed to stay out of a mixture of sentiment and tradition. My sons couldn't stand the old devil, nor could my wife. But I keep him to remind me of the unattractiveness of judgementalism. I expect he gave his parishioners a terrible time.' Swan looked from the painting to Simon and Longman and gave a quick grin. 'I hope I don't malign him.'

'You're obviously not afraid he'll haunt *you* then, sir,' Longman said.

'Not at all. It's a peaceful old house and wherever Joseph has gone to, I'm quite sure he has indeed gone, Sergeant Longman.' Swan gave Longman an ironical smile as if acknowledgement of their previous conversation at the funeral wake and directed them into a room on their right, its arched windows echoing those of the church next door, but letting in little light. This was simply furnished also, an old oak desk pushed sideways in to the window embrasure, a comfortable chintz sofa and chair diagonal to the fireplace and books filling the fitted oak book-shelves, both the books and shelves looking as if, like Joseph, they were survivors of the Victorian era. Simon, drawn as always by books, went to inspect them.

'I collect old sermons,' Swan said, waiting in the centre of the room.

'Riveting, I expect?' Simon smiled.

'Nauseating, a lot of them,' Swan's own smile lighted his dark features. 'But some of them can be instructive in a negative sense. And others are surprisingly enlightened. I enjoy the Victorians in particular. They were a curiously passionate lot. Even their cold puritanism contained some fiery heat. And their moral convictions are quite envi- able from the perspective of the age of uncertainty that we live in.'

'It was certainly an era of extraordinary characters.'

Simon pushed a book back on to the shelf and they all seated them- selves, Simon and Longman on the sofa, the vicar at a slightly higher level in the upholstered chair. This, Simon supposed, was where Swan spoke to parishioners who called. With a fire in winter it would be cosy and companionable.

He had noted Swan's use of the past tense when referring to his family. 'Do you live here alone?' he asked.

'The boys are both at university. Though at the moment they're still travelling before returning in October. Backpacking is the term, I believe. My wife became very ill at the end of last year and died.'

'I'm sorry,' Simon said. Removed from the professional context Simon had seen him in at the funeral Swan cut a lonely figure.

Swan took a breath. 'It's too big for me now, this place. It's a wonder they haven't moved me out sooner. I expect to be transferred to some smart little semi before long. These old vicarages have been selling for good prices and add a lot to church coffers, though ones very close to churchyards, like this one, can be harder to sell.'

'Bad chi,' Longman murmured.

'I'm sorry?' Swan leaned forward.

Longman cleared his throat and said more loudly, his face reddened, 'It's considered by some to be an unhealthy place to live next to, a churchyard. Supposed to give off bad energies.'

'Feng Shui,' Swan agreed. 'Yes, one of my sons got interested in that. It seems a lot of common sense to me, much of it. Certainly churchyards must be full of bad miasmas. But perhaps ours next door is old enough now to have passed that phase.'

Simon immediately thought of the poor Brontës, their home poised above that dreary churchyard. Bad chi or not, it would have been a depressing enough view.

'Interesting,' Swan murmured, 'but I'm sure you must be very pushed for time, Chief Inspector. As I said on the phone I am most desperately shocked and upset by what has happened to poor Kate. And now Sylvia is missing and you are concerned she may have suffered a similar fate, or that what has happened to them is somehow connected. How can I help?' He leaned forward, elbows on knees, hands clasped, his handsome face intent and concerned.

'We are trying to find out as much as we can about Kate and Mrs Gaston's private lives – in the hope that it may give us some lead, some explanation of what has happened to them. They were regulars at your church. We wondered what you might be able to tell us of them,' Simon said, leaning forward and making a mirror image of Swan's stance.

'I'm not sure how I can help,' Swan began uncertainly. 'We are not high church here. No confessions or anything like that, though even if there were—' He broke off, his gaze wandering to the window.

'But you did know them both fairly well, as regulars here?'

'Yes.' His gaze returned to Simon. 'I'm sorry, I'm of course weighing my knowledge of them against what possible use it might be to you. And that is not my job, it is yours.' He sighed and leaned back, clasping his hands now over his trim stomach. 'They've both been involved in work for the church. Sylvia was a church helper until the demands of her job made it impossible for her to keep to any commitments. Kate was keen on helping with any charitable affairs. She did a children's Christian camp for disadvantaged city children during the summer, by the sea in Devon. And she used to collect our charity envelopes. In fact she did one the day before she disappeared.'

Simon kept silent. If the man was allowed to keep talking he might manage to make some more personal comment.

Swan hesitated. 'I'm sorry. Just that it's painful to think of either of them being harmed. Sylvia nursed my wife after she came out of hospital. She was a wonderful nurse – supportive and very kind. You can understand that I feel deeply disturbed by her disappearance, and of course by the terrible thing that has happened to poor Kate. Even if Sylvia turns up safe she will be devastated by what has happened to her daughter. She was very proud of Kate, talked of her often. They were very close.'

So Swan had known Sylvia Gaston more closely than he'd known the ordinary run of parishioners. Simon was unable to avoid thinking of what Jessie had said about transference and wondering if this lonely widowed man had come to depend on the nurse to an unnecessary degree. He could see no unusual consciousness, though, in Swan's face.

'Did Mrs Gaston ever confide in you anything of her private life, or that of her daughter?' Simon asked.

Swan bit his lip, frowning.

'I understand you may feel inhibited about discussing private conversations, Reverend Swan, but in this situation I'm sure you know that Mrs Gaston would want you to give us every help.'

'Of course. Of course she would. One just gets used to a habit of discretion in my work. People do confide things and one must be very careful not to let slip things that one knows in the everyday run of things.'

'*Did* either of them confide in you, Reverend Swan?'

After a slight pause, Swan said, 'Sylvia did ask my advice about something that was troubling her. This would have been,' he raised his eyes to the high ceiling, 'about six months ago I would think.' His dark eyes returned again to Simon, 'I should have said this straight away, because it may well be relevant. She was being bothered by some kind of stalker.'

Something significant at last, and Swan had failed to let them know. 'What form did it take, this stalking?'

'Telephone calls mostly at first. I suggested she get her phone number changed, which she did, so she was relieved of that burden. But she thought she was being watched, followed. Sometimes the man left flowers for her on her doorstep.'

Longman's semi-recumbent form twitched slightly.

'And did she know who this stalker was?' Simon asked, keeping his voice even.

'She knew but she didn't give me any name.' Swan's hands began twisting in his lap, anxiety on his face.

'Did you give her any other advice, such as going to the police? A phone tap before she changed her number might have been helpful in tracking down whoever it was.'

'She really didn't want anyone official involved,' Swan said. 'She said that, if it was who she thought it was, it might cause distress to someone else.'

Simon thought again of the possibility that Jessie had raised. Had the stalker been a spouse of a patient, or a former patient himself, and had Sylvia been worried about the effect such a revelation or investigation might have on the partner? He recalled what Swan had just said. 'Was she willing to speak to someone unofficially?' he asked.

'I did suggest that she had a word with Jack Fielding, to see what he advised. She knew, knows, Jack and his wife through church. She also nursed Heather for a while, so I felt she would feel comfortable talking to him about it.'

'And did she?'

Swan frowned. 'I don't know for sure. You see, I've seen very little of Sylvia over the last months. She's been very busy with her nursing work. She lived in mostly and Sylvia was a very committed person.'

'But you must have seen her since the conversation you had with her about the stalker,' Simon said. 'Surely you made some reference to it?'

The cleric looked chastened. 'My reticence, I'm afraid. In the light of what has happened, it seems my scrupulousness about not prying or interfering with the lives of members of my flock must look like unconcern. It isn't that at all. It's just that I have believed it better to allow people to approach me freely for advice or whatever help they might feel I can give. I think if I bear down on them demanding some sort of follow-up, or enquire too closely into their well-being in any particular way, they might be less inclined to confide in me in the future.' Swan swept his dark hair back from his face and looked deeply unhappy.

Simon could understand his point of view, his diffidence, but could see that his attitude might occasionally appear uncaring.

'Did Jack Fielding say anything about it to you?' Longman asked, his voice loud in the sudden silence.

Swan shook his head. 'I hardly felt it appropriate to discuss Sylvia's private life with someone else, and as Jack never volunteered anything on the subject either, I'm afraid that was where the whole thing was left.'

So why, Simon wondered, hadn't Jack Fielding mentioned to him that Sylvia Gaston had been pursued by a stalker? He was a policeman, he knew that Sylvia had disappeared, surely he should have reported it to Simon and the team.

Echoing his thoughts, Swan asked, 'Has Jack not said anything to you about it, then?'

'He hasn't,' Simon said quietly.

'Maybe she decided not to speak to him about it after all,' Longman suggested. 'Perhaps she was afraid it would become official if she spoke to a policeman, that he would somehow force the issue, seeing it from a police point of view. Especially now that the law has really tightened up as far as stalking is concerned.'

'Jack's been going through a difficult time lately, with his accident and Heather's death,' Swan remarked. 'He may well have forgotten about it in his grief.'

'That's possible,' Simon agreed. 'We'll ask him about it, though.'

Swan straightened in his seat, pulling the sleeves of his neat clerical jacket down to almost the edge of his white shirt cuffs.

Simon, his eyes on the pristine cuffs, found himself wondering how Swan managed domestically now that he was alone. Who ensured that the vicar's clerical collars and cuffs maintained their unimpeachable whiteness? He couldn't quite imagine this urbane man up to his elbows in suds. But he knew that clerical salaries were distressingly low and hardly ran to paying the wages of a domestic help. Perhaps he had some private money of his own. Perhaps his wife had left him some? Simon became aware that a clock was ticking quietly, hypnotically, on the carved mantlepiece, and shook his thoughts free again.

'Did Mrs Gaston ever discuss her daughter with you? Was she ever troubled about Kate?'

Swan straightened to attention again. After a moment's hesitation he said, 'Yes, she did, she was.' He rubbed his chin, where a faint blue shadow marred his sartorial immaculateness. 'In fact it was probably on one of the last occasions I saw Sylvia. She said she was worried about a relationship that Kate had become involved in. She had asked Kate to talk to me about it and hoped I would be able to help her.' He looked across at Simon, his dark eyes shadowed as his chin. 'She never did, though, speak to me about it and I certainly didn't approach Kate on the subject.' He tilted his chin, a bit defensively, Simon thought.

'Did Mrs Gaston say what it was about this relationship that bothered her?' It must have been Bob Goodenough, the fact that he was a married man. Not a relationship a mother would wish for her daughter.

'She gave no details. But Sylvia did seem distressed about Kate's involvement with this man, whoever he was.'

'They were close, I understand, Kate and her mother?' Simon said.

Swan smiled, the expression lighting his face. 'They seemed to me more like sisters. Good friends. It's not always the case when the parents are divorced, but there was no question of Kate's loyalty to her mother.'

'You've known them a long time?'

'Since I first became incumbent here. It was shortly after Sylvia parted from her first husband, a very difficult time for them all.'

'What about the son, Ian? Did he also attend church?'

Swan gave a rueful smile. 'He came to Sunday School when he was young but stopped coming soon after the divorce and never attended services with his sister and mother. Sylvia never tried to force him. She believed, as I do, that religion had better come easily or not come at all.'

'To paraphrase the great Keats,' Simon added.

'Indeed.' Swan smiled.

'What was Keats really talking about, then?' Longman asked.

'Poetry,' they both replied.

'Of course.' Longman sank back again.

'You must have known Sylvia well because of her work for the church, Reverend Swan. Are you quite sure there's nothing you can think of that sheds any light on what has happened to her and her daughter?' Simon asked.

Swan gave a helpless shrug, the well-cut lines of his jacket falling smoothly into place as he lowered his shoulders. 'I only wish I could. We were friends, of course, through our mutual faith and interests in the church, but it was not an intimate relationship. I knew very little really of their day-to-day existence. I knew of their work, of Kate's success with her teaching career, Sylvia's involvement with her nursing. But they were after all among a fair number of parishioners. I had no reason to imagine that their lives would one day come under the microscope of a police investigation.'

And yet Sylvia had nursed Swan's own wife. She had surely meant a little more than the average run of his flock. Simon suddenly thought of Sylvia's second marriage. 'Did you know Sylvia's second husband?'

'He wasn't a believer, I'm afraid. I met him a couple of times when he came with Sylvia and Kate to church social events like the summer barbecue, though. He was a very quiet man, reserved. I didn't get to know him, though I believe he was well thought of. He was a local GP. Sylvia had known him for years. He had lost his own wife several years before.'

'Did he and Sylvia's children get along?' Longman asked.

Swan nodded. 'I believe so. Kate seemed affectionate towards him. He was much older than Sylvia. Died suddenly of a heart attack a couple of years ago. Strains of the job I think. He was said to be very conscientious.'

'I've met Dr Milliner,' Simon said. 'There seemed a remarkable coldness and indifference in him as far as his daughter and ex-wife were concerned. Do you know anything about the circumstances of the breakup of that marriage?'

'I'm afraid not.' Swan leaned back crossing his ankles and clasping his hands again. 'That marriage was over before I moved here and Sylvia never referred to Milliner, except in perhaps some passing reference.'

A shaft of sunlight suddenly cut through the room, motes danced in the air between them. Simon shifted forward in the comfortable chintz sofa.

'You last saw Kate at morning service on the Sunday she disappeared. How did she seem? Did you speak to her?'

Swan, whose eyes had been resting contemplatively on the carved clock, blinked suddenly. 'Only briefly, as she came out of church with Vanessa. I think I said Kate was doing some church work the day before, on the Saturday. It was in the evening actually. Not many young women would give up their Saturday evenings like that.'

But her boyfriend was otherwise occupied with his parents-in-law, Simon thought. Perhaps Kate had been glad of some virtuous occupation in the circumstances.

'She did the collection of charity envelopes for Christian Mission,' Swan continued. 'She called here at about half past nine and handed them in to me with the list but she didn't stay. I offered her a cup of tea but she said she had a lot of school work to catch up with so she was going home to her flat. The last thing she said was, "See you at the service tomorrow morning", and she was off.'

'Did she seem as normal?'

'Yes.' Swan eased his shoulders in his well-cut jacket and flexed his fingers. 'She seemed cheerful as usual. Didn't seem to have anything on her mind.'

'And Sylvia? When did you last speak to her?'

Swan's finely drawn mouth was pursed in thought. 'It must have been about three weeks ago. She came to the morning service. I spoke to her briefly at the church door as she was leaving. Apparently she was working that weekend but she had managed to have a couple of hours out so that she could come to church. Nothing of any significance was said.'

'Were you aware of any new relationship in Sylvia's life, any new man around?'

'No, not at all,' Swan said quickly. 'Was there one?' His dark eyes regarded Simon intently.

'We're not sure.' Simon paused for a moment, his eyes holding Swan's and then he rose slowly from the low sofa, his long legs making him awkward.

'I do hope you find out soon what has happened to Sylvia,' Swan said, also getting up. 'Nothing can be done for poor Kate now but it is dreadful to think that Sylvia may be alive and in trouble. Bad enough if she is merely out of touch for some reason and has yet to learn of Kate's death.' He followed Simon and Longman to the door. 'Is it likely you will be able to contact Ian, poor boy?'

Swan had slipped into his more familiar pastoral role and there was an evident air of relief about him as Simon and Longman paused at the front door prior to departure.

'We're doing what we can,' Simon said, pulling up his coat collar against a sudden flurry of cold wind. The sun, shining so warmly when they had arrived, had slipped behind heavy grey clouds and an almost tangible pall of depression descended over the house and garden.

'If you think of anything else I can help with . . .' Swan's voice trailed off. Simon nodded and turned away his last image of Swan as a lonely yet somewhat enigmatic figure.

'Well we got one useful lead out of all that,' Longman remarked heavily as they reached the heavy oak garden gate. 'There was a stalker. The one who sent those flowers.'

'Never be seduced by the obvious, Geoff.' Simon took off across the road to the car.

'Simple truth,' Longman objected.

'The truth is rarely pure—'

'I know, "and never simple", so said Oscar Wilde. And I don't happen to agree with him.'

'If that fact were particularly relevant,' Simon fell awkwardly into the driving seat, 'I'd be glad to spend time discussing it with you. But as things are, let's keep a little closer to the issues.'

'I thought I was,' Longman entered the car more ponderously. 'So what did you think of the Reverend Swan this time? Did he strike you as straight?'

'Why wouldn't he?' Simon's eyebrows rose in surprise.

'All those passionate sermons,' Longman said darkly. 'Do you think he's maybe a closet avenging angel? Maybe Kate did tell him about her affair with a married man and he killed her in a frenzy of moral outrage.'

Simon started the car. 'What a colourful inner life you lead, Geoff. I expect you'll have a theory to fit everyone in this case before we're finished.'

Simon's phone rang as he began to pull away from the kerb. 'Yes?' he answered, pulling up.

'Sir?' It was DI Stone, a new recruit to the team, a chillingly competent woman. 'A body's been found in a ditch in Cranton Plantation by some woodsmen. It's a middle-aged woman with blonde hair, could well be Sylvia Gaston.'

'That's on the Welby Road, is it?'

'That's right. Uniform have the area cordoned off so you won't have trouble finding it.'

Chapter 11

Cranton Plantation, as its name suggested, was an area of commercial woodland. About five miles north of the city, it was a depressing spread of dark pine woods, areas of which had been felled leaving roots ripped from the earth and an ugly desolation devoid of any green growth.

The police presence directed them along a forest track about half a mile into a dark section of woodland, deep ditches on either side of the track full of broken branches and pine needles. They were brought to a halt where a tent had already been set up over the body. As before, Evelyn Starkey had preceded him.

'Have you had a look yet?' Simon asked without preamble.

She nodded. 'It could be who you're looking for. She's been dead about the right time.'

'Cause of death?'

'Looks like strangulation. But she's been badly beaten.'

Simon swallowed. It was bad enough inspecting a body when you knew nothing about who the person was. But when you had already begun an investigation, begun to know the person and they had begun to take on their living identity, it was much harder. He pulled on his boots and overalls.

'Careful how you go,' Evelyn Starkey warned, 'it's slippery clay around there.'

'Any footprints?' Simon looked to the uniformed sergeant standing nearby.

'Nothing. Looks like they dumped the body from the path, which as you can see is well drained and dry enough. Then they slung some branches over.'

Simon manoeuvred himself into a crouching position and peered down. She was lying on her back, as she had been dumped, a leg twisted awkwardly beneath her. Her face was horribly bruised and suffused by the strangulation itself, but the hair was right, medium-length blonde, pine needles clinging to it. Her dress was low cut and she was wearing a light blue jacket, but what drew Simon's immediate attention was the pendant around her neck, slewed on to her shoulder by her fall. It was a silver star pendant and he had last seen it in the photograph of Sylvia Gaston at her home, the one he had extracted for publicity purposes. The image before him was a shocking contrast to the earlier one. He hadn't really doubted she was dead, but that didn't make the reality any easier.

'Looks like it's Sylvia Gaston,' he said, emerging back on to the track. 'Any evidence of identity on her?'

The sergeant produced an evidence bag. 'House keys by the look of it,' he said.

Simon took the bag from him and examined them through the plastic. They were attached to a key ring in the shape of a pill box with a medical cross on the side. 'I'll try these at her house,' he said. 'Where are the people who found her?'

'Just along there.' The sergeant gestured along the track to where a couple of men were leaning against their truck, one carefully grinding out a cigarette with his heel. He called to them and waved them over.

They came over quickly and in tandem, both still looking a little green around the gills.

'How did you come to find her?' he asked them.

'We were out marking up a new section for felling,' the taller one said, pointing to some red stakes beside the track. 'It just happens to be close to where she is.' He pulled a face. 'It was the smell made us look in the ditch. We thought maybe a badger had fallen in and couldn't get out.'

'Then her light blue jacket caught my eye,' Don agreed.

'Is the plantation accessible to vehicles generally?' Simon asked. 'I noticed a barrier that had been let down further along the track. I would have thought it would normally be locked to keep out the general public.'

'It is usually,' Don said. 'Obviously it's open today for you lot.'

'Usually. You mean sometimes someone forgets to lock up?'

'It happens,' the taller of the men said.

'You wouldn't happen to know whether it was locked during the weekend before last?'

They looked at each other. 'The padlock was broken a week or so back and the barrier thrown aside, wasn't it, Tone?' Don said. 'You'd have to ask Pete Ashbourne, the supervisor when it was exactly.'

'Do you get much of that kind of thing? Many members of the public in the woods?'

'It's not exactly pretty walking country, is it? No, there are nicer places in the area for people to walk.'

So it was not perhaps surprising that the body had not been found sooner. As it was it had largely been a matter of chance. 'If you'll give your statements to the sergeant here you can go. Thanks,' Simon said and turned again to Evelyn Starkey.

'Any other signs of injury?' he asked. 'Sexual assault?'

'Nothing obvious. But you'll have to wait until I've done a full examination. There's not much in the way of damage from animals, probably because she was difficult to get at under all those branches and leaves.' Her expression tightened. 'Do you think it is the girl's mother?'

'It looks like it.' Simon mentioned the silver star pendant.

'I gather you were expecting she'd been killed too.'

Simon nodded. 'Let's say it's no surprise.'

'It looks like the same killer,' she said. 'Same method of strangulation. But it looks as if it began with a violent assault.' She turned back to the tent. 'We'll get her out of there as soon as the photographer has finished. I'll be doing the autopsy tomorrow morning. See you there.'

There was no point in waiting around. He and Longman went back to the car.

'Shall we check the house keys at the house right away?' Longman asked.

'It has to be done, though I don't have any doubts it's Sylvia Gaston.'

As they pulled up outside the house Mrs Wright peered around the curtain at her window. She quickly emerged through the front door.

'Any news of Sylvia?' she asked, hurrying towards them.

'Good morning, Mrs Wright,' Simon said.

'Is there?' She ignored the courtesy.

The discovery of the body would be on the evening news and there was no point in alienating her. 'A woman's body has been found,' Simon said. 'It may be Sylvia's.'

Susan Wright put a hand over her mouth, an expression of horror on her face. She let out a breath. 'How terrible. Poor woman. Both of them murdered! Have you any idea what happened or who did it?'

'We're still interviewing people who knew them,' Simon answered, trying to edge his way past her.

'Some officers came here and asked me questions about them,' she said. 'But there wasn't much I could tell them. As I said before, Mrs Gaston kept herself to herself. She lived very quietly, I'll give her that.'

'Did you ever notice someone delivering flowers to her door?' Longman asked.

She put her head on one side. 'I have seen flowers on her doorstep once or twice and wondered if she had an admirer. But I've never seen who brought them. I've thought once or twice, though, that she had a visitor at night.'

'Oh?' Simon paused.

'Well I can't be sure, of course. I just thought a few times that I heard her front door bang shut late at night. This was after Ian went away – which I suppose is why I noticed it. I looked through the window but there was no strange car outside so I didn't think much of it.'

Susan Wright was an inquisitive woman. If Sylvia Gaston was, as it seemed, a woman who cherished her privacy, she would have been careful to excite no interest from that direction. In which case her neighbour might well be the last person to glean any details of her life.

Simon stood firm. 'Thank you very much for your information, Mrs Wright,' he said firmly. 'Now we really must get on.'

She lifted her pointed nose at him. 'Of course,' she said huffily. 'I have things to do too.' She turned on her heel and entered her house, banging the door firmly shut behind her.

It took only a few moments to confirm that the keys unlocked the front Yale lock and the mortice lock on the back door.

Both Longman and Simon were subdued on the way back to headquarters. Simon realized there had always been the slight hope that Sylvia might be found alive somewhere, despite the fact that they had acted with the assumption she was dead. Now, with Evelyn Starkey's belief that Sylvia had died approximately around the time they had thought, the same weekend as Kate, they could continue along the lines they had already begun, with the belief that the two deaths were closely linked.

Detective Superintendent Munro was leaving the building as Simon and Longman arrived back at headquarters. She looked even more splendid than usual in a stylish cerise dress and Simon smiled appreciatively. In the mostly uniform blues and greys at headquarters, her uninhibited adoption of cheering colour lifted the spirits.

'A working lunch,' she said, drawing him aside. Longman waited within earshot in the doorway.

'Well? Was it Sylvia Gaston's body?' she asked.

'It looks like it.' He explained why.

'I'm sorry to hear it,' she said. 'But I suppose it makes the case clearer. You can be pretty certain that the two deaths are linked. So, you carry on as before. Any other developments?'

Simon told her about the interview with Swan.

Eyebrows raised, she said, 'That sounds hopeful. If there was a stalker tracking Sylvia Gaston you may have found what is at the root of this. I assume you'll be speaking to Jack Fielding next?'

'On our way to find him,' Simon nodded.

'You don't seem very upbeat at the prospect,' she commented.

Simon paused in order to choose his words. It would be simpler to assure her that, of course, he was optimistic about this providing the lead they were hoping for. But he wasn't sure that it fitted with his earlier impression of the sequence of events that might have followed Kate's arrival at her mother's home that Sunday she disappeared. On the other hand, standing as they were on the edge of the car park didn't seem the place for any in-depth discussion of the implications of the evidence they had so far. Besides, Superintendent Munro might well be right: if there were a stalker in the case then he had to be the prime suspect. But he felt that there should have been signs of disturbance at Sylvia's house, some sign she had been taken by force rather than the appearance that she had merely left for an evening out with a trusted friend or lover. It was simpler, after all, to agree with her.

'No, it's promising,' he agreed.

She scrutinized his face, that familiar doubtful smile curving her lips. 'We'll talk later,' she said. 'I'll be interested to know what Jack has to say. I imagine in all his grief the whole thing has slipped his mind. Who will you get to identify the body? I assume Milliner is the only one you can ask?'

Simon said he would try to arrange it.

'She agrees with me,' Longman commented as Simon joined him. 'Why make things more complicated. If there's a headcase in the frame, why look elsewhere?'

'I didn't think we were,' Simon said shortly. 'Aren't we just about to follow it up?'

Jack Fielding was not in his office and a call to his home yielded only an answering service. 'Anyone know his mobile number?' Simon asked one of Jack's colleagues. It was handed to him, but the phone was switched off.

A uniformed sergeant in Fielding's section crossed to Simon and leaned close. 'You could try the churchyard. He's taking it harder than you'd think. Feeling guilty about Heather's death.' The sergeant, a homely and benign-looking man with an abundance of grey hair and an expansive midriff, stood straighter. 'It's not logical because it wasn't in any way Jack's fault, but grieving often takes people that way. He comes and goes at the moment and everyone is understanding about it, but it wouldn't do any harm for you to go and find him.'

'Thanks,' Simon said, 'We'll try that.'

'Back where we began today,' Longman observed. 'He might have been there when we were talking to the vicar.'

The plot in which Heather Fielding had been buried was some distance behind the church, the burial ground being a large and extended municipal one. Trees obscured any clear view of the area and it was a lengthy walk to the section where Simon remembered being for the interment the previous Friday. Elaborate tombstones with carved angels and lengthy inscriptions gave way to the simpler and more under-stated slab headstones of the modern age. Longman paused and rubbed his fingers over the lichen-encrusted words on a tall grey headstone.

'Miranda Lovelock 1813 – 1837. And her three children, Isobelle aged two years, James aged six months and Frances six days. Beloved wife of James Lovelock. A devoted wife and mother, dutiful in all her ways, now reaping her reward in the arms of our Lord in Heaven. May she and they rest in eternal peace. The Lord is thy Shepherd.' Longman looked up at Simon who had paused beside him. 'Hard times, weren't they? She was only twenty-four years old. You'd think the death rate would have undermined their faith more, but they were keen on the trappings of death and funerals. Didn't shovel it away like we do. Mourning was quite an industry.'

'Some people were never out of mourning,' Simon agreed. 'If I had to choose, I think I'd still prefer our current way of death.'

'But these modern tombstones often just have the name and dates of birth and death. As if we're glad to shovel them out of the way.' Longman ran his hand over the lichen again, brushing it from the etched wording.

'But *he's* not in there,' Simon commented.

97

Longman examined the tombstone again.

'You'll probably find his name on another headstone with a second or even third wife and a few more dead babies,' Simon said cynically. 'Off with the old and on with the new for all the fine sentiments.'

Longman's mouth pulled down at the corners. 'I suppose people don't really change, for all the surface appearances they give out. Ours is a less hypocrital age, for sure.'

'For sure,' Simon agreed. 'Though I'm not sure it makes it easier for us when it comes to dealing with other peoples' grief. Should we be approaching Jack at this moment, for instance?'

'If he's here. I expect a top-hatted Victorian policeman would have waited discreetly at the gate.' Longman cast a last glance at Miranda Lovelock's inscription and moved on ahead of Simon.

In the clear view beyond the last of the older trees the churchyard appeared empty and they both paused, about to turn back. Then a movement behind a distant headstone caught their eyes and they moved on. Jack Fielding stood up, his back towards them, the dark colour of his clothes distinct against the faded pastels of the floral tributes still lying on the mound of his wife's grave.

As they approached, he turned, apparently unsurprised and undisturbed at seeing them. His iron-grey hair was carefully brushed and he looked the upright policeman he was, despite his casual clothes, his dark sweatshirt and jeans neatly pressed and showing off his spare frame.

'I brought some fresh flowers,' he said in a dull voice, pointing at a stone vase containing white lilies. 'The others will be cleared away before long.'

They looked at the pure white flowers and could smell the scent of them from where they stood, overlaying the acrid scent of decay that the cellophane-wrapped sprays were giving off. A card was attached in the centre of the new display: 'To my dear love, in everlasting love, Jack.' Simon looked away, disturbed and moved.

'They won't be able to do the headstone until the earth has settled,' Fielding said conversationally, moving on to the path nearer to them. 'I wanted something special, but there are all sorts of regulations now about uniformity and so on. Sign of the times, eh?' he gave a humourless laugh.

His physical injuries must have been fairly slight, at least the ones that had shown, Simon thought. Fielding was still pale, but the scars showed as only a couple of pink lines on his forehead.

'It won't be long before none of us will get more than a small plaque after a mandatory cremation,' Longman said.

'So I suppose I'd better be grateful that she'll get a headstone at all,' Fielding said in a firmer voice. 'Anyway, what are you two doing that you need to track me down here?' He smiled to take away any implied resentment in his words.

'We're really sorry to intrude, Jack,' Simon said. 'Do you feel up to a few words? We've found what looks like Sylvia Gaston's body.'

'Oh? I'm really sorry. I hoped she'd turn up alive.' He looked away into the distance. 'I am sorry,' he repeated.

Simon thought it might be best to draw him away from any further contemplation of death. 'Jack, we've been talking to the Reverend Swan about her and we think you might be able to help us with something.'

'Sure,' Fielding said, turning finally away from the grave. 'There's a reasonable pub not far. Shall we go there?'

They followed as he led them to a side entrance to the churchyard and a narrow alleyway hemmed in with original Victorian railings. It was only a short distance to the rear entrance of a pub that stood on a corner of the main road the church was on.

'Let me. What will you have?' Fielding went straight to the bar and ordered their half-pints and his own pint then joined them in a quiet alcove.

'So what does Adrian think I can help you with?' he asked.

Simon swallowed his first mouthful of beer gratefully. 'He says he suggested to Sylvia Gaston that she spoke to you about a stalker she was having trouble with.'

Fielding put his hand to his forehead. 'God, I'm sorry. Whatever must you think of me? I should have told you about it.' His wide grey eyes were full of concern. 'I can only say that my mind's been on other things.'

'We understand that, Jack,' Simon said quietly.

Longman nodded agreement, placing his half-empty glass precisely on a beer mat.

'Yes, she did come to see me,' Fielding said. 'It was about six months ago, I should think. He had been making telephone calls to her and following her. He often didn't say anything on the phone, just seemed to be listening, though there was no heavy breathing or obscenity, she said. Sometimes he left flowers on her doorstep.'

'Was she aware of his identity?' Simon asked, impatient to know.

'She knew who he was, but she wouldn't tell me his name.' Fielding put down his glass and looked at Simon sympathetically.

So they were no further ahead, Simon thought, acutely disappointed. Even though he wasn't convinced that this man had actually taken Sylvia Gaston from her house, he realized it was possible he had been waiting for her if she had returned home after a night out on the Saturday.

'From what she said, though,' Fielding, added 'I gathered that he was the husband of one of her patients, a patient she had been nursing fairly recently. She said she didn't want to make anything official because it would hurt and upset the wife who had been very ill.'

Simon swallowed some more beer. Perhaps it wouldn't be too difficult to track this man down after all. They just needed a list from Thelma Jones that would cover the relevant time period. It might even be possible that he had been holding Sylvia against her will. But how did that link with the disappearance and murder of Kate? Had her mother told her the identity of her stalker and had Kate gone to look for him?

'Is it likely that Sylvia told her daughter Kate about this man? Might she have told her who he was?' he asked Fielding.

Fielding's eyes widened. 'You think he might have killed Kate as well?'

Simon said nothing. To him the inference seemed fairly obvious.

'Well, of course,' Fielding said, fiddling with his glass. 'The two cases, of Sylvia and her daughter, must be connected.'

'Did she say how long this stalking had been going on?' Simon asked.

'Not precisely,' Fielding narrowed his grey eyes in thought. 'I gathered it had been a month or so.'

'Do you think Kate did know about it, the trouble with the stalker?' Simon asked again.

Fielding pursed his lips. 'Hard to say. They were close, mother and daughter, from the way Sylvia used to speak about her when she was nursing Heather. But she was protective, too, so she might have not wanted to worry her about it.'

'What advice did you give Mrs Gaston, Jack?' Longman asked, pushing his empty beer glass away from him and leaning back on the bench seat.

Fielding gave a rueful smile. 'First off I advised her to be open about who he was. I offered to go and have an unofficial word with him to try to scare him off, but she wouldn't even allow that. She did follow my advice about having her telephone number changed, which helped a bit.

But living just with Ian in that large house and knowing he knew where she was did make her nervous. Of course, she was away at other people's houses working a lot of the time.'

'Was he a man she felt she had reason to be frightened of?' Simon asked. 'She must have got to know him a little if she was nursing his wife.'

'Actually she seemed a bit puzzled by his behaviour. Said he'd seemed a nice, pleasant quiet chap.' Fielding looked up with a frown. 'No, she didn't seem frightened exactly, but she was definitely disturbed and nervous, troubled obviously. I did point out to her that seemingly pleasant, quiet types can be just as dangerous as the more obviously violent ones, that some of the worst murderers have been charming types, but it didn't seem to change her mind.'

'Did she say anything about confronting him?'

'She was thinking about it. Again I urged her to make an official complaint and let us deal with it, but she was adamant.' Fielding let out a sigh and finished off his beer. 'I'm feeling very bad about it, Chris. I seem to have slipped up in giving the poor woman the kind of help she needed. But you know what it's like in our line of work, the hours and pressure—'

'And you had your own personal worries with Heather,' Longman said sympathetically.

Simon asked 'Did you speak to Sylvia subsequently about it? Did you ask her if she had indeed confronted this man?'

Fielding shook his head. 'I saw her at church a couple of times and asked discreetly if she was alright, if she was still having trouble, but she brushed me off. Said everything was fine and not to worry.'

'And did she *seem* unworried?'

'Hard to say really.' Fielding blew out his cheeks. 'She was a nice woman. It wasn't in her nature to trouble people with her own problems. She was too used to the boot being on the other foot. That was why, I suppose, she seemed more concerned for the stalker's wife than for herself.' He rubbed a hand over his chin, the faint growth of bristles making a rasping sound. 'I hope to God this isn't what's at the root of all this, the cause of what's happened to them both.'

'If it does turn out like that,' Longman said stoutly, 'you can hardly blame yourself. You couldn't force her to give the information to you. And you did all you could at the time.'

Simon nodded agreement. 'He's right Jack. It's pointless to think like that. And it may turn out that the stalker has nothing to do with what's happened. We're only a short way into the investigation as yet. 'We can't be sure of anything much.'

The pub was beginning to fill up with the lunchtime regulars and the noise level was rising as they were being elbowed on either side to make space for newcomers.

Longman asked hopefully, 'Anyone want another beer?'

Fielding shook his head, his eyes lowered. 'Not for me. I'm going home to get changed and back to work. Silly, isn't it?' he looked up at them. 'I don't like visiting her in uniform. It took me away from her too much, my job, and with her so ill for so long.' His voice faded away.

'We'll go,' Simon said, getting up and patting Fielding awkwardly on the arm. He didn't know what to say to the man still so clearly deep in grief. 'Thanks, Jack,' he said a trifle too heartily. 'Thanks for your help and sorry to disturb you as we did. You really have helped.'

Fielding gave a disbelieving smile as Longman grasped his hand.

They stood and watched as Fielding made his way back to the alley-way. 'Poor sod,' Longman said. 'He's taking it very hard, Heather's death.'

Chapter 12

Vanessa Peel's home was in a previously unfashionable area of town, now more prosperous looking, the windows and paintwork as glossy as the cars that lined the street and the small front gardens imaginatively landscaped, if such a term could be used of such limited spaces. The house was near the centre of the street, as neat and self-possessed looking as the rest, a new blue Vauxhall Corsa parked outside.

An attractive middle-aged woman answered the door, elegant in a pearl grey suit. She eyed them coolly, letting her light blue eyes run over Simon and Rhiannon for a moment longer than necessary.

'The police, is it?' she asked, and waited as they produced their ID cards. She knew perfectly well who they must be since Simon had telephoned to make the appointment. Then she gave a smile edged with amusement.

'Come in, I'm Vanessa's mother.' She stood back and let them into the narrow hallway.

Simon felt a moment's stab of sympathy for Vanessa in having a mother who was in such stark contrast to herself. The two could hardly be less physically alike. He wondered if Vanessa's rejection of any sartorial efforts, rejection of make-up and other personal adornment was indicative of rebellion against her mother, or whether she felt that the competition was just too great, and had given up.

He watched with interest for signs of interaction between the two as Mrs Peel showed them into the sitting room where Vanessa was seated in front of the television watching an Australian soap and eating a piece of cake, cup of tea on a table at her elbow. She was dressed in a shapeless skirt and cardigan in ill-matched colours of maroon and green, neither of which suited her colouring.

'Would you like a cup of tea and some cake as well?' Mrs Peel asked, the smile still hovering at her lips.

'That would be very nice, thank you,' Rhiannon said quickly, then glanced questioningly at Simon.

'Thank you,' he agreed. Rhiannon had missed her midday meal, as had he. Vanessa kept her eyes on the television screen with only the briefest of glances in the direction of himself and Rhiannon Jones.

'What about you, Vanessa?' her mother asked. '*More* cake?'

Vanessa coloured up. 'No thanks,' she said, without looking in her mother's direction. As her mother left the room, she spoke to Simon: 'Have you found Kate's mother yet?'

'It looks as if we have. A body was found this morning.'

'I'm sorry,' she said gruffly. 'She was a kind mother. What do you want to see me about?' she asked, as if she wanted to get things over before her mother returned.

'We want to know if Kate ever confided to you anything about her mother's personal life, or any problems that she might have had.'

Vanessa swallowed the last piece of her cake. 'What sort of problems?' she asked. She was as direct as her mother was subtle.

'Anything at all really,' Rhiannon said, her soft valleys accent more appealing than the clipped preciseness of Mrs Peel.

Vanessa frowned, her eyes back on the television screen. The sound was not loud but it was intrusive.

'Would you mind very much if we turned that off?' Rhiannon asked gently. 'I find it hard to concentrate with a television on.'

'Oh,' Vanessa said in surprise, as if such an idea would never have occurred to her. 'All right.' She picked up the remote control and, with a last lingering look at bronzed young bodies so unlike her own, made them disappear.

Rhiannon glanced at Simon and he nodded his agreement for her to continue. One of the reasons he had brought her along was for her non-threatening manner, her ability to empathize.

'Did Kate ever discuss whether her mother had boyfriends for instance?' Rhiannon asked.

Vanessa hesitated. 'Not in any detail, I don't think. I mean she might say something about her mother buying a new dress or something for a date. I never took a lot of interest.'

Did Vanessa feel so divorced from the usual concerns of women that, defensively, she ignored them? Simon wondered. And if so, did that mean she had missed any nuances in confidences that Kate may have offered?

'So Kate wasn't worried about her mother in the last few months or so?' Rhiannon tried again.

Vanessa appeared to think hard. 'I remember her saying she sometimes worried about when her mother was alone in the house with Ian gone.'

'Did she give any particular reason for her concern?'

'I can't remember. Why?'

It was as if she were being deliberately obstructive, Simon thought.

'Vanessa,' he said, 'you were one of Kate's closest friends, if not her closest. Surely she told you things about her family, her worries and concerns?' Perhaps a challenge over the nature of her friendship with Kate, a friendship she had seemingly guarded jealously, might prompt a more frank response.

'Why do you ask?' she said stubbornly.

'Well, obviously, Vanessa, we need to have some idea of Mrs Gaston's private life, the people she was involved with, if we are going to trace what has happened to her.' Rhiannon's voice was appealing.

'I suppose you do.' It was said grudgingly.

Was her problem the fact that she didn't like to admit openly that her great friend Kate had not, after all, confided in her at all? So that an air of uncooperative secrecy allowed Vanessa to convey the illusion of a greater intimacy then was actual?

'Perhaps Kate didn't confide in you at all,' Simon challenged her again, thinking that he and Rhiannon were forming the traditional team of nice guy and nasty one.

'She did,' Vanessa said pettishly. 'I'm not talking about her to anybody just for the sake of it.'

The inappropriateness of her words in the circumstances was allowed to hang in the air for a moment. Then Vanessa's mother entered with a trayful of crockery.

Vanessa watched on silently while her mother efficiently supplied Simon and Rhiannon with tea.

'How long have you known Kate?' Simon asked Vanessa after swallowing a mouthful of cake. It tasted like a supermarket brand but was welcome all the same. Mrs Peel looked as if she had other things to do than bake cakes.

'Since you were in the infants', wasn't it Vanessa?' her mother answered for her. 'Of course, Kate was always the brightest of the two.'

'Did you know Kate well, Mrs Peel?' Simon asked.

'Oh, I used to. When they were children. But I haven't seen much of her since she went to university. They took different paths.'

Vanessa's colour was up again. 'We were still friends. Kate used to write to me when she was away. And she phoned me as soon as she knew she'd got the job at Linden Road.'

'But you've only really been seeing her at church, dear, haven't you? Your social lives weren't exactly similar.' Mrs Peel smoothed her skirt and sat down to join them.

'We used to meet in town for coffee as well. You don't know all about my life,' Vanessa said hotly.

'Oh, coffee,' her mother said with sarcastic emphasis. 'You really know how to live, dear, don't you?'

Simon wondered how Vanessa bore such unkindness and contempt, and why she didn't move out and get some independence. Perhaps she was so undermined by her dominant mother she hadn't the confidence to take such an initiative.

It was unlikely, with her mother looking on, that Vanessa would say anything much, for fear of being ridiculed. On the other hand, perhaps the rivalry might prompt Vanessa into being more forthcoming.

'So you didn't know Kate in recent years, Mrs Peel,' he said. 'Did you know her mother, Sylvia Gaston? Perhaps you met at church?'

She gave a snort of laughter. 'I don't go to church, Chief Inspector. It was Vanessa's father who was the religious one and got her started at Sunday School. He left some time ago.'

Vanessa cast her mother a look of dull resentment.

'In that case, Mrs Peel,' Rhiannon said softly with the right degree of apology, 'as you didn't know Kate or Mrs Gaston, we don't need to waste any more of your time. The cake is delicious by the way. Did you make it yourself?'

Simon glanced down, suppressing a smile.

With a look of combined suspicion and aggrievement, Mrs Peel got to her feet. 'I've certainly got plenty to be doing. I work full time and run the house singlehandedly,' she said, looking pointedly at her daughter. 'I'm sure Vanessa can manage to let you out,' she shot at them as she left the room.

Her daughter, colour still flushing her cheeks, gave Rhiannon a grateful smile, lightening her face for the first time and making her fine blue eyes sparkle.

She was pretty, Simon realized, under all that awkwardness. What a pity she didn't break away and find a life for herself apart from her mother. He remembered Jessie talking about the habit-forming nature of relationships, how people seek out and stay with relationships that allow one to continue to behave and react in ways that had become habitual. It was why women repeated a pattern of abusive relationships in adulthood, having been accustomed to it as children. He suddenly wondered if something like that had been the basis of Vanessa's relationship with Kate Milliner. Had Kate, confident and obviously attractive, been a dominant partner in that friendship, Vanessa patronized and condescended to? In which case, if Kate had felt a degree of contempt for her less attractive friend, she might have thought her too unimportant to worry much about what she confided in her.

'You were saying,' he said to Vanessa, 'that Kate did confide in you, as I'm sure she must have done. But you didn't see why you should tell just anyone. Well, we're not *anyone*, Vanessa. We're investigating Kate's death and the death of her mother. I'm sure that you, after a lifetime's friendship with Kate, must want to help us in any way you can to catch the killer.' He picked up his cup of tea which had been growing cold. Vanessa had her eyes on the slab of cake that Rhiannon was eating.

Rhiannon patted her flat stomach. 'I'm afraid I can't finish that. Can you help me out?' She pushed her plate towards Vanessa who eagerly seized it.

It was an heroic gesture on Rhiannon's part.

Vanessa, her mouth full of cake, met Simon's eyes fully for the first time. She swallowed hastily, as if having come to a decision. 'I can't remember everything Kate said about her mother – I'm afraid I don't always pay attention like I ought to.' She looked apologetically at Rhiannon who gave her an encouraging smile.

Vanessa settled herself more comfortably in her chair, leaning on the arm and facing them. 'I remember Kate saying that her mother was having trouble with some man following her around. I'm pretty sure Kate said it was an ex-patient of Mrs Gaston's. She said that it was a problem sometimes that patients get a bit fixated on people who care for them.' She pushed her fine hair back from her face. 'I suppose it's not surprising really. People must get very isolated when they're ill and they must find it hard to discriminate between professional care and personal interest.'

Her pose of dull indifference was falling away under Rhiannon's sympathetic interest, Simon thought. Given half a chance, Vanessa was articulate and intelligent.

'I hadn't thought of that,' Rhiannon said, 'That's very perceptive.'

Vanessa brightened a little more.

'Did Kate say who this man was?' Rhiannon added.

'She might have done,' Vanessa said, 'but I can't remember, I'm sorry. I know it was why Kate was worried about her mother being alone in the house though.'

'Do you know anything about any boyfriend Mrs Gaston had, someone who Kate thought might look out for her?' Rhiannon asked.

Vanessa nodded. 'She did have some man friend but he wasn't available enough, Kate felt.' She hesitated for a moment. 'I wondered if he was married. Kate wouldn't like to admit something like that. She wouldn't approve of it,' she said solemnly.

Then Kate would most certainly not have confided in her friend that she herself was having a relationship with a married man, Simon thought. She had let her think her only male friendship was with her squash partner, Rupert Colville. In fact, there seemed to be a number of things that Kate had not confided: Vanessa was seemingly ignorant of the fact that Kate's father had been back in town for the last two years. He decided to ask her about that.

'Vanessa, I gathered from something you said the other day that you thought Dr Milliner, Kate's father, was still living up north. Is that right?'

Her smooth brow furrowed. 'Yes, that's right. Why?'

'He's been working in Westwich at the Royal Hospital for the last two years. I've spoken to him,' Simon said.

She looked puzzled, then upset as the implication sank in. 'Why ever didn't she say?' she wondered aloud. 'She didn't like him,' she added, her voice hardening. 'That's probably why she didn't say anything. She preferred to behave as if he didn't exist.'

'Probably that was it,' Simon agreed, hoping he hadn't damaged her more compliant mood.

'Why was Kate killed?' Vanessa suddenly asked. 'You do think it was something to do with her mother's disappearance, don't you? Maybe Kate's father's involved. He was a very jealous type, Kate told me. He used to hit her mother.'

'Because of other men?' Rhiannon asked.

She shook her head. 'There weren't other men, Kate said. It was just him and his imagination.'

'Mrs Gaston did, of course, remarry,' Simon remarked.

'That wasn't anything to do with how Dr Milliner came to leave. She wasn't involved with Dr Gaston at the time. She wasn't involved with anyone, Kate said. But Kate's mum was working at the same hospital as Dr Milliner was and if he caught her talking to any men, nurses or doctors or whatever, he used to freak out when they were at home together.'

Simon thought of Jessie's analogy of the caged bird. 'How did it finally come about, the marriage breakup?' he asked.

'He got a job in a hospital up north – Manchester I think it was.' Vanessa licked a finger and picked up a crumb of cake with it from the plate beside her.

'And she didn't follow?' Rhiannon asked.

Vanessa glanced at her. 'That's right,' she said with a small smile. 'She let him think she would, that she was selling the house and so on, while he was settling in his new job, and then she told him she was staying put and divorcing him.'

'And he accepted that?' Simon somehow doubted it.

Her eyes widened. 'Oh, no. He came down from Manchester and there was a really bad row. I think he did Kate's mum some real damage that time and she had to go to hospital. She threatened him with the police and he backed off and went back where he came from. I thought that was the end of it.'

'And it wasn't?' Rhiannon asked.

'It was as far as I knew. I didn't know he was back in town.' Vanessa looked meaningfully from Simon to Rhiannon.

'And this was about ten years ago, when Kate would have been in her early teens?' Simon said.

She nodded, her lips compressed. 'We were still at school together – at the comp. I remember how upset Kate was at the time. She was frightened for her mother.'

'And she never mentioned him turning up again?'

'Mrs Gaston got all the medical evidence together, threatened a court order against him.' She sniffed. 'I expect he valued his career too much to risk any more.'

'Kate's brother Ian, how did he cope?' Rhiannon asked.

Vanessa's expression softened. 'He's a lot younger than Kate, so he was about eight at the time. I don't think he really understood too much of what was going on. Mrs Gaston just wanted to close the book on that part of her life so she didn't want any contact between Ian and his father, or Kate and her father for that matter. Not that Kate wanted to know him after the years of behaving the way he did.' Vanessa leaned towards them. 'I think that was part of the deal, that he let go of the children. He wasn't too happy about that apparently.'

He wouldn't be, Simon thought. They were *his* children and he was obviously a control freak.

'Was Kate aware that her father had remarried and has another son?' he asked.

Her eyebrows rose. 'I don't think so. But then, she didn't tell me he was back working in Westwich. Poor woman – and son – is all I can say.'

'Kate didn't have anything to do with him. Though Ian apparently visited him,' Simon said.

'He'd be curious, I suppose,' Vanessa said thoughtfully. 'After all it was a long time ago for someone his age, and he'd want to see for himself what he made of his father. Have you had any news of Ian?'

Simon shook his head. 'We're vague about where he might be by now. I think our best hope is that he will see the British newspapers when he next hits the right kind of town.'

'Poor Ian,' Vanessa said sorrowfully. 'What a terrible thing to find out so far from home.'

'He's not alone, though?' Rhiannon asked.

'He's with a friend I think. I had a postcard from him a couple of months ago.' Vanessa got up slowly and went to a bookcase near the other end of the room. She handed it to Simon. It was a view of a temple in Nepal, mountains in the background. On the back it read, in large jagged words, *Having a great time. Going south to Cambodia after this, then Oz. Love Ian.*

'He's fond of you?' Simon smiled, handing the card back to Vanessa.

'He was a dear little lad. I knew him from a baby,' she said, her eyes softening. 'It was difficult for him at first, not having a father around. But Dr Gaston was a nice kind man and more than made up for things when he married Ian's mother.' She sighed. 'And after all that, Ian was a vulnerable age when his stepfather died. Still,' she turned to put the postcard on the mantelpiece, 'he's turned out all right. He's doing OK. Though I don't know how he's going to be after all this happening. He's had a difficult life, poor Ian.'

The sound of music turned up loudly came suddenly from another part of the house. Vanessa turned back, a wry expression on her face. 'I think that must be my mother signalling that the evening meal is ready.'

'Thank you Vanessa. You've been very helpful,' Simon said, unfolding from his chair with his usual awkwardness of height and limb.

'I just hope you catch whoever it is,' Vanessa said. 'I miss Kate. And I shall miss her even more as time goes on. I should check on Dr Milliner if I were you,' she added fiercely. 'He's quite capable of murder, I'd say.'

She showed them to the door and waited as they drove off, a lonely and rather forlorn figure in her sagging unflattering clothes.

'Poor kid,' Rhiannon said, buckling her seatbelt. 'What a mother! No wonder she's so awkward. The woman must undermine her confidence all the time.'

'She probably envied Kate's relationship with her own mother,' Simon agreed. 'It would seem to have been a bit of a contrast.'

'She should strike out on her own,' Rhiannon said stoutly. 'Like I did. My own mam is a bit of a tyrant.'

Simon looked at her with interest. He knew very little of Rhiannon's background, except her obvious nationality. 'They breed them tough in the valleys I understand,' he said.

'True enough. It's in the blood. When life's hard you have to be strong and unsentimental. It's my mam's upbringing, and that of her mother's before her. But times change and I didn't want to be part of all that any more.' Rhiannon sounded understanding rather than judgemental.

'Well you've chosen a hard enough job to move on to, if you're trying to escape the gritty realities of life.'

'Ah, but the breeding comes in handy, sir. And I'm not as soft as I may look,' Rhiannon said solemnly.

He glanced at her and saw that she was smiling. It was on the tip of his tongue to say that she looked just right to him, but realized that it might be unwise. 'Just as well,' he said instead, non-commitally.

Rhiannon gave a small cough and changed the conversation. 'When you spoke to Dr Milliner,' she said, 'what did you make of him? As bad as Vanessa suggests?'

'Not a man one warms to,' Simon admitted, turning the car right at the end of the street. 'He struck me as cold and arrogant.'

'Well, he's a consultant, isn't he?' Rhiannon sounded amused. 'The power goes to their heads.'

'So I've been told. But I've met the occasional agreeable one.'

'This one certainly isn't,' Rhiannon said sharply. 'He's a wife beater.

111

Do you think he might really have anything to do with his ex-wife's or his daughter's deaths? Vanessa seemed very keen he should be investigated.'

'We'll check him out of course. I just can't see why, after ten years of being apart, he should suddenly flip. Where's any motive?'

'That'd be for us to find out I suppose. But strong emotions can simmer for a long time. It's been known for ex-husbands to murder their ex-wives after years apart, even when they've remarried and apparently got another life.'

'True. But I can't see someone like Dr Milliner taking too many risks with his life and career, jeopardizing them in such a way.'

'He's a man who can't control his feelings too well, though, obviously, sir,' Rhiannon said cautiously.

Her admiration for Simon had long tended to inhibit any contentiousness on her part when she was working with him on a case. He was conscious of it and, aware of his own vanity, never failed to feel touched by her solicitousness. Whereas he might have been more dismissive of her remarks if they had come from Longman he was careful to treat her remarks with the courtesy they deserved. 'I don't deny that,' he said. 'But where's any evidence that Sylvia, or Kate, had angered him again to such a degree that he would attack and kill either or both of them?'

'We haven't got any yet, but it might be there. It's early days in the investigation.'

'We'll bear it in mind, and check him out, as I said,' Simon agreed. 'I think the stalker is a more promising lead to follow though.'

'And Sylvia's patients and their partners have got to be the best bet.'

'I want you to check out the medical backgrounds, Rhiannon. Get as much information as you can. And we need to find Mrs Gaston's boyfriend. Who and where is he, I wonder?'

'We need a friend of Mrs Gaston, someone she's likely to have confided in.'

Simon changed gear and turned left. The rain was heavier now and the sweep of the windscreen wipers was cosily soporific. He enjoyed Rhiannon's company, despite feeling vaguely guilty that he did so. He knew it was largely because she was so unfailingly uncritical of him and therefore such a soothing presence, but he should do more to disabuse her of any illusions she had about him.

'You think the murderer might have removed evidence?' Rhiannon asked.

'Could be.'

'But there's no sign of any break-in at either place?'

'None that's evident. But that doesn't necessarily mean anything. Sylvia's house keys are missing and so are Kate's. The murderer could have returned later and removed any evidence that might have implicated him.'

'He wouldn't be able to fix the phone calls they made, though. That's the best way to find any friend of Sylvia's that might know more about what was going on in her life. Someone she was in contact with a lot.'

Simon pulled into the car park at headquarters just as Longman was leaving to take Milliner to the mortuary. Milliner got into the car after casting a baleful look in Simon's direction, while Longman hurried over to speak to Simon.

He rolled his eyes. 'That took a bit of persuasion. I don't know what he'll say when he sees her face so battered. Probably refuse to give an identification.'

'He'll be within his rights,' Simon said. 'On the other hand, from what Vanessa Peel just told us, he should be quite familiar with his ex-wife's face after a battering.'

The legendary eyebrows shot up. 'Wife beater was he? Well I feel even less concerned about inconveniencing him then.' Longman went back to his car and shot off, barely giving Milliner time to fasten his safety belt.

Chapter 13

There was an unfamiliar car parked outside Jessie's cottage when Simon arrived that evening, a bright yellow VW Beetle. As he let himself in through the back door he heard female voices, the low easy tones of Jessie and higher, more excitable notes. The other voice was familiar, but he couldn't put a name to it. He looked around the sitting room door.

'Chris! How nice to see you again!' It was Hermione, flame haired, green eyed, lounging on the sofa and displaying her long legs to advantage. He had not seen her since she had offered help in a previous case he was working on. She lectured in Jessie's department in psychology and had a particular interest in the paranormal.

'Hi,' he said cautiously, emerging slowly into the room. His earlier encounters with Hermione had proved a trifle overwhelming.

'Hermione's eating with us tonight,' Jessie said, a knowing smile in her eyes.

'Lovely,' he said. 'Anything I can do?'

Jessie got up from her usual position on the floor where she had been resting her back against one of the armchairs. She had lit the fire now that the evenings had grown autumn cool and she carefully put another log in place. 'You can keep Hermione entertained while I check the meal,' she said, turning to him and planting a kiss on his cheek.

'What an offer!' Hermione said with her cat-like smile and usual provocative manner.

Her back to her friend, Jessie gave Simon an ironic smile and lift of the eyebrows and left the room.

Hermione moved her legs a little and patted the sofa beside her. Simon pretended not to notice and eased himself into the armchair opposite her.

'It's been quite a while since I've seen you,' Hermione said. 'Not since that case you were working on about the missing student. I notice you haven't called on me for help in any cases since.'

Simon cleared his throat. 'Haven't really needed to,' he said.

'You have to admit that my psychic was pretty accurate, though.' Hermione picked up her glass of wine and took a sip.

'She was,' Simon agreed. 'Unfortunately, what she said only really made sense retrospectively, once the case was solved.'

'I think if you'd had any faith in what she said it might have been more help.' She gave him an arch smile.

'Possibly.' He had no wish to be drawn into an argument with Hermione. This was partly because she would win. And that was largely because she would be determined to.

'And now you've got another missing person, I understand. The mother of the girl who was murdered.'

'Has Jessie been discussing it with you?' he asked. His inhibitions about sharing his cases with Jessie may have for the most part disappeared, but he was dismayed at the idea of her passing anything on to anyone else. And Hermione was not, he guessed, the most discreet of persons.

'Not guilty', Jessie said, entering the room and handing him a glass of red wine.

'Sorry,' he said uncomfortably.

'Chris,' Hermione said with exaggerated patience, 'the news is all over the newspapers and on television. Don't you ever look?'

'Not much.' He took a mouthful of wine, 'Detective Superintendent Munro usually deals with the media, along with the media liason officer. I find it all a bit distracting.' It was in fact more than distracting. It could become deeply disheartening to read press criticism of the way a case was being conducted. And that was not conducive to doing one's best work.

'But appeals are useful,' Jessie said, still standing at his side. 'They bring in a lot of information.'

'Too much sometimes,' he said with a grimace. 'You can get bogged down in following thousands of pieces of information and miss the more obvious lines of inquiry.'

'It does happen,' Hermione agreed sagely. 'It must be difficult sometimes to be sure what's best. But in a case like this where someone is apparently missing and you can't be sure she's dead, I'd have thought using appeals for information from the public must be necessary.'

'You haven't watched the news this evening though, I gather.'

'Why? You've found her?' Hermione said eagerly. 'Is she dead?'

'We've found the body of a woman who appears to be Sylvia Gaston,' Simon said, his voice restrained in the face of Hermione's enthusiasm.

She tilted her head to one side and tapped her glass with blood-red nails. 'You're not comfortable talking about it,' she observed.

'I'm not entirely free to,' he said.

'Dinner's ready anyway,' Jessie announced.

They went through to the kitchen, cosily warm from the stove and fragrant with herbs from Jessie's garden. Hermione accepted another half-glass of wine. 'I'm driving' she said, casting a look at the policeman in their midst. Jessie filled up her own glass and Simon's and they helped themselves to a rich vegetable casserole and salad and newly heated crusty bread.

'For a veggie, you do quite well,' Hermione commented with a smile at Jesssie.

There was silence for a while as they all began eating. Then Hermione dragged up the case again. 'The dead woman,' she said. 'she's the ex-wife of Dr Milliner, isn't she?'

Simon nodded, his mouth full.

'I know him,' Hermione continued. 'Through his work that is. I was one of his patients.'

Simon remembered Jessie mentioning it. He waited for Hermione to continue. If the conversation consisted of Hermione's account of a possible suspect, without input from himself, he could have no difficulty with that.

'He's a bastard,' Hermione said taking another mouthful of wine.

'Why do you say that?' Simon asked, having a perfectly good idea of why.

'You know of course that he's a gynaecologist? Well I had to see him about some problems I was having and of course he had to examine me.' Hermione appeared to swallow bile rather than wine. 'It was probably one of the most humiliating experiences of my life.'

Simon would have liked to ask what the other ones were. 'I imagine it can feel pretty humiliating in the best of circumstances, even with decent doctors,' he said instead. 'Men aren't happy about exposing sensitive parts of their anatomy for examination.'

'It's worse for women,' Hermione said hotly, 'they're made differ-ently and they're much more vulnerable. That man coldly and deliberately left me in a very exposed position and walked out of the room for quite some time. It was inexcusable.'

Simon wondered if Hermione had annoyed Milliner by something she had said, or her manner. As an apparent control freak he would have reacted in some way. 'That must have been pretty awful,' Simon said, meaning it.

'Exactly. I'm sure there was no reason for him to leave me like that except for the feeling of power it gave him to humiliate a woman.'

'So you didn't think it was more personal in any way?' Jessie asked.

'What difference does that make?' Hermione hastily swallowed some food.

'None at all,' Jessie said, 'in terms of it being inexcusable. I just wondered if he might be more inclined to behave in such a way with a woman such as yourself, a professional, articulate self-assured woman than, say the kind of woman who never questions what a doctor says.'

'You think he may have treated me like that because he felt threatened by me?'

'The thought has surely occurred to you?' Jessie said with a slight smile.

'Not really,' Hermione shook her head. 'I just thought he probably hated all women.'

'Because he feels threatened by them,' Jessie said. 'Possibly true. But what a branch of his profession to choose in that case.'

'The perfect one perhaps,' Simon said mildly. 'A lot of jobs involving some kind of responsibility over people have people in them who are there for the wrong reasons as far as their clients are concerned, for the opportunity of forms of abuse that they offer. As we know, the police force isn't immune. Any job that involves a degree of power over others can attract such people – caring professions of all sorts, teaching, the armed forces—'

'Yes, we do know that,' Hermione said impatiently. 'We are psychologists, remember?'

'Then I'm surprised at your surprise about Milliner's behaviour,' he responded, realizing that Hermione's heatedness had more to do with her reliving Milliner's treatment of her than anything he himself had said.

'You told me that you had decided to go private after the experience,' Jessie said, 'but you didn't tell me in any detail what happened next. What did you say when he came back into the room?'

'I told him to release me from the contraption I was held in immediately.'

'And?'

'He smiled down at me very patronizingly and said, "Miss Hastings, you can have no idea what the life of a busy doctor involves if you think—" 'I said, "My name is Dr Hastings and what's more I am probably the only real doctor in the room since yours is merely an honorary title".'

'I bet he liked that,' Jessie said approvingly. 'Unless he has a higher medical degree, which is quite possible.'

'I didn't give him a chance to tell me,' Hermione said. 'He stood there refusing to do as I asked so I told the nurse to get on with it. When I was finally on my feet again I told him I would be complaining to the medical authorities about him.'

'And how did he respond to that?' Simon asked.

'He asked me how I expected to get treatment afterwards. I said, "I beg your pardon! Are you insinuating something you haven't the courage to say clearly?" He replied that the medical estabishment was a small world in many ways and that it looked after its own. Can you believe it? He looked thoroughly sinister.' Hermione tossed off the remains of her wine. 'I said I would be sure to report everything he had said to me. Then he positively shouted at me to get out of the room.'

'And have you had any difficulties with subsequent treatment?' Simon asked.

'None at all. As Jessie said, I've gone private, rather against my principles but my present gynaecologist is a dear, sweet man.'

'He presumably knows Milliner, though,' Simon said. 'He does private too.'

'I expect he does,' Hermione said. 'But if you've met Milliner, you can't imagine anyone exactly warming to him, can you?'

Simon had to agree.

'Have you had any reply to your complaint?' Jessie asked.

'Only a preliminary one. They're looking into it they say. But I don't intend to let it drop. And I gather that Milliner doesn't have a particularly good reputation medically as well as personally.'

'Oh?' Simon said.

'No details really,' Hermione said. 'Just odd hints I've heard here and there. I'll let you know if I hear anything that might interest you.'

Simon nodded his thanks and finished the remains of his meal.

'His second wife works as his secretary, did you know?' Hermione added, eying the bottle of wine. 'Do you think it would be over the limit if I had a little more of that lovely wine?'

'You've only had the total of one glass full with a meal,' Jessie said. But she eyed Simon questioningly, the bottle poised.

'Don't ask me. I don't work in Traffic. But I'd think you'll be below the limit with another half-glass. You have enough body mass,' Simon said thoughtlessly.

'Charming way you have of putting things,' Hermione said sardonically, holding her glass out.

It was true that Hermione was built on fairly voluptuous lines, but he had not meant to imply that she was in any way fat. He said so.

Hermione smiled at him. 'Dear Chris, I am not insecure about my appearance. Hadn't you noticed?'

Jessie suppressed a laugh.

'Have you met Milliner's present wife then?' he asked quickly.

'Only spoken to her on the phone. She has one of those little girl voices – soft and a bit tremulous. It doesn't surprise me that he's married a passive type and that he has her working where he can see her and shut up a bit from the general run of the hospital. He's a control freak.'

'I wonder if he had anything to do with his first wife's disappearance?' Hermione said, eyeing Simon closely. 'He's nasty enough.'

'If you can discover any reason why he might have, be sure to let me know,' Simon said.

She brightened at that so he added hastily, 'But we've no reason to think so. There are much more likely possibilities.'

'I don't suppose you'd tell us what they are?' Hermione rested her chin on her hand and looked at him appealingly.

He smiled. 'Not a chance.'

Chapter 14

Another postmortem behind him, Simon was feeling a bit more cheerful when he went into the incident room. Evelyn Starkey had informed him that the level of insect activity in the body was consistent with the woman having been dead for the same period of time as Kate, give or take a matter of hours. But beyond that she had nothing much to add, apart from the fact that the facial bruising had taken place both before and after strangulation, indicative of real anger on the part of the killer.

Milliner had given the official identification, apparently satisfied that it was his ex-wife despite the distortion of her face.

'I think he just wanted to get out of there,' was Longman's opinion, 'after he'd enjoyed himself kicking up a fuss.'

Tremaine came up to them. 'Thought you might like to know, sir, that the college has reported that a Miss Kate Milliner didn't turn up for her archaeology evening class.'

What world are they living in? Longman wondered.

'Anything else?' Simon asked.

'We checked Mrs Gaston's email, easy enough as it was automatic dial up. But there was nothing there. Either she didn't use it, because perhaps her son set it up for her and she couldn't be bothered, or she deleted them after reading and sending.'

'Or someone deleted them for her,' Simon said. 'What about her computer files? Anything there?'

'A lot of stuff, mostly medical information that she'd obviously down-loaded from the net. I skipped through it but there wasn't anything that looked personal. I've checked out Mrs Gaston's address book by phon-ing the names in it. A lot of them are former patients or business numbers, but so far I've come up with two who were friends of hers. They both appeared on her phone records as being contacted quite frequently.'

'Well done. I'll speak to them.'

Savage said, 'We've spoken to Goodenough's wife. She confirms he was there all day on the Sunday that Kate disappeared.'

'Did she show any suspicions about his relationship with Kate?'

'No, sir. She just seemed shocked in a normal sort of way about what had happened to Kate. And we told her we were checking on all the men that Kate knew through work or socially, not her husband in particular.'

'I'm sure Goodenough will be eternally grateful to you,' Simon said. 'Had she met Kate?'

'Once at some social do at the school, she said.'

Simon nodded. 'Well there's enough to be going on with.'

'She could be a suspect, Mrs Goodenough,' Longman said as the two DCs turned away. 'Suppose she did know about Kate and killed her in a fit of jealousy?'

'And Kate's mother's death is a mere coincidence?'

Longman pulled at a bushy eyebrow thoughtfully. 'Suppose things are the other way around from what we thought,' he said slowly. 'Suppose Mrs Gaston was there all the time when Kate was phoning her boyfriend and Mrs Goodenough turns up, attacks Kate and does away with her mother as well?'

'I haven't met Goodenough's wife but I'd suppose her to be an Amazon to have managed the pair of them,' Simon said dryly.

'No, it's possible,' Longman argued. 'Sylvia could have popped out to a corner shop or something, come back and found Goodenough's wife there and been attacked herself.'

'Then she presumably bundled them into her car in broad daylight and trundled off to bury them? Come on Geoff!'

Simon was used to Longman's flights of fancy when it came to suspects: before they had finished he would have fitted a theoretical motive to everyone who featured in the case.

'She didn't have to take them away in daylight, did she? Kate wasn't found until nearly a week later. She could have come back at any time and removed the bodies.'

They were at the car by now. Simon pulled open his door and threw himself into his seat. Longman heavily got in beside him.

'Which is true whoever the killer is,' Simon said, starting the engine.

'He or she must have come back to the house later. There's so little personal stuff there.'

'But Mrs Goodenough would have no reason to remove personal

letters and so on from Sylvia's house.'

'True.' Longman subsided for the moment.

It was a glorious autumn morning again. The first people from Thelma Jones's list lived in the countryside north of the city and Simon was looking forward to the drive.

They were on the outskirts of the city before Longman spoke again. 'If it was the stalker who killed Sylvia, why hasn't Sylvia's boyfriend come forward?'

'The usual reasons I imagine,' Simon said, winding down the window as the sun grew hot on the driver's side of the car. 'He'd know he'd have to be investigated and, if he is married as Vanessa suspects, he wouldn't want to risk his wife finding out about the relationship.'

'If it *was* the stalker who killed Sylvia,' Longman said thoughtfully stroking his eyebrow again, 'when did he do it? Did he wait for Sylvia to be dropped off at home by her boyfriend and then leap out at her from behind the shrubbery?'

'Seems a likely scenario,' Simon commented.

'So who was Kate planning to visit when she rang for Goodenough's support? We've assumed until now that it was a boyfriend, that her mother would have told her who he was – something Vanessa seems to think.'

'I think what we've suspected is that Kate was going to see the killer, and got killed in turn for her effort,' Simon said, turning off the ringroad at a roundabout and taking a narrower road. 'We've assumed, as you say, that Kate's mother would have told her who the boyfriend was. But Sylvia seems to have known who the stalker was and she wasn't telling anyone else, except Kate maybe. She might have confided that to Kate so that when her mother disappeared Kate might think it was the stalker who was responsible. Of course,' he said slowly, 'there is always the possibility that the boyfriend and the stalker were one and the same.'

'Eh?' Longman said, startled, turning to Simon.

'It could be,' Simon's tone was still exploratory. 'Suppose Sylvia decided to confront this man and ended up forming a relationship with him – so that he and the married boyfriend became one?'

'Is that really likely?' Longman said doubtfully. 'Perhaps it's something you ought to discuss with Jessie, but I've always understood that stalkers were not moonstruck lover types, but the kind of men who need to dominate and threaten the women concerned. They want the feeling of power, they're obsessives and they're often dangerous.'

'You're right of course,' Simon said, conceding. 'But Sylvia had refused to try the official route in dealing with him. Didn't Jack think she might have confronted him? She may have thought she could persuade him to behave more reasonably, tried to form some kind of relationship with him to get him to leave her alone. It might have encouraged him in some way and given him more access to her.'

'That's possible. Sylvia Gaston was by all acounts a sympathetic, kind, caring individual. And if she knew the man's wife, which seems to be the case, she might have tried to do all she could to bring the thing to halt without having to resort to the police.'

'So we can't be sure that the boyfriend was a separate person from the stalker,' Simon said, slowing down to examine a road sign and taking a left turn on to a long straight lane. 'If she did risk letting him get closer to her she was making herself vulnerable.'

Longman looked at a list he pulled out of his pocket. 'This is one of the patients from around eight months ago, a Mrs Framley and her husband. Do we know anything more about them?'

'You didn't manage to wrest much more from Thelma Jones, did you?'

'It wasn't easy,' Longman said defensively, 'getting this much. But I thought Rhiannon was going to be doing a bit of research before we started.'

'I didn't want to wait about,' Simon said. 'She is doing some checks on the others on the list. We're starting here because of the time period involved. Sylvia talked about the stalker to Adrian Swan about six months ago, he thought. It would have taken a little time for her to real-ize she had a problem, say as much as a month maybe, depending on how active the stalker was, and two months before that she started nurs-ing Mrs Framley and was with her for three weeks, leaving approximately a month over. These two are at the early end of possibil-ities I would think, which is why I've started with them, without much background to go on.'

'I like to be forearmed,' Longman said. 'It's a bit too much like fumbling in the dark, this.'

'We can come back again if necessary.'

'And we've got how many more to see?' Longman said, consulting the list again. 'Four couples in the relevant period. Depending on how long it was after the stalker started work that Sylvia spoke to Swan.'

'It would be useful to speak to some of her more recent patients as well, as we originally planned. She might have had some personal conversations with some of them. They might know something of her recent social life.'

'Well if they all live in countryside like this it will be some compensation,' Longman said, tucking the list away. He folded his arms and gazed out of the window at the undulating fields and small copses. 'I've never been out here before, have you? I saw a sign back there to some ancient chapel.'

'I think it's in the same hamlet we're going to. Always meant to turn off and have a look at it.'

They were close now. A small river ran alongside the road then turned under it so that they crossed an ancient stone bridge before reaching a small group of cottages. On their right was a surprisingly large church for so small a community, its graveyard well kept, with huge old horse chestnut trees, their remaining leaves crisp and shredded. Rooks and crows crossed from church spire to trees, flying up to tumble in the air between, delighting in the breeze that had sprung up.

Simon drove on slowly around a bend in the road. 'The house is called Watt's Barn.'

'That it?' Longman pointed to a red brick L-shaped building ahead and to their left. It was, as might be anticipated, a converted barn – a huge one and one on which evidently no expense had been spared.

They went through double gates into what had probably been a farm or stable yard in former years and was now cheered with tubs of brilliant yellow rudbeckias. A large black four-wheel-drive was parked at the open doors of an integral garage, part of the upper end of the upside-down L. As he stopped the car a man appeared at the outsize arched glazed door and waited for them. Simon had phoned earlier and they were expected.

'Lovely place you have, sir,' Longman said, looking around appreciatively as they approached.

'We like it,' the man said with the briefest of smiles. He held out a hand directing them into the vast space of his home. 'Charles Framley. Do come in.'

He was a big man, broadly built with thick grey hair, dressed casually in chinos and a Shetland sweater. His skin was lightly tanned, his brown eyes expressionless and his mouth firm and straight. Not a face to give anything readily away, Simon thought.

He ushered them into a part of the open-plan ground floor space towards some well-upholstered sofas set around a huge wood-burning stove giving out a good heat. The area was in part open to the A-framed roof and gave one the sense of being in a cathedral-like space. Framley, with his impressive dimensions, seemed undiminished by all the grandeur, but his wife, a slight figure sitting in a corner of one of the huge sofas, seemed overwhelmed. Simon noted the pair of crutches propped by her side.

'May we offer you coffee, Chief Inspector?' she asked, her eyes including Longman, her voice seeming to come from far away.

'Thank you,' Simon agreed.

'Will you have some, Jean?' Framley asked his wife.

'No thank you, Charles,' she said without looking up.

'I've got the kettle boiled,' Framley said and strode off.

Mrs Framley gestured for them to be seated on a sofa opposite her. 'I understand you want to speak to us about poor Sylvia Gaston,' she said, her voice trailing away. 'I gather you have found her body.'

Simon nodded. 'We're speaking to everyone she had anything much to do with in the last nine months or so,' Simon said. 'We've been able to find out very little about her private life.'

She looked puzzled. 'I'm not sure how *we* can help,' she said.

Simon said. 'Perhaps you can't, but you probably learned a few things without being aware of it. How long was she here with you? And did she live in?'

'Yes she did. She was here about three weeks.' Mrs Framley smiled reminiscently. 'She was a lovely woman, so very kind and understanding. Nothing was too much trouble for her. I have MS,' she said, 'and sometimes I have periods when I just can't manage on my own. Charles is away a lot on business and it is rather isolated here. I'm having one of my better times at the moment.'

She looked desperately tired and worn though, a complete contrast to the rude health of her husband, and almost mocked by the strength and lines of the building around her, diminished amid the dimensions and vigour of it. Her hair was a faded blonde, shoulder length and lank, her face with its small delicate nose and hooded deepset eyes, pale and lacklustre.

'We tried to get Sylvia back again a little while ago but she was busy working elsewhere. I gather she was much in demand,' she went on, making an effort to straighten herself in her seat.

'Three weeks is quite a long time to spend in someone's company,

125

fairly intimately,' Simon said. 'I imagine you must have had some personal conversations, she must have said something to you of her private life?'

'Well, a little, of course. She told me about her children and she talked about losing her husband, who was a GP, a few years ago.' She gave a faint deprecating smile. 'But I imagine you must know all this sort of thing.'

'We know the basic facts, but did Sylvia make any comments about the people in her life?'

'She obviously missed her husband a lot – she said he was the reason she had decided to work as a private nurse. That he had been worn down by the system and all the bureaucracy and lack of time he had to spend with patients doing his job properly. She realized it was the same for her, working in an NHS hospital as a nurse – that she didn't have the opportunity to truly nurse patients, the reason she had gone into nursing in the first place. Working in people's homes allowed her to look after patients properly, as she would wish.' She gave a sad smile. 'It did bother her a bit, though, believing as she did that health care should be available equally to all. But she said she had done her bit in the system and was looking for a little satisfaction herself now.'

Framley returned, rattling cups on a tray. Simon had been hoping, in this relatively opulent household, for coffee that might be better quality than the type they were usually offered and was disappointed to smell a cheap instant brand, kept especially perhaps for unimportant people such as himself and Longman. The idea caused him to cast a more jaundiced eye at the big man.

'Right!' Framley said, straightening up. 'I'm off to catch up on some paperwork.'

'We'd be glad of some of your time, Mr Framley.' Simon replaced his cup and saucer on the tray.

Framley's slanted eyebrows inched up a degree or two. 'But I had very little to do with Mrs Gaston you must realize. Don't think I ever had any real conversation with her, did I Jean?' He glanced down at his wife.

She looked away, hands gripped in her lap. 'No,' she said hesitantly, 'I don't suppose you did, really.'

The big man brought the full force of his personality to focus on Simon, who was poised on the edge of the sofa and forced to look up at him. 'I was away for much of the time that the nurse was here,' he said, as if to a child hard of hearing and comprehension. 'That was why she was here, mainly, because I wasn't. I really have nothing to tell you. Now may I get on with my own life?'

Simon shrugged. There was nothing he could do to keep him. Besides, he couldn't imagine Framley in the role of some lurking stalker. That being established in his own mind, the only remaining purpose in being here was to gather what he could from Framley's wife. Simon nodded his agreement and turned to Jean Framley again. Framley's leather-soled brogues sounded loudly on the polished floorboards.

'You were saying, Mrs Framley, that Mrs Gaston was looking for some satisfaction in her own life – that this sector of nursing was more satisfying for her. Did she ever talk about her personal life with you? The two of you, out here alone, must have found time to talk, perhaps confide in each other?'

She flushed slightly, her eyes turning in the direction her husband had gone. 'I suppose we did,' she said vaguely. 'But, you understand, I wasn't too well at the time. In bed and so on,' she trailed off again.

Simon tried again. 'Did she receive any phone calls when she was here?'

'Yes,' she said almost eagerly, as if relieved to find something to offer him. 'Her daughter phoned a few times. She was in her first year of teaching, Sylvia said. Sylvia was proud of her children,' she said almost wistfully.

Simon wondered if she herself had not had children and perhaps envied Sylvia's own experience of motherhood. 'Did she have her own phone? A mobile phone? We haven't been able to find one that belonged to her.'

'No, she was wary of them she said, and the health risks. Kate didn't have one either, her daughter, for the same reason.'

'Did Sylvia ever receive any calls from a man friend do you know?'

The tired hooded eyes opened more fully. 'Not that I'm aware. In fact from what she said, I got the impression she was rather lonely since her husband died. No,' she shook her head, 'I'm sure there wasn't anyone.'

If so, Simon thought, any relationship that Sylvia had established had been after she left here. 'What did you both talk about, Mrs Framley?' Simon tried again. 'I'm not prying into your own life, just hoping that I might trigger some memory.'

She managed a faint smile. 'Of course I understand, Chief Inspector. I'm sorry I'm not being of more help.' She put out a hand to one of her

127

steel crutches as if for support, then let it drift back to her lap. 'The fact is, Sylvia encouraged me to talk about myself and my life, rather than try to gain sympathy for her own. Not that I had much to tell, but she was a very comforting, comfortable person, someone it was easy to unburden oneself to. As you can imagine, it's not easy being long-term ill. Or perhaps you can't,' she said with a wry smile. 'Most people in rude health can't even begin to imagine how it erodes your life, destroys who you thought you were.' She swallowed. 'Well, Sylvia did understand. And I think she was a clever psychologist. She knew just how long to allow one to give out and then managed to lighten things with some anecdote or remark. She had a great sense of humour. Made me laugh so much, more than I have in years.' She wiped at her eyes. 'Sorry. I missed her terribly when she left.'

'It must be lonely out here when your husband is away,' Simon remarked gently.

She sniffed and pulled out a snowy handkerchief. 'Charles was back by then and I was feeling much better. The agency had been on to Sylvia asking her when she'd be available, so it seemed time for her to go.'

'Did Mrs Gaston keep in touch with you afterwards?'

She gave a quick smile. 'Yes, yes she did. That was a part of her kindness, to check and see that I was alright mentally as well as physically, even if she couldn't meet up with me.'

'*Did* you meet away from your home?' Simon asked.

'Yes, didn't I say? When I'm well enough I can drive so we used to meet for a coffee, sometimes for lunch, in Westwich.'

'And when did you last meet her?' Longman asked, speaking for the first time and startling her.

'Oh!' She turned her eyes on him, pale and reflective. 'It was in June.'

'And how did she seem,' Longman leaned towards her, placing his coffee cup on a low table.

'How do you mean?'

'Did she seem worried about anything for instance? Anxious perhaps?'

She frowned, her small forehead puckering in thought and gazing at her delicate hands. 'Actually, now you mention it, I'd say she was quite the opposite. She seemed to be positively glowing with health and vitality.'

'Did you comment on it?' Simon asked.

She looked up, her eyes far away. 'Yes, I think I did. I remember her laughing and saying that life was a little less lonely these days.' Her eyes came back to Simon. 'So perhaps she did have a man in her life. I hope she did. She deserved some happiness. I'm so sorry. I should have remembered that when you asked me earlier if she had had calls from a man. I probably get too self-absorbed at times.' She shifted in her seat, plumping the cushion at her right shoulder. 'Anyway, she was certainly happier then when I saw her the time before.'

'And when was that?' Simon asked.

'In April I think it was. She seemed a bit distracted, worried about something. Didn't have her usual sparkle.'

That would have been, Simon reflected, about the time that she had reported her worries about the stalker to Swan and Fielding. 'She didn't volunteer an explanation for her low spirits?' he asked.

'No. And I felt it would be insensitive to probe if she didn't want to tell me of her own inclination,' Mrs Framley said, her voice a shade cooler in tone.

Longman was not put off. 'Did you ask her if she had a new boyfriend when she seemed so happy in June?'

'Certainly not. If she had wanted to she would have volunteered to tell me. I wasn't going to intrude, or pry.'

'Can you remember what you did talk about?' Longman persisted.

She shrugged. 'Just my own rather uneventful existence. And her work. She mentioned a few of her patients. In fact I seem to remember she was a bit worried about something to do with her work.'

'Any idea what?' Simon asked. 'Did she elaborate?'

'No, no she didn't. But she was very discreet so I wouldn't really expect her to. So sorry, I'm not being a great deal of help to you, am I?' She sighed and said impatiently, 'I feel so useless sometimes.'

'No, it all helps,' Simon tried to reassure her. It was difficult not to pity this woman and her situation, though he tried not to show it. Pity was not a reaction that many people craved of others and, though Jean Framley made no effort to hide her fragility, she seemed a woman of pride and dignity.

'Your husband said he was away most of the time,' he said, aware that despite her denials she probably did spend an unacceptable amount of her time alone. 'What does he do?'

She gave a soft laugh. 'Not much use asking me for any details. It's an import-export business. He works from home but it involves him being abroad quite a lot.'

129

'Your husband certainly has a lovely home to work from when he's here,' Longman said. 'Did you have the barn converted yourselves, or was it already done when you moved here?'

'It was already done. I certainly couldn't have coped with being around the work that must have been involved. Charles thought the country air would do me good, I believe, which was why we moved here,' she said with a wistful glance through the tall window at the end of the room.

Simon and Longman's eyes followed hers to where the almost naked yellow stems of willows trailed sorrowfully in the slow-moving river. Simon felt that the isolation of his wife in this lonely hamlet and mournful landscape was not the most sensitive of Charles Framley's decisions.

'Is that the old chapel that's signposted?' Longman asked, getting up and going over to the window. Simon could see the corner of the old stone building from where he was sitting.

'Yes,' she said and gave a small shudder. 'I think it's rather a brutal sort of place, very primitive. But it's one of the earliest of its kind apparently still standing. Sylvia used to like it, though, on its mound above the river. She used to go out there on a fine day and sit there when I was asleep, she told me.'

Longman continued to stare and the room fell silent.

Simon gave a small cough, needing to break the air of melancholy that had descended. 'Did Sylvia ever mention her first husband to you?' he asked.

The hooded eyes opened wide again. 'Did she have two husbands then? Did he die as well? How awful for her.'

'No, she was divorced from her first husband,' Simon said.

The eyelids lowered. 'That must have been hard, too. Her religion meant a lot to her.'

All the time there were hints that this woman had known more of Sylvia Gaston than she was admitting. Or to be charitable, perhaps she was merely unconscious of things that might be considered significant by others.

Jean Framley leaned into the corner of the sofa, her hand raised to cover a yawn. Simon was aware that they had probably talked to this frail woman for longer than they should.

'Did *he* divorce *her*?' she asked suddenly.

'The other way around I understand.'

'Things must have been very bad, then,' she said sombrely.

130

Chapter 15

'D'you mind if I go and take a quick look at the chapel while we're here?' Longman asked as Simon drove slowly through the gates of the Framley residence.

Simon was inclined to an irritable answer along the lines of there being an investigation to carry out and time being of the essence and so on. But he realized that he too could do with a break of fresh air after the sad and, despite the spaciousness of the building, claustrophobic atmosphere of Mrs Framley's home. He drove on without speaking until he reached the gates of the church and parked there. 'Give me the list,' he said. 'I'll find myself a tombstone.'

Longman heaved himself from his seat and set off back towards the chapel.

Rooks and crows were still throwing themselves into the high air and the breeze was cool as Simon made his way along the side of the church to where a green secluded area scattered with leaves and ancient tombs made a sheltered place. He found a lichen-covered tombstone – Daniel Barrington 1726–1789 – and seated himself facing a view over meadowland.

He ran his eyes down the list. There were names, a cryptic note of the illness or need that had brought Sylvia Gaston to them, and the dates she had been there, along with addresses and telephone numbers. Somewhere among these names was perhaps the name of Sylvia's stalker and, maybe, the name of the new man in Sylvia's life. Mrs Jones had given no helpful dates of birth of clients so he couldn't begin to discard possibilities by that method, eliminating the much older ones.

It seemed likely, from what he had been told, that the stalker was either a former patient or the husband of one. And Sylvia had first mentioned him six months ago – around March or April. This tied in with Mrs Framley's remark about Sylvia seeming to be troubled when she had met her in April. So the stalker would be from the client list prior to that time.

He looked at the list again. In March itself Sylvia had spent two weeks with a post-operative gynaecology case and two weeks with a post-operative ovarian cancer patient. Both women then, and did both have husbands or partners? Sylvia had made the remark to Fielding about not wanting to upset the wife of the person who was stalking her.

In February she had spent two weeks with Mrs Fielding, Jack's wife, and time running into the beginning of March with Mrs Framley. She would hardly have accepted Swan's advice to speak to Jack about the stalker if he were the problem in the first place. And besides, he recalled, Jack had been in hospital after the accident on the relevant weekend. Neither he nor Charles Framley seemed likely stalkers. Simon, though, was aware he could do with some more in-depth understanding of stalkers and their psychology, as he'd forgotten most of what he'd learned on some distant training course. Jessie might be able to help, or might know someone who could.

Discarding February's patients, Simon moved back to January on the list. There was a post-operative heart case, male, another ovarian cancer, two weeks respite care – presumably of an elderly person? Though it could be to give a break to any carer at any age. But the whole point would be that the carer was away and not in the house while Sylvia was there and so forming a perverted form of attachment to her. Before that was another post-operative gynaecology patient, Mrs Swan, the Reverend Swan's wife who had died at the end of last year. And, quite apart from the fact that Simon could not envisage the Reverend Swan in the role of sinister stalker, that was surely going back too far. And besides, there was the comment of Sylvia's about not wanting to hurt the wife of the person concerned. And Mrs Swan was beyond such earthly concerns.

No, the stalker would surely have begun pursuing Sylvia much sooner after he had encountered her. So, he glanced back over the list, March itself offered the most likely clients, both patients being female and probably middle-aged with middle-aged partners. These would be the ones to follow up first.

He folded the list and put it in his pocket, aware once more of the cawing birds overhead, feeling a lift of spirits in the clean fresh breeze, and pleased that he had placed his thoughts in some kind of order. But he was uneasy that he was going ahead in this investigation too much of the time with insufficient knowledge and preparation. It was true that any interview with previous patients of Sylvia Gaston's might furnish him with some item of information that proved valuable, so need not be a waste of time, but he might be wrong in his assumption that March was the most likely month that she met the stalker for the first time simply based on his reasoning so far. He thrust his hand into his pocket and brought out the list again. They had to come first, though. They were still the most hopeful cases for him to interview, given the time factor.

He was about to replace the increasingly crumpled papers when he realized he hadn't considered the issue of Sylvia's boyfriend in relation to her client list.

Jean Framley had remarked on Sylvia looking 'glowing' in June. If the new boyfriend was the reason, it suggested that he had appeared in her life between April and June. In April Sylvia had attended yet another gynaecology case, but Thelma Jones had marked deceased against this. If Vanessa's suspicion that Sylvia's new man was married was right then it excluded this one. There was a short gap, during which she had met up with Jean Framley, going forward into May when she had a busy month: she spent a week with a patient with arthritis and flu followed by ten days with a post-operative (non-specified) case, and one week of elderly respite care. In June itself she spent two weeks with a post-hysterectomy patient with infection complications. Thelma Jones's notes were inconsistent in terms of the information she provided.

So the boyfriend could have been in any of the households except perhaps that of the deceased patient and the elderly respite care case, leaving three others to follow up, at least as priorities. The list shoved heedlessly back in his pocket once again, Simon was once more assailed by doubts. It was always possible that the boyfriend wasn't connected with Sylvia's patients. Though she seemed to have had little opportunity to meet someone other than at work or perhaps church. But evidence might yet turn up. He would just have to wait. There were still the two friends of Sylvia's whom she might have confided in. He was unfortunately still at the stage of firing sufficient bullets in the hope they hit a target at some point.

The chill of the tombstone he was sitting on was beginning to penetrate so he got up and walked around the church. On the north side he discovered a huge sculpture of an angel, wings spread and carved in a white marble, integral to the wall of the building. Its feet were a foot or two above Simon's own six foot three and it was about twelve feet high. For a moment he had thought he was seeing the real thing, so luminous did it seem. It was beautifully formed and despite its context, unexpected. He stood and stared up at it, oddly comforted by this private experience. At some time, long ago in the history of this old church, had lived perhaps close by a quite sublime artist who had given to this remote and unimportant parish a work of great beauty: such quality of work was usually reserved for the great cathedrals. Not for the first time Simon found himself comparing himself unfavourably with those whose manifest love of their work shone as a bright light in a dark world. While this long-forgotten sculptor had contemplated messengers of heaven, he, Simon, was grubbing around in the darker recesses of man's soul. He turned away, conscious of the egotism of his discontent, as Longman came puffing around the corner of the church.

'That's quite something,' he said, staring up at the luminous angel, bushy eyebrows bristling with interest.

'How was the chapel?' Simon asked, turning away.

Longman didn't reply at once, his attention still absorbed. 'Do you believe in angels?' he asked Simon, receiving no reply.

'People are afraid to think of the implications,' Longman said, undeterred. 'They'll talk loftily enough of the art and skill of something like this, but they don't really like to confront its meaning.'

'Superstition? A hope of something better out there than the harsh grind of life in the Middle Ages?'

Longman sighed. 'If you say so,' he said, turning away from the angel and joining Simon where he leaned against a tall tombstone.

'We seem to be spending a lot of time in churchyards,' Simon said. 'Was the chapel worth a visit?' They started walking back, the wind in their faces as they moved from the shelter of the church.

'There's nothing like that there,' Longman said, casting a glance back at the angel. 'It's a bit grim really, just a shell with the upper floor gone. It says on the board that it's one of the oldest Christian places of worship left more or less intact, but any decorative work is gone, if it was ever there. If it was like it is now in those days they must have worshipped a pretty grim God.'

'The one of the Old Testament rather than the New?' Simon suggested. 'So it was a bit of a waste of time?'

'Not entirely,' Longman said thoughtfully. 'I went back along the road on the Framley side so I couldn't be seen from their house.'

'Didn't want them to think the police are an idle lot?'

'Partly. Anyway, I could get into the chapel itself without being seen from their house. But I could see into their place, the room we were in, from one of the slit windows.'

'And you saw?'

'They were having a row.'

'You could *hear* them?' Simon asked.

Longman glanced up at the expression of amused scepticism on Simon's face.

'No, and anyway the place is double-glazed. But it was obvious. He was standing over her looking threatening and she was shrinking back in her seat, away from him. I thought she looked pretty scared.'

'How long did it go on?'

'About five minutes. I saw him come into the room just after I got into the chapel.'

'Did he start intimidating her straight away or was there some kind of conversation first?' Simon asked. If the row were an ongoing one, Framley might have been continuing where he left off. But if some initial questions had led to him getting angry with her it might well have been connected to the fact that she had been talking to the police, and what she might have said.

'They talked fairly normally at first,' Longman said consideringly. 'Then he put his hand on the back of her seat and leaned over her and you could tell he was getting agitated.'

'I wonder if he was listening in from that gallery upstairs. Perhaps he objected to something she'd told us?'

'I didn't think she told us anything really. Certainly nothing he could object to, did she?' Longman said.

'*He* might have thought so.'

They had reached the gate and both turned to glance up at the wheeling birds before getting into the car.

'But what?' Longman said, shifting his bulk to buckle up. 'I mean, what would he have to worry about? He doesn't strike me as the type to be the stalker. Did he seem like that to you?'

No, he hadn't. 'Boyfriend, then?' Simon suggested, starting the car engine.

After a pause, Longman said, 'Sylvia Gaston was with the Framleys in February. It wasn't until June that she says she seemed happier. "Glowing" was the word she used, I think.'

'She might have been "glowing" earlier than that and Mrs Framley unaware of it.'

'But she wasn't in March when they met up. Sylvia still seemed to be troubled at that time. Probably the stalker problem.'

'Didn't she say that they had tried to get Sylvia back again at some point, but that she was too busy?' Simon said.

'Yes, why?'

'Just wondering about any contact Framley might have had with her subsequently.' At the thought of telephone contact, something else became obvious to Simon. 'He can't be the stalker.'

'Oh? Why's that?'

Simon was pulling up at the junction with the main road. 'Because,' he said, turning right and straightening up, 'Sylvia changed her number in March because of the stalker, after which the calls to her home stopped. The Framleys obviously had her telephone number – the new one – and Framley could have continued making unwanted calls.'

'Except that, as one of the few with the new number that might have pointed the finger at him,' Longman objected, 'he wouldn't have been able to continue.'

'True but unlikely. Stalkers are obsessives.'

'So, he's possible boyfriend material but not stalker material,' Longman said. 'He's very domineering though, isn't he? I wonder if Sylvia would be that willing to get involved with another control freak, after her first husband.'

'I wondered the same thing. People do repeat abusive relationships. It seems to be a pattern they find hard to break. But she apparently did break it in her happy second marriage.'

'Mmm.' Longman's interest was taken up by the scenery again and there was silence for a while.

'But we have got a tentative guide now to the time periods we're looking at as far as boyfriends and stalkers are concerned,' he said finally. 'Did you decide anything from the list?'

Simon shifted awkwardly and took the list from his pocket. He handed it across. 'See if you come up with the same possibilities as I did.'

Longman shuffled the papers and read for a while, glancing out of the car on a regular basis. 'I get sick reading in a moving car,' he grumbled.

Simon gave him his reasons for believing they should begin with the March patients as far as the stalker was concerned.

Longman risked another glance at the list. 'Both female patients,' he concurred, 'but Thelma Jones gives us no ideas of ages.'

'The Barringtons are just off our route back. We'll call on them first,' Simon decided.

The four-square red-brick house was in large grounds in a narrow road just off the main road into Westwich. The garden was well-tended and landscaped and there was the tang of burning leaves in the air, drifts of smoke coming from somewhere at the far end of the garden behind the house. They stepped inside the glazed porch and Longman rang the bell. There was no response so they stepped back outside and heard the crunch of feet on gravel. A man in late middle-age appeared.

'Can I help you?' he asked incuriously. He was carrying a leaf rake and dressed in well-worn gardening clothes, a waxed waistcoat over check shirt and baggy canvas trousers. Wisps of grey hair escaped from a battered baseball cap.

Simon introduced himself and Longman. 'Could we perhaps have a word with you and Mrs Barrington?'

'What's it about?'

Simon explained and saw the man's expressions change to sympathetic concern.

Barrington glanced at the house. 'I'll just check inside first if you don't mind.'

They stood back to make way for him as he entered the porch and kicked off his boots.

He was back soon and gestured to them to come inside, leading them towards the back of the house.

'This is Mollie, my wife,' he said, gesturing to them to sit at the kitchen table where his wife was already seated, a cup of tea and a broadsheet newspaper in front of her.

She looked up, a faint smile on her face. She and her husband were of an age, her own hair thin and greying, her skin with a yellowish tinge.

'Would you both like some tea?' she offered, lifting her cup in enquiry.

Simon agreed for the sake of conviviality than a desire for any more caffeine. Barrington filled the kettle and switched it on and there was a pause as the kettle began to stir into life. Simon glanced round the room, taking in the old but cared-for wooden cupboards and shelves. It was a cosy room, the Rayburn in the corner making the room overly warm.

'I feel the cold rather, so I'm afraid it is a little hot in here,' Mollie Barrington said, watching Longman run a finger around his collar. 'Do feel free to take your coats off.'

Simon and Longman did so, pushing the coats over the backs of their chairs.

'I don't think we can be much help to you,' Barrington said, pouring hot water into a big brown teapot.

'Though we wish we could be,' Mrs Barrington added. 'Sylvia was here for only two weeks after my operation but we felt we had made a friend. She was a very kind person.'

Simon reflected that, for a woman who seemed to be so highly thought of and considered a friend by her patients, she had apparently volunteered very little about herself.

Barrington placed the teapot with milk, sugar and biscuits in the centre of the table and handed out cups and saucers. He gave a fresh cup of tea to his wife and removed her used cup. Simon saw his watchful glance at her face, the way he touched her shoulder as he sat down and joined them, her fond glance. He could not picture this man making furtive telephone calls, calling unwanted at Sylvia's house with little gifts or notes, tracking her movements obsessively. Nor could he imagine him being unfaithful to his wife in the more conventional way: they were obviously a very loving couple.

'You've retired, Mr Barrington?' he asked, pouring his own tea as invited.

His wife gave an amused laugh. 'I think he works harder now than ever.'

'The garden,' he smiled. 'Always something to be done. I used to be a dentist and after all those years it's a relief to be more concerned with growth than decay.'

'Nonsense,' she teased, 'it's all decay at this time of year.'

A fleeting look of sadness passed over her husband's face, as if he had heard more in what she had said than the others had. Mrs Barrington's name had appeared on the list as post-operative cancer/gynaecology, and by her present appearance, the yellowish tinge to her skin, the threat was far from over.

There was little to be gained here, Simon thought. His instinct was to drink up his tea and leave these two in peace.

'How did Mrs Gaston seem when she was here?' he asked. 'Was she happy, troubled? Did you learn anything of her personal life?'

'She was a very peaceful person,' Mollie Barrington said. 'And if she was in any trouble I don't think she would have dreamed of burdening me with it.' She hesitated. 'I got the impression though that she was worried about her daughter. Kate rang her a few times and Sylvia always seemed a bit subdued afterwards.'

'I saw little of her really,' her husband said. 'I was still working at the time and retired soon after Sylvia left here. I wanted to be able to spend more time with Mollie but couldn't leave the partnership any earlier.'

'It was Sylvia's ex-husband who was my consultant,' Mollie said. Her mouth turned down. 'Not a very charming man.'

'I've met him,' Simon said and she gave an answering smile.

'Did she have any current relationship with anyone, did you think?' Longman asked.

She pursed her lips. 'I didn't get that impression. Certainly no man ever rang her here as far as I know. It was only her daughter. Oh, and her son. He was fending for himself at home, Sylvia said, taking his A levels and then planning to go off backpacking around the world,' she said a bit wistfully.

It seemed, if they had discovered nothing else from this interview, that things in Sylvia Gaston's life had been equable enough in the last couple of weeks of March.

'Was there anything else you learned about Mrs Gaston?' Simon asked.

'She talked about work a bit. She seemed troubled about something that had been going on.'

'Anything specific?' Simon asked.

Mollie Barrington shook her head. 'She didn't say what it was but she asked if I minded her using the phone a few times and it was almost always former patients that she semed to be contacting, as if she were still worried about them.' She frowned. 'Sylvia *was* an extremely conscientious nurse, I realize that. But she seemed overly cautious at times. She was very particular about dressing my operation scar, making sure no infection had set in.'

She hesitated. 'Yes, I remember her remarking on former patients who had died due to post-operative infection. It wasn't her fault, it was something to do with these hopital bugs we're hearing so much about I suppose.'

There was silence again and Simon became aware of the ticking of the clock on the wall. It was an unwelcome reminder of time running on – and perhaps running out for the woman opposite him. He stirred, thanking them for their time. 'If you do think of any other detail about

Sylvia, even if it seems nothing much, please give me a call.' He handed his card to Mollie Barrington who studied it carefully.

She looked up, her expression sad. 'I'm so sorry about Sylvia and her daughter. We both are,' she said, reaching to clasp her husband's hand. 'Such a lovely woman. What a waste. And that poor boy will have to come home to such terrible news. I do hope you catch whoever did this and they put them away for a long time.'

Barrington saw them to the door and hurried back to his wife, his garden obviously forgotten for now.

Chapter 16

Simon was looking so distracted as he and Longman entered the incident room that DC Rhiannon Jones, ever sensitive to Simon's feelings, hesitated to approach him.

She said quietly, 'Sir, I've been to see Thelma Jones at the agency to see what additional information I could get from her.' She paused, her eyes on Simon's face as he gazed out over the terracotta roofs of the old part of town, seemingly not listening to a word she was saying. Sergeant Longman had sunk into the nearest available chair and was twiddling thoughtfully with one of his bushy eyebrows.

'Mmm?' Simon turned and looked down at her, frowning.

'Mrs Jones, sir, at the agency,' she began again.

'Sir!' DC Savage came through the door accompanied by DC Tremaine and hurried over to Simon, ignoring Rhiannon. Simon turned his attention to them.

'We've been getting some results from the house-to-house inquiries, sir,' Tremaine said. 'An old guy who walks his dog around Mrs Gaston's area saw Kate when he was coming back from the pub around 1.30 p.m. on the Sunday. She was walking towards the North Gate. There's nowhere much else to go in that area except further into the housing built up around Telbury Avenue.'

'There's more, sir,' Savage said. 'He's noticed a couple of cars outside Mrs Gaston's when he's been out with the dog.'

'Any description, number plates?'

Savage got out his notebook. 'One was a black four-wheel drive. He said you didn't see many of those parked around his area. Not really townie cars, he said.'

'When was this?'

'This one wasn't on the night or day in question, sir. It was around a week before. But it was after dark at about ten when he usually takes the dog out for a last run.'

So Charles Framley had omitted to mention that he had been visiting his wife's former nurse: it was unlikely there could be any other black four-wheel drive connected to the case. Mr Framley would have to be interviewed again. Simon had dismissed the man as the possible stalker. And he had not really considered him as the possible boyfriend because of the timing: Sylvia's transformation, according to Jean Framley, had been several months after her first meeting with Charles Framley. But perhaps his wife had manipulated the truth in an effort to draw suspicion from him. It was, after all, entirely likely that she might in the circumstances. If there was some association between Sylvia and Framley it might explain Framley's argument with his wife after he and Longman had left them, though he couldn't think of anything she had said to justify her husband's anger. Maybe it had been about something entirely unrelated.

'Did he note the number plate?'

'No sir. He doesn't do number plates,' Savage answered solemnly.

'The other car?' Simon asked.

Tremaine answered. 'A blue Vauxhall Corsa. Now that,' he said, 'was there when he was on his way to the pub at about half an hour before he saw Kate walking away from her mother's house.'

'Vanessa Peel has a blue Corsa. Or perhaps her mother,' Simon said. Why hadn't the young woman mentioned following Kate back after their meeting at church that morning? It was before the last sighting of Kate, though, so unlikely to be relevant to her death.

'Speak to her about it,' Simon said. 'One of you go with Rhiannon to her house after she finishes work. Find out why she didn't mention it when we interviewed her.'

He told them about their interviews that morning. 'Charles Framley has a black four-wheel drive. But I think I'll speak to him myself. We'll leave him for now.' Simon wanted to be as well informed as possible before he spoke to the overbearing Framley again.

Tremaine said, 'The two friends of Mrs Gaston, sir, that I tracked down, have you spoken to them yet? I left the information on your desk.'

'I'll see to it,'

The two DCs moved away, Rhiannon remained waiting.

'Sir?' Grayson, a young DC new to the team, called. 'We've got one of those friends on the line now, a Mrs Temple.'

Her voice was an attractive contralto. 'Lorraine Temple here. I want to apologize to you for not having contacted you before. Your officer caught me almost as we got through the door. The fact is that we've only just got back from a holiday in Crete. I saw the British newspapers of course. It was terrible to read about Kate, but now you've found Sylvia dead as well and I just can't believe it. It's all an awful shock, I'm very distressed. I can't think though of anything I might know that would be useful but I'm sure you are the best judge of that.'

'When did you last see Sylvia, Mrs Temple?' Simon asked.

'It must be about three weeks ago, about a week before we went away. We had lunch together. She'd just finished with a relief care job.'

'How did she seem? Did she have any worries that she mentioned?'

There was a pause before she answered. 'She was happy enough. A bit tired perhaps. You're often rather on your own with respite care. It can be quite demanding. But you want more than generalities, don't you? I'm trying to think of what we talked about.' There was a moment's pause again. 'I remember she was worried about Ian. Said she didn't hear from him often enough and she felt backpacking was becoming more dangerous, apart from the obvious risks of catching some horrible disease. She was concerned about Kate, too. An unsuitable relationship was the problem there.'

'Yes, we know something about that. What about Sylvia's own relationships, Mrs Temple?' Simon asked.

'Didn't her boyfriend contact you?' She sounded indignant.

'What boyfriend, Mrs Temple?' Simon said steadily.

'Ah,' she said. 'His name I cannot tell you because Sylvia was being very discreet about him.'

Simon's heart sank. 'But she was definitely involved with someone?'

'Yes. Though she didn't volunteer the fact. It was only because she was obviously buoyed up so much that I challenged her about it and she agreed she was seeing someone. That was a few months ago – that it first started, I mean. Isn't it rather strange that he hasn't been in touch with you? Of course, you must wonder if he is involved in her disappearance, in that case. But maybe that's why he's keeping out of the way.'

'It happens,' Simon agreed. 'But we do need to find him, Mrs Temple. Can you think of anything Sylvia said that might give us some lead to his identity?'

'He was married,' she said with certainty. 'That's why she was being

143

so quiet about it. I admit I was surprised at Sylvia for getting involved with a married man. She's always been so principled about that sort of thing. Especially since she was on the receiving end when her first husband got involved with someone. Not that she wasn't glad to get rid of Milliner anyway.'

'Did she actually tell you the man was married, or did you assume it?'

'Not in so many words I suppose, because she obviously didn't want to talk about the fact. But I was sure that was what was meant.' She sounded defensive.

Simon's heart sank further. Trying to get to grips with Sylvia Gaston's life was like trying to grapple with gossamer. 'Do you have any idea when this relationship began?' he asked, not hopeful of any clear answer.

'I'm not being a lot of help, am I?' she said sharply. 'Of course, had I realized that my conversations with Sylvia would be needed in evidence at some point I might have been rather pushier with her. Perhaps another reason Sylvia didn't want to admit to an affair with a married man was because she'd been making such a fuss about her daughter being involved with one.'

'That could be so,' Simon agreed. It was more than likely. It was a change to hear a hint of criticism of Sylvia Gaston and he regretted that he was having this talk over the phone: nuances were lost, facial expressions invisible.

'Anyway, why all the fuss over the boyfriend?' she asked abruptly. 'What about the man who was bothering her on the phone, leaving her little gifts? I'd have thought you'd have been more interested in him.'

'We're very interested, Mrs Temple. What do you know of him that might help us? We've not yet been able to identify him.'

There was a moment's silence at the end of the line. Simon, after a brief foolish hope, felt it fade again. This woman didn't know the stalker's identity, either.

'I've just been trying to remember his name. Something like Cave, Hole? No, that's not right.'

Simon wrestled the list of patients from his pocket. There was nothing like those names on his short list of possibles.

'He was someone whose wife Sylvia had nursed after an operation. It started back in the spring as far as I remember. Sylvia didn't want to make an official complaint because of the wife being in poor health. But it really got to her, you know? She got really jumpy and nervous. Of course, Ian was still at home then. Some of the time at least. Like most young men he was out a fair amount and Sylvia hated it when she had to be at home on her own. But being Sylvia she wouldn't put on Ian.'

'I understood that the nuisance calls stopped after Mrs Gaston changed her telephone number,' Simon said.

'Yes, they did. But he was still around. She was still getting bunches of flowers on the doorstep and letters and she felt she was being watched. But I think after the boyfriend came along she felt a bit less anxious, as if she'd got someone to call on when needed.'

It was perhaps a dangerous situation for Sylvia to have allowed to continue without intervention. Perhaps she *had* tried to deal with the man herself – and with fateful consequences.

'Thank you, Mrs Temple, you've been very helpful,' Simon said, a touch mendaciously. 'If there is anything else you think of that might be of help we'd be glad if you'd let us know.' He rang off.

'Any help?' Longman, who had been lingering close by, asked.

Simon gave him a short account of the call.

'Not a lot, then,' Longman grunted. 'She was a very cagey woman was Sylvia Gaston. Too cagey for her own good as it turns out.' He sank down on to the nearest chair. 'And what about the black four-wheel drive seen outside her house that night? Puts Framley in the picture.'

Simon tipped his chair back. 'He might have been trying to get hold of Sylvia to come and stay with his wife again.'

'Funny time to call on her if so,' Longman objected. 'After all, why not just phone her? We know his wife must have had Sylvia's number.'

'Which was why we decided he couldn't be the stalker, because the stalker's calls stopped. But we don't know for sure, do we, that Jean Framley *did* have Sylvia's number? Sylvia may have phoned Jean Framley to make the arrangements to meet, without giving out her own number.'

'But,' Longman said slowly, 'that means that Framley could still be the stalker because if we decided that the calls stopping was some kind of indication that he wasn't, that no longer applies.'

'I think I got the gist of that,' Simon said after concentrating his mind for a moment. 'But I'm not sure any of it means anything now.'

Simon's chair landed back on its four legs. 'Framley doesn't sound like Cave or Hole, if Mrs Temple's memory is anywhere near right.' He stood up, pushing the chair back.

'Have you asked Jessie for any insights about stalkers?' Longman asked.

'She said she'd do a bit of research today if she had time. She may have something for me tonight.'

Chapter 17

Simon was later arriving at Jessie's cottage than he had intended to be, delayed by paperwork and an update meeting with Detective Superintendent Munro. He found Jessie in the sitting room, seated in her favourite position with her back against the sofa and her bare feet on the edge of the hearth of the open fire, a book in her lap and her cat prostrate beside her, belly-up to the fire.

Jessie gave him a brief glance. 'Your dinner's in Floss.'

Such a reception was unusual. He wondered whether his transgression was immediate and minor or whether her obvious annoyance with him was a symptom of something deeper.

'If I were to consider only the evidence of her vast and hairy abdomen I might believe you,' he said calmly. 'But vegetarian Floss is not.'

He saw a flicker of amused response turn to a frown as she paid closer attention to her reading. Should he confront the ominous signs or behave as if nothing were amiss? As always he chose non-confrontation. 'I'll go and make myself something, shall I? Anything you want. A drink? I picked up a good wine on the way home.' Even the word *home* resonated with danger. It was her cottage, her home and was he offering her an opportunity to remind him?

She threw her book aside. '*Why* can't you ever let me know what time you'll be home? *Why* do I make so many meals that are wasted or forgotten because you can't be bothered to let me know what you're doing and when you'll be here? Why are you so bloody inconsiderate?' She glared at him, hostile and implacable.

He was at a loss. He had had no idea that she was harbouring so much resentment over his anything but regular or predictable work life. So unexpected was the attack that he just stood there open-mouthed. He was not practised in conflict with Jessie. Her behaviour was unfair, he told himself. He had never expected her to prepare meals for him – it was just that Jessie was almost always home before he was. On the rare occasions when it was he who was home first then he prepared the meal – a simple one no doubt but still adequate for its purpose. But the fact remained that most meals were made by Jessie and most times she prepared something that could be kept warm without spoiling in case he were late.

'I don't expect you to have a meal waiting for me,' he said quietly.

'You eat the meals I make without much comment!' she flung at him.

'So don't make me any more!' he retorted. He felt a mixture of shame at his apparent insensitivity and righteous anger at her duplicity in not expressing any of this before.

'That's not the point!'

'What *is* the point, Jess? Please tell me. Is this really about meals and my irregular timekeeping or is something else behind this? Have I transgressed in some other way that I'm as yet unaware of? Because if so I wish you would tell me. I don't have time to play guessing games, because I've spent my day trying to work out who killed a young girl and probably her mother and talking to people who all seem to want to keep some little detail hidden from me so that I have to spend my time trying to figure out what it might be and why and when I come home I don't want to have to do the same thing with you!'

'That's just it! You think about other people all the time and you just don't have time to think about me! Or consider whether I might have the smallest interest in what time you might decide to wander in.' Jessie picked up her book again and slapped it into her lap.

Such petulance in Jessie was unheard of: Simon was almost inclined to laugh – and fortunately managed to restrain himself. 'What's behind this, Jess? Are you not feeling well?' he asked carefully.

She frowned up at him. 'Don't you dare mention hormones.'

'I've never known you be a martyr to them,' he denied.

'And what is this?' she said with a toss of her hair. 'Suddenly *I'm* the one who's in the wrong? *I'm* the one whose behaviour is being criticized. This is about you and your behaviour, not about me.' She stared fiercely at the fire, the cat, who had raised her head at the noisy altercation, staring at her in dismay.

'It's about you because you're the one who's upset,' Simon pointed out.

'It would be too much to expect you to be I suppose!'

Abandoning any idea of sustenance for the time being Simon flung himself into the archair opposite her. 'Of course I'm upset that you're upset. And I'm very sorry that I have failed to let you know when I am likely to be home and now that you've reminded me I shall do so in future. I'm also sorry that you needed to have to tell me to do so. But you know what my job is like, Jess. I can't pick it up and put it down like a regular office job. There are too many people involved and—'

'And I'm "people" too!'

'No. You're far, far, more than just people.' He stopped, at a bit of a loss how to continue. Suddenly he had found himself, he realized, in the role of reassuring Jessie. Unheard of. He was the one who needed reassuring all the time, even if he didn't admit it. And in this new role he had no idea how to proceed, the concept of Jessie being the one in need being alien to him.

In a sudden fusion of understanding the same realization seemed to come to Jessie. 'Just a minute,' she said. 'How did my anger at you for not letting me know you would be home late, or when you would be home at all, somehow become a cue for you to reassure me that I am more than "just people"?'

Silence seemed the safest course. Simon looked at her blankly.

'Is that what you think is behind my anger?'

'You're the psychologist, Jess,' he said cautiously. He leaned to place a log on the fire.

'So my anger at your lack of consideration simply means to you that I must be feeling insecure in this relationship?' Her eyes were on the fire, her face expressionless.

'No. But more was said than that.' Simon bit his lip unsure whether to continue. 'It's just that you've never reacted like that before I suppose, and God knows I've transgressed often enough.'

'I suddenly saw it as being taken for granted, you mean? And therefore not cared about enough.'

'I don't know,' he said, out of his depth. 'I suppose only you can know.'

There was silence for a few minutes, apart from the crackle of logs on the fire and the faint snoring of the cat who had resumed her supine position. 'It's true. In a way,' Jessie said quietly.

He wanted to reassure her again. The idea that he could ever take her for granted was so far from the truth. But he realized she couldn't know that. So morbidly aware had he always felt of the inequality of their feelings, so aware that his need of her was far greater than hers of him. And to say so now would seem insincere, as any declaration forced out of such a situation, somehow seemed twisted or false.

'I'm sorry,' she said. She gave a brief laugh and glanced up at him. 'Projection, perhaps.'

He knew what she meant and it bothered him. They had discussed projection before – the habit people have of judging others for faults that are reflections of their own shortcomings. He said, as lightly as he could, 'So, you were only angry at my lack of consideration of you because you are conscious, or not, that you lack consideration for me?'

'Could be something like that.'

'I hadn't noticed,' he said. But perhaps after all he had, on some level. Was it the reason for his constant insecurity in his relationship with Jessie, all the agonizings over whether to ask her to marry him, his fears that she would refuse because her career was too important to interrupt? Was this the time to face up to his doubts?

She shifted her position and laid her book carefully beside her. 'Well, whatever that little interlude was about I do apologize. If it was about a simple desire to be informed of when you are likely to be home I had only to say so without any histrionics.'

'And if it wasn't?' he felt impelled to ask.

'Time will tell, I suppose,' she said.

The power shift had been for a short duration, Simon thought.

'In fact, I haven't eaten yet,' she admitted.

'I'll get something, shall I?'

'Open the wine first.'

It was a sexist-based myth Simon thought, as he prepared the meal of Spanish omelette with green and potato salads, that he was incapable of cooking a decent meal. It was being in the force with its irregular hours and pub and canteen culture that had allowed the rot to set in. Cooking didn't have to be rocket science and he vowed to make an effort to make more of the meals that Jessie and he ate. Except it just wasn't practicable so much of the time because they would both have to wait longer to eat if it were left up to him.

He called Jessie and she came into the kitchen to eat with him. The feeling of unease between them had returned, Jessie seeming lost in her own thoughts. The wine seemed to have some effect after a while and Jessie began recounting a few incidents at work that day.

'I did a bit of checking on the subject of stalkers too,' she said. 'Unless that's no longer relevant?'

'Very much so. Thanks Jess.'

She took a mouthful of wine, eyeing him over the rim of her glass. 'Please don't go all abject on me because of my little outburst.'

He cleared his throat, her scrutiny making him nervous, 'I think we've narrowed down when Sylvia may have come into contact with the stalker. We might even get to him tomorrow, so any prior information would help a lot.'

'Don't get too excited because there's not a vast deal of research published, as far as I can gather. In fact there's little comparatively, probably because it's only in recent years that it became a crime. A lot of the research is American, not surprisingly, and there doesn't appear to be any psychiatric profile of stalkers.'

They had both finished eating their meal and Jessie pointed to the fruit bowl. Simon shook his head and she topped up their wine glasses.

'I'll go and get my notes. As it is,' she said as she came back, 'there isn't even complete consensus on classifying the different types.'

'Just give me what you think may be useful,' he said, not wanting to be overwhelmed with too much detail. Jessie would anyway have made her own assessment of what might be most relevant.

She took a sip of wine. 'The most dangerous stalker is one who has had a previous relationship with the victim. This is the "simple obsessional stalker" who refuses to let go and let anyone else have a relationship with the ex-partner. It's often an extension of domestic violence.'

'Milliner?' he said. 'He used to beat Sylvia when they were married.'

'Possibly,' she agreed. 'But they had been apart, living a long way from each other and each had remarried.'

'It might have flared up again after he moved back to the area,' Simon suggested.

'You can bear it in mind then. The "love obsession stalker" has a love obsession with a person with whom they have no previous relationship. This can overlap with the "erotomania stalker". They convince themselves that their victim loves them in return but that some external influence prevents them from expressing that love. They may find their victim through a variety of ways, a passing contact, someone at work, medical treatment, whatever.'

'So that would fit with your idea about Sylvia meeting someone through the work she does.'

'Could be quite likely. These are also the types who become celebrity stalkers. The love obsession and the erotomania type are distinguished between by the fact that the first type are obsessed without usually believing their feelings are returned and they often suffer from major psychiatric illnesses – which would make it more likely such a person would stand out in your investigation.'

'They're not likely to show any immediate appearance of mental illness though,' Simon said. 'Not to my untutored eye. But it could be useful I suppose if we are checking a suspect's background.'

'As a general rule, though,' Jessie said, 'stalkers are no more likely to suffer from psychological symptoms than any other group of criminals. They often don't have a previous criminal history but on the other hand they do score high on testing for anxiety and emotional withdrawal and marital disfunction is common.'

'I'll look out for that then,' Simon said dryly. 'Anything else?'

'The other categories of stalkers are the sexual deviant types, who are paedophiles and rapists, the "organized harrassment type", and the Munchausen Syndrome type who see themselves as the victim and are likely to report their victim as stalking them, though they have a lot of admiration for their victims. This last type has inferiority problems.'

'So these last types are a bit different in that they have a different agenda?' Simon suggested.

'That's one of the confusions with trying to classify stalking behaviour,' Jessie said. 'Some classifications are made on a basis of motivation while others are made on behaviour only.'

'If her stalker were the sexual deviant type he's more likely to have picked Sylvia quite randomly then?'

'More likely. But since Sylvia appears to have been receiving calls and letters and tokens of affection, your most likely category is going to be with the love obsession or erotomania type.'

'And I'm not sure where that gets me,' Simon said.

'Nor I,' Jessie said with a smile. 'But I'd say you will be looking for a mildly depressed man with a none-too-good relationship with his wife, who probably was someone Sylvia met through her work and who may or may not have believed that Sylvia returned his love.'

'I'll look out for him. Anything else?'

Jessie looked at her notes. 'There are other methods of classification based on both motivation and needs and wants of the stalker – if you want to hear them?'

'Go ahead.'

'There's the "predatory", which would equate more or less with the rapist and paedophile type; the "resentful", similar to the organized harrassment type, who seek vengeance for a perceived slight or insult; the "intimacy seeker", equating with the erotomania type and the "rejected", who fall into the same sort of category as the simple obsession type. The only slightly separate category here are the "incompetent" type who stalk as a way to obtaining a partner.'

'That seems much the same as the obsessional or erotomania type.'

Jessie shrugged. 'I suppose so. They're just as terrifying.'

'Well thanks,' Simon said. 'I'm sure it will help.'

She laughed. 'A bit perhaps, if only in a negative sense. You'll be more comfortable being aware of just how limited is the information on what you might need to know.'

Chapter 18

Valerie Pitt was a patient of Sylvia Gaston's in March, the month during which she might have encountered her stalker. There had been no mention of a husband in the sparse notes supplied by Thelma Jones but when Longman had made their appointment with Mrs Pitt she had mentioned that her husband, Owen, would be there when they arrived.

The house was an ugly detached box painted a stark white with huge plate glass windows and an integral double garage. The garden was large, mostly laid to shrubs and grass and approached by a short drive off the main road.

Valerie Pitt opened the door and stood holding on to its edge as she glanced at their identification.

'Come in,' she said and led them across the parquet floor to the sitting room at the back of the house. She walked stiffly, as if she were in some pain.

'Have a seat.' She indicated a wide brown sofa and chose an armchair by the huge picture window for herself, lowering her body carefully while holding on to the arms of the chair.

'Oh, I'm sorry. Would you both like a cup of tea or something?' she asked.

Both Simon and Longman had observed how stiffly she had walked, as if in some pain. Both, out of consideration for her lack of mobility, shook their heads.

She was dark haired and bright-eyed, her face and body showing the rounded curves associated with middle age. 'It's about poor Sylvia I understand,' she said, looking at Longman. 'Your sergeant explained on the telephone. And her daughter murdered! Poor, poor Sylvia.' Her eyes clouded. 'Such a lovely woman, Sylvia, and so kind. And she was so proud of Kate. I am so, so sorry.'

Simon explained their purpose in visiting her.

She looked at each of them, evidently puzzled. 'But it's some time since I last saw Sylvia. Let me see, it was way back in March when she came here to look after me. I'd had a hysterectomy and there were some complications, an infection afterwards, and I was quite ill. And what with my arthritis and my husband not being available to look after me because he has his business to run, I had to have help. And no one could have been more gentle and kind than Sylvia.'

'What does your husband do, Mrs Pitt?' Simon asked, unhappily aware of some of the more pointed questions he might need to ask regarding her husband. The name suddenly struck him more forcibly. Pitt. Was that the name Lorraine Temple had been struggling for when she came up with Cave and Hole?

'He's a photographer. He has a studio and shop in town but he also works at home. He's got a place up in the loft that we had converted for him. I can't get up there,' she said with a quick laugh, 'not with my hip the way it is and the steep ladder contraption he uses. He pulls it up shut just as if he's on a ship, only battening the hatches upside down, if you know what I mean.'

'He's here today, you told Sergeant Longman?' Simon asked.

'Yes, he's up there working as usual. Why? Did you want to speak to him? I was the one who had most to do with Sylvia.'

'In a while, yes we would. But meanwhile can you tell us what you remember about Sylvia while she was here. Did she talk to you about any personal matters for instance?'

She looked away at the view through the window to where a bird table stood in the vast expanse of lawn, birds fluttering and clinging on to peanut feeders.

'I suppose it's a bit early to be putting food out,' she said inconsequentially. 'But I do so love watching them. A real bit of life they bring, don't they?'

'They do,' Longman agreed. 'I've got a lot of feeders myself. D'you know, I even had a great spotted woodpecker on my peanuts the other day.'

'Did you?' she breathed, turning a delighted smile on him. 'I mostly get the blue tits and great tits, and I've even had some siskins already, but I also had a flock of longtailed tits at the table the other day. So tiny they are, and so pretty.'

She must have observed Simon's glance at Longman because she

155

smiled apologetically. 'I'm so sorry. You're busy people and you must want to get on with this.'

Simon immediately felt contrite, as if he had deprived this friendly woman of a chance to share some pleasure in what seemed a lonely existence. He had noted that there were no family photographs on surfaces of furniture, or hanging on the walls. And with a photographer for a husband one might have expected them to be there if such an extended family existed.

She straightened herself awkwardly in her chair, bringing a cushion around to the small of her back. 'Sylvia wasn't a gossipy woman. Just as well in her line of work I suppose, she wouldn't want her patients thinking they had to be careful what they said to her. It's partly why she was so much in demand I expect. She did volunteer a few things about her family. I never had any children myself, so I suppose I wasn't the best person for her to confide in, not having had any experience of what it's like.

'She was worried about her son, Ian I think his name was, using his gap year to go backpacking. I remember her saying, "They grow up but they're always your children and you go on worrying about them". Ian was living at home with her and she always tried to get home to make sure he was managing all right. And as I said, she was very proud of Kate, felt she was settled in her job and her flat.' She paused and looked at them uncertainly. 'Now I feel as if I am being a gossip but I suppose you have to be told whatever I know . . . ?'

'Yes?' Simon leaned forward, hoping that at last he might hear something he did not already know.

'She was worried about Kate. I think it was some relationship she was in that Sylvia wasn't happy about.'

'Yes, we know about that, Mrs Pitt,' Simon said, disappointed. He added, 'Did Sylvia ever talk about her own private life? Any relationship she was in?'

Valerie Pitt shook her head. 'No. I would have remembered. She was such an attractive woman, you see. I was surprised she was on her own. She did mention her husband who died and the fact that she had been married before. But I expect you know all about that too?' She looked at Simon questioningly.

Simon and Longman nodded. 'Did she receive any phone calls when she was here, personal calls?' Simon asked.

But what she told them was more or less a repetition of what they had already been told by Jean Framley and Mollie Barrington: calls had come from Sylvia's children.

'Apart from the agency trying to arrange her next assignment I can't remember anyone else ringing. She was even apologetic about that – I mean having any use of our phone – but she didn't trust mobile phones she said. Thought they would prove to be unhealthy. I haven't got one myself. But that's because I don't go out enough to have much use for one.' She looked at them wistfully.

'So there were no calls that upset her in any way?'

'None that I can think of,' she replied, looking puzzled.

'And did Mrs Gaston seem relaxed, happy enough while she was here with you? Nothing was bothering her?'

Her look of puzzlement turned to a frown. 'Well, perhaps I didn't know her well enough to judge how she was compared with normally, but she seemed cheerful and relaxed as far as I could tell.'

So it was unlikely that the stalker had begun his attentions prior to her period with Valerie Pitt or she would have begun exhibiting some of the symptoms common to victims of stalkers that Jessie had described the night before. The question now was whether they had begun immediately afterwards.

'You said your husband would be at home this morning, Mrs Pitt,' Simon said.

Her eyebrows twitched higher. 'Why do you need to speak to Owen? As I said, I was the one who saw most of Sylvia. I was the one who was her patient.'

Simon took a breath. 'We are having to question all the men Sylvia came in contact with in the course of her work over the last several months, Mrs Pitt. We don't mean to alarm you or your husband, it is just a routine collection of alibis for the time that Sylvia disappeared.'

'Oh, I see,' she said, sounding more disappointed than alarmed. 'I'd better go and call him for you then.' She got up stiffly and walked awkwardly to the door. They heard her uneven steps across the hallway and then there was silence. If she had to climb the thickly carpeted stairway every time she needed to speak to her husband, Simon thought it was an insensitive arrangement on his part. He noticed a pair of walking sticks propped behind the door. Either vanity or courage kept Valerie Pitt from using them as she perhaps needed.

They heard a muffled thumping and Simon got up and walked out into the hallway. He could see Valerie Pitt in the upstairs hall, a long rod in her right hand, knocking at a hatch in the ceiling above. 'Owen?' He heard her call. Simon stood back out of sight and watched as after a few moments the hatch was raised and a man appeared, crouching in the entrance. There was something intensely demeaning, Simon thought, for the woman in having to summon her husband in such a way.

'What is it?' he heard the man ask irritably.

'The police are here, love. You remember I told you they were coming to talk about Sylvia Gaston.'

Her husband gave a grunt of exasperation. 'I'll be down in a minute, tell them.' He let the hatch door fall back and Simon slipped back into the sitting room as Valerie Pitt began her slow journey back down the stairs.

Longman was standing at the window watching the birds. 'Look,' he said, 'they've got a pecking order just like at HQ. The bigger birds just push the smaller ones out of the way.'

'Owen will be down in a moment,' Valerie Owen said from the doorway. 'Now that I'm on my feet would you like me to get you a cup of tea or coffee? I'm sure my husband will want one, though he has got the facilities to make his own in the loft.'

Yet another opportunity for an excuse for company denied her, Simon thought.

'Let me help, Mrs Pitt,' Longman said. 'Just show me where things are. Tea or coffee?' he asked, turning to Simon.

Simon watched the birds while he waited. It was a bright sunny day and the light caught the startling iridescence on a flock of starlings that had just arrived and were busy seeing off the competition. A blue tit swept in almost beneath the wing of a starling and flew off with its booty while a robin arrived and fluffed itself up, facing up to the competition aggressively. Stealth and sheer cheek, Simon thought, survival methods for the weaker members of the species. He wished human beings could achieve their ends with such charm.

'I'm Owen Pitt,' a voice said softly behind him. Simon had not heard him approach.

Simon turned and introduced himself, holding out his hand. Owen Pitt was medium height and slightly built, with pale hair, pale eyes and pale skin, as if the time spent in his darkroom had had an etiolating effect. His longish hair was combed across his head as if to hide a sparseness of growth on top. His hand, as Simon clasped it, felt unpleasantly damp, perhaps from handling fluids in his darkroom rather than any sign of nervousness.

The man seemed calm enough as he took the armchair adjacent to the one his wife had been sitting in. 'I understand you're talking to people about Sylvia Gaston,' he said, crossing long thin legs. 'I'm not sure how I can help you. I didn't see much of her in the two weeks she was here. Obviously, she was here to look after my wife. Running my own business meant I couldn't look after my wife after she came out of hospital after her operation.

'She can't manage too well at the best of times with her arthritis. And it gets worse when winter comes on. Last March it was pretty bad after the wet winter we had. So,' he uncrossed his legs, 'we got Mrs Gaston in and she was very good Valerie said.'

'You must have seen something of her yourself,' Simon said. The man and his wife were such a contrast: she all warmth and friendliness, he cold and watchful. Simon wondered how he tempered his personality to succeed with a photographic studio business where a certain ease with people must surely be a necessary asset.

'Not much,' Pitt said dismissively, flicking an imaginary speck from the arm of his chair. 'She seemed very pleasant, though. Valerie certainly liked her.'

There was a rattle of crockery as Longman came through the door, preceeding Valerie Pitt. The tray was placed on the coffee table and she insisted on pouring and distributing their drinks and offering them all biscuits before sitting down next to her husband.

Pitt said, after Simon had intoduced Longman, 'I saw on the news that Mrs Gaston has been found. You think her death and the death of her daughter are connected do you?'

'It seems unlikely that they're not,' Simon said.

'Well I fail to see how we can help. We haven't seen Mrs Gaston since last March, have we Valerie?' Pitt said without looking at his wife.

'Not seen her, no,' she replied.

They all looked at her.

'She phoned, to see how I was going on, a few times. She was very kind like that,' Mrs Pitt said, reddening a little.

Simon remembered Mollie Barrington saying that Sylvia had followed up her former patients' progress.

'Can you remember when it was that she called?' Longman asked.

She looked flustered. 'Let me see, she rang a week or so after she left to see if I was recovering well and then in May or June. And she rang in August as well.' She turned to her husband. 'You must remember. You answered the phone and had a few words with her.'

He shrugged. 'Can't say I remember.'

'How did she seem when she rang?' Simon asked her.

Mrs Pitt looked into the distance, as if trying to see into the past. 'Actually, the first time she rang I thought at first that I must have done something to offend her.' She sounded surprised at the memory. 'But then she relaxed a bit and we had a chat and I asked about her children and she rang off.'

Simon suddenly wondered if Sylvia's purpose in ringing might actually have been to try to speak to the husband rather than the wife. Had she perhaps rung to tell him that she was aware he was stalking her and that she would be taking steps about it if he didn't stop? Owen Pitt seemed to him a good candidate for the stalker and he fitted what they so far knew in terms of the time frame. Also he was married to a kindly woman whom Sylvia would have been anxious to protect from knowledge of her husband's behaviour.

'How did she seem the other times she called?' Longman asked.

'Happy enough, I think. She said she was busy and all was well. Mostly she was asking about how I was. She thought more could be done to help with my arthritis. She was very kind, as I said.'

Simon turned to Owen Pitt. 'We're asking all the men we know to have had contact with Sylvia Gaston since last spring to account for their whereabouts on the weekend that she disappeared. Can you tell us what you were doing then?'

The man looked taken aback, a not unsurprising reaction perhaps, but Simon thought a little overdone. 'When was it?'

Simon gave him the date. 'We're interested in the period between the Saturday midday and the Sunday around the same time.'

'I'll have to look in my diary,' he said unwillingly, standing up and looking towards a bureau in the corner of the room.

It was not so long ago, Simon thought. Surely he could recall it easily enough?

'It was the weekend you went to your car rally, Owen,' Mrs Pitt reminded him. 'Owen is an MG enthusiast, Chief Inspector Simon. He's always going to these things. They all admire each other's engines and swap parts. You know the sort of thing.'

'Where was this?' Simon asked her husband.

'Yes, of course I was there,' her husband said glaring at her as if there had been some argument about it. He shoved his hands in his pockets and sat down again. 'It started on the Saturday morning and we finished late afternoon the next day. We had the rally at that big motel outside Bristol, The Wayfarer.'

'You got back here around five, didn't you Owen?' Valerie Pitt said.

He nodded.

'Then we had a meal in the evening and watched television. We went to bed at about ten, Chief Inspector,' she said.

'As far as the rally is concerned I expect you can give me plenty of names of people who can witness you were there,' Simon said pleasantly. Though how much such an alibi would really be worth he wasn't sure. Bristol was only about forty miles away and with such a crowd and with drinking in the evening no doubt, it was unlikely anyone could swear clearly to Owen Pitt's presence for the whole of that time. It was a similar alibi to Milliner's and likely to be as difficult to establish clearly. He'd heard nothing so far either way on how the Milliner alibi was shaping up.

'I expect you were supplied with a list of people attending the rally, Mr Pitt.' Longman said. 'Perhaps you could mark off the names of those you spent most time with, the ones you spent the evening with and so on.'

Pitt stood up again abruptly and sighed. 'It's probably all in the bureau. I'll have a look. Though I must say I think this is ridiculous. Good God, I hardly spoke to the woman!' He went over to the desk and began rifling through some papers.

'Owen is absolutely obsessive about that MG of his,' Valerie Pitt said brightly, as if trying to ease tension her husband had created. 'He's forever cleaning and polishing and tinkering with it. I always say I wish he'd pay me half as much attention.' She gave a nervous laugh as her husband turned to cast a baleful glance in her direction. 'But I expect all the wives feel the same. Though I think there are some women owners in the club, aren't there Owen?' Her husband ignored her.

Simon thought of what Jessie had said about stalkers, that they were often depressive and withdrawn and had marital disfunction. Pitt seemed to comply reasonably neatly with those criteria. And as far as the obsessional stalker type went, Pitt certainly showed obsessiveness in relation to his car, if nothing else. Presumably obsessiveness transferred from the inanimate to the animate and was a general character trait. The time Pitt evidently spent alone in his darkroom was another indication of the loner and at least deeply committed if not obsessive.

On the other hand an MG sports car was hardly an ideal vehicle in which to ferry around dead bodies. For that matter, it was hardly ideal for the man's wife, incapacitated as she was by arthritis.

'Is that the only car you have, Mr and Mrs Pitt?' he asked.

'We've got a Mondeo as well,' Valerie Pitt answered. 'I can't get into the MG any more. But I can even drive the Mondeo myself on my better days.'

Simon was glad to hear that the poor woman had at least some opportunity to get out of the house. She was very different, but her life had strong parallels with that of Jean Framley.

'But mostly Owen uses it,' she added. 'He needs the bigger boot for his photographic equipment when he has work to do outside, or he's ferrying things from here to his studio in town.'

So, if Pitt's need for the car coincided with her 'better days' she was probably as imprisoned as Simon imagined. But it occurred to him that although a Mondeo had a large enough boot to conceal a body, Pitt would not have had that car with him that weekend if he were attending a rally with his MG. He would have had to return home and collect the Mondeo. Would his wife have heard him return? Less likely if he'd come back at night when she was asleep. The double garage was to the far right side of the house, integral to it. It would depend on where her bedroom was.

If he had taken Sylvia Gaston some time on the Saturday night, he would have had to return for her daughter the following afternoon. Which meant a gap in his attendance at the rally on the Saturday night – a relatively easy time to slip away – and on the Sunday would only have meant leaving a little earlier than the official end. But *why* would he have gone back for Kate? Perhaps he hadn't. Perhaps he had gone back to the house to remove anything that might incriminate him.

But Kate had been seen walking safely away from her mother's house in the early afternoon of the Sunday. Had she gone back to the house and encountered Pitt? Or whoever the stalker was, Simon reminded himself.

Pitt came back grasping a couple of leaflets. He held them out to Simon, a printed list of names uppermost.

'I've marked the names of the people I spent most time with,' he said.

'Addresses? Telephone numbers?' Simon asked.

'Well you'd have to get those from the organizers, wouldn't you?' Pitt answered irritably. 'I've probably got some of them somewhere but—'

'In your address book, perhaps?' Longman inserted. 'You must have one of those, especially in your line of work, Mr Pitt.'

'It's probably at the studio in town.'

Pitt was obviously hostile and Simon didn't feel inclined to push him too much. If this did turn out to be their stalker and even murderer, it would be wiser initially to let him feel complacent rather than threatened.

He took the papers carefully to avoid confusing his own fingerprints with Pitt's. They would be able to check them against the ones on the cellophane wrapping round the flowers in Sylvia's bin.

'Is that all?' Pitt asked. 'I'd like to get back to work.'

Simon wanted a look around the house. He wanted to know where Mrs Pitt slept and he didn't want Pitt feeling too alarmed by their interest. 'You've been very helpful, Mr and Mrs Pitt,' he said, standing up and apologizing for their intrusion. 'I hope you realize that it is all just routine.' He smiled, his smile lighting in less of a rictus as it moved from husband to wife.

Pitt looked slightly mollified. His wife said, 'I'd do anything I could, Chief Inspector,' she said, 'to help you find out who killed Sylvia.'

They all made their way to the hallway, Valerie Pitt bringing up the rear. Simon paused, looking around him. 'This is a lovely house,' he said mendaciously, his tastes running to more traditional style. 'Not everyone admires seventies architecture but I love the openness and light you get. It's so spacious.' Longman was peering at him, frowning.

'We like it, don't we, Owen?' Valerie Pitt said, placing a hand through her husband's arm and receiving no response. 'We've been here since it was almost new.'

'My fiancée and I are looking to buy somewhere soon and it's just the kind of place I'd like,' Simon said, smiling down on her. 'Is it as pleasant upstairs as down?'

'Would you like to have a look? You're very welcome,' she said eagerly. Simon felt ashamed.

Her husband shrugged her hand away and stared stonily at Simon.

'Do you mind, Mr Pitt?' Simon asked.

Pitt shrugged coldly. 'Help yourself. But, if you'll excuse me.' He took off up the stairs at a speed which made a mockery of his wife's painful progress.

Simon watched guiltily as Valerie Pitt began her painful effort to climb the stairs again and offered her his arm, which she accepted with a smile.

Pitt had disappeared into his loft space and drawn up the hatch by the time the three of them reached the landing. Valerie cast a glance upwards before leading Simon and Longman into a corrridor on their left, lit by a tall window at the end, Simon murmuring appreciative comments. Longman kept close, maintaining the fiction of Simon and Jessie's prospective house purchase by making comments and asking questions based on an entirely imaginary concept of Jessie's tastes, particularly with regard to the en suite bathroom in the main bedroom. It was quite quickly established that Mrs Pitt slept in this room which was at the end of the corridor at the back, the opposite end from the garage, 'overlooking the garden', as she pointed out to Simon.

The inspection was over quite quickly and Simon felt contrite as he walked with her down the stairs, the pain showing in her face. She managed another of her bright smiles though as they left, wishing them every success in discovering what had happened to 'poor Sylvia and her poor daughter'.

'He certainly looks worth investigating,' Longman said firmly as they got into the car. 'He could have got back from Bristol that weekend easily enough.'

A light breeze was stirring fallen leaves on the yellow gravel of the drive. It felt good to be out of that troubled household: Pitt's curt dismissiveness of his wife, her seemingly isolated existence, had been depressing.

'She wouldn't have heard him if he came back for a bigger car,' Simon said, squinting into the lowering autumn sun and driving carefully through the entrance on to the main road. 'Not with her bedroom at the other end of the house from the garage.'

'I wondered if that was the reason for your eccentric interest in their house,' Longman chuckled.

'Thanks for your support in that,' Simon said dryly.

'I don't think Owen Pitt believed in it,' Longman said. 'And she's a nice woman. I was just trying to make things more comfortable.'

'No need to overdo it, however.'

'Are we going to see the Kylands now?' Longman asked, ignoring the comment.

'May as well. That was where Sylvia went next. I wonder, if the stalker was Pitt, whether he started phoning her during her next job. She would have begun showing some signs of anxiety if so.'

'The job with the Kylands ran into April and it was during that month that Sylvia approached Adrian Swan for advice, so the timing has to be fairly tight.'

'I'll bet Owen Pitt's the one,' Longman said.

Having met Valerie Pitt, Simon's feelings were mixed. She didn't have an easy life with her husband by all appearances, but she seemed attached to him and life could only be worse for her if their suspicions were true. He told Longman what Jessie had said about the current thinking on stalkers and how Pitt seemed to fit the type, probably of obsessional or erotomania.

'As I said, he's likely to be the one.'

Chapter 19

It was immediately evident to Simon that the Kylands were highly unlikely to be implicated in the fate of Sylvia or her daughter. The husband answered the door, aged somewhere over seventy and leaning hard on a walking stick.

He welcomed them inside, apparently as keen for company as Valerie Pitt had seemed. His wife was in a sitting room at the rear of the house, her high, straight-backed chair drawn up close to a flickering gas fire. The immediate impression of the room was of order, cleanliness and a liberal use of polish. It seemed all ochre and brown, as if they had stepped into an old sepia photograph, the impression increased by the bowl of bronze chrysanthemums placed on a side table, their pungent odour overpowering that of polish. The furniture itself was old and good quality and, apart from the chairs and a sofa, was pressed back against the walls, probably to aid ease of movement about the room. The only colour was in the photographs displayed on a high sideboard, the fleeting glance Simon managed taking in images of sunshine and exotic plants smiling on healthy, strong-limbed young couples and children. These stood next to a very formal black and white picture of what must have been the Kylands on their wedding day in postwar austerity Britain. But Simon had no time for more than a fleeting glance: it, was immediately apparent to him from the demeanor of the woman sitting in the chair that curiosity would be considered vulgar and intrusive.

'We read about Mrs Gaston and her daughter,' she said. She was a thin, elegant woman with a fine head of carefully styled iron-grey hair and a face lined with pain.

Simon and Longman took the high-seated sofa she directed them to, her husband in the seat opposite her, his back to the French windows overlooking the large rear garden.

'I can't think of any way that we can be of help,' she said. 'Mrs

Gaston was with us for two weeks after my knee replacement operation. The operation was not a great success and my husband, as you may have observed, has his own joint problems and was unable to be of much support to me at the time. He is due for a hip replacement next month, and I hope it will be a greater success than I have experienced. We were planning to ask for Mrs Gaston again. She was excellent at her job.' She spoke very precisely, her accent clear and clipped.

She was not perhaps the kind of woman to whom one would offer any confidences, should the desire or need arise. Her manner was of one accustomed to command servants and such might have been her attitude to a hired nurse.

'Did Mrs Gaston live in while she was attending you, Mrs Kyland?' Simon asked. 'I noticed that her own home is very close by.'

'No, but she was here to see me to bed and get me up in the morning, and for the rest of the day of course. I am afraid we shall have to look for more suitable accommodation very soon, a bungalow somewhere. We have kept putting it off because we have lived here for some time and also because we couldn't face all the upheaval. But it will have to come.' She looked across at her husband, a fleeting expression of defiance in her eyes.

Simon was afraid that the self-absorbtion of old age made it unlikely that this couple would have noticed anything less than the clearly overt in Sylvia Gaston's behaviour and was resigned to asking a few routine questions before leaving.

'How did Mrs Gaston seem when she was here?' he asked, glancing at each of them. 'Apart from being a satisfactory nurse, as everyone seems to agree, did she seem troubled to you?'

'She did strike me as a bit anxious.' It was the husband who answered. He was less patrician than his wife, with a gentler expression and voice. 'I thought she was perhaps worried about the son. People have so much trouble with their offspring these days. So many frightening things like drugs that they get caught up in.'

'We didn't have any problems like that with our own children,' Mrs Kyland said, as if to correct any wrong impression her husband might have given. 'But then, they were away at good schools a lot of the time.' Her expression fell. 'And now they are away abroad and we never see our grandchildren.'

Despite her starchiness it was impossible not to feel sympathy for them, ageing and frail, lacking the support of any close relations, and in fear of what the future might bring. Perhaps they had bought their own children's future at some cost to their own.

'Mrs Gaston didn't discuss her family or any other personal issues, I suppose?' Longman said.

'I wouldn't encourage such a thing,' Mrs Kyland said stiffly.

'She wasn't the sort,' her husband said in a more kindly tone. 'I talked to her a fair bit while Beatrice was resting. She was very sympathetic and caring. She understood a lot about long-term illness and disablement and how it eats up one's life and sets you apart.'

His wife gave an audible sniff, her expression disapproving, but he continued speaking. 'What I mean is that she struck me as a woman who was thinking of others' needs more than her own, so she wouldn't be the sort to say anything readily about her private life, whatever the circumstances, unless invited to do so, I suppose.'

'Did Mrs Gaston receive any telephone calls while she was here?' Longman asked.

'I made it clear that that was not encouraged,' Mrs Kyland said, her eyes on the view through the French windows.

It was not a direct answer, Simon realized. But there seemed little point in prolonging this interview. He stood up, thanking them for their time.

Mr Kyland accompanied them to the front door.

Out of earshot of his wife, the husband volunteered, 'Mrs Gaston did have a couple of telephone calls. Fortunately they came when Beatrice was resting. They seemed to upset Mrs Gaston.' He leaned against the door jamb, obviously in some discomfort.

'Do you know who they were from?' Simon asked.

'I was the one who answered the phone but he didn't give a name, just repeated he wanted to speak to Mrs Gaston. It was a man's voice but certainly not her son, I wouldn't think.'

'And you handed her the phone. Did you overhear any of the conversation?'

'No, of course not. I left her to some privacy.'

'Did she say anything about it afterwards?' Simon asked, conscious of keeping the old man lingering on the cold northerly doorstep in a cutting breeze.

'She apologized,' Kyland said, shifting his weight a little to the support of his walking stick. 'But she didn't say anything, just looked a bit distracted and upset.'

'And the second call?' Longman asked.

'Same voice as far as I could tell. I was a bit hesitant about passing on the call to her after the last time, but I didn't want her to think that I was censoring her use of the phone. And it was always possible there was some sort of an emergency.'

'How did she react on that occasion? Did you hear anything of the call?'

Kyland's colour heightened a little. 'Actually, I did linger a bit closer this time because I recognized the voice and didn't want her upset again. The phone's here in the hall,' he pointed behind him, 'and I went into the dining room just there,' he indicated the door of a room at the front of the house.

'What did you hear?' Simon asked.

'That was the odd thing. Nothing really. She spoke into the phone, giving her name and then she just listened for a minute or so, if that. All she said was "No!" and put the phone down. Slammed it down. She was a bit pink in the face when I came out of the dining room, just standing there, still looking down at the phone as if it had bitten her. I asked her if everything was all right and she apologized again and said it was nothing important. But I could see she was upset. I asked if there was anything I could do to help and she just said she would try to see that it didn't happen again.'

It was surely the stalker, Simon thought, just at the beginning of his campaign, since there had been no reports of this sort from her other patients. And if Sylvia had stated she was going to try to see there was no repeat of the phone calls, had she decided to contact the stalker to tell him to stop? Which would be just what he would want, a response from her and a corresponding feeling of power and control. Given the timing and lack of earlier reports of anything like this, Owen Pitt looked more and more like the culprit. Simon wanted to get back and start some serious investigation into the man and his supposed alibi.

'That had to be Pitt, surely,' Longman echoed Simon's own thoughts as they drove off again. 'How would he have got hold of Sylvia's number at the Kylands? Surely Thelma Jones at the agency wouldn't pass on a client's telephone number.'

'We can ask her.'

'She might deny it. Maybe it was that dozy receptionist.'

Simon turned left towards the centre of town. 'It's possible he rang her home number and the boy, Ian, gave him the number. His mother was bound to leave it with him, in case of trouble. Pitt, if it were he, only needed to say it was an urgent message.'

'That would seem easy enough. We should check if it happened again, when Sylvia was with later clients.'

'I imagine Sylvia would have told her son to never pass on such information again, so I doubt it,' Simon said. 'Anyway, we don't need to do any more checking on that score. We just need to find out if Pitt is the stalker. And we've got a nice set of prints from the list he gave me. We can check those against the cellophane wrapping on the flowers Sylvia received.'

'Unless they were sent by a flower shop. We've had no news on that, I suppose?'

'We may have when we get back.'

Chapter 20

On the way to the team meeting, Simon spotted Jack Fielding along the corridor and called out to him.

Jack turned and waited. 'How's it going?' he asked. 'Any developments?'

'We spoke to someone today who may be the man who was stalking Sylvia. I don't suppose you can be a bit more precise about when it all started?'

The Inspector frowned, folding his arms. His scars were healing nicely but he still looked pale and unwell; it was still early days yet for the inner wounds to heal. He stared at the floor in thought for a moment or two then looked up apologetically. 'Sorry. I can't remember precisely when it was. All I can remember is that it was in April. Is it so important?'

'Not vitally, I suppose. If our man is the right one it won't matter at all. Just wondered how many other of Sylvia's clients we might need to speak to.'

'You could try asking the Reverend Swan. Sylvia spoke to him first, if you remember.'

Simon thanked him and carried on to the incident room where the others were waiting.

He began by filling in everyone on his own activities and then turned to Detective Inspector Rebecca Stone, the new member of the team replacing the lugubrious and contentious DI Monkton.

She was tall – only a couple of inches shorter than Simon himself, very slender, and dressed neutrally in formal trousers and jacket. Her smooth auburn hair was drawn back with a hair comb and she wore severe reading glasses. Beneath the carefully cultivated businesslike exterior she was probably quite striking, but she was ambitious and clearly had no intention of distracting from what she considered her greater assets: an analytical mind and total focus on the job. Hence she had requested in her first meeting with Simon that, in the main and unless otherwise ordered, she took care of the paperwork and direction of inquiries, in consultation with him, of course. She would, at least, ensure that reports got filed on time, and for that Simon was already grateful to her.

'I'll give you a brief outline of results of inquiries to date, sir,' she said, pushing her glasses into position. 'And then people can add any parentheses.'

'Vanessa Peel has been interviewed,' she went on, barely glancing at her printed notes. 'She was upset at being questioned about her presence at Mrs Gaston's house on the Sunday that Kate disappeared. She said that she and Kate had had "words" after coming out of church that morning, but she didn't want to talk about the subject of the disagreement. Insisted it was private and not relevant to the case.'

'I see,' Simon said, unconvinced that Vanessa should be allowed to be the judge of what was or what was not relevant to the case. He said so.

DI Stone nodded and glanced over to Tremaine and Savage who had apparently interviewed Vanessa. 'She wouldn't explain, sir,' Savage said. 'We couldn't budge her. She just said that after she had simmered down she drove to Mrs Gaston's house at about one o'clock to make it up with Kate and apologize. She went into the house and spoke with her but she said Kate seemed to have forgotten about the row and seemed preoccupied.'

Nothing new there, Simon thought. The last sighting of Kate was still that of the man with the dog around half past one in the afternoon. 'I'll speak to Vanessa Peel myself,' he said. 'We can't let witnesses decide what's relevant to us. Try and keep that in mind you two, will you?'

'Sorry sir,' both Tremaine and Savage replied, looking resentful. 'But she was so adamant, it would have been like bullying to keep on at her.'

'I approve your sensibilities more than your sense,' Simon said dryly. 'If it was important enough, emotive enough, for her to want to keep quiet about the altercation she had with Kate, then it's possible it has some bearing on the case. Not necessarily likely, but possible all the same, so take charge of interviews in future and try to learn a few elements of persuasion where all else fails.'

'Sir,' they murmured.

Simon turned to DI Stone. 'Next?'

'We haven't managed to arrange an interview with Charles Framley about the presence of his vehicle outside Mrs Gaston's house.

Apparently he has gone away for a few days. I believe you want to follow that up, sir.'

'We haven't come across anyone else who might be a possible boyfriend of Sylvia's. And while the stalker remains our likeliest hope we still need to find the elusive married man Sylvia was seeing,' Simon said to the room in general.

'Anything else?' he asked DI Stone.

'They've found tissue under Kate Milliner's fingernails, which will be a help when we have a suspect.'

'And not before. It's about two weeks since Kate was strangled. Any scratches she inflicted are likely to have faded by now,' Simon commented. Still it was good news, providing them with proof if and when they arrested anyone.

'Inquiries have begun on Dr Milliner's whereabouts for the weekend in question,' DI Stone continued. 'We have obtained a list of associates at the conference and are working through. We should speak to him again for a list of names that might vouch for him. Shall I designate that?'

Simon nodded. If any real progress had been made DI Stone would have begun with that. 'Anything else of interest from forensics or pathology?'

'Nothing of note – just the presence of some fibres on the clothing of both women which they are comparing with fibres from her mother's house and her flat. Oh,' she said, shaking her pages of notes into place, 'we have discovered where the flowers in Sylvia's kitchen bin came from.' She named a well-known high-street supermarket.

'And we have good fingerprints on the cellophane?'

She nodded. 'A few sets, but nice and clear.'

'Excellent.' Simon drew out from his pocket an evidence envelope with the list Pitt had given inside. 'Get them checked against Pitt's prints on these, after you've copied the list for checking. He's given us names of people he spent most time with that weekend, but overnight on the Saturday to Sunday when Sylvia disappeared is more of a problem. As I said earlier, he could have got back to Westwich and used the Mondeo to move any body. The Sunday when Kate disappeared is more of a problem. She wasn't seen as far as we know after she was walking away from her mother's house at about 1.30 p.m. And the girl downstairs says she didn't see her come home again, or hear her. It's possible she went back to her mother's house and the killer found her there. So as far as Pitt is concerned, we want his whereabouts after the early-afternoon sighting of Kate.'

Stone nodded and added the envelope to her pile of notes. 'The autopsy report came in. It's on your desk. I don't think there's anything new on it.'

'What about house-to-house inquiries in the area?' Simon asked.

'Nothing more of any interest so far.'

'No news of the son, Ian?'

She shook her head. 'DC Jones has something she wants to say, though.'

Rhiannon looked up, her face pink, her demeanour and appearance contrasting with the cool and immaculate DI Stone. She was a pretty young woman, but her rounded figure couldn't compare with the elegance of the inspector and untameable Celtic hair made it an impossible competition when it came to a businesslike exterior. Simon, fond of the rather emotional DC, knew which of the two's shoulders he would prefer to cry on in a crisis, as some of their customers in traumatic moments felt the need to.

'Rhiannon?' he said encouragingly.

She cleared her throat, and hesitated, never one to wish for the centre stage. 'I tried to mention it to you before, sir, but you were busy,' she began. 'But you may remember that you asked me to check on the health records of Mrs Gaston's patients as far as I was able.'

Simon nodded. It had seemed possibly relevant at the time, but, apart from Rhiannon feeling the need to shine a little in the daunting presence of the new DI, he couldn't think why she should think this topic of any particular interest any more.

'Go on,' he said, anxious that she should not feel rebuffed for her obvious efforts. Apart from his affection for her, there was a very real need to keep a team encouraged and together during an investigation.

'Sir, I found that there were a surprising number of deaths of people that Mrs Gaston had looked after.'

'Why surprising? How could you judge that?' he asked, perhaps a little too quickly.

Her colour rose again but she continued. 'I spoke to Mrs Jones about the cases. She's thawed out a bit with me talking to her a lot and she agreed that the deaths were unexpected in the circumstances.'

'And what were the circumstances?' Simon asked.

'Otherwise healthy women died after operations, most of them middle aged, sir.'

'What are you suggesting?'

'I'm not suggesting she was doing anything deliberately wrong,' Rhiannon said, a hint of defensiveness in her voice, 'but it's always possible that someone else, a husband for instance, thought that she had.'

'You mean Sylvia Gaston might have been murdered in revenge for the death of a wife?' DI Stone said coolly.

'It's possible, isn't it?' Rhiannon said, her voice rising on the repetition of the second word.

DI Stone glanced at Simon. It was outside any of their thoughts on the case at the moment. Simon realized that he was guilty of falling into the trap of trying to make things fit his own theory as far as the likely guilt of any stalker went. Despite his gut feeling that he, rather than Rhiannon was on the right track, he smiled and nodded to her. 'Good work, DC Jones. Keep at it and see how far back these deaths go. Get as much background as you can.'

'Thank you, sir,' she said, sitting up straighter in her seat.

'But wherever we go, all we hear is what a good and conscientious nurse Mrs Gaston was. In fact, one or two mentioned how concerned she was about possible infection after their operation,' he added.

'But it didn't need to be deliberate neglect or anything on her part, sir,' Rhiannon said earnestly, 'for someone to blame her for a death of a much-loved spouse.'

'True.'

'And we know she was unhappy about something to do with her work,' Rhiannon persisted.

Simon held up his hands. 'Just get on with it, then,' he conceded. He had no knowledge of any of Sylvia Gaston's clients that had died; their information having been that her stalker had been married, her boyfriend too, he had concentrated only on still-married couples during the relevant periods of time.

'Anything else?' he asked the room in general. He realized that he had not yet spoken to Sylvia's other close friend. The first had mentioned Sylvia's worries on the work front, maybe the second knew more.

Savage spoke up. 'Sir, we seem to have Pitt in our sights as the possible stalker, though I know we've still got some checks to do. But I'm not quite clear on how that would involve Kate. We know she was around and seen leaving the house in the early afternoon. If Pitt disposed of Sylvia, why come back for Kate?'

'Because he thought she might know who he was,' Tremaine said. 'So he'd have to get her out of the way in case she pointed the finger at him.'

'But how would he know where to find her?' DI Stone interjected. 'Or was she in the telephone book? Perhaps he followed her that day, bundled her into the car after she left her mother's house.'

Simon said, 'He would have been absent from the rally for most of that morning in that case. It's possible that he was going to Sylvia's house to remove any evidence that might point at him and spotted Kate leaving.'

'How would he get into the house?' Longman objected. 'That is, if he did go there.'

'Sylvia's keys were probably on her when he picked her up,' Simon said. 'He could easily have put the keys where we found them after letting himself out of the front door. It's a Yale.'

'And Kate could have come back to the house after she was seen walking away from it,' Longman said. 'But all this in broad daylight?'

'It didn't have to be,' Simon commented. 'He could have strangled Kate in the house and removed her later that night, after dark.'

'We were thinking in the beginning that Kate had gone off to find her mother's boyfriend, on the supposition that her mother was out with him the night before. And it's still a priority to find out who the boyfriend was. But, as Tremaine says, Kate might have known who the stalker was. Her mother might have spoken to her about him, and it might have been Pitt, or whoever, that she went to see, to confront.' Longman let out a long breath, puffing out his round cheeks. 'It's a lot of suppositions, though.'

'Even so,' Simon said, 'we've got plenty to follow up, and the fingerprint evidence may give us a real lead at last.' He drew the meeting to a close and decided to try the other friend with whom Sylvia had been in frequent contact.

The phone was answered on the third ring by a breathless voice with a Scottish accent.

'Mrs McEvoy?' Simon introduced himself.

'Hester McEvoy speaking. So you've finally got around to contacting me,' was her immediate observation. 'I had half a mind I should come in and see you myself at the police station. And you've caught me at a bad time an' all because I am just this minute off to work so you'd better make it sharpish. Unless you'd prefer me to see you at your office? I'm free in the morning if that would suit?'

'I suppose that depends on whether you think you have any useful information for me,' Simon said cautiously.

'Och, well that's for you to determine, is it not? How would I be able to judge?' she said briskly.

'We're trying to establish who Sylvia's boyfriend was. Do you know his name?' Simon decided to be equally to the point.

'She never told me. I know he was married and she wavered for some time about involvement. Then she decided to plunge in, you might say. I don't know what changed her mind, but she seemed happier, especially after all that awful business with that damned stalker upsetting her so much. She got in an awful state about it, as I believe people do. Perhaps it was that that made her succumb to a friendly male's attention. I'm divorced myself,' she added in a tone that suggested the foolishness of any woman who sought refuge or support in a man.

Simon sighed inwardly. This looked like being another pointless conversation. 'Mrs McEvoy – ' he began.

'Miss McEvoy,' she corrected. 'I reverted to my maiden name after making the mistake of marrying a Sassenach.'

'But you decided to stay in Sassenach country all the same,' Simon couldn't resist commenting. Perhaps her almost incomprehensible accent was cultivated as a rejection of all things south of the border.

He heard her chuckle. 'Ah, well, y'see, my children were born and brought up here. I shall go home when I retire. You were saying?'

Simon had lost the thread for a moment. 'Ah, yes, I wondered when it was that Sylvia became involved with this boyfriend of hers. Do you know?'

'It was ages ago now.'

'Years you mean?'

'Och, no. But months, way back. In the early part of this year anyway. That was when she told me the man was married and she couldn't in all conscience get involved. Not having gone through the same kind of treatment from that first husband of hers.'

So, Simon thought, instead of looking at spring onwards for the time when Sylvia found her boyfriend, they should have been looking at an earlier period at the beginning of the year. 'So she didn't actually begin a relationship with this man until after the stalker started bothering her?' he asked.

'That's what I said, isn't it? He was married to one of her patients, and she kept it very discreet. And she was a lot happier for it I have to admit.'

'What about the man who was stalking her? Did she name him?'

'She did not. That was another complication arising out of her type of work. You do get this sort of botheration with home nursing at times. Of course the randy older buggers you can cope with and you don't take it too seriously, but the middle-aged ones can be more of a problem. And this one certainly was. I told her she should go to the police, but she wouldn't have it. Didn't want the wife upset, she said.'

'Is there anything else you can think of that might help us? Anything that Sylvia talked to you about in recent weeks?'

There was silence for a moment. 'Not really,' she said, for the first time sounding less ebullient. 'Just the usual stuff of worries over kids and concerns over young Ian going backpacking.' Her voice rose. 'Has Ian got back yet? Has he been contacted? The poor wee lad will be utterly devastated, so he will. Imagine having to come back to this! I don't suppose his father will mind, however. He'll be glad to get Ian back in his grip, he's been trying for long enough.'

'We're still trying to contact Ian, but it's proving difficult,' Simon said. 'We think he's somewhere in Australia by now.'

'I can tell you one thing, though,' she said. 'Sylvia was worried about things at work. You might look into that. I'll say no more,' she added quickly. 'I really have to go now or I shall be late.'

'Are you a nurse yourself, Miss McEvoy?' Simon asked.

'I am.'

'Home nursing like Sylvia?'

'Westwich Royal,' she said. The line went dead.

Simon was left staring at the phone wondering whether her haste was merely fear of being late for work, or whether she had decided she wanted to say no more about Sylvia's problems at work. Mrs Temple had made a similar reference, and Sylvia had been reported as checking on former patients in a way that surely went further than duty required. Perhaps Rhiannon's investigations might prove more important then he had thought.

He looked at his watch, anxious to give no further offence to Jessie tonight by being late or failing to phone. He had still to key in his reports and make a verbal one to Detective Superintendent Munro.

Chapter 21

The following morning Simon was forced by a traffic diversion to enter the city by the North Gate, obliging him to pass by St Biddulph's. Approaching the vicarage gate was Adrian Swan, clutching a carton of milk and a loaf of bread. Simon pulled over.

'Good morning Chief Inspector!' Swan called, casually dressed in jeans and sweater, his hair uncombed and looking quite unlike Simon's earlier visions of him. 'Are you coming for a cup of tea? Breakfast?'

Simon had had only the briefest of breakfasts, Jessie being out in her garden at an early hour planting spring bulbs, denying them their usual more leisurely Saturday morning meal. He accepted, locking the car door and following Swan into the vicarage.

Swan led him through to the back of the building into the kitchen, warmed by an old Rayburn and in a homely state of disorder.

'Sorry about the mess,' Swan said, moving a pile of church magazines from one of the chairs. 'I can only offer you toast and marmalade with a pot of tea. Will that do?'

'Admirably.' Simon settled himself, looking around the room while Swan put some sliced bread in the toaster and moved the kettle on to the hotplate of the Rayburn. It looked as if Swan did much of his written work for the parish here: papers and books scattered the dresser and one end of the long kitchen table was taken up with other piles of papers and writing materials. The room was fairly dim, being on the north side of the house and looking out on to a looming, dense shrubbery.

'How are things progressing?' Swan asked, placing a butter dish and jar of marmalade on the table, after brushing aside a few more papers with his elbow. He stopped and looked at Simon, his expression serious. 'I heard that Sylvia's body had been found. I had hoped she might still be found alive.'

'We've had no real breakthroughs as yet,' Simon said. 'We're still

179

trying to identify the man who was stalking Mrs Gaston. Actually, I was wondering if you had a clearer date of when she first told you about him. Jack Fielding can't say more than that it was some time in April that she spoke to him.'

Swan stood with a piece of toast in each hand. 'I should be able to help. You get stuck into these and I'll get my diary from my study.'

He was back before Simon had finished buttering his first piece of toast, waving a thick black book in his right hand. 'I keep a record of just about everything these days. My memory isn't what it was, and it matters to people that you can readily recall things they've discussed with you. So, when someone comes I can do a quick check to revive my memory on what we discussed last time.' He sat opposite Simon and began to flick through the book.

'Please,' Simon said with some compunction, 'have your breakfast first.'

Swan waved his words away. 'It was April, I know. Ah, here it is: the twelfth. She came to see me in the morning.' He had put on his glasses and now he peered over them at Simon. 'She really was very disturbed and upset, you know.'

'She would be,' Simon said, quickly swallowing a mouthful of toast and jotting the date in his notebook. The date given fitted with Pitt being their man. He coughed on a crumb.

'Let me get you some tea,' Swan leapt to his feet. 'Tea is essential with toast, I always think.' He took down the tea caddy and heaped spoonfuls of leaves into the waiting teapot, stirring it while reaching for some mugs that hung above the stove. While it brewed he put on more toast and opened the carton of milk, pouring some into each of the mugs.

'I'm sorry,' he said to Simon, 'you do take milk?'

Simon nodded. 'You're very efficient,' he said, observing Swan's economic movements.

Swan smiled. 'Ergonomics. It's become a bad habit of mine. There never seems to be enough time for all the things that need doing, especially since my wife passed away, so I try to not waste a second when I'm doing anything: never wait for the kettle to boil, work out what you can do while it's coming to the boil. Don't get the butter out before you put the toast on, that can wait until it's toasting, and so on. It must sound a bit obsessive, but it's become a bit of a game of mine.' He pulled a self-deprecating face, pushing Simon's mug of tea in front of him, along with a sugar bowl. Simon declined the latter until he had tasted the strong bitter tea. At last Swan sat down to begin his own modest meal.

'I used to insist on the full English breakfast,' he said with a smile, 'but,' patting his stomach, 'I'm losing weight around the middle after months of this meagre beginning to the day.'

They continued eating for a minute or so, the ticking of the old clock on the wall adding to the tranquility of the moment, then Swan swallowed and asked, 'Do you think this stalker is responsible for Sylvia's, and Kate's, death?'

'He has to be a suspect.'

Swan nodded, taking another mouthful of toast. He swallowed. 'It's terribly distressing. I can't quite believe it's happened so close to home, to members of my flock.'

'There doesn't seem to be any such thing as immunity,' Simon remarked. 'Bad things happen to good people.' He remembered saying the same to someone before.

'Sometimes, it seems, more often than to bad people.' Swan wiped his lips with a napkin and pulled another out of a drawer and threw it to Simon. 'You and I seem somehow to be at oppostite ends of a spectrum. I spend my time extolling goodness and virtue, looking for it wherever I may find it. While you are forced to suspect the worst in everyone.'

'Not quite,' Simon protested. 'I like to think that I try to discriminate between the good, the bad and the merely ugly.'

'Are you asking if I would feel bound by the secrecy of the confessional, even if we don't officially have one here? You wonder if I would report it to the police?' Swan narrowed his eyes against the billowing smoke.

'No. That completely aside.'

The priest frowned, examining the tip of his cigarette. 'It would depend on the circumstances. There seems to me a vast distance morally between someone killing with a blow in anger, not intending the outcome, and someone who kills deliberately out of some perversion or for his or her deliberate gain.'

'The latter then? You must have had thoughts about the nature of the evil that men do.' Simon sniffed at the tobacco smoke and was strongly tempted to ask Swan for a cigarette. 'You do believe in evil, I take it?'

'The other side of your sergeant's question about whether I believe in God? Yes, I believe there is such a thing as evil, a force for evil as there is a force for good.'

'How would you look for it in my position? Would you see it as inherent in one suspect rather than another because you discerned the

181

potential for evil action?' Simon leaned back in his seat, his eyes on Swan's face as he gazed into the distance through the grey swirling smoke. He reflected how much Longman would have enjoyed this conversation. But with him here the talk would have gone on all morning and – Simon glanced at the old kitchen clock – he couldn't be too late for the interview that he'd arranged with Charles Framley.

'I don't suppose my instinct would be any better than yours,' Swan said. 'You are probably fairly unconscious of how you manage to discriminate when it comes to suspects. It comes with experience. For my part, and at the risk of sounding utterly world-weary, I would say that most people have within them the capacity to do evil and that circumstances will largely influence whether they ever succumb to temptation to any significant degree.' He seemed to warm to the subject, leaning forward and resting his elbows on the table. 'My understanding is that the further we are from God in our consciousness, the greater the likelihood of our committing some dreadful crime against another human being.' He stubbed out his cigarette.

'But how do you tell how far a person is from God?' Simon asked.

Swan hesitated. 'Ego?' he said. 'The tension between the ego, the false self, and the soul that belongs to God, is the drama of our lives here on earth. The greater the grip the ego has the greater the potential for harm being done.'

Simon reflected that the majority of his clients had only the vaguest of notions that they were in possession of a soul. He said so to Swan.

'That's part of the problem. It's why we need religion in some form to remind people of their true identities,' Swan smiled.

'So murder, being the ultimate crime, would be carried out by a supreme egotist? I should always be looking for signs of egotism in suspects?' Simon had a fleeting thought of Jessie devising some sort of psychological test to see which suspect scored highest in egotism.

'It's not that simple. The act itself is one of supreme egotism and arrogance, but as I said, circumstances can make it more likely sometimes that a lesser egotist on the whole may commit the crime. The circumstances may bring the egotism to the fore, particularly for instance if the ego itself is threatened in some way. It may appear more latent in everyday life. But either way, God isn't in the picture. It's called free will.' Swan leaned back, lighting up another cigarette.

'We don't know why Kate, or Sylvia, were killed,' Simon said soberly. 'I can't imagine what kind of a threat they were to the killer. Though it's likely, I think, that Kate died because she knew something about him. But I do wonder why anyone would want to kill a woman like Sylvia.'

'Because she was a good woman, you mean? And she was. As good a person as one is likely to meet. She had compassion, sensitivity, gentleness, kindness and a form of selflessness that is rare in this self-centred age.' Grey swirls of smoke drifted between them. 'But evil is very attracted to good. It fears it, cannot let it pass unchallenged, seeks to destroy it. It is the threat to the egotism of evil, mocks it by being separate from it, unownable, remote. To kill it seems a solution at times.'

'She wasn't perfect,' Simon protested, a bit fazed by this muscular language. 'She seems to have had little forgiveness for her first husband. And it seems she was having an affair with a married man.'

Swan's eyebrows twitched. 'She was? How do you know that?'

Simon felt some compunction under the priest's clear gaze. 'I don't for absolute certain, but her friends have indicated it.'

Swan looked down, his lips pursed. 'She had forgiven her husband, Dr Milliner. She was just wary of his influence over the children and she was still afraid of him.'

'Oh?' Simon said. Perhaps he should be looking more closely at Dr Milliner.

'I don't mean in fear of her life,' Swan corrected his thoughts. Though—' he shook his head. 'No, Milliner was a bully when they were married. He needs to be in control always.' He smiled, 'A clear egotist, of course. But probably too self-protective to do anything drastic which might threaten his ambition.' He gave a quick laugh. 'You see, there are plenty of egotists around. Perhaps you need to be looking for a very frightened egotist, killing out of self-protection in some way.'

'He'll be frightened by now, for sure, with a murder investigation under way,' Simon said.

'I gather that the man who was stalking Sylvia is your main suspect, and stalking does sometimes end in murder. The act of stalking is supremely egotistical, one of dominance and a desire to control his object. And, of course, if he met Sylvia as a spouse of one of her patients he would have seen Sylvia's finest qualities in operation. He would have wanted some of her attention and care for himself, but would have to be blinded by egotism to the fact that his tactics could not work.'

'Not all stalkings end in murder, by any means,' Simon replied. 'Why Sylvia?'

Swan gave a small shrug. 'Perhaps she had had enough and decided to

183

go to the police despite the man's wife. Perhaps she threatened him with that.'

'But she seemed to have been less upset by the stalker since she got involved with her boyfriend.'

'Your job is a little like mine, as I said. You have to go on only what people choose to tell you. I imagine that sometimes just one small remark may underpin any cherished theories you have—' Swan broke off as a loud banging was heard at the front door, startling Simon.

'Probably a parishioner wanting me.' Swan stood up. 'I'm sorry Chief Inspector, but we'll have to end our very interesting conversation here. I'm never off duty.'

Simon accompanied Swan to the front door where an elderly man waited anxiously. The priest gave Simon a warm smile of farewell as he placed an arm around the old man's shoulders and escorted him indoors.

The sun had emerged through the autumn mists and shone brilliantly once more in a clear blue sky. Simon looked at his watch, wondering if he had time to get some fresh air in his lungs before seeing Framley. He could manage another ten minutes before attending to his own duties, and set off through the churchyard, reflecting that churchyards and cemeteries were the most numerous open spaces in the city, there being only one central park.

After passing through hosts of marble angels and cherubim he arrived at the memorials to members of a more secular age, their headstones uniform and without kerbs or other decoration, to make keeping the place tidy, cutting the grass, more efficient, he assumed. Market forces reigned supreme even in God's real estate.

He passed by Heather Fielding's grave, the flowers in their cellophane wrappings wilted and brown, the bright ribbons garish in contrast, and continued along the path idly reading the headstones of other parishioners recently departed. Julia Swan's headstone was as uniform as the others, the inscription secular rather than religious as he would have expected:

All losses are restored and sorrows end.

He moved on, then struck by some anomaly he couldn't name, he returned to look again. Julia had died in the current year, not at the end of last year as he had understood. Perhaps he had misheard, perhaps he had assumed that she had died at the time she was ill, when Sylvia had attended her. He should check his notes. But, he mentally shrugged, there was no reason for Swan to lie, the evidence was here for all to see.

Chapter 22

Charles Framley was pacing the reception area when Simon arrived at headquarters. He greeted Simon angrily. 'You may enjoy the luxury of a lie-in on a Saturday morning, Simon, but those of us who are self-employed never have time off like you lot do!'

The desk sergeant raised an eyebrow at Simon and gave a shrug.

Simon was annoyed at Framley's seigneurial use of his surname, though the sting was always taken from it by the fact that it was also a first name, something that had always frustrated his ebullient former senior officer, Detective Superintendent Bradley.

'Ah, but you can take time off when you choose, Mr Framley, whereas I have been on duty already for some hours this morning.' Eating toast and drinking tea in congenial company, he did not add.

'Why on earth have you dragged me in here, anyway?' Framley protested, following Simon up the stairs.

Simon ignored him.

Longman was on the lookout and followed them both into Simon's office. Framley ignored the seat offered and towered over Simon at his desk, his height and bulk dominating the room.

'Take a seat, Mr Framley,' Simon repeated. 'If you want this done with quickly then let's get on with it. I too have other things to do.'

Framley hesitated before slumping into the chair.

Simon decided not to offer coffee or tea. He could imagine the response. Framley was looking less groomed than at their last meeting, his colour high and his clothes creased as if he, rather than Simon, had had to abandon a lie in.

'Well?' Framley said agressively, folding his arms across his massive chest.

'You car was seen outside Sylvia Gaston's house at night, a week before her disappearance. Can you tell me why you were there and at such a late hour?'

Framley's colour deepened and he seemed taken aback. 'Who says so?' he blustered.

'Are you denying it, Mr Framley?' Simon asked quietly.

'When was this? What date did you say?'

'Oh come, Mr Framley. Either you were there regularly or it was a one-off, and as such, you are likely to recall the reason for you being there. Which is it?'

'Of course I wasn't there regularly. I just can't recall when it was. I remember now how it came about. Jean had asked me to call on Mrs Gaston to see if she could possibly come back to look after her. She'd been having a bad time and didn't want anyone but Mrs Gaston. She thought a personal approach might be more persuasive than telephoning.'

This somehow seemed unlikely, given the friendship between the two women. Sylvia Gaston was surely more likely to respond to a plea from Jean Framley than her husband. Unless there was a relationship there that they were unaware of.

'Why did you call at such a late hour?'

'Did I? If you say so. I suppose it was because I had been out on business and called in on Mrs Gaston on the way home.'

'You suppose? It's only about three weeks ago, Mr Framley.' Simon found Framley's manner and behaviour puzzling. He must surely have considered that the police might find out about the visit and would be likely to have got his story straight. Instead of which he was floundering around like an errant schoolboy.

'All right, I *don't* suppose. That *was* what happened,' Framley said in a firmer voice.

'And what did Mrs Gaston say?'

Framley scowled. 'Nothing. She wasn't in. There was nobody there.'

'And did you call another time?'

'No. Jean tried her by phone and eventually got hold of her. She was booked up for the time being.'

'Have you met with Sylvia Gaston on more social occasions?'

'What? Are you implying that I had some sort of relationship with the woman?' Framley leaned forward and placed his large fleshy hands on Simon's desk, his face suffused.

'Someone did, Mr Framley. We're just trying to find out who it was.

We know it was the husband of one of her patients. I am merely asking if it was you. It doesn't imply any culpability, but it might help clarify what happened to Mrs Gaston.' Simon kept his voice even, but it did nothing to placate Framley.

'Well it wasn't me! Good God! I don't have time for messing about with affairs. I have a business to run and a sick wife to care for.'

'No offence was meant, I assure you.' Simon said a little untruthfully. 'But we do have evidence we need to clarify, such as fingerprints in the home of Mrs Gaston. You are sure you never entered her house at any time? We may need to fingerprint people who knew her.'

There seemed the slightest of hesitations before Framley replied, speaking slowly as if to the mentally impaired. 'I have never been inside Sylvia Gaston's house in my life. There, does that satisfy you? Because I'd like to go now and get on with some work.'

'We have the same ambition, Mr Framley,' Simon said with a disingenuous smile. 'Thank you for your time.'

Framley quickly got to his feet.

'Before you go, however, we need a statement from you as to your whereabouts on the weekend Sylvia Gaston and her daughter disappeared.'

The big man sank back into his chair. 'And what if it's not convenient?'

'Then we shall have to inconvenience you again tomorrow.'

'Oh, very well,' Framley said impatiently. 'Let's get on with it!'

Simon left him to Longman.

'Something smoky about that man,' Longman said when he rejoined Simon later.

'Anything interesting in his statement then?' Simon asked.

'Not a thing. A conventional and virtuous claim that he was with his wife for the whole of that weekend. I meant the way he behaved generally.'

'He was a bit edgy,' Simon agreed, 'if he's as blameless as he claims.'

'Perhaps he's got a guilty conscience.' Longman got up and went over to the window, hands in pockets.

'How so?'

'Maybe he fancied Mrs Gaston. He may have tried it on with her and is afraid that somehow we'll find out.' Longman turned from the window. 'It's too nice a day to be winkling out people's grubby secrets.'

Simon joined him, looking out to the cathedral and the small part of the precinct visible where crowds of tourists gathered in colourful groups. 'We should check his story with his wife,' he said.

'Framley's a bit of a bully. He'll have her primed as to what to say if we come asking.'

Simon had to agree. 'Has to be done though. Quick coffee in the canteen?' he suggested.

'How can you grace it with the name!'

There was a quick knock at the door. It opened to reveal DI Stone, looking more animated than was usual. 'Sir, we've got a match on the fingerprints! Pitt's are on the flower wrapping from Mrs Gaston's kitchen.'

It was Valerie Pitt who opened the door to Simon, Longman and DI Stone. Simon had asked the members of uniformed branch, which included a woman police constable, to keep their car out of sight for the time being. 'Detective Chief Inspector Simon,' she said, her smile fading as she took in the ominous presence of DI Stone.

'May we come in, Mrs Pitt?' Simon asked gently.

'Yes, of course.' She turned awkwardly, holding the door for support.

'It was your husband we wanted to speak to. Is he at home?' Simon asked as soon as they were in the hallway with the door closed.

'I don't know,' she said. 'I mean, I haven't seen him since last night when he went up to his studio in the loft. I took a sleeping tablet and slept rather heavily.' She was now clinging to the lower banister.

'Shall we go into the sitting room?' Simon asked, offering his arm.

She reached for her walking stick that she had left propped beside the door, but clung to him all the same. 'For all I know, he's still up there. He has everything he needs – kettle, telephone, even a small bed.'

'We'll call him,' Simon said, settling her in her armchair by the window. Birds, their foliage bright in the autumn sunshine, still fluttered about the feeding table.

'Why have you come back, Chief Inspector?' she asked anxiously. 'Do you suspect my husband of something?'

She looked pale, but whether it was caused by the shock of their arrival or the pain she was obviously suffering, it was impossible to tell.

'We need to ask your husband some questions, Mrs Pitt,' Simon said.

He and Longman went upstairs while DI Stone went through to the kitchen. Simon picked up the rod that he had seen Mrs Pitt use and knocked on the door to the loft. 'Mr Pitt! May we have a word please?'

Absolute silence.

Simon tried again and still there was no reply. The rod was obviously also intended for use in opening the door so he pressed upwards on the catch and the door fell open to reveal an extending ladder. He pulled it down and went up into the loft space. Pitt was not there. He shook his head at Longman who waited below and Longman ascended to join him.

The space was, as Mrs Pitt had said, equipped to make a tolerable living as well as working space. Windows at both ends gave good light, added to by a dormer window in the rear roof. A boxed-off area provided the darkroom and most of the space was taken up by photographic equipment. At a quick glance, many of the photographs on view were studio portraits of young women, some of young families. Longman, looking through some display boards leaning against one of the walls, called Simon over. 'Take a look at this!'

There were three boards of photographs featuring Sylvia Gaston, mostly in black and white, shopping, getting out of her car, entering her house, walking in town with her daughter Kate, drinking coffee with a woman friend at a table outside one of the city cafeterias. One enlarged colour photograph was a close up, vividly expressing her vitality and glowing good looks.

'Not much doubt he followed her around then,' Longman said soberly.

They carefully descended the steep steps and returned to the sitting room. 'Is it likely your husband has gone to his studio in town?'

DI Stone was just handing Valerie Pitt a cup of tea. She took it, her hand shaking so that the cup rattled in the saucer. 'It's quite possible,' she said. 'If he's not up there, I suppose that's where he must be. He's not likely to have gone for a walk.'

'You haven't looked to see if his car is in the garage?'

She shook her head.

'Is it unlocked, the garage?'

'I don't know. But the keys are usually kept on the hook by the front door.' Before Simon could move, she said, her face puckered with anxiety, 'Chief Inspector, please tell me what this is about. You surely don't suspect Owen of anything?'

'We just need to ask him some questions,' Simon repeated, making a cowardly retreat through the door, Longman following closely.

There were no keys on the hook, they found them in the lock of the first of the two garage doors. Simon lifted it, peering into the internal gloom, his eyes still dazzled by the bright sunshine outside. He continued peering, Longman beside him, unable at first to believe what his eyes were trying to tell him.

Owen Pitt was hanging by a narrow blue cord from one of the rafters, a couple of feet from his beloved MG sports car. Simon hastily climbed on to it, reaching to feel for a pulse in Pitt's neck, but it was obvious from his horribly suffused and swollen face that he had died some time before. It looked as if he had jumped from the Mondeo saloon parked next to the MG, dusty footprints from his trainers showed on the roof.

'Look,' Longman said, pointing to the breeze-block wall behind Simon.

Simon, not trusting his precarious balance, climbed down.

'I KILLED THEM' was sprayed there in red paint.

It was some time before Simon was able to leave, having arranged for Scene of Crimes officers, the examination of the body prior to post-mortem examination and for a sister of Valerie Pitt to arrive to keep her company. There was no sense of relief for a case solved, not one with such a messy ending. It was always a risk, in interviewing possible suspects, that someone whose mental balance was already on the edge might do something desperate. But they had neither the resources nor manpower to guard against something like this happening.

Longman, noticing Simon's glum expression as they drove away, said cheerfully, 'Well, he's saved us a bit of work.'

'Very considerate of him,' Simon said dryly.

'Well it was, in a way.'

'I shall still want all the ends tied up.'

'The routine stuff,' Longman said placidly.

Simon frowned. 'I want it done properly.'

'Of course.' Longman looked away, apparently admiring the colours in the autumn trees.

'I don't understand it,' Simon said quietly, forcing Longman to lean back towards him.

'What don't you understand?' Longman said irritably. Sometimes Simon's fastidiousness in investigations annoyed him, seeming to seek difficulties when there weren't any.

'I don't see how Pitt could have killed Kate. He was with his wife after he got back from the car rally that Sunday, right up until they went to bed.'

'Unless she's lying,' Longman said, he thought, reasonably.

'She had no reason to lie. She doesn't know our estimates on when Kate was likely to have been killed.'

'No,' Longman agreed patiently. 'But the more time she could give him an alibi for, the better, I expect she thought.'

'That's possible – and we shall have to speak to her again. But I don't think she was lying. She obviously felt pleasure remembering a rare evening spent in the company of her husband.'

'Hang on,' Longman said, puzzled. 'He doesn't have an alibi for before the time he arrived home. He could have left the rally early afternoon and still caught Kate.'

'On the street, in broad daylight?'

'He could have told her her mother needed her or something, to make her get in the car.'

Simon nodded. 'He could. But I still want his alibi followed up.'

They drove on into the centre of town in a tense silence, which Longman finally broke. 'You realize what you're saying, I suppose?'

'What?'

'That if Pitt didn't kill Kate, then we're looking for two killers.'

'It might be possible,' Simon said steadily.

'You think he might not have killed both women?' Detective Superintendent Munro's finely marked eyebrows lifted.

Simon was in her beautifully appointed office, drinking an excellent cup of coffee and attempting to relax in one of the informal chairs.

'That's not what I'm saying.' Simon tried unsuccessfully to adopt a more upright position. These comfortable chairs had as much going against them as for them when it came to interrogation by his sharp-eyed senior officer. 'All I'm saying,' he continued, hooking an arm over the chair's low back, 'is that we can't be sure until we have his alibi checked thoroughly.'

'But you surely think he did kill them both? He's committed suicide, he left his confession on the wall in plain English. What more do you want?'

'Yes, of course he must have done it. I just want to be sure all the ends are tied up. It's proper policing, that's all.' Simon leaned forward to place his empty coffee cup on the low table.

'I am aware of what is proper policing, Chris,' she said, her use of his first name taking some of the sting out of the rebuke.

'Of course.' Simon had no desire for any clash with Munro. Conflicts

191

with senior officers invariably resulted in closer inspection of what one was doing, usually meaning a lot of wasted time.

'DI Stone seems to have been having a positive effect,' Munro remarked. 'It's been a treat to get regular reports on time. Even yours.'

'She's a tartar,' Simon said with a smile. 'Scares me to death.'

'More than I do?' The look Munro gave him could hardly have been considered flirtatious. Perhaps it irked her, the idea that an officer of lower rank might have greater influence over his conduct than she.

'It's merely her omnipresence,' Simon said truthfully.

'I hope I'm with you in spirit even so.' She smiled, making him wonder just how much she did try to tantalize him, how much she used her sexuality in her job. Not that she could avoid it: her smooth brown skin, high cheekbones, big dark eyes and sensuous mouth, her tall shapely form and clothes that were, unlike DI Stone's, designed to flatter rather than conceal, made it impossible for any man of heterosexual persuasion to be unaware of her as a woman before anything else. So she didn't have to try. No, when she stepped just a little over that tenuous line it was done in order to confound, to confuse and thence to dominate.

'Chris?' she prompted him.

'You are,' he said picking his words carefully. 'It's good to have a senior officer who requires me to think about what I'm doing rather than just try to justify it afterwards. Uncomfortable at times, though.'

'I've had no influence over your sartorial shortcomings however,' she said, ignoring the compliment.

He had no answer to that, except 'Perish the thought', which he did not utter.

She stood up, interview at an end. 'So, you still have a few ends to tie up and plenty to get on with.'

'We haven't had time to do a proper search of Pitt's studio at home and the one in town.'

'The post-mortem is on Monday?'

Simon nodded.

'You'd better get back and finalize the evidence. We'll postpone any press comment until you feel more comfortable with what you find from the post-mortem and checking Pitt's alibi.'

Simon was grateful for that. Bradley, her predecessor, would have been all for announcing a joyful conclusion to the murder investigation, leaving them open to accusations of hounding an innocent man to his death if the evidence failed to accumulate in the way they hoped. But, despite his reservations, he had no real doubt that Pitt was a murderer.

Chapter 23

Valerie Pitt had been persuaded to take some medication and had retired to her bedroom, watched over by her sister, the woman police constable informed Simon.

'She was in a bit of a state, sir. Won't accept Pitt had done anything wrong, said he wouldn't hurt anyone. She can't seem to come to terms with his death at all, poor woman.'

Simon and Longman went back to the loft studio to begin their examination of Pitt's papers and other belongings. There was a full computer set-up with a phone beside it and filing cabinet. While Longman leafed through the papers on Pitt's small desk, Simon took in the general arrangement of the room with more leisure than earlier. The living quarter was at the far end of the loft space, beneath a square window and comprised a camp bed with small table beside it and a table with electric kettle and single electric burner. Pinned to the sloping wall by the bed, unnoticed earlier because of the small wall buttress that obscured it, was pinned a large colour photograph of Sylvia Gaston in casual clothes, her hair lifted by the breeze, walking through the centre of town. On the small bedside table a photograph frame had been turned face-down. Simon picked it up and turned it to the light. It was a black and white portrait of Sylvia seated with Pitt at a table outside a cafeteria. Sylvia's head was turned with a smile to Pitt, who gazed lovingly into her eyes. The image shocked Simon, destroying all his preconceptions.

'Come and look at this!' he said to Longman.

Longman took it from Simon, his bushy eyebrows shooting up to his hair. 'Looks like you might have been right and she did make friends with him.' His eyes narrowed. 'Just a minute,' he took the picture to the window. 'It's not real,' he pronounced.

'What d'you mean, it's not real?' Simon took the frame from him and studied it again. It looked real enough to him.

'It's a doctored picture. He's taken a photograph of Sylvia with some-one else, perhaps her son, and transposed his own head where the original was.' Longman nodded in the direction of the computer set-up. 'He's got all the gear. I mean, he would have, wouldn't he, he's a photographer.'

'But how can you be sure?' The picture had made such a vivid impres-sion on Simon that he was not willing immediately to let it go.

Longman pointed. 'It's not that obvious, but it's proportion. Pitt's head is slightly small for the body. And the body is that of a taller male.'

Now that Longman had pointed it out, the illusion vanished. The picture became merely grotesque. Simon replaced it in its original posi-tion, face-down, wondering if Pitt had placed it that way after he killed Sylvia. Perhaps that was why the boards with photographs of Sylvia had been turned to the wall. There had been no need to hide anything from the possibly prying eyes of his wife: he knew it would be impossible for her to climb up to his private domain. Simon couldn't even begin to get inside a mind that could stalk, with the illusion of love and wooing, a woman he was obsessed with, only to destroy her: to destroy her because he couldn't have her. Simon wondered if he had discovered that Sylvia had formed a close relationship with another man, and that had been what made him decide to kill her. Or perhaps she had threatened to report him to the police finally. From what Jessie had said, a high proportion of certain types of stalker was psychotic, with genuine prob-lems of mental instability. It had proved possible to break the obsessive behaviour of some stalkers, given the right treatment. Sylvia, in her desire to protect Valerie Pitt from knowledge of her husband's clandes-tine behaviour, had not been doing either Pitt or his wife any favours in the long run – and certainly not herself.

They continued sifting through the loft, finding many more photographs of Sylvia. From one of the desk drawers Longman produced a diary and began to flick through it.

'Just look at this,' he said in his turn, holding the book open for Simon to view. 'It's a journal, addressed every day to Sylvia. He pours out all his thoughts, how much he loves her, the lot.'

Simon took the book. 'What do the last entries say?' The very last was dated on the Friday night of the weekend of Sylvia's disappearance:

I realize that despite all that I have said, you will not stop seeing that man. I cannot bear to think of him touching you, holding you, kissing you, doing all the things that you and I have done for so long. How could you turn away from what we have known together? What does it take to make you see that it is all wrong with this man? I am the one who loves you. I would give my life for you. But instead it is not to be. You are so gentle, so wonderful, so beautiful. Why can't you see that it is me you should be with? Together we would both be so happy. But if you keep on with this behaviour I shall have to do something desperate. I can't bear the pain, you see. I have done all I can to convince you, but you just won't take any notice. I watch over you to make sure you are safe but it won't be like that any more. You are going to be sorry, I know that you are. You will regret it my darling. I am determined to bring a stop to this once and for all. This time I really mean it. I know that you'll be sorry.

It was rambling, somewhat incoherent, emotional. Simon handed it to Longman to read. Longman grunted. 'Looks like he'd had enough and had decided what he was going to do with her. Good evidence.' He flipped the book closed and handed it back to Simon who continued to read it.

'I suppose it is all just his imagination, all that stuff? You don't think it's possible they did have a relationship of some sort?' Longman said, turning back to Simon.

'I don't think so,' Simon said. 'This fantasy stuff is fairly typical of the erotomania stalker.'

He read on. Much of it was made up of imaginary events that Pitt had shared with Sylvia, a lot of it erotic and even downright pornographic.

'It's totally delusional,' he commented. 'You wonder how a man can live an outwardly normal existence, going to work, sharing a home – in a manner of speaking – with his wife, and have all this sick lunacy churning away inside his brain.' It was not an elegant phrase: he could imagine Jessie wincing at his words. But it was how he saw it – rather than in the neat language of psychology, sanitized and stripped of any visceral meaning or impact.

After a while longer they called a halt.

'There might be something from the examination of the cars,' Longman said. 'Clothing or carpet fibres, soil samples and so on.'

'Let's hope so.'

They went on to town, to Pitt's studio in North Street. His assistant, who said his name was Nat Swinton, was about to close up for the week-end. He had been informed about Pitt's death and waited nervously for Simon's questions, his hands behind him clinging on to a chair. He was a thin spotty youth, wearing a T-shirt and jeans, both of which hung off him and served to emphasize his skinny frame. His hair was waxed and gelled, standing in irregular spikes, making his state of fright more emphatic.

'I didn't know what to do,' he said in a rush, his voice cracking. 'When Mr Pitt didn't come in this morning I just kept the shop open and explained what had happened when people turned up for their appointments. I s'pose I could have done some of the work but there didn't seem much point.' He brought his hands to the front of his body and twisted them anxiously.

'So you did telephone Mr Pitt at home to find out why he wasn't in?'

'Oh, yes I did,' he said, nodding his head vigorously. 'But he didn't have any appointments till nearly midday and when I did phone was when the police were already there.' His face twisted in an awkward grimace. 'Mr Pitt didn't like me chasing him up all the time. He said he was self-employed and he didn't want to have someone on his back.' He took a nervous breath. 'What happened? All they told me was that Mr Pitt was dead.'

'That's right,' Simon said, unwilling to give any more details than necessary at this juncture. 'Have you noticed any change in Mr Pitt in recent weeks?' he asked him.

The boy's eyes widened. He was probably no more than nineteen, and an immature nineteen at that. 'Well,' he hesitated, 'he wasn't in here as often as he had been. And when he was he seemed really down, like.'

'He didn't say why?'

'No,' the eyes widened further. 'And I wouldn't like to ask.'

'Was he a difficult employer?'

Nat gave an awkward shrug, his eyes elsewhere. 'He was a bit picky, yeah. And he got a bit more so recently. He didn't allow any slacking.'

'How long have you worked here, Nat?' Simon asked.

'About a year. He was s'posed to be helping me learn a bit about photography, but I spent most of the time doing a bit of office work and setting up the props. He did let me do some darkroom work, he showed me some of that. Meant I could help out with it. And I learned to use the computer for graphics and all that.' He pointed to another desk, deeper into the long narrow room, where a state-of-the-art computer shone in the gloom.

Neither Pitt nor young Nat, Simon thought, had quite the personality one might expect for work in a photographic studio. He couldn't imagine either of them cooing over recalcitrant babies, persuading them to beam at the camera. Perhaps for both of them the real interest lay in the technical side of the work.

'And how was business? Plenty of customers?' Longman asked.

'Uh,' Nat chewed at a ragged nail. 'Not so good lately.' He said, in a characteristic rush, as if afraid he might fail at the last fence, 'Mr Pitt seemed to have lost interest a bit.'

He might well have done, Simon thought. First through his obsession with Sylvia Gaston and, more recently, with the aftermath of what he had done to her and her daughter.

'He was out a lot more, was he?' he asked the boy.

Nat chewed more furiously at what was left of his nail. 'Yeah, he was actually.'

There was no point in asking Nat to confirm a pattern of behaviour in Pitt that they could already guess at. He would have no evidence to offer as far as Pitt's alibi was concerned. But there was always the possibility, unlikely as it seemed, that Pitt might have confided some details of his private life. 'Did Mr Pitt ever mention anything that was going on in his life, of a more personal nature?' Simon asked.

Nat looked worried. 'No, I don't think so. How d'you mean?'

'Anything at all, lad,' Longman said robustly. 'I mean, did you know anything about his private life?'

The boy looked even more hunted. 'No. I mean I knew he was married but he never talked about his wife. He never mentioned anything really.'

'What about his car, his MG Sports?'

'Oh, yeah,' Nat pointed unenthusiastically behind them to where a set of photographs of the car were carefully arranged. 'Yeah, he'd talk about that. Always tracking down spare parts.'

'Did he mention the car rally he went to a couple of weeks back?'

Nat's jaw drooped as he cast his mind back. He turned abruptly to the calendar hanging near the desk. 'He kept the weekend free. Told me not to make any appointments.'

'Did he talk about the rally afterwards?'

'Not really. I asked if he'd had a good time but he didn't say much.'

'We're going to have a look around Nat,' Simon said. 'Look through

Mr Pitt's papers and so on. Can you show us where things are?'

Nat made an effort to straighten his long, thin body. 'Yeah. I'll sort of show you around, shall I?' He gestured with a limp hand to a desk piled with papers. On the wall above the desk were notices in capitals in red felt pen, with arrows pointing to baskets of paperwork – GET THESE SORTED! SEND OFF FOR! and so on. The blood-red capital letters recalled the horror of Pitt's body in the garage and Simon felt a shadow of unease cross his mind. Perhaps it was the brutal peremptoriness of the commands.

Nat, watching Simon, gave an awkward smile. 'Yeah, he could be a bit tough to work for. Wanted things done yesterday. Anyway,' he turned away, contriving to chew on another nail and talk at the same time, 'this bit is the office section as you can see. You've seen the reception already. Off to the side of the reception,' he eased past Simon and Longman, 'is where we take the photographs and keep the props.'

Simon and Longman followed him to a pleasant room furnished with items designed to add the illusion of gaudy luxury to the images Pitt created: velvet upholstered gilt chairs and chaises longues, various extravagant drapes and, for a more rustic appeal, bales of straw. A number of panoramic backdrops were hanging from the walls and there was a number of period props – plant stands and even an upright piano.

'He had been doing quite well with some period theme portraits,' Nat said, seeing Longman examining the props with interest. 'But he'd not even bothered with advertising for a while now. Tell you the truth, I was thinking of looking for a job somewhere else. S'pose I shall have to now,' he said glumly.

'Did he ever do glamour photography?' Simon asked, vaguely wondering if that sleazy branch of the business might have reflected in Pitt's fantasies about Sylvia Gaston.

'What?' Nat replied, looking as if the term was a mystery to him. 'We've done makeovers. Got an arrangement with the beauty salon up the street.'

Simon nodded. He noticed that Pitt had displayed a good selection of his range of photographic work in this area, as well as in the reception room outside. As well as family portraits, gurgling babies, wedding scenes and well-endowed but discreetly dressed 'made-over' young women, he had displayed a range of black and white as well as colour landscape photographs, and it was here that Pitt's very real skills became apparent for the first time, and for the first time Simon felt a very genuine pang of regret for Pitt's death. They were very good indeed and covered a variety of subjects county-wide – barns, rolling hills and fields, rivers and streams, colour, texture and form were all vividly present. Most of them were priced, with a brief pencilled indication of where the photographs had been taken. He stopped at an excellent picture of a bluebell wood, light dappling on the grey bark of beech trees, the brilliant blues true to colour. Simon had tried with his fairly ordinary camera to take similar pictures and had failed. Then he noticed, all his pleasure evaporating, that the picture had been taken in Eltham Woods, where the body of Kate Milliner had been found in its shallow grave. He pointed it out to Longman.

They went back to the office and Simon asked Nat for the office keys. 'Leave your address and telephone number on the desk before you go,' he added.

Nat did so in a long sloping hand and had quietly disappeared before they realized it.

'I don't think we're going to find anything here,' Longman said, taking a seat and leafing through what looked like invoices. 'He wouldn't leave anything smoky for the boy to find.'

It had to be gone through all the same. After an hour or so Simon called a halt. 'I think our best hopes for evidence will be with the car and any fibres. Meanwhile I'm taking the rest of the weekend off. We've got the post-mortem early on Monday, don't forget.'

'As if I could,' Longman said glumly. It was disheartening work when you found little or nothing to tighten up a case. The portrait of Eltham Wood's bluebells could hardly be regarded as evidence.

When Simon arrived at Jessie's cottage the yellow VW was there again and he heard voices coming from the small terrace at the rear. He felt a small edge of annoyance. He had been hoping that they might both go out for a meal tonight, partly in celebration of the closure of the case.

'Hello!' Hermione said in her rich low voice, raising a glass at him half full of golden wine. 'Isn't this lovely!'

It was warm, certainly, the heat from the lowering sun still filling this sheltered space. The honeysuckle that Jessie and his mother had planted early in the summer had flourished and was still putting out richly perfumed blooms, scenting the area as they had intended it should. Jessie, relaxed in one of the cane chairs, smiled up at him. 'Can I get you a glass?'

Only the thought of being left alone with the overpowering Hermione made him hesitate for a moment. But a drink was just what he needed. 'I'll get it,' he said.

'In the fridge!' she called over her shoulder.

He rejoined them, placing his back to the sun and facing the two women.

'How's the case going?' Hermione asked before he could draw breath.

He was not about to tell her what had happened today, despite the fact that she would be aware of his omission later when the news did get reported. 'So, so,' he replied with a smile.

'Is he always this reticent?' Hermione asked Jessie. 'It would drive me insane!'

Jessie cast Simon an understanding look. 'He likes a break from it now and again,' she said.

'Of course! Oh, I'm so sorry! How thoughtless of me.' Hermione's contrition was genuine but usually evanescent, so Simon remained guarded.

'Is Hermione staying for a meal tonight?' he asked, making an effort to make his words friendly.

'There's no need to be polite. No, I'm not. I've got a hot date as a matter of fact and I shall be leaving soon,' she said, a note of triumph in her voice.

'Anyone we know?' Simon looked from one woman to the other.

'No. No one from the department, if that's what you mean. He's a doctor.'

'A medical doctor?' Simon asked, his voice rising in surprise. 'After all you've said on the subject of doctors, Hermione. You surprise me.'

Hermione lifted her long red hair, flaming in the late sun, and tossed it over her shoulder. 'Prejudice is best rejected by the mature mind,' she said, lowering her eyelashes at him. 'I used not to like policemen either, but *you* soon changed my mind.'

Simon doubted if that had been the case. Hermione was incapable of avoiding flirting with any male, whatever his calling, age or life circumstances. Jessie had once remarked that Hermione had done some research into interpersonal behaviour and got hooked on the power potential. Flirting was just a branch of it. Simon thought himself immune, but she still managed to discomfit him.

'You should meet some of my colleagues,' he said.

'Is that an offer?' she asked, taking a sip from her glass and raising her eyebrows.

Jessie laughed. 'Get a grip, Hermione.'

'Sorry darling.' Hermione straightened up and put her glass down. 'There are mutterings,' she said in a low voice, 'about Dr Milliner.'

Of little interest to him now, Simon thought, but had no desire for Hermione to be aware of the fact. 'Oh?' he said, injecting as much interest as he could into his voice. 'About what?'

Hermione gave a languid shrug, indicative perhaps that she didn't know as much as she implied. 'Incompetence?' she said.

'Or medical negligence?'

'Could be,' she said, pursing her blood-red lips.

'I'll bear it in mind,' he said, hoping to deflect her from any further interest in the case. 'So where are you going tonight?'

She smiled a knowing smile, aware that he was heading her off. 'That new restaurant that everyone is talking about in Chawston.'

'He's not a junior doctor, then.' Simon had heard reports of the place, a former minor stately home on the banks of the river at Chawston, with plans to hold outdoor picnic concerts. The food was excellent and the prices were similar to a deposit on a medium-sized house.

'I'm exercising greater discrimination as I grow up,' Hermione grinned, glancing at her watch. 'Heavens! I must go and have a scenty soak and tart myself up. I've bought myself the most divine dress,' she said turning to Jessie.

'You're always buying yourself the most divine dresses, Hermione,' Jessie said, unimpressed. 'Isn't it time you found some value in attracting a man with the beauty of your mind rather than your body?'

'Easy for you to talk.' Hermione sniffed. 'You'd look good in any old rag. Whereas I'm the type that requires adornment.'

Simon noted with amusement that Jessie was still dressed in her gardening clothes, a stained pair of combat trousers, disreputable T-shirt and sleeveless jerkin, its pockets sagging with balls of string, secateurs and who knew what else, while Hermione could have walked into the swankiest restaurant dressed as she was in a hip-clinging dress and well-fitting jacket. But Hermione was right: Jessie did not need adornment.

'So you tell yourself,' Jessie answered Hermione with a wry smile. 'It helps justify shopping.'

'Think what you like, darling.' Hermione leaned over and planted a kiss on Jessie's brow then moved purposefully towards Simon, kissing him fully on the lips.

He was still coming up for air as Hermione disappeared around the side of the cottage. 'Are my lips red?' he asked Jessie.

'Not from the lipstick,' she said solemnly. 'More wine?'

They continued sitting for a while, relaxed in the unseasonable warmth and each other's company. Any experience with other women tended to increase Simon's gratitude for Jessie. She declined his suggestion that they go out for a meal and brought out a cold salad for them to share.

'Something happened today?' she finally asked, always sensitive to shifts in his mood.

He told her about Pitt, the blood-red confession on the wall of the garage, the diary, everything that had happened that day, glad to recount it, as always with her, helping him to get a perspective on an experience.

'You're sure he did do it?' she asked a few moments after he had finished.

As he started to react, he realized that she had only articulated his own unease but still felt driven to defend the obvious. 'Why wouldn't I be?' he asked.

She gave a small shrug. 'It's unusual to have a stalker kill when he's had no previous intimate relationship with the victim.'

'It happens. What about John Lennon?'

He stretched out his legs and emptied his glass as the last glowing edge of the sun slipped behind the distant hill. 'We're trying to get evidence that confirms Pitt did it, of course.' Now he was being defensive.

'And you don't need me to tell you the dangers of trying to fit the facts to the theory,' she said quietly.

He felt irritated, and troubled, but he knew she was right. 'Why kill himself then?' he asked. 'Why spray his confession all over the wall?'

'People confess to crimes they didn't do all the time, don't they?'

'They don't usually go so far as to kill themselves.'

'But he knew he was under suspicion for stalking,' Jessie said reasonably. 'Maybe it was the thought of all of it coming out, the effect on his business maybe? And he may have got it in his head that he was in some way responsible for what had happened to Kate and her mother, because of his own behaviour.'

'You're the psychologist,' he commented glumly.

203

'I'd just hate you to forget it,' she said more lightly.

Simon searched his mind for a change of subject, remembering his conversation with Adrian Swan earlier in the day. He told Jessie about it. 'He even had me wondering if we could do a psychological test on suspects, measuring their levels of egotism. What do you think?' he asked with a smile, not really intending being taken seriously.

'It might help,' she said, surprising him. 'After all such tests are used after convictions to assess criminals for appropriate treatment. Psychopaths, for example, are the ultimate egotists, lacking totally in empathy, absolutely focused on what they want. But for the majority of criminals it's the circumstances of the crime that evoke the degree of egotism displayed. I mean, you couldn't just take people off the street and test them and be able to reliably predict which of them would be likely to be murderers, barring the extremes – the psychopaths. Most murders, outside the gangland type for example, are committed when circumstances arise that represent a threshold for that individual. By definition, to take another person's life deliberately, or even otherwise sometimes, is an act of supreme egotism. But it just depends on their flashpoint – the event that makes any other action at that moment intolerable. The flashpoint is going to happen more readily in those who are the greater egotists, though, people who are most focused on what they want, what is their right, at the expense of anyone else. When something that matters to them is threatened, they are more likely to kill. The greater egotists take less account of the other in any given scenario.'

After swallowing that Simon said, 'So it would be a matter of only being able to be wise after the event.'

'For professionals like us, yes. Someone in Adrian Swan's position, who has access to people's thoughts and emotions, might be a better judge of an individual's potential for sin.'

It was odd to hear Jessie use such a morally loaded word as 'sin'. He said so.

She pulled her jerkin more closely around her. 'It's not a term of preference for psychologists,' she agreed. 'We increasingly search for terminology that robs words of any gut meaning. It's the scientific method that's the reason for it, keeping things objective no matter how objectionable they may be. It has to be done if psychology is to be taken seriously, but I sometimes wonder how much damage it does in undermining any moral judgement in society.'

'Judge not that ye shall not be judged, though?'

'Discrimination, then, or discernment. Right and wrong get blurred when everyone's behaviour is interpreted in objective terms, the causative impulses and so on.'

'And burglars sue their victims?'

'Exactly!' She laughed. 'Don't let me go on. I shall be forced to resign.'

'I have to admit it was a sort of relief to hear Swan speak with such conviction on the subject of sin. Neither you nor I have it in our remit to make judgements about people's behaviour. We're both supposed to be objective, though I admit few of my colleagues are, particularly in certain circumstances.'

'I'm relieved to hear it,' Jessie said. 'I imagine the job can be unbearable at times, particularly where the very vulnerable are concerned. Police officers surely need to have some feelings about their job, and to vent them at times. They'd hardly be human otherwise.'

'Yes,' Simon said solemnly, 'they're not prone to standing about sympathetically discussing the deprived background of someone who's just beaten up an old lady.'

'And yet,' Jessie sighed, 'there is undoubtedly a causative link. Those who have been brutalized are the most likely to brutalize others.'

'But that doesn't make it all right.'

'Explanation not expiation.' Jessie shivered. 'Let's go inside.'

They retired to the sitting room where the fire was already laid. Jessie put a match to it and announced her intention of having a long soak in the bath. While she did so, Simon put on some Mozart in the hope of stimulating his brain cells and stared at the growing flames of the fire over a glass of brandy.

When Jessie had questioned his acceptance that Pitt was the murderer, she was merely articulating his own sense of unease. Beyond the brief confession sprayed on the wall of the garage, they had proof only that Pitt was the person who had been stalking Sylvia Gaston: no real proof that he had killed either of the women. Given the circumstances, though, he might well get away with closing the case on the assumption that it was solved. It was tempting, but he realized he would find it impossible. They would have to keep questioning and searching for the proof that would have satisfied a court of law, had Pitt come to trial. He couldn't even begin to articulate what the implications were if Pitt had not done the killings. Did it cast a doubt over whether Pitt had even killed himself?

Chapter 24

Simon and Longman looked elsewhere as Havers performed the post-mortem on Pitt's body. Simon's attendance was always more of a formality than anything else since he could never, despite his years of experience, bring himself to focus on the details of each event. He took in the gruesome sounds of saw on bone, fleshy organs slapped into containers and on to weighing scales, the click of the camera handled by an assistant, the never-ending enthusiasm of Havers' commentary, but his eyes were anywhere else, as were Longman's. And his stomach rebelled.

Simon remembered little afterwards, except that Pitt was a healthy male in his forties, and that he had thought to ask a question. 'His wife said they had their evening meal together that evening. How much later do you think he died?'

Robin Havers, plump and bright-eyed as his namesake, paused to consider. 'Some sort of meat pie with mushrooms, potatoes and vegetables. From the state of digestion that would put his death at around five hours later, give or take an hour or two.'

He had summed up, 'Death from broken neck and asphyxiation. I'll get the report to you as soon as possible. A tidy wrapping-up of your murder case, I gather?'

Havers always took an interest in the story behind the bodies he cut up. Simon decided that if it were he, he'd prefer to know as little as possible about the erstwhile human being who was now suffering such indignities. But Havers was not without respect for his clients, as he called them, and an intelligent interest in the case made him more professional in his job.

'Looks like it,' Simon said with as much cheer as he could muster. They thanked Havers and left. Longman, who possibly enjoyed post-mortems even less than Simon did, beating Simon to the outside door and taking several deep breaths of the keen autumn wind.

Back at headquarters, DC Tremaine was waiting, his expression anxious.

'Sir,' he said, 'I don't see how Pitt could have done it. At least I can't see how he can have killed Kate.'

Simon closed his eyes and muttered a silent expletive. He had conveniently tucked to the back of his mind Jessie's point that proof of being a stalker was not proof in itself of being a murderer, despite the painted confession, hoping, expecting that the extra evidence would be forthcoming. 'Tell me upstairs, Tremaine,' he said.

In his office, Longman took up his favourite position by the window and Simon lowered himself into his chair. Tremaine sat on the edge of his seat in front of Simon's desk, clutching some papers to his chest.

'Well?' Simon asked him.

'As far as I can see, sir, Pitt has an alibi which covers him for the time we're interested in. I spoke to the people he referred us to from the list of people at the rally. He didn't leave the place until about four and then he and another bloke,' he glanced at the top page of his notes, 'Brian Mowbray, travelled up the motorway to Westwich. I gather they were racing each other.'

'He admitted that to you, a policeman?' Simon asked sceptically, still reluctant to believe this sudden shift of reality.

'He didn't at first,' Tremaine said. 'But I suggested he couldn't have known where Pitt got to once they were on the motorway, that they must have lost sight of each other. And he said, they were in sight of each other all the way, because they were seeing who could get to the Westwich turn-off first. He'd even seen Pitt pull in to his house as he drove past on the way to his own house a mile or two further on around 5 p.m.'

Simon forebore to comment on the stupidity of racing on motorways. 'It's all very convenient for Pitt, or might have been,' he commented. 'How can you be sure it wasn't cooked up? Maybe Pitt got in touch with him and asked him to tell this tale.' That was surely the most likely explanation for this perfectly squared alibi.

'Two things really, sir,' Tremaine said earnestly. 'First, Brian Mowbray obviously didn't like Pitt much, called him a bit of a prat and said he was a speed fanatic. Said it was his fault they got into a race in the first place, kept nudging him from behind until he increased his speed.'

'And second?' Simon raised his eyebrows.

'Well really it's just a confirmation of what Mowbray said to some extent. Another person at the rally, Jim Hastings, confirmed that Pitt and Mowbray did drive off from the rally together.' Tremaine lowered his papers to his lap.

'What about the Saturday night? Any sign of an alibi for then?' Simon couldn't keep the sourness from his voice and he was ashamed of it. But the whole case looked as if it might be back to square one.

'Everyone I spoke to said they were up drinking until after one in the morning, Pitt included,' Tremaine said, sympathy rather than triumph in his voice.

Which also made it unlikely that Pitt had had anything to do with Sylvia Gaston's disappearance, Simon thought glumly. She was unlikely to have arrived home at around two in the morning at a convenient time for Pitt's arrival back in Westwich. And there was no sign of a break-in at her house.

'Well done, Tremaine,' he said. 'Write it up, will you?'

'While we write it up to experience,' Longman said, turning from the window as Tremaine left the room. 'Where do we go after this? I can't see that Pitt can have been involved in the deaths of either of the women.'

'I think what bothers me most is the alibi itself,' Simon said. 'An apparently perfect alibi for the weekend in question looks more suspicious to me than anything else.'

'You can't get away from the fact that it's real enough. Pitt couldn't be in two places at once,' Longman said, irritated that as he often did, Simon was digging in his heels when it came to anything straightforward.

'Unless we're not looking at things properly.' Simon lapsed into silence, the full implications slowly sinking in. 'Does this mean that really Pitt didn't kill himself?' he said. 'Why confess and kill himself if he wasn't responsible for their deaths?'

Longman said what Jessie had pointed out. 'People do admit to crimes they haven't committed. Happens all the time.'

'But they don't usually go so far as to commit suicide. There may be some latent guilt there, or some desire for attention, but surely the guilt couldn't feel so overwhelming as to drive him to suicide? The guilt for having stalked Sylvia, I mean.'

'In his diary,' Longman said solidly, easing himself into the chair in front of Simon,' he said he was bringing things to an end. What did he mean by that then, if he didn't mean her death or his?'

'Maybe he meant that he was going to stop stalking her.' Simon bit his lip in thought. 'If you think about it, if Pitt *didn't* kill Sylvia, he wouldn't know she was dead, would he? No one else seemed to notice, for sure. No one reported her missing. Yet there were no notes at her house during her absence that week, no letters, no flower deliveries since the one she pushed in the bin.'

'So he either did know, because he did it, or he didn't know and the tokens of his esteem weren't left at her house because he had decided to stop,' Longman summed it up.

'We need to get this alibi business really straightened out,' Simon decided. 'We'll have to speak to Mrs Pitt.' There was something else he must do also. He picked up the phone and called Havers.

'Is there any way this might *not* have been suicide?' Simon asked.

'I assume you're not postulating accidental death?' Havers asked solemnly. 'Auto-erotic strangulation for example?'

'The only accidental example possible I would think,' Simon said. 'No, what I'm asking is whether it's possible that someone strangled him and strung him up.'

There was silence for a moment. Havers disliked answering any such question without his questioner recognizing that the full weight of his expertise was being brought to bear. 'I would have to say that it was possible,' he finally said. 'Of course there are no signs of a struggle with any putative attacker. But if someone had come at him from behind with a noose and quickly broken his neck and followed it up by speedily stringing him up, it would be very difficult to tell the difference.'

'So you can't be positive either way?' Simon said bluntly.

'I imagine evidence in this case is more likely to be found from your area of expertise than my own. Forensic evidence, for example. I hope you have been vigilant in that respect?'

'We have,' Simon confirmed. He thanked Havers and rang off. The forensic evidence had been collected and filed by the book. His own vigilance was another matter. He had assumed death by suicide and, as a failing of his was to retreat from dead bodies as soon as was feasible, he had not examined the scene with any suspicion in his mind that what he was seeing was anything but an image of the reality of Pitt's death – especially with the confession sprayed so insistently on the wall.

With Havers' opinion not firm either way, he still needed to speak to Owen Pitt's wife.

She was seated as before in the chair by the window. Her sister, thinner and older with short grey hair, was seated opposite her knitting something in purple wool. As Simon and Longman came in Valerie seemed reluctant to turn her eyes from the birds outside. Despite the total upheaval in her life she had not forgotten to feed them.

The sister introduced herself as Celia Winston. Her small dark eyes fixed Simon with a glare. 'Do you have to bother Valerie now? She can't sleep, won't take any more medication, and just wants to be quiet and stare at the birds. It seems to comfort her.'

A still, if moving, point in a whirling world, Simon thought. He addressed himself to Valerie Pitt. 'It is important, Mrs Pitt, that we speak to you, if you feel you can cope with it.'

She turned to him with a bitter expression on her face, her eyes red from recent tears, her face pale and strained. 'So that you can prove my husband murdered Sylvia Gaston and her daughter, Chief Inspector? So that, after hounding him to commit suicide, you can tidily wrap up your case? Do you really think I shall help you?'

He hesitated for the right words, troubled that she should have blamed him for her husband's death. He could not protect her from the fact that Owen Pitt had terrorized Sylvia Gaston, but he might be able to save her from some worse possibility, even if it seemed to her at the moment that nothing could be any worse.

'Mrs Pitt,' he said gently. 'We don't yet know the truth of what has happened to your husband. And the truth is all that I am trying to find. I promise you that I have no interest in closing the case at this time, nor of holding your husband responsible for anything he didn't do. But I cannot find the truth of what has happened here without your help. I promise you that it is in helping me that you can best help your husband's memory.'

She regarded him sceptically, all her earlier good humour and tolerance gone. 'I think my husband is beyond help now, don't you?' A spasm of pain crossed her face and she began to rub at her knees, massaging them.

Simon considered the effect of being open with her about her husband's obsession with Sylvia Gaston, unsure whether it would help or hinder his efforts. She would have to know about it at some time, particularly when it came to the inquest on her husband's death.

'Mrs Pitt,' he began, speaking quietly, 'we don't know who killed Sylvia Gaston and her daughter for sure. You've been told that a confession of guilt was sprayed on the wall of the garage where your husband was found, but we do not always take things at face value. Your husband was not "hounded" by me or any other police officer – he was asked the same questions as other men we have interviewed in this case.' Not entirely true, but it might have been.

'There is plenty of evidence, though, that he did have an abnormal interest in Mrs Gaston – that he telephoned her, sent her flowers and generally stalked her movements.' He paused, trying to gauge her reaction. Celia Winston had stopped knitting, her eyes on her sister.

It seemed to take a few moments for what he had said to sink in. Then she lowered her head and pressed the heels of her palms into her eye sockets, her shoulders trembling. Her sister threw down her knitting and put her arms around her. Valerie pushed her aside and took a quick breath.

'I am so sorry to hear that Owen did that to Sylvia. It was a terrible, shocking thing to do. But why didn't she report him? She did realize it was him I suppose?'

Simon nodded. 'Apparently it was out of concern for you. She didn't want you upset.'

She sighed. 'How like her. Not very wise though, was it? What is it they say about the road to hell being paved with good intentions? If she'd spoken earlier it might not have come to this. I understand that you just have to do your job. But it still feels as if Owen was pressured into killing himself. He may have stalked Sylvia as you say, but I'm sure he couldn't have killed her. He must have thought that if you could prove he was the stalker, you would make a good case he was the murderer.' Her eyes filled with tears. 'He'd been so depressed lately.'

What she had said was close enough to the truth. It had seemed obvious that if there was a stalker in the case then he was likely to be the murderer. The problem here was that he did not want to suggest possibilities that might be more palatable to this poor woman only to let her down afterwards. On the other hand the alternative interpretation of what had happened was unlikely to comfort her. The idea that her husband might have been murdered, rather than committed suicide, was hardly likely to cheer her up. The only possible relief she might get was in helping to clear her husband of murder.

'It may well be that your husband proves not to be responsible for what happened to those two women, Mrs Pitt. But we need to have some more information if that is to be proved. You said when we spoke to you before that your husband came back from the rally at around 5 p.m. Is that right?'

She inclined her head, keeping her eyes on his.

'And you said you spent the evening together, had a meal and watched television?'

'Yes. If I remember rightly I said something about having spent more time in Owen's company than I had for a while.' She blinked back tears.

'You did. And afterwards?'

In the age of reckless sexual abandonment in which they lived, he was touched to see the colour rise in her neck. She gave a quick glance at her sister. 'We went to bed together.'

'And did Owen stay in the bedroom all night after that? Or did you perhaps take a sleeping pill?'

'I slept well afterwards,' she said, her colour still high. 'I didn't need to take a pill. But I sleep lightly. He was with me all night.'

And even if he weren't, it would surely have been way past the time that Kate had been attacked: Kate had gone to see someone at half past one that Sunday afternoon. It could hardly have been Pitt since he was still at the rally. And if he hadn't killed Kate, but had killed Sylvia, they were looking at the highly unlikely situation of having two murderers attacking two different members of the same family on the same weekend. Quite apart from the fact that Pitt had enough of an alibi for the Saturday night to make it highly unlikely that he could have been Sylvia's killer. No, there couldn't surely be two killers.

He felt he had to offer her what crumb of comfort he could. 'If that is so, Mrs Pitt, it isn't possible that your husband had anything to do with Kate Milliner's death.'

She relaxed a fraction. 'And what about Sylvia?'

He hesitated and Longman, often exasperated by Simon's tentativeness, spoke up. 'It's not very likely, Mrs Pitt. Only one person is likely to have been responsible for what happened to the two women. If your husband didn't kill Kate, he's not likely to have killed Mrs Gaston, either.' He moved to sit in the chair beside her, placing his hand over hers. It was the right thing to do. Her expression softened and she smiled up at him. 'Thank you,' she said, her voice firmer than before.

The sister, Celia Winston spoke up sharply. 'If Owen wasn't involved in any murders then why did he kill himself?'

Simon answered quickly before Longman could whitewash the whole case as far as Valerie Pitt was concerned. 'We don't know that,' he said ambiguously. 'There are other factors that we need to look into.'

'And what "factors" might they be?' she asked with a hint of sarcasm. She was harder than her sister, her clicking needles arousing an image of the *tricoteuses* at the guillotine. There was a sense more of relish in the situation than sympathy for her sister in the woman's expression.

'Owen may have felt guilt over stalking Sylvia,' he said cautiously. 'Mrs Pitt says he'd been depressed.'

'He'd have to have been extremely depressed,' she said sceptically. 'Unless he was being pressured by the police more than Valerie here was aware.'

'I promise you he wasn't,' Simon said firmly.

He directed his attention to Valerie Pitt again. 'Mrs Pitt, you told us that on the night your husband died he had been working in his studio. Did you see nothing at all of him that night?'

She seemed miles away, but finally focused on Simon again. 'No, I told you I didn't see him. He came in a bit late from work and said he was going to develop some photographs in the loft.'

'What time did he eat?'

'He heated himself a microwave meal at about half past seven.'

'Did he come down from the loft later?'

She shook her head a fraction. 'I went to bed early and took a sleeping pill. I had been in a lot of pain that day and needed a good rest. When I take the pills I sleep quite heavily.'

'But would it have been unusual for him to go out late?' he asked. Celia Winston frowned at his persistence and stabbed angrily with her needles.

'Not really,' Valerie said, a little calmer now. 'It wasn't unusual for him to go out and have a little tinker with his beloved MG at any time if he couldn't sleep. He said it always calmed him down a bit. I remember him saying that mechanical things had a soothing logic.'

'And the following morning, weren't you worried about him?'

'As I said before, he has, had, everything he needed up there in his studio. And if he wasn't there, I assumed he'd have gone to work or something.'

There were no bathroom facilities, Simon reflected. 'You slept late, then?' he asked.

213

She swallowed. 'Yes, I'm afraid I did.'

'You said he had been a bit depressed. Was he on any medication? Had he seen a doctor?'

Celia Winston laid down her knitting in her lap. 'What possible difference does it make now, Chief Inspector? I really think you should leave Valerie in peace.'

Valerie waved an unsteady hand at her sister. 'No, it's all right. I'd rather he got to the truth behind all this. When I said he was depressed,' she said, turning to Simon, 'I really meant he was a bit low. He had been for a couple of weeks, but it wasn't full depression. I didn't even suggest he see a doctor and I would have done if I had thought there was something serious wrong.' She bit her lip. 'I must have been mistaken, though. Perhaps I should have taken more notice. It's just that we all go through times when we get a bit down and I thought that was all it was. It's terrible to think I might have been able to help him and didn't.'

It seemed grossly unfair to Simon that she should carry any guilt. Her husband, as far as Simon had been able to tell, had not been the kind of character who would have welcomed advice or expressions of concern from his wife. He tried to articulate this to her. 'People more often than not won't accept any advice like that. Part of the problem, if it's real, is that they can be in denial over it. I doubt if there was anything you could have done.'

She gave him a watery smile. 'It's kind of you to say so, but I shall probably go on thinking it. And now, if you don't mind, Detective Chief Inspector, I think I really am not up to any more questions.'

Her sister was on her feet more quickly than Simon and Longman, ready to show them to the door.

'We shall just be taking a quick look around the garage before we leave,' Simon said over his shoulder to Valerie Pitt.

'You will let me know of any developments, will you?' she asked. 'My sister will take a message if I am resting.'

'What are you looking for?' Longman asked curiously as Simon raised the first garage door. 'You're not really thinking Pitt *didn't* kill himself, are you? I gathered Havers wasn't going for it. Besides, it seems a bit unlikely to say the least.'

Simon didn't reply, his eyes again accustoming themselves to the dim light. He found the light switch and flicked it on. Without Pitt's body the scene was innocuous and peaceful, until you noticed the blood-red words on the wall. He wandered between the two cars, examining the

Mondeo and the dusty imprints of the soles of Pitt's trainers on the bonnet and roof. With a last glance round, he joined Longman who waited in the sunshine outside.

They got in the car and drove off, Simon silent and obviously uncommunicative. Longman folded his arms across his chest and stared stolidly ahead. He found Simon's silences irksome. 'What are you thinking about?' he asked.

'Nothing in particular,' Simon said. But he was trying to pinpoint what it was that didn't fit in with what he had seen. Something had registered as not right and the only way to work out what it was, was to just let the images float freely through his mind until he found a focus.

'I suppose they took the paint spray can for fingerprinting?' Longman said, refusing to take a hint.

'Of course,' Simon said irritably. Then it came almost as a click in Simon's head. 'That's it!' he said.

'As in *Eureka!*?' Longman asked.

'Pitt didn't write that message on the wall,' Simon said positvely.

'How come?' Longman asked, refusing to show any excitement.

'The Greek Es.'

'Eh?'

'At Pitt's studio in town, do you remember the notices he had up, reminders for Nat Swinton to get on with jobs Pitt wanted done?'

'Yes,' Longman said slowly.

'All the Es he printed were in Greek form. The Es in the message on the wall were not, they were the normal E made with an L and two horizontal forward strokes. The Greek form of the letter is made with a forward-facing curve in one stroke and one horizontal forward stroke. In other words, only two movements of the pen. Strictly speaking, I suppose, the Greek form is a V on its side, rather than a curved U shape, but most people use one movement of the pen to shape the curve because it's quicker.'

'You think that's pretty conclusive then?' Longman sounded a bit doubtful.

'We can get a graphologist to give an expert opinion if you like,' Simon said cheerfully.

'It might be as well. I thought when capital letters were used it was harder to be sure about the identity of the writer.'

'That's only because it can be easier to fake writing using capitals because the form of the letters is simpler. That doesn't apply here.

Whoever wrote that confession on the wall didn't know that Pitt used the Greek E form, and he would have assumed that using a spray can in itself would disguise any slight differences in the formation of the letters. But the different E form that Pitt used, apparently often used by creative types, by the way, is not something that Pitt would have changed, particularly at a time of acute stress. Which he would have to be under if he were really committing suicide.'

'So,' Longman said, 'it might turn out to be a true confession after all.'

'How do you mean?' Simon glanced at him with a frown.

'Well,' Longman said reasonably, 'whoever killed Pitt must have killed Sylvia and Kate. And wrote his own confession in his attempt to frame Pitt. And he won't have been daft enough to leave his fingerprints on the can of paint. He'll have wiped his own and left a nice set of Pitt's in their place.'

'But who knew about Pitt being a possible suspect, the stalker?' Simon said.

'Quite a lot of people knew we were looking for her stalker. What we don't know is how many of them knew the stalker was Pitt. We've asked a number of people who have denied that she told them his name.'

'One person she surely would have told was her boyfriend, whoever he is,' Simon said.

Chapter 25

The team meeting that evening was noisy with speculation and theories.

'It's got to be Sylvia's boyfriend behind it, surely?' DC Rogers said, to a general murmur of agreement. 'I mean, who else would most likely have known that Pitt was the person easiest to frame?'

'Yes, finding the identity of her boyfriend has to be one priority,' Simon said.

'Who was likely to have known the identity of Pitt?' Tremaine asked, reverting to the point that Rogers had made. 'That's surely got to be the main starting point?'

'The problem with that is that we simply can't know,' Simon said. 'We can't be sure who Sylvia might have confided in. Yes, her boyfriend, whoever he was, is the most likely person, but whoever it was wasn't going to admit to us that he, or she, knew about the stalker's name, not if they were planning to use him as a scapegoat for his own crimes. Almost everyone we have spoken to knew that we were trying to find out who the stalker was, so they knew of our suspicions about him. We're going to have to go through our reports again.'

'Sir?' DC Jones spoke up, and unlike the others, as always she waited for Simon's attention.

'Yes, Rhiannon?'

'I've been following up on the people who died who were in Sylvia Gaston's care.'

'With the idea that Sylvia's death might be a revenge killing by a spouse or partner of one of the people who died in her care,' Simon explained for those who had not been there when Rhiannon had first mentioned her idea. 'Go on, what have you found?'

'There were six deaths in the last nine months, all from post-operative infections, though Mrs Swan's death in February came later on after Sylvia Gaston's care, some very nasty complications apparently caused by poisoning of the abdominal cavity. I've spoken to all of the partners except for the Reverend Swan.'

'Oh? Why did you leave him out?' Simon asked.

'Well,' her colour heightened, 'partly because he's a vicar,' she began and was interrupted by the odd howl of derision.

'You haven't been reading the newspapers lately, Rhiannon,' DI Stone said, a note of derision in her voice. 'There seem to be proportionately as many sinners among the clergy, or priesthood as in their congregations.'

'Yes, ma'am,' Rhiannon said, getting redder but keeping her voice calm, 'but the main reason, I was going to say, was that Detective Chief Inspector Simon has already had an amount of contact with the Reverend Swan and I thought he might prefer to speak to him himself.'

'That's all right, Rhiannon,' Simon agreed. 'But how did you get on with the other people you spoke to? Any angry partners wanting Sylvia Gaston's scalp?'

'Well, they *were* all men, sir, but none of them had a bad word to say about her.'

'They hardly would, would they, if they were the guilty one?' Tremaine said.

'That's part of the trouble,' Rhiannon agreed. 'But most were late middle-aged to old and not very agile. One even confessed that he was rather enjoying the single life.'

More laughter followed this.

'Was there anyone, then, you thought it worth following up?' Simon asked.

'Perhaps one or two,' Rhiannon said doubtfully.

Simon hated to undermine her further by questioning the validity of her theory in the face of recent evidence, but he had no choice. 'But how would any of this fit with the idea that the killer knew who Pitt was?'

Rhiannon defended herself. 'Well it all depends on who Sylvia told, doesn't it?'

'Sylvia's friends did remark that she was very concerned about some issue to do with her work,' Simon said. 'By the way, how did you get the information about ex-patients? I thought Mrs Jones was being very strict about medical records.'

'I was a bit dishonest,' Rhiannon admitted. 'I suggested that the agency had made a serious error of judgement in giving out Mrs Gaston's number to the stalker when she was staying with a patient.'

'But we thought he got the number from Ian, her son,' Simon said.

'Yes I know.' Rhiannon pulled an apologetic face. 'But it got her to open up a bit when I pointed out that it had showed the agency wasn't as security-conscious as it should be. I think Mrs Jones thought that it was that dozy receptionist's fault.'

'Pity if it means the girl loses her job,' DI Stone remarked.

'Not really ma'am,' Rhiannon said coolly. 'She's more of a liability than a help in that place.'

'You have depths I had not suspected,' Rebecca Stone said.

'There's something else about all this, sir,' Rhiannon said, bypassing DI Stone. 'All the women who died were gynaecology patients. And all of them were operated on by Dr Milliner, Sylvia Gaston's ex-husband.'

Simon had a sudden and colourful vision of Hermione, red nails clasped around her wine glass: 'There are mutterings about Milliner,' she had announced.

'Was Sylvia stirring up trouble for her ex?' he asked, his interest quickening for the first time.

'That's what I was wondering, sir,' Rhiannon said, unable to resist a faintly triumphant glance at Rebecca. 'I was going to have a look at her computer and see if she had kept any kind of file on him.'

'I thought it had been checked for anything of interest and nothing worth noting had been reported.' Simon looked round for confirmation.

DI Stone said, 'She had a large number of files on medical issues that she had downloaded from the Net. We didn't think they were a priority.'

'I think we should take a look at them,' Simon said to Rhiannon. 'It's definitely worth following up.' If Sylvia Gaston had been building some kind of case against Milliner for medical neglect or incompetence, it gave him a clear motive for getting rid of her. Whistle-blowing was not readily undertaken in the medical profession, but Milliner would have been aware that her personal hostility would override any qualms about solidarity. And if whispers had got about already, enough for Hermione to have got wind of them, he might have been very worried indeed, especially if his wife had threatened him with carefully documented evidence.

Leaving DI Stone to rationalize the other aspects of the investigation, not forgetting a properly investigated alibi for Charles Framley, Simon took Sergeant Longman, who was comfortable around computers, along with himself and Rhiannon Jones.

219

Empty houses always had an air of melancholy, Simon thought as he opened the front door of Sylvia Gaston's house, but his knowledge of what had happened since anyone had last lived here intensified the atmosphere a hundredfold. Outside the grass had grown long and leaves littered the lawn, adding to the sense of abandonment. He wondered what Ian Milliner would do when he returned home and whether he would find it possible to live with his father's new family. He might not even have that choice if what they were here for should end in implicating his father in the murder of his mother and sister.

A coloured postcard lay on the mat inside the door, along with a pile of junk mail. The mail was collected every other day and taken to headquarters. The card was from Ian and showed a low white hotel by a turquoise sea on South Island, New Zealand:

Dear Mum, I've been working here at this hotel now for a month and plan on staying a month more at least. I love it here. They let me use their email address and I sent you an email about a week ago. Why no reply from you? I'll try again next week if I don't hear from you. Hope everything's OK with you and Kate? I'm having a great time, love, Ian.

So, after all their efforts to locate the young man, he'd finally made it simple for them.

Longman was already booting up the computer in the former dining room, Rhiannon at his side.

'Check the email,' Simon said, putting the postcard on the desk so that they could read it.

The promised email from Ian had arrived. It was the only email there.

'Tremaine said there was nothing here when he checked,' Rhiannon said. 'Does that mean Ian's previous one had been wiped?'

'Along with any other emails that were here,' Simon said. He studied the postmark. 'This was sent a week ago, so Ian would have first emailed around the time his mother and sister were killed.'

'So the killer got in here and cleaned up her mail because it might have contained references to him?' Longman examined the postcard again.

'That's what it looks like,' Simon said. 'Which means that she must have been communicating with someone at least that she confided in.'

'Well they haven't told us that,' Rhiannon said. 'Why haven't they been in touch with us?'

Longman shrugged. 'It could have been the killer himself she was emailing.' He checked the address book on the screen. It was blank.

'See what you can find in the files,' Simon suggested.

They watched as Longman scrolled through the very large number of files in Sylvia's documents section. It would take a while to check each one individually and all appeared to have medical titles.

'Think of what she might call the file,' Longman said. 'A lot of them have got "report" in the title, so it's not a lot of help using that as a search word. Any suggestions?'

'Gynaecology?' Rhiannon suggested. This turned up quite a few files, none of which were relevant.

'Try "Milliner",' Simon said. But that yielded nothing.

'Infectious or infection?' Rhiannon said, followed by a number of other possibilities, all of which got them nowhere.

Simon, never happy around computers, was beginning to feel his usual irritation with this one as well. 'We need to think more laterally,' he suggested. They all paused to think.

Longman keyed in 'incompetence'. Again nothing.

'What about "Nemesis"? Rhiannon said.

Nothing. Longman folded his arms and leaned back. 'This could take a while.'

'Try "Medical Nemesis",' Rhiannon said, undeterred.

And the report appeared, to Rhiannon's and their delight. She looked up at Simon, unconscious as usual of her habit of appeal to him.

'Well done,' he said.

They all peered to read the document. It was formally addressed to the Medical Complaints Authority, with copies to the local relevant body. As Longman slowly scrolled through it was obvious that Sylvia had relied not only on her own client cases but had obtained evidence from colleagues at the agency she worked for: there were several other deaths linked to operations performed by Milliner.

'She hadn't mentioned any of this to Thelma Jones?' Simon asked Rhiannon.

'Mrs Jones certainly didn't say so. I don't think Mrs Gaston would have said anything, though. She probably thought Mrs Jones would think it was bad for the agency in some way.'

Longman printed off some copies and handed one to each of them.

Simon remarked, 'She's even done a comparative study of operations and post-operative care of patients operated on by other gynaecologists. It shows the statistics are significantly different. Not all of Milliner's who died were affected by infections. There were other mistakes.'

'I wondered about that,' Rhiannon said. 'I mean, there are so many cases of deaths from infections in hospital with this super bug about you wonder if the problem in this case can be traced to Milliner himself. But they obviously can, according to what Mrs Gaston discovered.'

'I remember reading once,' Longman added, 'that hospitals are the third most likely place you'll die from an accident – after mines and high-rise construction.'

'In this country,' Simon remarked dryly, 'hospitals have probably moved up to second place.'

'We'd better go and get Milliner in as soon as possible,' Simon said. 'Who was supposed to be checking out his alibi for that weekend?'

'DC Rogers I think,' Rhiannon said.

'Let's hope he's still back at HQ and not gone haring off to London.' Simon locked up behind them, handing Ian Milliner's postcard to Rhiannon.

It took a little while but Milliner was finally brought to Simon and Longman's presence. He had with him his solicitor, Jonathan Redman, a portly man with slickly greased-back hair. Milliner, with his usual air of a man who had to be about much more important business, sat down fussily and faced Simon.

'What on earth is all this about, Detective Chief Inspector? I have spoken to you once already and told you where I was on the weekend that my daughter and ex-wife were murdered. And, as if it is not enough that you should have suspicions that a grieving father has in some way done harm to his daughter, you are piling on the agony by forcing me to come in once more and face your ridiculous accusations.'

As Milliner drew breath Simon said mildly, 'Nobody forced you to come in, Dr Milliner, and by bringing your solicitor you have assumed that the purpose of this interview may be in some way inimical to you.'

'When it comes to the police, one is wise to assume any eventuality,' Milliner replied pompously.

He certainly was not showing any indication of guilt or awareness that he had anything to hide, Simon thought. And irritability seemed be a part of his personality.

'What is it you want with Dr Milliner?' Jonathan Redman asked smoothly.

Unfortunately Rogers was nowhere to be found and was apparently not responding to his mobile phone. Rhiannon had text messaged him and Simon was hoping to receive some message from him before this interview had to be terminated. Milliner had not, in their first meeting, given much precise information about his conference in London and Tremaine would have had to have thrown a fairly wide net to come up with anyone who could confirm Milliner's presence for the period of time they were interested in. Simon decided that he had no option but to be upfront with Milliner. Without some explanation for his interest in him, Milliner and his plump solicitor would probably start talking about police harrassment.

'Dr Milliner,' he began, 'how much do you know about the complaint against you that your ex-wife, Mrs Sylvia Gaston, was proceeding with?'

Milliner blinked. 'Was she?'

'You can't be unaware that she had grounds. Can you Dr Milliner?'

Milliner glanced at Redman whose expression was impassive.

'Well, I . . . .' He looked down at his white perfectly manicured hands clasped on the table in front of him.

'Would you respond to the question, please, Dr Milliner,' Simon said firmly. He was puzzled by Milliner's reaction. He would have expected him to have blustered and protested immediately that there was no substance in his wife's piece of research into his medical competence.

'I can't believe that she would have done it,' Milliner said, his pomposity deflated. 'It was several weeks ago, before she disappeared. Why had she left it so long? And why haven't you mentioned it before?'

Simon was stalled. They were talking at cross-purposes, obviously, but it might be best if Milliner remained unaware of the fact.

'Why would you have imagined she would not have reported it?' he asked.

'She never did before. Because of the children.' Milliner's voice was indistinct as he lowered his head.

He had attacked her again, Simon realized. He must be unaware of Sylvia's real efforts to sabotage his career.

'Perhaps you wouldn't mind keeping your head up so that we can hear you more clearly, Dr Milliner,' he said. 'And would you give your version of what happened at the time?'

Milliner cleared his throat. 'It was over Ian. She wanted me to stay away from him. But I'm his father and I have a right to have a relationship with my son. She'd found out that Ian had been to see me.' He gave a thin smile. 'I realized of course that Ian was planning to get some money from me for his backpacking trip, that that was his real interest in contacting me. But I didn't mind. I thought we could build on it, develop a proper father and son relationship. He'll be needing extra funds anyway for university and I shall be in a better position to help him than my ex-wife was.'

'So she said to you that she wanted you to keep away from Ian and you beat her?' Simon's carefully neutral tone made it sound worse.

Milliner's pale face flushed. 'It didn't happen quite like that,' he said stiffly. 'She said a lot of very personal things, too. She could have a cruel tongue.'

'What was it she said that made you hit her, Dr Milliner?' Longman asked, placing an emphasis on Milliner's title.

'I can't remember! A lot of things were said, things from the past came up, she mocked me, she was poisoning my children against me.'

'Perhaps she felt you were not the best of role models,' Longman suggested, 'particularly for her son. Being a wife batterer and so on?'

Milliner clenched his fists.

Simon wanted to ask exactly when this row between Milliner and his wife had occurred, but was aware that it would reveal the fact that no official complaint had actually been made. He had to introduce the subject of the real complaint that Sylvia had had in train.

'During this, ah, altercation with your wife, did she perhaps mention that she was compiling a complaint against you for medical malpractice, Dr Milliner?' he asked.

Both Milliner's and Redman's heads jerked up at this.

'What did you say?' If Milliner was acting, he was very convincing.

Simon repeated his words.

'That's preposterous! Stupid, silly little woman! What does she know? So that's the way she thought she'd try and get back at me, did she? Who'd listen to the opinion of some stupid little private nurse!'

Simon could swear that Milliner had known nothing of what his wife had been up to. 'Her research was very professional and thorough,' he said, hating Milliner's arrogance.

'And you'd be some judge of that, would you? A plodding policeman!' Milliner jeered.

Redman nudged Milliner in an effort to restrain his outburst. Milliner angrily brushed him away.

If Milliner had not been aware of the revenge that Sylvia had devised to try to ruin him, where was any motive for him killing her? Unless it lay in what Milliner had first believed he was here to account for: their violent disagreement over their son. Had Milliner disposed of his wife to rid himself of the person who stood in the way of that relationship? A man's relationship with his son could have atavistic depths of pride, genetics, ambition and so on, particularly for a control freak like Milliner.

'What is your son going to be studying at university next year?' he asked Milliner.

'It was supposed to be medicine. But now he's going for bioengineering. Her fault of course, suggesting he might be more suited to pure research.' Even talking about it Milliner was stiff with rage.

'Perhaps she thought *he* wouldn't be so good on the people side of the business either,' Longman suggested.

'What would you know?' Milliner retorted contemptuously.

'As a consumer, as they now term it, I can tell a good doctor from a bad one,' Longman said smiling easily. 'One quality in a good doctor is a genuine interest in his or her patients, and their welfare of course.'

Milliner ignored him, saying to Simon, 'Ian would have made a very fine doctor.'

'There's always the possibility he'll change his mind,' Simon replied, believing that under his father's control Ian might well do that, particularly with financial inducements. 'But, to get back to the purpose of the interview, Dr Milliner, I am sure you can understand that, taking into account your violent interaction with your ex-wife, her report against you, and your strong disagreement over your son, you have motive for wishing your wife's death. We need a convincing alibi from you in the circumstances.'

Milliner gave an odd jerk of the head. 'I've already given you a statement about the conference in London that weekend. All weekend,' he said firmly, as if that were enough explanation and evidence combined.

'Yes, and you gave us a few names of colleagues. But we want more detail, for example of what talks you attended, the people who were near you or with you at the time and so on.'

'But I went to various seminars and speeches.' Milliner spoke as if to someone mentally challenged. 'We all have our particular specialist interests, different seminars and talks and so on. I can't remember all the people who were there at the time.'

'Then you had better make a very thorough statement of exactly what you did and the persons who can vouch for you doing them,' Simon said, imitating Milliner's manner. 'I shall want information on how you spent the Saturday evening and night, if you went out anywhere and who with and so on. I'd also like you to give us an account of where you were from last Saturday evening until Sunday.' He stood up. 'I'll leave you with Sergeant Longman to make sure you know how to do it.'

'What has last Saturday got to do with anything?' Milliner asked in a wearied voice.

'We don't have to tell you that,' Longman said with some satisfaction.

The rotund Mr Redman gave a small cough. 'I think that's not quite true, Sergeant. My client has a right to know what he is accused of. Last Saturday night is not relevant to the fate of his ex-wife and daughter more than two weeks ago.'

'Are you suggesting that I killed my only daughter?' Milliner broke in. Redman gave him a pained look. 'How could you believe that? Are you intending to arrrest me? Because if you are not then I don't think I have to provide you with any statement.'

Redman sighed and rubbed his face with his hands.

'We can arrest you, if you prefer,' Simon said. 'If that's what it takes to encourage you to comply with a simple request. You can surely see that we are trying to eliminate people from our inquiries in order to arrive at the person who is guilty in all this. You may see that, if you refuse to cooperate, it will not help us uncover the truth and certain questions may arise over your deliberate unhelpfulness.'

Milliner opened his mouth to protest, then gave a curt nod.

'Perhaps we might have some tea sent in?' Redman asked smoothly.

Simon went back to his office, he put his feet on the desk, leaned back and closed his eyes. If extreme egotism were a pointer to the criminal mind then he had surely got his man in James Milliner. And, if he were going to arrest someone for these crimes then he would be happy that, out of all the people he had interviewed, it should be he. Except when he thought of Ian Milliner, now being contacted by the New Zealand police and probably due home some time tomorrow. However obnoxious the boy's father was, he was all he had left.

But Simon had none of the sense of conviction that usually was there when he had solved a crime. Milliner fitted the statistics all right: most victims of murder being killed by a member, or ex-member of their own family. He could well have waited for Sylvia when she came home after a night out, attacked her and killed her. His motive for killing his daughter could only be that she knew or guessed what he had done. And that was the hazy part of his case that bothered him. Had Kate gone looking for her father on that Sunday afternoon when she found her mother was not at home? Did she know about the row that had become physical between her father and mother, and was it he she had gone looking for when she couldn't find her mother? If Kate had feared her father, which she was likely to do given his past behaviour, it would explain why she had asked Goodenough to go with her that afternoon.

Milliner's motive was real enough: if Sylvia had decided to report his recent assault on her it might well affect his career quite seriously. But Simon could have sworn that Milliner hadn't known about the report she had compiled, so that couldn't be Milliner's motive, unless Sylvia had made threats of producing something like it in the future. And the killer had removed Sylvia's emails. If Milliner had known about the report he would surely have found it and removed it from her files.

But where did Pitt's death fit into this? Milliner might be the type who enjoyed hitting women, but that type usually stayed well away from any physical confrontation with men. They were cowards by definition. Simon couldn't imagine him loitering outside Pitt's house, or inveigling him to meet him outside, noose in hand. And would Milliner be likely to know about the stalker? It was not something that Sylvia was likely to confide in her despised ex-husband.

Unless Ian had told his father. It was likely that Ian was fully aware of Pitt and his unwelcome attentions. Sylvia would have had to speak to him if he had been the one to pass on her location at the Kyland's to Pitt and he would surely anyway have been aware of the trouble his mother was experiencing. Ian might have mentioned this to his father, but would he have passed on Pitt's identity?

At this stage it was all speculation. Simon got up and went to the window, looking out at the lit-up cathedral, a sight that always soothed. He decided to go home to Jessie's.

Chapter 26

'Pitt received a telephone call at half past eleven last Saturday night,' Longman said as Simon arrived next morning. 'It was from a public call box in the centre of town, so it's no help to us.'

'Except that it tends to confirm our idea that someone probably enticed Pitt outside that night after calling him with some offer he couldn't ignore.'

'S'pose so.' Longman looked glum.

'You look tired, Geoff.'

'That statement took a while with Milliner protesting all the way,' Longman complained. 'I'm glad I'm not a woman. I'd hate to fall into his hands, especially with such a sensitive portion of my anatomy.'

'Me too,' Simon agreed and Longman gave a quick laugh. Simon thought of Hermione and her trials, and how pleased she would be that her prime suspect was being more thoroughly investigated.

'But if his statement is correct, there's no way he could have been here that weekend,' Longman said. 'He's got enough witnesses, he claims, that he was there for a late dinner on the Saturday night of the weekend the two were killed. And on the Sunday he says he didn't leave until late afternoon. I suppose it's possible he could have managed it, but it doesn't seem likely.'

'What did he say about last Saturday night, when Pitt died?'

'Says he went out to dinner with his wife at a friend's house and got home around quarter past midnight.'

'According to the time Valerie Pitt says her husband had his last meal, he must have died around half past twelve. So he could have made the call around midnight and gone to Pitt's after that.'

'Not if what he says is true. His friends live in Minborough, which is a village five miles from his house on the north of Westwich. He wouldn't have had to go through the centre of town to get home.'

'So, effectively, his wife is his alibi, so not a particularly strong one. Milliner being what he is, she's hardly likely to contradict him,' Simon pointed out.

'I suppose so,' Longman said unenthusiatically.

'You don't sound too keen on Milliner being our man.'

Longman gave a sharp laugh. 'I'd love it to be, pompous ass. But I just don't like the feel of it somehow. It's going to depend on how his alibis check out but can you really see Milliner going out to garrotte Pitt in the dark? It's just not his style. I can believe he might have killed the women, but not a man.'

'I had the same thought,' Simon agreed.

'Sir?' DI Rebecca Stone entered the room, looking slightly less in control than usual. 'I'm so sorry I'm late. There was a pile-up on the road into town. It held up the traffic for over half an hour.'

DI Stone seemed more concerned with her reputation for timekeeping than the fate of the victims of the crash.

'Anyone hurt?' Simon asked.

'Hmm?' she asked, tidying a loose strand of hair into her tortoiseshell comb.

'In the crash?'

'Oh! I don't think so. I used the time going through the reports.'

Which reminded Simon that he had failed to update Detective Superintendent Munro. He gave Stone an account of the events of the previous evening and Milliner's statement.

She said, turning a sympathetic look on him. 'I had a verbal report from DC Savage last night. He seems to think that Milliner is covered for the relevant time. He has spoken to colleagues from the conference enough, he thinks, to uphold any alibi Milliner claims.'

'I don't suppose he used a hitman?' Longman suggested.

'I don't either,' Simon said.

'It does happen, sir,' DI Stone said reasonably.

'Check his bank accounts then,' Simon said, irritated.

'Do you mean that?' she asked.

'If you like,' he said grudgingly. 'It happens. And he's the type who might do it. But if he did use a hitman, why would Kate be killed? The only motive for her death, surely, is that she knew, or suspected, who had killed her mother.'

'If she only suspected something had happened to her mother, and thought her father was responsible, she could have gone looking for him

229

and he could have killed her while the hitman killed Sylvia.' Longman sat back and folded his arms over his expanding stomach.

'Except that he wasn't there for her to find,' Simon said dryly.

'True.' Longman's shaggy eyebrows lowered. 'Then he could have sent the hitman after Kate.'

'Anything from forensics or pathology?' Simon asked Stone.

'Pitt's prints found on the can of red spray paint. But as we know that's easy enough for the killer to fix. And the results of the tissue match. It confirms that Pitt was not the killer.'

'So we're no further forward with anything.' Simon finally sat down.

'Eliminating suspects is some progress, sir,' DI Stone said encouragingly. 'Ian Milliner will be arriving at Heathrow tomorrow evening by the way. He might know something of use.'

'We're going to have to give the poor lad some time to recover from the bad news first,' Longman said. 'Quite apart from getting over the journey.'

'What about Framley's alibi?' Simon asked. 'Has his wife supported his statement he was with her for the whole of the relevant weekend?'

'I wonder just how valuable such an alibi can be with a woman who is so obviously ill,' Longman said. 'She must have to rest a lot, surely? And it would be easy enough to slip a sleeping tablet in her cocoa.'

'Actually, we haven't been able to speak to her to confirm or deny her husband's account of that weekend,' DI Stone said. 'Every time we try to get hold of her her husband answers the phone and says she's not well enough to talk to anyone.'

A police officer's life was a surreal one in some respects, Simon reflected. It was a bit like trying to live in several parallel universes all at the same time – the reality of what you were able to observe, and the accounts of the truth that were supplied to you by people involved in the investigation, accounts which might vary greatly. And all the time you were trying to reach an objective truth which explained and took into account the varying perception of truth or deliberate lies of those people, untangling them into a recognizable picture of reality.

'I suppose we'll have to go out there and see Mrs Framley,' he said. 'Though her husband may be telling the truth. I'll try her later.'

'So where are we at now, sir?' DI Stone said. 'Is Milliner off our list?'

'I suppose that depends to some extent how reliable his wife seems. You'd better tie up the ends, I suppose. Take Detective Sergeant Longman with you.'

'Bit of a waste of time if you ask me,' Longman grumbled, rising from his seat.

'And after that you can follow up on Milliner's accounts. See if any large sums of money have been taken out lately.' Simon turned to the computer and began to organize his report for Detective Superintendent Munro. He hoped it might clarify his mind a little, the strands of the investigation all seeming at the moment to be thinning to an infinity of nothing in particular.

He took his time over it and was no clearer in his mind, except to see that Framley was the person with probably the weakest alibi when DC Grayson called over that Jean Framley was on the line for him.

'Detective Chief Inspector Simon?' She sounded hesitant.

Simon injected some warmth into his voice. 'Thank you very much for calling, Mrs Framley.'

'I understand you wanted to speak to me.'

'Yes. We're just trying to clear up a few points and you should be able to help.'

'I'm sorry I haven't been able to speak to you sooner. Charles has stopped me. It's about Charles, isn't it? You want to know where he was when Sylvia disappeared.' Her voice was very faint. Simon wondered if she were trying to conceal this call from her husband somewhere in the house, and felt some concern. She was too frail to withstand too many angry onslaughts.

'Is your husband there?' he asked her.

'No, he's gone out for a while. He told me not to speak to you, but it's silly. He doesn't realize I know, you see.'

Simon's heart seemed to skip a beat. 'Know what, Mrs Framley?'

'About his affair. He was with *her* that weekend and he thinks I don't know about it. So he thought if he admitted to you where he was that it would get back to me and I would find out about it.' She gave a soft laugh. 'I've known about it for ages.'

Simon was about to protest that she should have told him before this, but realized that in her situation that was not so easily done. 'So he was with Sylvia Gaston the weekend she disappeared?' A hundred thoughts flowed in quick motion through his head. Was Jean Framley aware of what she was admitting to as far as her husband was concerned?

'No!' her voice caught raggedly. 'He has a woman, not Sylvia. Someone he's been seeing for a couple of years. He must think I'm as feeble in my mind as I am in my body. She's the one you need to speak to if you still think he needs an alibi.'

'Do you know her name, her address?'

'I know them because she used to be a friend of mine. Her name is Gillian Harris and she lives at 119 Beecham Road. I was hoping you wouldn't feel the need to follow this up because I don't want them to know I know. It's a little fiction between us, you see, that Charles is the devoted husband of a sickly wife. It's better kept that way. If he knew I knew all about her he might decide to leave me and I would prefer to keep things as they are.' Her voice was unsteady. 'You probably think it's very selfish of me.'

'No,' Simon hastened to reassure her. He couldn't imagine being in this woman's situation. 'No, I don't think that at all,' he said firmly. 'I think you have a lot of courage, Mrs Framley.'

He heard a faint derisory laugh. 'Quite the contrary, Chief Inspector. So, will you need to speak to Charles or can this be left as it is? You surely don't regard him as any serious suspect in the case?'

If what she had said was true there could be no need to follow up any further on Charles Framley. He couldn't believe that she was lying, she had seemed too proud a woman to stoop to deceit in this particular form. It wasn't any cast-iron proof of Framley's innocence as far as the killings were concerned because Jean Framley couldn't be certain that her husband was with the mistress she knew about that weekend. But it was indicative enough. 'I can't foresee any reason to take any of this any further at the moment, Mrs Framley. And in the unlikely event of things changing I would speak to you first.'

She gave a little sigh. 'Thank you, Chief Inspector.' The line went dead.

Simon sighed too as he replaced the phone. He got up and wandered off to his office, disinclined in the circumstances to attempt any verbal update with Detective Superintendent Munro, despite the reminder to do so that had been left on his desk. He leaned back, his arms linked behind his head, working his way back through the investigation, trying to find a point of significance he must have missed.

Much later in the day he was back in the incident room updating himself on the sparse information that was coming in, none of it of any seeming relevance.

'Sir?' Rhiannon Jones put her head around the door. 'Vanessa Peel is here to see you.'

'Show her in,' he said.

The period of warm autumn sunshine had brought Vanessa out in a loose flowery dress. She appeared more confident than before, walking straight into the room and seating herself in front of Simon without waiting to be invited to do so. Simon wondered if her earlier uncertainty had owed a lot to the shock of Kate's death and, of course, in their previous meeting, the presence of her dominant mother. Perhaps now she was here he could press her a little more closely than the others had managed to do about what had happened when she had followed Kate that Sunday.

'I've had a postcard from Ian,' she announced, taking a large colour postcard from her capacious bag. 'He's got a job in New Zealand for a while so you should be able to contact him there.'

'Excellent,' he said warmly, not wanting to deflate her by saying he already knew where Ian was. He picked up the card and read through it. It said little more than the other card had said, barring the email address.

He passed the card to Rhiannon who was waiting by the door. 'Deal with that then, right away, will you, DC Jones?' he said.

Rhiannon, her expression puzzled, took the card. As she went through the door her face cleared and she cast him a nod of under-standing.

'We should have Ian back here very soon now,' he said, keeping his expression pleased. 'Though I wish that we could have had the case cleared up before he came home. It's going to be very hard for him either way.'

Vanessa's head drooped in agreement.

'Have you had any thoughts since I last spoke to you, about the case? About what may have happened that weekend, Vanessa? The weekend they disappeared?'

'Have you checked on Dr Milliner?' she said uncomfortably.

'We've checked on just about everyone.'

'Oh.' She made a slight move, as if to leave.

'Vanessa, you were obviously a close and loyal friend to Kate and to her mother. There may be some things you felt you didn't want to tell us because of that loyalty. But now that they've gone you have to think about who's left behind. Surely you can see that you owe it to Ian to do everything you can to help us catch whoever is responsible for what happened? You're fond of him, a friend, aren't you?'

'Course I am,' she said gruffly. She looked up. 'I don't know what you

233

mean,' she said. 'I don't know anything that can help you.'

'You may not think you do,' he said gently. 'But there may be something that was said that doesn't mean anything to you but it might mean something to us, in the context of what we know so far.'

She raised her head and looked towards the window as if seeking escape.

'When my colleagues spoke to you last time,' he continued, 'you told them about when you followed Kate to her mother's house after church, didn't you?'

She gave a slight nod, still not looking his way.

'But you indicated that certain things were said that you didn't want to talk about, that they were private. I need to know exactly what was said, Vanessa.'

He watched the colour creep up her cheeks and wondered what could have been so controversial, so shaming, that this young woman found it so difficult to talk about. 'Is it embarrassing to you, Vanessa?' he asked.

'No!' She turned back to him, frowning. 'It's no big deal. I was upset about it that's all, because of the row Kate and I had. That's why I didn't want to talk to you about it in the first place. And I thought that if I told you I'd had a row with Kate you might suspect me or something.'

It had never occurred to him.

'So, really,' he said slowly, 'you'd have no objection telling me all about it now?'

'I s'pose so,' she shrugged. 'But I can't see how any of it can help you. It's a bit of a fuss about nothing.'

'So you talked to Kate outside church on the Sunday morning and had a bit of a disagreement. What was that about?' Simon asked.

'She stood me up the night before and I was angry about it.'

Simon frowned. 'But she was out collecting charity envelopes, wasn't she, until quite late?'

'Yes, but there was an Irish Folk group on at the Wheatsheaf in the East Gate starting at half past nine and we were supposed to meet there. I hung about outside until quarter to ten but I didn't want to go inside on my own. Anyway, she didn't turn up and I felt a bit conspicuous waiting there so I went on home.'

Simon recalled Adrian Swan saying that Kate had returned to the vicarage at around half past nine, so Kate should have been in plenty of time to catch up with Vanessa: the Wheatsheaf was about a ten-minute walk away.

'Did Kate say why she didn't turn up?' he asked.

'She said she felt tired and decided to go home. But I didn't believe her. She knew I really wanted to see that particular group and I guessed that she'd found something different to do. Found someone else to go out with.'

The resentment Vanessa had felt was imprinted on her face. Simon could imagine that the awkward young woman sitting in front of him would have been deeply hurt by the neglect, especially if she had few friends on whom to call to go for a night out in Westwich. Her more attractive friend would have rubbed salt in the wound by demonstrating she had a choice of company, and preferred that to Vanessa's.

'She told the Reverend Swan that she was going home to catch up on some school work,' Simon said, remembering. 'Are you sure she was with someone else?'

Vanessa tossed her head. 'She wouldn't admit it at first, but I could always tell when Kate was lying.' Her lips twisted. 'She wasn't very good at it. Besides, I called her flat on my mobile at quarter to ten when I left, and again at half past ten after I got home.' Vanessa squirmed on her seat, making it creak. It was obvious she was very uncomfortable with giving this account.

'Who was it she was with?' Simon asked sympathetically.

'I said I supposed she'd gone off with Rupert Colville, her friend from school. She denied it, but there was something in the way she said it. I knew she'd gone out with someone. She looked really uncomfortable, and it was more than just having let me down. It struck me that she'd been seeing someone that she knew she shouldn't have and I said so, but she just got obstinate and walked away.

'Then I said what I really shouldn't have said. I accused her of being like her mother. Something along the lines of keeping secrets for the same reason.' Vanessa's eyes filled and she started scrabbling in a side pocket of her dress for a handkerchief. Simon passed her a tissue from the box on his desk.

'It was a terrible thing to say,' she sniffed into the tissue. 'And it's even worse now that she's dead.'

'How did she respond, Vanessa?'

She blew her nose and cleared her throat. 'She gave me a really angry look and went off without speaking to me. I was supposed to give her a lift back to her flat, but I didn't go after her. I was upset, too. I was upset she'd let me down and I was really sorry soon after for upsetting her.'

'So she didn't deny what you'd accused her of?'

'No, but that wasn't the point. I'd insulted her mother as well, and it was like I was breaking any confidence between us. I'd used the little she'd confided in me to throw back in her face.'

Her guilt at her sense of betrayal of Kate was plain. Simon could understand why, despite Kate's treatment of her, Vanessa had felt the need to follow her and try to make peace between them. Kate had been the dominant one in this particular friendship and it would always have been Vanessa who would have sought to heal any breaches in the relationship.

'And when you caught up with Kate at her mother's house later?'

Vanessa's memory of the event still had the power to make her colour rise again. 'She wasn't very friendly, but she let me into the hall. I apologized to her and told her I hadn't meant to hurt her, it was just that I'd felt hurt myself.' She swallowed, dabbing at her nose with the tissue again.

'Did she accept your apology?'

'Actually, she didn't seem too bothered. She was thinking about her mother by then and why she wasn't home as she'd promised. Actually, she seemed more angry than anything about it. I asked her what she was going to do and if she wanted me to give her a lift back to her flat, or come back to our house and have a meal with me and my mother. But she refused and said she was going to find her mother.'

'Did she say where she thought her mother was?' Simon's interest quickened. If Vanessa had not been so fastidious about some schoolgirlish quarrel with her friend, the case might have taken a different turn much earlier.

'I asked her that. She didn't tell me though. She said she had a pretty good idea, something about something she'd seen the night before that made her realize where her mother must have been. But she went quiet after that because she didn't trust me any more I expect. But she said something about not understanding why she hadn't come home.'

'Could you try and remember the exact words she used, Vanessa. It might be very important.'

Perhaps he shouldn't have added that last sentence: Vanessa's expression became paralysed with uncertainty. 'Just take your time,' he urged quietly, 'try and think yourself back to the situation.'

The uncertainty turned to agony. 'I can't,' she pleaded. 'I can't remember any more than that. I can't remember exactly what she said, just the gist of it.'

'Don't worry,' he said. 'It's more likely to come back to you if you don't try too hard. What happened next?'

Vanessa looked relieved. 'I remember that I didn't like to ask her any more about it, about where her mother might be, because of what I'd said to her earlier. I didn't want to say the wrong thing, and I didn't want to seem curious in case she got angry with me again.'

'And then?'

She gave a small shrug. 'She said I'd better go because she would be going out. So I went. Kate was picking up the phone as I let myself out through the front door.'

Probably to phone Bob Goodenough, Simon thought. If Kate *had* stood Vanessa up the night before in favour of someone else, he was probably the person she had been with. And if so, he had failed to speak of it when he was being interviewed. Not suspicious in itself, of course, Goodenough had been more concerned that his wife shoud not find out about Kate than concerned that Kate's killer should be caught.

Vanessa was clutching her bag tightly to her chest and glancing towards the door. 'I'll let you know if I do remember anything else,' she assured him.

He let her go. The poor girl had suffered enough domineering treatment in her life without a lecture from him on how her reticence may have affected the case.

He checked his watch. Goodenough should be home from work by now, but he tried the school first and got one of the cleaning women who told him they'd 'all cleared off'. He grabbed his jacket, deciding he couldn't care less at this stage if he caused Goodenough embarrassment by going to his house.

The Goodenough home was in a terraced row on the southern edge of the city. The man himself answered the front door, still dressed in his work outfit, though some recent stains on his tie indicated current efforts at feeding an infant. His face was a picture of dismay at seeing who was on his doorstep. Simon could hear the sound of young children's voices chattering in the background. Goodenough pulled the door to behind him. 'Can we talk in your car?' he asked in a low voice, calling over his shoulder to his wife somewhere in the background, 'Just something to do with school, love. Won't be long.'

Simon decided to go along with it. Making Goodenough more hostile wouldn't help.

'What do you want?' he asked almost before he had settled into the passenger seat. 'I've told you everything I can,' he added intensely, glancing back at his front door.

'You didn't tell me about your night out with Kate on the night before she died.'

'Who told you that?' Goodenough asked fiercely, glancing quickly at Simon's face.

'That's irrelevant. Where did you go?'

Goodenough was quick. 'If you don't know that, how do you know if I was out with Kate?'

Simon was not inclined at this moment to bandy words. 'I'm the one asking the questions. Answer them,' he said sharply.

The young man looked sulky. 'It wasn't for long anyway. I waited for her outside the vicarage, picked her up and we went to a pub for a drink. We were only out for an hour, I had to get back,' he said grudgingly, 'with my parents being here. I dropped Kate off on my way back.'

'What pub did you go to?'

'The Oarsman down by the river.' Goodenough was keeping his eye on his house, obviously in fear of his wife appearing.

'You evidently want to get back into the house as soon as possible,' Simon said, 'in order to avoid more awkward questions than those I have to ask. So I suggest you answer me as fully and accurately as you can, or I may need to take you in to headquarters for a fuller interview.'

Goodenough cast him a look of dislike. 'Go ahead, but there's nothing to tell.'

'Did Kate see anyone she knew when you were out with her?' Simon asked.

He gave a quick frown. 'Not that I'm aware of.'

'Did Kate mention her mother that night?'

The frown deepened. 'Why would she? We had other things to talk about.'

'Did she say anything about what she'd been doing earlier? She had been collecting charity envelopes, but did she make any remarks about anything that had happened?'

'No! I told you. We had other things to talk about.'

'Your relationship with each other?'

'That's what two people who fancy each other usually do.' Goodenough turned a sneer on Simon. 'Perhaps it's too far in your past for you to remember.'

'I remember juvenile self-absorption quite well,' Simon said equably.

'I just don't want to recall it too often.' Simon wasn't sure whether he might have despised Goodenough more if he had talked of love between Kate and himself, but the word he had used instead left a bad taste.

'What sort of mood was Kate in?' Simon asked.

'A very good mood. She was with me wasn't she?' He folded his arms and sighed. 'Look, nothing happened, nothing was said that could be of any interest to you. So can I go now?'

Simon wasn't satisfied, but he realized that Goodenough was so absorbed in himself that he was unlikely to have noticed, or listened, if Kate had had anything on her mind. Reluctantly he told Goodenough he could go. The car door slammed hastily behind him.

Chapter 27

Simon crashed the gears in his haste to put distance between himself and Goodenough's repulsive indifference to what had happened to his late girlfriend. Simon could understand the man's fear of his wife becoming aware of the relationship with Kate. It was his sheer lack of concern, utter lack of interest in how Kate had come to die, who had killed her and why, that offended Simon deeply.

What had Kate seen, or registered, that Saturday night that she had found significant the next day, when her mother had failed to materialize as expected? According to Goodenough, nothing had occurred when the two of them had been at the pub. The other place she had been that night was at Adam Swan's returning her charity envelopes.

Had she noticed something at the vicarage that night that she recalled next day? A scarf, or some other item belonging to her mother, perhaps? What if Swan were the elusive boyfriend? A chill settled over Simon as he registered the idea. There had been so much confusion over the timing of Sylvia's involvement with the new man in her life, some believing it had not happened until later on, around mid-summer, her friend Miss McEvoy being sure it had been as early as February. And Swan's wife had died in February. The chill increased as Simon registered the full implications and possibilities. He had been sure Swan had led him to believe that his wife had died at the end of last year. Believing that, any talk about Sylvia's compunction over her new relationship on the grounds that the man was married to a woman who was ill, had led Simon to discount anyone without an ailing wife and not consider anyone with no wife at all. Besides, Simon had just not registered a vicar as a potential love interest, and he should have. He was reminded of DI Stone's amused comment on the scandals of men of the cloth in this day and age.

Once Swan was free of his wife the relationship could have gone ahead without Sylvia feeling any guilt. Though her continued reticence would be explained by the fact that it would be even less seemly for a recently bereaved vicar than a lay person to be seen to begin a relationship so soon after a spouse's death. The relationship would have had its beginnings, though, when Sylvia had been nursing Swan's wife and daily proximity had drawn them together.

If it was Swan it explained so much: the obfuscation concerning the date of his wife's death, Sylvia's secretiveness, even Kate's sensitivity on the subject. And he had known about the stalker, had admitted the fact to Simon. He would have felt he had no choice since Sylvia had subsequently spoken to Fielding, who was bound to mention the fact to Simon.

Simon's image of Adrian Swan was subtly altering, the man's apparently open and ingenuous face took on a darker image. Perhaps he had spoken so intently on the subject of the ego and evil because he was familiar with their workings. Simon still didn't want to believe it. He had liked Swan, warmed to the man, enjoyed talking with him.

Why would he have killed Sylvia? Had she threatened him in some way? Did they have a quarrel that might have ended in her threatening to report him to the bishop about his adulterous behaviour, if their relationship had been physical before his seriously ill wife had died? Or had she known, because of their intimacy, something more about him that might lead to his professional ruin?

When Kate had returned to the vicarage the following day, demanding to know where her mother was, Swan would have felt compelled to kill her to cover his first crime. And, knowing about Pitt, much more fully than he had admitted to Simon, he had tried to set up Pitt as the murderer.

Simon suddenly came to the realization that, instead of arriving at headquarters as he had intended, he was approaching St Biddulph's and the vicarage. He pulled the car to a slow halt and stared across the road. He really should not go in there and confront Swan without taking someone with him, but at this moment the urge to do so was a pull as strong as gravity. He got out of the car and locked it, leaning against the car studying Swan's home for any sign of activity.

The clear blue skies of the sunny day had evolved into a wonderful indigo pricked by a few early stars and there was a scent of frost in the air. Simon pulled his coat more closely around him. He noticed in the gathering dark that light from the kitchen was shining on the shrubbery at the rear of the building. He felt a renewed lurch of dismay that Swan might be the one who had emerged from a carapace of deceit to reveal himself as a very different creature from the one he had portrayed.

Simon could hear one of Mozart's symphonies playing as he waited for the door to be answered. Swan looked surprised, even pleased, to see him. 'Come in,' he invited. 'I've had a rather quiet day so I'll be glad of your company.' He closed the door behind Simon, seeming not to notice anything different in his manner, though Simon felt as stiff and awkward as a mannequin.

Swan was dressed in a worn pair of corduroys and an equally scruffy sweater. 'I've got a very nice single malt I was planning on sampling any time now. Can I offer you one?' he said, leading the way to the kitchen, warm after the chill air outside.

Simon decided to accept: he was in no position to make an arrest. And, besides, the man was owed the chance to answer a few questions.

Swan turned down the music and handed him a cut crystal glass with an inch of whisky in it. 'I've just been talking to a couple who are due to be married soon,' he said. 'We're doing a lot more of this pre-marital counselling now. Time will tell, I suppose, whether it does any good, or has any effect.'

Ironic, Simon thought, but could trace no sign of consciousness in Swan's expression, which remained open and friendly as usual. 'I saw your wife's headstone the other day,' he said. 'I hadn't realized she died as late as February. Somehow I had the impression she had died at the end of last year.

Again there was no quickening of awareness on Swan's face as he sat down opposite Simon at the kitchen table.

'She did, in a way,' he said quietly, rolling his glass between his palms. 'She never recovered from the operation and she was very ill. Not the person she had been. I can't condone euthanasia, but when you see someone you greatly love suffering so much pain it does make you understand how witnessing something like that for a long period would be quite unbearable.'

He sounded entirely sincere. But Simon supposed you could continue to love someone you had loved for a long time and still fall in love with someone else, especially if your first love were changed by illness.

'She was my soul mate,' Swan added, a pained smile on his face. 'I miss her terribly.'

'I'm very sorry,' Simon said inadequately, wondering for a moment if he had got things horribly wrong. But he supposed it was possible that if the void left by his wife's loss had been so great, Swan might have even more readily looked for comfort with Sylvia Gaston.

'So am I in a way' Swan said, the smile turning crooked. 'It's made it impossible to think there could ever be a replacement for Fay.' He took a sip from his glass, savouring it for a moment. 'But I mustn't bore you. It's just that these marital counselling sessions make it even more raw for me. I find myself wondering if these young couples will ever find what Julia and I did in our marriage. Do you believe in soul mates, Chief Inspector?'

'Call me Chris,' Simon found himself saying. He took a moment before answering. His relationship with Jessie was too important to him, too private to be readily discussed with anyone. Yet to deny a complete affinity with what Swan was expressing would seem like denying Jessie herself. He limited himself to agreeing that he did indeed believe in soul mates.

'Psychologists would explain it away,' Swan mused, absently shaking a cigarette from a packet on the table and lighting it. 'They would say it was a mere accident of genetics, attracting like to like, or a rare complementing of distinct personalities or some such thing.'

Simon had never broached the subject with Jessie so he had no idea of her own views. He knew that he regarded Jessie in the same light, though, as Swan had his own partner: she was his kindred spirit. But did his uncertainties about her feelings for him mean that they could not be kindred in the way Swan was describing? Surely the feelings must be entirely mutual? So on the whole he preferred not to put Jessie's thoughts on the concept to the test.

'But they would be wrong,' Swan said, blowing his cigarette smoke towards the Rayburn. 'I suppose it's like a lot of things that matter – they have to be experienced to be believed. And when you have experienced such a sublime affinity with another human being you can never imagine doing with anything less. I suppose I shall get greater comfort as I live on, knowing that at least I was blessed with such love, so much more than most people seem to experience. But meanwhile the loneliness is intense sometimes.'

Simon was feeling more and more uncomfortable with his reason for being here, and increasingly unsure that Swan could be guilty of even *post mortem* infidelity to his wife, let alone anything truly sinister. 'I imagine your faith is of some help?' he suggested.

'I've tried to imagine how I would have been without my faith, though it's difficult to imagine myself as I am not. But I'm sure it's helped. I believe that we will meet again and that comforts me, of course. It must be terrible indeed for any bereaved person without that belief. But I'm in human form and she is not. Nothing assuages the pain of not being able to touch her, hold her, comfort and be comforted. Though I often sense her presence around me.' He took another mouthful of whisky and laid the glass down. 'She was my friend, my very best friend.'

Simon recalled the words Swan had had carved on her headstone. He remembered thinking it slightly ambiguous, but it was of course a statement about profound friendship from one of Shakespeare's sonnets, the full rhyming couplet being: *But if the while I think on thee, dear friend, All losses are restored and sorrows end.* Simon nodded. 'I noticed the words you put on her headstone.'

'I'm not doing too well at sticking to the sentiment, am I?' Swan said with an apologetic smile. 'I really am sorry, Chris, to burden you with my woes. I hope you haven't minded too much?'

Simon found it easy to reassure him. 'I imagine it's difficult when you are the person always expected to be giving out comfort. Perhaps it gets forgotten that you, too, have needs of the same kind.'

Swan drew on his cigarette again. 'We members of the clergy each have a spiritual counsellor, of course. But I sometimes think we are expected to put up and get on with things rather more than our lay sisters and brothers,' he said with another wry smile. 'But enough of me. What was it you came to see me about, while I've been using up your valuable time?'

Simon was conscious of a hot feeling of shame at his misjudgement of this warm-hearted and sensitive man. He found it impossible to believe that he was anything other than utterly sincere in his feelings about his dead wife. Yet still he wondered uneasily if Swan had nevertheless sought comfort in Sylvia. Could it even have been his revulsion at feelings of betrayal of his wife that had fired any quarrel they might have had, leading to her death? He took his time finishing his whisky and placed the glass carefully on the table in front of him.

Swan said, as if picking up something of Simon's thoughts, 'Sylvia understood a lot of what I was going through. She had a wonderful marriage with her second husband. That's why I was a little surprised when you said that she had become involved with another man.' He frowned. 'I hope she didn't feel she couldn't confide that in me because of the talks we had had. She needn't have felt like that, if so. I would have been only too glad for her to find love and companionship again.'

The man simply could not be that duplicitous, that much of an actor, Simon thought, watching him closely, his unselfconsciousness, his relaxed posture.

'So was there anything in particular you wanted to ask me?' Swan asked again. 'Not that you're not very welcome to call by any time.' He raised his eyebrows, the frankness and openness of his gaze dispelling Simon's last doubts.

'I wanted to ask you about the night before Kate disappeared. The Saturday night,' he said.

Swan's gaze didn't waver. 'When Kate called in with the Christian Mission envelopes,' he confirmed. 'I'm not sure there's much I can add. Kate wasn't here long. She seemed anxious to be off.'

She was probably aware that Goodenough was already waiting for her outside, Simon thought.

'We understand now,' Simon said, 'that Kate saw something that night that led her to guess where her mother might be, when she wasn't home as Kate was expecting her to be the next day. Can you think of anything that you might have said about Sylvia, for example?'

Swan looked entirely at a loss. 'I'm sure we didn't mention her mother.'

'Can you remember what you did talk about?'

'Well, not much really. Kate came with me into the study and handed me the envelopes and the list of people who had signed against their names. I have a small safe in there and I put the envelopes in immediately. Kate remarked that she'd been pleased to catch so many people at home on a Saturday night. She said she hadn't expected to. I remember she made some remark about being sorry she couldn't do it on weekday nights but she was too busy with school work and keeping on top of that.

'Which reminds me that I haven't yet sorted and banked the money so that I can send off the cheque.' He stubbed out his cigarette in an old saucer.

'Nothing else you remember?' Simon asked, disappointed.

'No,' Swan shook his head, frowning in thought. 'She was here a matter of a few minutes, that's all.'

'Perhaps it was something she saw when she was out collecting the envelopes,' Simon said slowly.

'If so, she certainly didn't mention it to me,' Swan said.

'I wonder, might I have a look at the list of people Kate called on that night?'

'Of course.' Swan stood up. 'If you'll bear with me. It will be somewhere on my desk in the study.' He disappeared through the door.

He returned in a few minutes with two stapled sheets of foolscap and handed them to Simon. 'You'll see that each of the people she called on signed their names at the end of the line that has their name and address on.'

Simon read down the list of totally unfamiliar names. Kate had managed to find at least two thirds of them at home that night. He turned to the second sheet and one name immediately stood out as well known to him. It was the only one he knew. Simon continued to stare as the full implications of what he was seeing began to dawn on him.

'What time did you say Kate got back here?' he asked Swan.

'About half past nine.'

'And she started out?'

'Just after eight I think.'

'Do you know in what order she would have called on these people? Where would she have started?'

'The lists are drawn up according to the proximity of the houses to each other, obviously,' Swan said, pulling towards him the list that Simon had laid on the table. 'They're based on the catchment area for St Biddulph's and divided into six approximate sections. Kate covered the north-west section from the church and she would have started on the outer limit and moved back towards the church. This was the usual practice because it meant they were nearer to home base when they were carrying the most money.' He pushed the list back to Simon. 'I didn't like Kate doing the collection after dark but she insisted.'

So Kate would have called on that familiar address much nearer to half past nine than eight because it was very close to St Biddulph's. Simon stared at the name again, the signature that should not have been there at all. He felt sick as the understanding of what must have happened fell into place in his mind. One of the ironies was that Sylvia had not been murdered after all.

'You seem to have found something of significance,' Swan said quietly. 'I suppose I had better not offer you more whisky, if you're driving. But you seem upset.'

Simon shook his head. 'Thank you, no. I have some telephone calls I need to make. Things I have to do. May I borrow this list?'

'You can let me have a photocopy of it if you like,' Swan said help-fully.

Simon patted Swan absently on his shoulder as he left the vicarage, his mind still in turmoil.

Chapter 28

As Simon stepped out into the sharp frosty night he was clear about one thing: he could not afford to wait until tomorrow before he made the arrest. At this stage evidence might still be destroyed, especially if the murderer had become aware that they were not pinning the deaths of Kate and Sylvia on Owen Pitt.

Back at headquarters he called in Detective Sergeant Longman and DI Stone. Then he phoned the hospital and finally managed to track down the doctor he needed to speak to. After that he contacted Detective Superintendent Munro. She was deeply shocked at first, concerned that Simon was sure he had got it right, and still bemused as he rang off.

After Longman and Stone arrived he arranged for a squad car to go with them and they set off, Simon explaining to them on the way.

Longman was unbelieving at first, even hostile, reluctant to accept the conclusions Simon had drawn, but finally he conceded. 'My God,' he said finally, subsiding back into the passenger seat.

'You'd better be right about this, sir,' DI Stone said, almost disapprovingly from the back seat.

'I am,' Simon said grimly, no happier than they were.

'So whose was the body we found in Cranton Plantation?' Longman sat up straight again.

'I don't know. It may have been any random blonde middle-aged woman who more or less resembled Sylvia Gaston, once she'd had her face battered. Or it's possible that some friend who knew about Sylvia's relationship with the killer went looking for her at his house that Sunday when Sylvia didn't arrive home.'

'I should think it must have been the latter,' DI Stone said. 'No point in complicating things. Without Sylvia's body we would have always had to wonder whether she were really dead, which would suit the murderer. Whereas once you had the body there was always the chance you would do more stringent tests than you did and not rely on Milliner's identification.'

The undisguised reproof in her voice was well-earned, Simon thought. He said, 'He wiped Sylvia's emails because he was mentioned in them.'

As they drew up outside the house Longman said, 'To think, we actually went to Sylvia Gaston's funeral.'

'By some form of proxy, I suppose,' Simon agreed, his memory of the day vivid in his mind, his sympathy for the bereaved husband so utterly misplaced. It had been just another small deceit beside the other greater one.

Fielding answered their knock at the door with a genial smile. 'Chris? Geoff?' But the smile faded as he saw the squad car drawn up by the gate.

He turned away from them and they followed him into the house. The television was on in the sitting room showing some lightweight comedy show, a cigar burning in the ashtray and a half-full glass of whisky on the table beside Fielding's chair. The very normality of it offended Simon as much as anything.

'What can I do for you, Chris?' Fielding said with an attempt at bravado.

'We're here to arrest you, Jack,' Simon said evenly and Longman began the formal words: 'Jack Fielding I am arresting you for the murder of your wife Heather Fielding and for the murder of Kate Milliner . . . .'

Fielding reached for his cigar and took a mouthful of whisky.

When Longman had finished speaking Simon said, 'Jack, it may go better for you if you tell us where Heather is. You may as well cooperate and save us time.'

He had shown no emotion, offered no protest. Now he said with a smile, 'You know where Heather is Chris. You came to her funeral.'

Simon experienced a surge of anger followed by revulsion. 'I came to Sylvia Gaston's burial,' he corrected him. 'There will be no difficulty over an exhumation. Is there perhaps a cellar in this house?'

'Come off it, Chris. All I have to say is that I want my solicitor.'

'Go ahead,' Simon said, nodding at the telephone on the side table.

Fielding picked up the phone and calmly pressed the buttons. He spoke quietly for a few minutes then replaced the phone while Longman fidgeted and glanced anxiously at Simon. DI Stone stood silent and still as her name, taking in everything and saying nothing.

'Shall we go?' Fielding said, as if they were on some amiable social mission.

They led him out to the squad car and put him in the back seat.

It was not an interview that Simon could expect to feel any satisfaction in: a policeman gone to the bad always produced a deep sense of betrayal in his colleagues. Fielding remained at first monosyllabic until his solicitor, a cadaverous man called David Thompson, asked for some more time alone with him, now that he was more clear about the charges being made and the evidence likely to be made available.

When Simon and Longman returned to the interview room, Fielding's expression had changed from impassive to resentful. But he was now willing to speak. He was familiar enough with the law to know that remaining silent would do him greater damage than cooperation.

Simon switched on the tape and spoke the date, time and names of those present again.

'Jack,' he began. 'You went out that evening for a meal with Sylvia Gaston. Did you pick up Sylvia from her house?'

'Yes.'

'At what time?'

'Eight o'clock.'

'And you arrived at the restaurant in Chingford at what time?'

'Around half past eight.'

'And you left there at what time?'

'About ten.'

'So you were approaching the outskirts of Westwich at twenty-five minutes past ten when the collision with another vehicle occurred, in which Sylvia Gaston died?'

For the first time a flicker of emotion crossed Fielding's face. 'Yes,' he said more quietly.

Simon covered the emergency service's arrival, the journey to the hospital where Sylvia was pronounced dead.

'They assumed she was my wife,' Fielding said, pressing his lips together. He swallowed hard. 'It would have been like denying her, disowning her, to let them think anything else.'

Both Heather and Sylvia had been middle-aged women with blonde hair. Any other lack of resemblance had been disguised by the facial injuries that Sylvia had sustained. Jack himself had only minor injuries, the vehicle that had hit them crushing only the passenger side.

'I found myself formally identifying her. They let me go home after patching me up. I was still in a daze. It was like Heather was dead too. I'd just said so. And when I got home Heather was waiting up for me.' Fielding frowned and started picking at a thumbnail. He flickered a glance at Simon. 'She started accusing me of being unfaithful to her. She was so bitter, so contemptuous.' His voice rose. 'She had no idea what it had been like for me these past years: Heather's illness, Heather's tests and treatment. Her so tired we could do nothing together. It was no marriage any more. Suddenly I just felt so utterly weary with all the years of illness and struggle and worry with Heather. The endless tests, the tension over results, her exhaustion, the ending of any real life we had shared.' His voice quickened. 'And Sylvia was so alive. I loved her, I was shattered by her death. I hated her that it was Sylvia who had died. So I hit her. I hit her stupid sickly face. And then I hit her again. And again until she was dead.'

Simon had known it must have happened like that, that there must have been some such motivation. But Fielding's words had the power to shock him profoundly. Even Fielding's solicitor looked away, and he felt Longman tense beside him. Shock gave way to deep sadness, pity for Heather Fielding, regret for Sylvia Gaston who had apparently struggled against involvement in this relationship. She should have followed her first instincts, Simon thought. She had enough knowledge and experience of long-term illness and the strains it must put on relationships to know she was trading in inflammable territory. But she had probably thought she could keep it all under control. And she would not for a moment have forseen the chance of a fatal accident. The contrast of Fielding's words with those of Adrian Swan earlier underlined the chasm that exists between a truly loving relationship and one that had gone so sour.

'What did you do then, with Heather's body?' Simon asked.

Fielding smiled a sardonic smile. 'Such a cliché. But a basement can be so convenient. As you thought, Chris, she's in the cellar.'

David Thompson leaned and spoke quietly into Fielding's ear. Probably to warn Fielding against the use of unfeeling language, Simon thought, in case the tape should be used in evidence.

'Would you repeat that for the recording please, Mr Thompson?' he requested. Thompson briefly did so, obfuscating his meaning as much as he could, then asked for another brief conversation with his client.

Outside the room Longman was subdued. 'I'm not enjoying this,' he said. 'I'd never have believed it. I've known Jack for years, and Heather. Shows you never really know what goes on inside a marriage.'

Simon's mind had become more focused. 'I was afraid he might have moved Heather's body when he realized we had rejected Pitt as the killer.'

'Sylvia's body will have to be exhumed anyway,' Longman said. 'Her family, what's left of it, will want a proper funeral for her. So that's bound to clear up what really happened.' He seemed to register the rest of what Simon had said. 'You think he's been checking on what we've been doing? Of course he was!' Longman's eyebrows shot up. 'He must have planned it all. He waited until we had Pitt in our sights so that he'd know when to kill him and set him up as the murderer.'

'It would have been easy enough for him to check our reports, see where we were at,' Simon said with a trace of bitterness.

'You don't expect to have to guard what you're doing in the name of the law inside a police headquarters,' Longman said angrily.

'*Quis custodiet ipsos custodes*? Who will guard the guards, or watch the watchers, indeed.' Simon looked grim.

'So we'll begin on the cellar tomorrow morning I suppose?'

Simon nodded. 'That first. And we want fibre matching from Kate's clothes and we can do the tissue match from her fingernails. We may find some cord to match the piece he hanged Pitt with.'

'But we've got a confession anyway,' Longman said.

'Only for Heather's murder. We'd better get back inside.' Simon pushed open the door.

He restarted the tape. 'Can you describe to me what happened the next afternoon, on the Sunday when Kate Milliner came to see you,' he addressed Fielding.

Fielding hesitated for a moment, then a subtle nudge from Thompson encouraged him to speak. 'She turned up demanding to know where her mother was. I was still in a state of shock. I'd had a bang on the head you know, in the crash. I didn't know what I was doing. That was how I came to hit out at Heather.'

So that was to be the defence, Simon thought acidly: all done while the balance of Fielding's mind was disturbed by a traumatic road accident. Simon wondered whether the defence experts would be able to extend the evidence of disturbance of mind to the murder of Owen Pitt.

'Go on,' he said coldly.

'I panicked. I hadn't thought about Kate. I didn't know she knew about me and Sylvia. But I realized that since she did there was no way I could get away with what I'd done. I asked her inside. She was really hostile and accusing towards me. She asked me where my wife was. I grabbed her in a panic to shut her up and before I knew it she was dead.'

If the injuries to Fielding's head had not been the cause of him becoming homicidal, they had certainly affected his judgement in other ways. He could have fobbed Kate off and then followed her, perhaps arranging something that looked like an accident. They had no real concerns over pinning the murders of Heather Fielding and Kate Milliner now anyway – there was evidence enough to provide for conviction, in addition to Fielding's confession. It was getting Fielding convicted for the murder of Pitt that now concerned Simon most: they had no real evidence unless they found that matching cord. It was all entirely circumstantial.

'When did you take her to Eltham Woods?' Simon asked, getting back to more solid ground.

'That night.'

How ironic, Simon thought, that Kate's murder had been announced in Fielding's house during the supposed wake for his wife.

'Now tell us about the murder of Owen Pitt,' Simon said.

'Who's Owen Pitt?'

Longman spoke. 'Owen Pitt is the man who you knew had been stalking Sylvia Gaston. She told you about him, asked your advice on how she might deal with the situation. You decided he would make the ideal suspect for the supposed murder of Sylvia Gaston and the actual murder of Kate, her daughter. So you telephoned him last Saturday night and got him to agree to meet you outside his house. You then strangled him with a cord and strung him up from a beam in his garage. Then you used a spray can to write his confession on the wall. But you didn't know his handwriting and it was obvious that Pitt had not put those words there. Come on Jack, we've got a fingerprint on the can that doesn't belong to Pitt.'

'That's not possible—' Fielding snapped.

'Why's that Jack? Because you thought you had wiped the can clean before you pressed Pitt's fingerprints on it?' Longman said smoothly.

Fielding bared his teeth in a tight smile. He had fallen for one of the oldest tricks. 'It's not possible because I wasn't there, ever,' he said.

But his response had been indicative enough. It wasn't much to be going on with, but it was something.

'And the woman we found in the plantation, in the ditch, Jack? We have fibres on her clothes that we expect to match with fibres from your home. Who was she?'

Fielding deliberated for a moment then his posture slumped. 'She was Sylvia's sister,' he said. He leaned forward and put his hands over his face, as if the enormity of all that he had done had suddenly overwhelmed him.

The sister in Scotland, Simon thought, who Milliner had said was not in contact with Sylvia. But there had been a lot of years go by since Milliner knew much about Sylvia's life.

'I'd forgotten completely,' Fielding said, wiping his hands over his face as if washing away a memory, 'that Sylvia had said she was visiting that Sunday. She'd moved down south a year ago and they had been in close contact again. Sylvia was very happy about it.'

'And Sylvia had told her all about you.'

Fielding nodded. 'She was careful not to talk about us to anyone local. I hadn't realized she'd told her sister so much about us.'

'When did she come to your house?'

'That evening on the Sunday. She said she was worried about Sylvia and did I know where she was. She said she hadn't been able to get Kate on the phone either.' Fielding sank back in his chair.

'So you felt you had to kill her, too.'

'She knew too much. She knew I was going out with Sylvia the night before.' Fielding looked at Simon, his eyes empty of anything.

'And after you'd killed her you put Sylvia's pendant around her neck to lead us to believe it was Sylvia's body.'

A nod of agreement.

'Then you realized you had better wipe Sylvia's emails.'

'They gave me Sylvia's belongings at the hospital. I had her keys. I knew I had to remove any evidence of our relationship.' Fielding bowed his head. 'She hadn't told her sister that I was married, but obviously she'd told her my name, which was how she found me. Until I read what she'd written in her emails to her sister I hadn't realized just how much I meant to her.'

'She didn't know you, did she Jack?' Longman said harshly. 'I wonder how she'd feel about you, knowing you had killed her daughter and her sister, left her son alone?'

The man suddenly began to sob uncontrollably. His solicitor took out a white handkerchief and handed it to him, a look of distaste on his face.

Simon decided to call a halt. It would be tempting, but not reliable police practice, to continue to question Fielding while he was in his current state. And anyway, by tomorrow he might have some more solid evidence to challenge Fielding with and get him to confess to Pitt's murder too. He told the constable waiting at the door to take Fielding to a cell when he had recovered some equilibrium. The young man was obviously uncomfortable at having to perform this duty for a senior officer. In fact the whole of headquarters was behaving like a stirred up ants' nest. Word had got around and some officers had come back to HQ to find out what was going on, even at this late hour.

Simon and Longman walked out to the car park together and stood on the steps for a few minutes breathing in the sharp air.

'I still can't believe it,' Longman said, breathing deeply.

'We find it difficult to believe what we don't want to believe.'

'How was it you realized it was Jack? I would never have considered him, quite apart from the fact that he seemed to have the perfect alibi.'

Simon explained how he had seen Heather Fielding's signature, signed in a time and place where it should not have been possible. 'It was simple. If Heather was in, and we knew Jack was out and that the woman with him was killed that night, there *was* only one explanation.'

'Simple,' Longman said. 'All the time the answer was on some innocuous list in a vicar's study.' He turned his head quickly to Simon. 'But what were you doing at the vicarage in the first place?'

Simon became hot in the frosty air as he remembered what had taken him there: he had no desire for Longman to know that he had sped there in the belief that Swan was their murderer. But he could tell something of the truth. He told Longman about his conversation with Vanessa earlier. 'She seemed to think that Kate had seen something on the Saturday night that made her realize where her mother might be. The only place we knew Kate had been was collecting charity envelopes and at the vicarage handing them in. I got Swan to show me the list of people Kate had called on. Heather Fielding's name obviously leapt out.'

'Simple,' Longman said again.

It wasn't until Simon was starting the car that he realized to his dismay that he had completely forgotten to get in touch with Jessie, to tell her he would be late back. And he was very late, so late that he even considered a cowardly retreat to his flat. But something propelled him onwards.

This whole case had centred around relationships between men and women, in sickness and in health. It had shown the best and the worst of marital relations, their strengths and their great frailties, their potential for good and their dangerous tides of destructive emotions. None of the couples he had met had known when they embarked on their relationships how they would turn out, from the murderous rejection by Fielding, through the contemptuous indifference of Pitt and the domineering tolerance of Framley to the devotion that Swan had expressed. And admittedly the admirable in marriage had been mostly outweighed by the far from admirable, but marriage was a mystery to even those within one it seemed. What he came to realize as he drove through the starry night was that, whatever marriage might turn out to be for them, he could no longer tolerate the indecision that had plagued him for so long in his relationship with Jessie.

She was still up, sitting in her usual place, her back against the sofa, in the dark by the log fire, a book on her lap, eyes closed.

'*When you are old and grey and full of sleep and nodding by the fire,*' the words of Yeats's poem came into his head and his fears of her anger at his lateness were replaced by infinite tenderness. He sat down quietly beside her and put an arm around her shoulders. She shifted sleepily towards him.

'Jess?' he said softly.

'Mmm?'

'Will you marry me?'

She opened her eyes and turned her head towards him. 'Yes,' she said.